TRAGEDY

The Erinnan Legacy

Treason and Truth
Book 4 of 12

J.A.Cauldwell

Dedication
For Mark

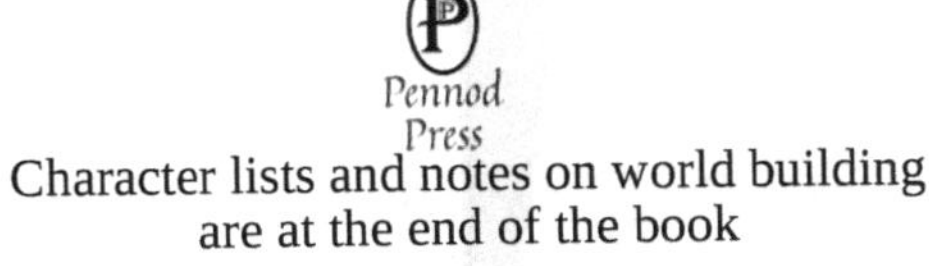
Pennod
Press

Character lists and notes on world building
are at the end of the book

The Erinnan Legacy

Treason and Truth

FROM THE PAST COMES MAGIC, FROM THE PRESENT, DANGER, GRADUALLY COLLIDING

1	TREASON	5	THROWN
2	TERA		
3	TRAPPED		
4	TRAGEDY		

Stories From Erinna

EVERYBODY HAS A STORY AND SOMEBODY KNOWS IT

Standalone stories that may link to characters from other series.

TIES

TRAGEDY

From the past comes magic, from the present, danger, gradually colliding.

As peril prowls the empire's roads and halls of power, bandits strike with chilling precision. When Prince Arkyn is ambushed, murmurs of betrayal stir, old friendships fracture and trust erodes. Even the army cannot escape scrutiny.

King Adeone dares not risk civil war, but restraint has its price. Every cautious choice leaves room for ambition and treachery to fester.

In the shadow of growing unrest, Prince Tain's path to Justiciar is littered with doubt and frustrations, but his resolve remains. He will become the weapon they need.

Lord Scanlon's schemes rise and fall, but power is patient – and tragedy never comes uninvited.

Copyright

Trigger Warning

This book is set in a pre-Victorian-inspired world with elements of fantasy. It includes references to difficult themes such as loss, hardship, and moral dilemmas. Some events explore the consequences of harm, societal oppression, and personal struggles, including grief and guilt.

This book is written in British English. The lack of Z might keep you awake but we like U. If you prefer a different flavour of English, I hope you find your next read soon.

MAPS

THE OEDRANIAN EMPIRE

ENVIRONS OF OEDRAN
Paras Road
Torport Road
Carregshore Road
River Edra
River Edra
EDRA FERRY
Garth Road
WHARF REACH
Port Road
TWO WAYS
OEDRAN
CRABTREE
River Carn
CILFORD
Dallin Road
DELLWOOD
5
1
4
2
3
River Encil
Hill Beck
REX DALLIN
7
6
N
0   1 mi
1: Pillars of Alcis
2: Ceardlann
3: Encampment Field
4: Wishing Tree
5: Fitz's Inn
6: The Pools
7: The Warrens

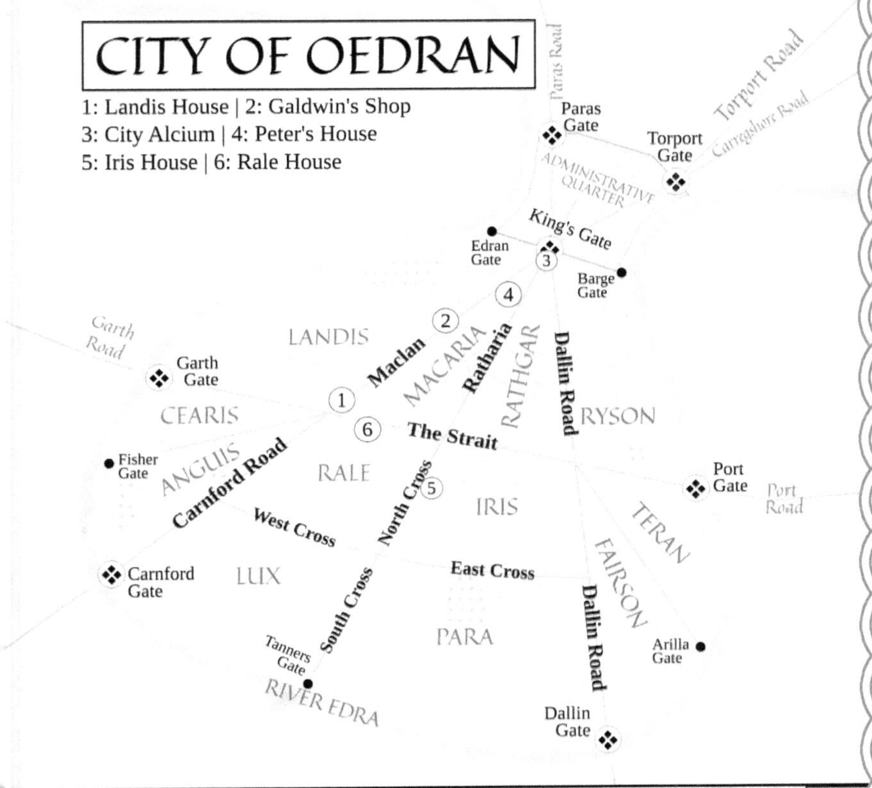

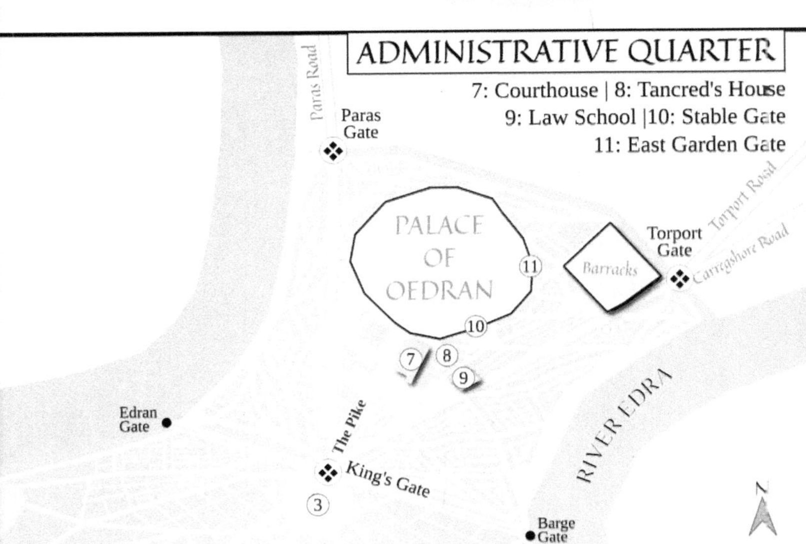
CITY OF OEDRAN
1: Landis House | 2: Galdwin's Shop
3: City Alcium | 4: Peter's House
5: Iris House | 6: Rale House
Paras Road
Torport Road
Carregshore Road
Paras Gate
Torport Gate
King's Gate
ADMINISTRATIVE QUARTER
Edran Gate
Barge Gate
Maclan
MACARIA
Ratharia
RATHGAR
Dallin Road
RYSON
LANDIS
Garth Road
Garth Gate
CEARIS
ANGUIS
Carnford Road
The Strait
RALE
Fisher Gate
West Cross
North Cross
IRIS
Port Gate
Port Road
TERAN
FAIRSON
Carnford Gate
LUX
South Cross
East Cross
PARA
Dallin Road
Arilla Gate
Tanners Gate
RIVER EDRA
Dallin Gate
ADMINISTRATIVE QUARTER
7: Courthouse | 8: Tancred's House
9: Law School |10: Stable Gate
11: East Garden Gate
Paras Road
Paras Gate
PALACE OF OEDRAN
Barracks
Torport Gate
Torport Road
Carregshore Road
Edran Gate
The Pike
King's Gate
Barge Gate
RIVER EDRA

ARCHIVE

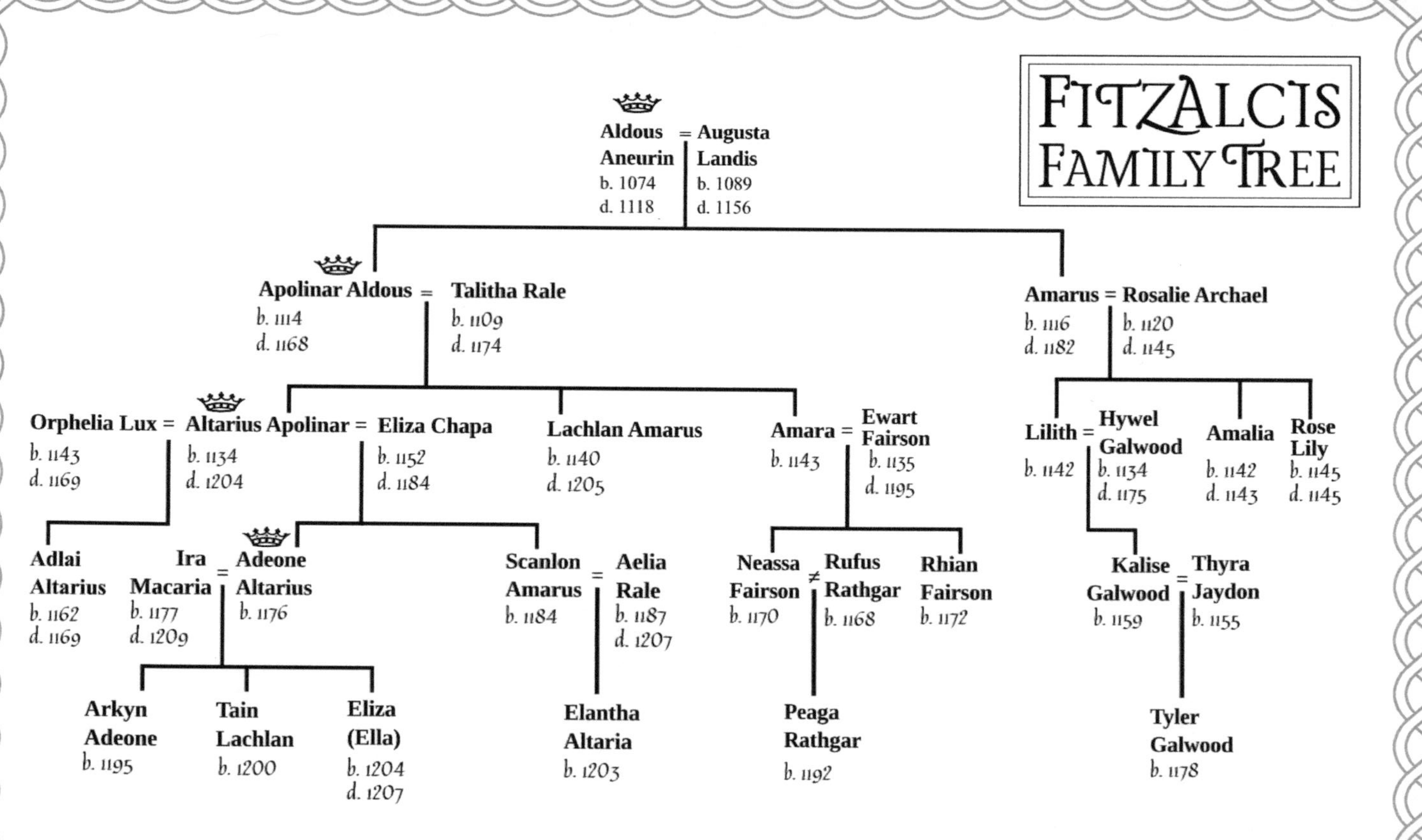

FITZALCIS FAMILY TREE

Aldous Aneurin b. 1074 d. 1118 = Augusta Landis b. 1089 d. 1156

Apolinar Aldous b. 1114 d. 1168 = Talitha Rale b. 1109 d. 1174

Amarus b. 1116 d. 1182 = Rosalie Archael b. 1120 d. 1145

Orphelia Lux b. 1143 d. 1169 = Altarius Apolinar b. 1134 d. 1204 = Eliza Chapa b. 1152 d. 1184

Lachlan Amarus b. 1140 d. 1205

Amara b. 1143 = Ewart Fairson b. 1135 d. 1195

Lilith b. 1142 = Hywel Galwood b. 1134 d. 1175

Amalia b. 1142 d. 1143

Rose Lily b. 1145 d. 1145

Adlai Altarius b. 1162 d. 1169

Ira Macaria b. 1177 d. 1209 = Adeone Altarius b. 1176

Scanlon Amarus b. 1184 = Aelia Rale b. 1187 d. 1207

Neassa Fairson b. 1170 ≠ Rufus Rathgar b. 1168

Rhian Fairson b. 1172

Kalise Galwood b. 1159 = Thyra Jaydon b. 1155

Arkyn Adeone b. 1195

Tain Lachlan b. 1200

Eliza (Ella) b. 1204 d. 1207

Elantha Altaria b. 1203

Peaga Rathgar b. 1192

Tyler Galwood b. 1178

CHRONICLE

1168
Accession of
King Altarius

1169
Bayan
Rebellion

1175
Altarius marries
Eliza Chapa

1176
Birth of
Adeone

1184
Birth of Scanlon
Death of Queen Eliza

1203
Scanlon marries Aelia
Rale, Birth of Elantha

1200
Birth of
Tain

1195
Birth of
Arkyn

1193
Adeone marries
Ira Macaria

1204
Scanlon drops title of Prince
Birth of Ella
Accession of King Adeone

1205
Death of
Prince
Lachlan

1207
Death of
Princess Ella
and Aelia

1209
Death of Queen
Ira. Promotion of
Wynfeld

1211
Arkyn undertakes
Terasian Review. Roth
murders Portur.

1210
Gad attacks King
Adeone at the
Guild Banquet

1209
Triniculum Plan.
Haster life-bound

1211
Anonymous notes left.
Secretaries dismissed.

1211
Landis House
burns down

1212
Tancred starts
teaching Tain

1212
Arkyn undertakes
Anaparian Review

1213
Tancred's history
revealed

1212
Neassa divorced

1212
Daioch life-bound
Landis history
discovered.

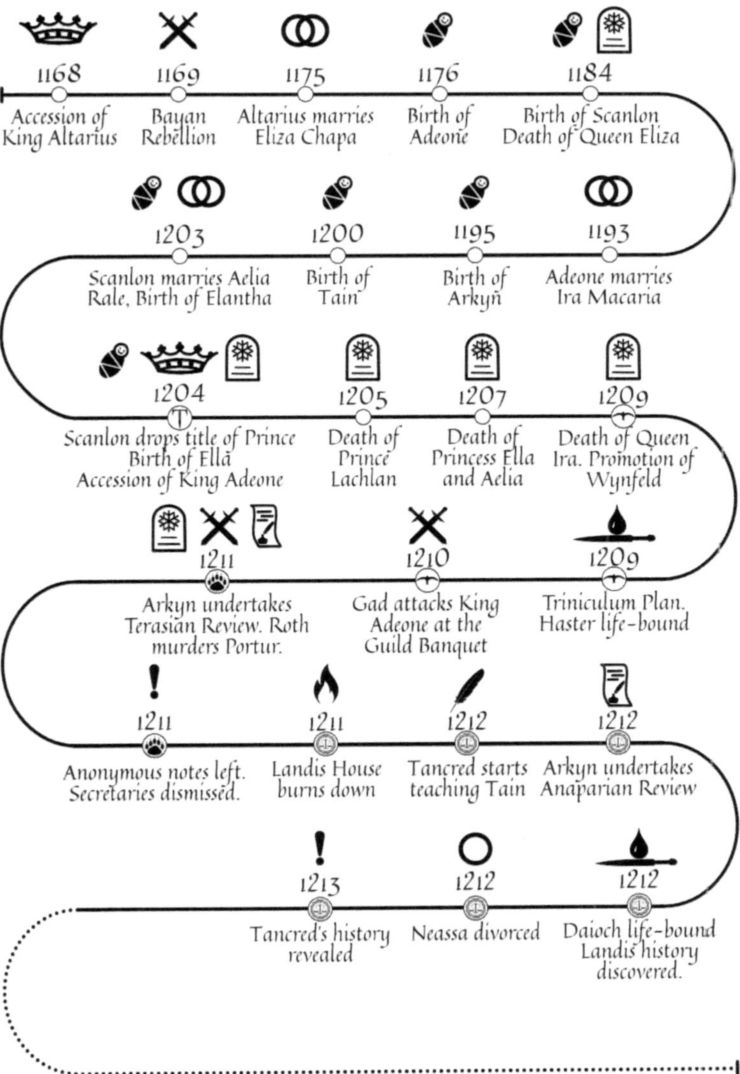

TRAGEDY

PART 1

Chapter 1
PRICE OF LOYALTY
Tretaldai, Week 43 – 17th Geryal, 3rd Geryis 1204
Anapara – Black Hills House

DEEP VALLEYS, dark and forbidding forests, fast flowing water and sparse fertile ground characterised the Raven Hills of Anapara. Tamed in the tenth century with bandits routed out and forest cleared, small settlements and lords' estates grew to prosperity where once there had been fear. Each lord bound to pay tribute to the ruling FitzAlcis and sworn to uphold the peace.

After the clearing of land started in 1050, the first large house was built on the edge of vast grounds surrounded by a stout wall, designed to hinder bandits. Less than a mile from the gates, Thornwood village developed, the rents filling the Black Hills House coffers. By 1204, the house and its situation offered an income and complete privacy and that was what Lord Scanlon Amarus FitzAlcis, Justiciar of Oedran and the Empire, wanted.

Lord Abbas, heir of Lord Atgas of Anapara, met Scanlon at the gates of Black Hills House. His bow, precise and unhurried, was calculated to please the Justiciar.

Dismounting in the stableyard, Scanlon assessed its practicality. There were ten stalls for horses and two coach houses. He pursed his lips. "This isn't large enough, Bantling!"

"It could be expanded, Greatness; there's land to the rear," explained his advisor.

Lord Abbas said, "The Thornwood inn has large stables also, sir, which you might use in need."

"Hmm. Are the current tenants here?" asked Scanlon.

"No, sir, they are visiting relations."

Scanlon stripped off his riding gloves, tossing them at Bantling. "Good. I don't want distractions. Show us the house, my lord."

So Abbas did. At one point, he enquired if the Justiciar would like to inspect the servants' accommodation. Rather tartly, Scanlon pointed out he didn't intend to be using it personally. After that, Abbas concentrated on the spacious family areas. Finally, they entered the sunny drawing room and were served refreshments; once the footmen left, Scanlon gave Bantling a nod.

"Lord Abbas, the Justiciar is willing to open negotiations—"

"I deal directly, not through some flunkey," snapped Abbas, eyes flashing.

"You'll deal how I say!" retorted Scanlon

"Then the deal will reflect that, Justiciar."

They eyed each other, two strong-willed men with a single purpose.

Scanlon waited long enough for Abbas to break eye contact before he snapped, "Get out," without even looking at his advisor.

Once Bantling had left, Abbas said, "Thank you, Your… my lord."

"Do you therefore still recognise me as a prince of the FitzAlcis?"

"As all men must, sir, in our hearts."

Scanlon sneered. "Courtly talk for one so scarred. The house is private?"

"There is only Thornwood for a couple of miles."

"Would you relinquish rights on the village and surrounding land as well as the house?"

"For the right price, Justiciar," confirmed Atgas.

Scanlon's blue eyes narrowed. "Your audacity is extraordinary. Don't forget I *am* FitzAlcis."

"As is my ancestry, sir," Abbas reminded him.

"Time can matter for views of ancestry."

"Ancestry is many things, sir. As I'm sure you know."

Scanlon held his gaze. "What is your price?"

"It is a matter of necessity, sir. I am in need of a wife, so that I may inherit when my father dies, but I am no courtier. Can you suggest a beautiful lady to me? All I require is that she is obedient and fertile. I have no wish to be made a fool of by my goods."

"You talk from the past," said Scanlon.

"It is what I believe is the right way of doing things, my lord. Traditions are important – in family life as in the empire. It means, also, that I am my liege's to command as much as I command my household."

Scanlon eyed him; was the man offering what he appeared to be? "You say, therefore, that you expect absolute loyalty from your household and family. What would you do if they broke that expectation?"

"How does one punish the unruly, sir? With a whipping or something equally as poignant. It keeps them exact and obedient. My servants know where they stand. I would like to say I pay them well but, what with one thing or another, few ever get their full wage."

"You have a love of money?"

"Don't we all? Money *can* buy anything: a man's loyalty, his freedom, even his honour, sir. Men would be bound to your service or mine without thought for anything else, for a few darl and a fulfilling of their desires."

Scanlon paused, liking Abbas' attitude but unwilling to show it. "We have digressed. What of the servants? Would they come with the house?"

"I could negotiate it, sir, but sometimes it is better to start afresh."

"You'll have my decision within a week."

"Thank you, sir. Will you accept my hospitality tonight? My manor… That is, my father's manor is only a couple of hours' ride away."

Scanlon paused. "Yes. I will have to talk with your father to ensure he has no objection to relinquishing the house and possibly the village."

"Certainly, sir, but he's getting rather senile in his old age."

"What you mean is that you've not told him."

Lord Abbas simply smiled.

* * *

Two days later, Scanlon was saying to King Adeone, "I've found a house: Black Hills; they want ten thousand to release it."

Adeone paused, eyeing his brother. "That seems a little steep."

"Yes, but it's a fair price, given the land they'll lose through no fault of theirs. I did negotiate. It includes the village and environs."

"I'll get an appraiser to make an assessment. If there's a discrepancy and you still want it, you'll make up the difference."

"Don't you owe me this?"

Adeone considered the implication and recriminations behind that. Their father had refused to grant Scanlon entry to their private retreat after his death, and had made Adeone promise to uphold that decision. Unfortunate though the circumstance was, Adeone considered there was no unforgiving blame to be attached to him. The fact he and Scanlon had rarely found common ground was just an added complication.

"I'm not going to sign over ten thousand darl without good reason or proof it's worth it. Debt in families always runs high, but there are many calls on our purse. If you hadn't been extravagant for years, you would be able to afford it, so I'll do what I think is right. You must learn the empire doesn't have limitless funds for you to fritter away. I will also not remove the land and house from Lord Atgas. I'll get my lawyers to deal with the paperwork, if you're not taking it on as a tenant. You'll pay, but the family will reclaim the land. I'm not going to indulge your excess as father did."

"What he did and didn't do would astonish you, Adeone. Oh, I'm sorry, *Your Majesty*."

"Take your tantrum elsewhere."

Scanlon left, saying, "Feeling headachy, are we? It must be the stress of being officious."

Once outside the office, he whistled good-humouredly. It was a shame the bluff had failed, but he'd get income from elsewhere.

* * *

19

Lord Abbas never blinked when the King's Appraiser appeared. Giving exaggerated information, he wheedled out of the man how much Scanlon had claimed he'd requested and carried on embellishing, intrigued that the King had fallen for his brother's lies and also that the King's Lawyers would deal with the matter. Was *Lord Scanlon* really so restricted?

When he next spoke to Scanlon, he carried on the act and mentioned they could come to an accommodation over the money, where most of it would remain with the Justiciar if he, Abbas, got a wife of his choosing. He'd tell the lawyers he'd received the payment, or return most of it to Scanlon if the lawyers sent it to him independently.

"Who do you wish to marry then?" enquired Scanlon, having no intention of handing over any money.

"Lady Malinda Teran."

"She's already married to my *wed-brother*!"

"Yes. Rather unfortunate that," mused Atgas. "How much privacy and money do you need? Is it worth sacrificing a few scruples for my silence? Your plans will require much more—"

Scanlon eyed Abbas. "What do you know of my plans?"

"What I know is up for sale already. You're playing a dangerous game, *Justiciar*, but I could rather like your aims. I wouldn't like to be forced into betraying you for something as sordid as money, but I like its sparkle."

Scanlon nearly called his bluff but one look into those dark eyes made him realise that it was no bluff; Abbas would tell everything he knew for the right price. A few painful questions should ascertain who had spoken of his private plans. There weren't that many privy to them.

"No member of your staff has betrayed you, Justiciar. I suspect they don't even know that they are working for a man who will become king. With my arm through yours, sir, you will be king."

Scanlon cursed. What had given him away? The need for privacy? Whatever it had been, it was too late now. Maybe he could use the situation to his advantage. "You will not speak of such things to me again, Lord Abbas. You will, however, I hope, be my guest at Black Hills one day soon. I'll take possession on the first day of 1205."

Lord Abbas said, "Very good, Justiciar, and our *arrangement*?"

"Have patience!"

* * *

Scanlon talked with several of his closest acquaintances and one day Lord Finn Rale and Lord Osbern Teran, his first cousin by marriage, had some swordplay.

After half an hour, Finn said, "Alcis, Os, that was close. Are you trying to kill me? I think the sun has got to you. Let's go in."

Osbern inwardly swore, he'd been promised a lot if Finn died. "Why would I want to kill you? You're cover for mine and Malinda's affair…"

Finn coloured. "Stop clowning around, Os."

Osbern's face set. "I'm not clowning, Finn. Didn't you know? Everyone else does. She's good, isn't she? I'm amazed you've only one son. I can't keep my hands off her. I mean, she *really wants* it. Are you sure the boy's yours? I've heard talk that maybe he isn't—"

Finn drew his sword. "You squat little—"

"Why deny the truth, Finn? I mean, look at us. Is it any surprise that she prefers me? I've certainly got more than your runty stature implies."

Their swords clanged. Rage coursed through Finn. Osbern's lies were obvious, but he had to stop him voicing them again. He wanted to punish Osbern, wanted to slice the immutable Teran sneer off his face. He wanted to see fear in his supercilious eyes, but Osbern was still laughing at him. Rage made him careless and he didn't anticipate the low blow. He fell, letting out a curse that would raise his ancestors' wrath. Grasping at his leg, trying to stop the pumping blood pooling around him, he gasped,

"Get help."

Osbern knelt, apparently to see what he could do. He whispered, "Not just yet. Let's make certain you won't survive; Lord Scanlon wouldn't want that. Malinda's the price he's got to pay for a little project. Don't worry, Finian is yours."

"Is that what you call letting me die easy, you bastard?"

He grasped at Osbern's tunic with one hand and tried to retrieve his dagger with another but was becoming too weak. Osbern grasped his hands and shouted for help. It took two minutes until anyone got there and they had to leave again to get more help, a stretcher and the doctor. Osbern held Finn down and tied what appeared to be a tourniquet around his leg, but it wasn't tight.

Finn fumbled, trying to tighten it himself. "Let me see Malinda…"

Prising his hands away, Osbern said, "She's visiting Aelia. There's no-one to tell. Your father's at Iris House and you're obviously hallucinating if anyone asks. I'll tell them you were seeing dragons."

"You bastard! What had I done?"

"Nothing, and that's the point. Times are changing, Finn, and you were in Lord Scanlon's way; my liege is demanding."

"I can't… believe… the King—"

"Do you think I can't change my allegiance? Oh dear, you really are naïve, aren't you? Or did Adeone buy your loyalty?"

Finn, slipping into unconsciousness, managed, "Commend my loyalty… to the King… and my love to… family."

Osbern didn't say anything. By the time the doctor arrived, the tourniquet was tight, but Finn was dead.

* * *

When the news reached Malinda and Aelia, the distraught wed-sisters held each other, racked by sobs. Lord Scanlon appeared a couple of hours later to find them still sitting together.

He said to his wife, "It's true, Aelia. An accident in a sword fight. Your father wants the family together tonight."

Aelia couldn't stop her flowing tears. Her brother had always been there, supportive, willing to listen and tease. "Can I… Can I go?"

"Of course. You must. I'll be there as well. Come on. Malinda, Finian's been told, but he's asking for you."

Malinda started. "I must go to him…"

Aelia nodded. "I'm coming as well. Scanlon, can we take the coach?"

"It's waiting. Adeone's ordered the Court into sober clothes in respect."

* * *

1205 arrived. Aelia and Scanlon moved to Black Hills with their daughter, Elantha. Within a fortnight, Scanlon suggested that Aelia ought to invite Malinda for a change of scene. Abbas was a regular visitor, and well-constructed comments meant Malinda began to believe Abbas cared for her. By the Mundimri she was remarried, to the scandal of Oedran but the pleasure of her friends who knew she needed support and mistakenly believed Abbas loved her.

Chapter 2
NEGOTIATION
Hexadai, Week 47 – 20th Lufial, 13th Lufis 1212
Black Hills House – Lord Scanlon's Study

SEVERAL YEARS LATER, sitting in his imposing study, Scanlon eyed his guest. Had he been right to confide in him? A ruthless right-hand man he might be, but was he too ruthless? There were stories that made Scanlon wary, but he needed the expertise of one of the lord's men and that would cost, but success would be sweeter than gold.

Betraying nothing of his mindset, the empire's Justiciar said, "I'll give him his orders. There's to be no failure."

"What if he's captured, Greatness? What then? If you give him orders he might reveal—"

"I doubt my cellarer could make him spill any information. He's already

22

a marked man. Most of the army's trying to locate him thanks to the Oedranian Major. Didn't you know? Think what he could reveal with the right incentive and the King's men don't rely on pain."

Dark eyes met blue. "I'll give him his orders, sir. He'll understand them and I'll face the consequences if things go wrong. My eventual arrest is a certainty, I know that."

Scanlon held his gaze, the air between them crackling with suspicion. "Such pessimism isn't normally your style. Do you not trust your liege?"

"No," came the succinct reply.

"How wise. What is your price for your man's services? We'll settle other matters later."

The lord's lips twitched as he named his price. "That includes his *supplies*, which I'll provide."

"Don't take me for a fool!"

"Never, Justiciar. Very well. He'll need a decent lawyer if he's arrested." He doubled the earlier figure, watching Scanlon's face with satisfaction. "Six hundred darl. I wouldn't insult Your Greatness by underestimating the job in hand, and my man's services would cost far more to others."

"So you're doing me a favour?" mocked Scanlon.

"I am your vassal, Greatness. I'd say I am doing my duty. If you don't like the price, you can risk the head of one of your men."

"My men will be there as well. Later there will be a lone mission—"

The lord smiled humourlessly. That had told him enough to have an inkling of what was planned. "So you're hunting for a leader as well... Hmm. Leading costs—"

Scanlon's eyes narrowed. "I'll give you four hundred darl and not a crescent more. If you still wish to refuse that more-than-generous offer, maybe you should reconsider your employment—"

"I'm your vassal; I cannot reconsider that without going to His Majesty."

"I didn't say reconsider your loyalty but your employment," growled Scanlon. "Do you think I pay every vassal I've *persuaded* into working for me? Now, four hundred – take it or leave."

Enjoying the effect he was having, the lord flourished his hand. "How can I refuse such a generous offer? Compensation will be forthcoming should he not return to Misol?"

"If he should not return, we shall discuss our position at that point," conceded Scanlon, mindful of the man's skills. "Send him here for orders. I don't have much time."

The lord rose, when standing he dominated the room with both height and bearing. He used it to his full advantage. "He is *my* man. He stays in my employ; *I* shall give him orders. Write them out if you must but it shall be my hand that passes them over. I'm sure as Justiciar of the Empire you do not wish to muddy your hands with anything dubious. When will the orders be ready?"

Scanlon rose, eyes flashing. "Do not forget to whom you speak!"

"I thought the emphasis of your illustrious position was the point of my words. What would His Majesty say if he heard his brother plotting? The fact he's no actual *proof* is the reason that you're not under arrest, Greatness. Will you hand it to him after all this time?"

Scanlon took a deep breath. "He cannot arrest me. I would have to try myself for a start—"

"Would you? He has judges he could trust as a group—"

"Who? If you're so knowledgeable, tell me, who?" Laws were not as easy to remember as some supposed, especially with his men's skills.

The lord smiled disingenuously. "That old goat Tancred? Maybe Judge Fairson too. Your old mentor, sitting in judgement on whom you have become. The thought is invidious, isn't it? I'll need those orders by tonight. Scarsy is expected at Misol tomorrow."

Scanlon frowned. "How do I know the orders will be destroyed?"

"I suppose you'll only have my word for that, Greatness, but I'd hardly want them in my house, would I?"

Chapter 3
ATTACK
Tretaldai, Week 4 – 24th Cearal, 3rd Middis 1213
Lufian – Lord Faran's Land

A WARM BREEZE brought the scents of summer, of wildflowers and cut hay, through the coach's window. The landscape passed by in a rumble of wheels and clopping hooves. The jangle of harness and the men's conversation became the music of the moment. Birds soared far above, rabbits hopped towards hedges and home and butterflies flitted between meadow flowers. The tranquil atmosphere relaxed the mind and senses, lulling the travellers into contentment.

Prince Arkyn, heir to the Oedranian Empire, gazed out of the coach window, watching the rolling Lufian countryside pass. Had he been right not to ride? The day was glorious, sunny with a decent breeze. It would have been enlivening to be riding, but his aching body had other ideas. They were due to arrive at Lord Faran's by mid-afternoon. It would be far better if he didn't look shattered.

He glanced back at his disordered companion. As courtiers went, Lord

Kensal Parchi wasn't typical. More interested in history than current affairs, he didn't worry about trifling things like appearance. Since meeting Arkyn the year before, he was getting better at knowing when formal wear was expected but obviously considered that travelling wasn't one of those times. He wore an unbleached linen tunic, his cracked and mottled leather belt was adorned only with an undecorated belt pouch. There was no need for a dagger or sword with such informal wear and Kensal hadn't decided to break with convention, but his sword was thrown idly on the seat next to him.

All too conscious that he wouldn't have time to change before Faran greeted him, Arkyn wore a formal white silk tunic with narrow red stripes. It shouted he was a FitzAlcis Prince and King's Representative. Part of him envied Kensal's more relaxed manner but there were reasons he didn't emulate him. He pulled his mind back to Kensal's monologue.

"You can't know that. You're just grasping at air."

Kensal grinned. "Not quite air, sir. Look, you've got three significant buildings in Oedran before the Fall of the Cearcall. The old palace, the Justice Hall and the King's Hall, now in the Palace of Oedran. Fine. Why did the kings need both the old palace and the King's Hall? They didn't. Oedran wasn't even the capital of Anapara until later in the Age of the Cearcall. Before that it was Paras. So why did they need those two buildings? I'd suggest they didn't. That the so-called King's Hall had a different purpose. When you start looking at it without preconception, you start seeing anomalies. There are globes of magical power at the Palace – globes, plural, now lost—"

"There are globes at other significant buildings, or there were."

"Yes, sir, but normally history talks of them in the singular. 'A globe was gifted by the Cearcall to the city of Amista on the occasion of…' that sort of thing. They never say the old palace had multiple globes gifted to it. Yet it's said there are globes at the Palace of Oedran."

Arkyn's gaze wandered again. The unharvested hay fields were growing well. A copse was drawing closer, cut wood left drying in the sun.

"All right, try telling me without all the ramble."

"Look at the King's Hall, sir. Imagine it without the Palace enclosing it. It's on the high point of the hill, the Justice Hall just below it. The city looked up at it. If we dispense with the idea it was about the Kings of Anapara, then who was it about? The only other power that could fill such a spot at the gates of Oedran, and get away with it, is the Cearcall. The early accounts say they had many meeting places. So, when examining the premise the hall is Cearcallian, it begins to make sense. Not just the hall itself, with its symbolism carved into the rafters but with the fact that the Imperial Garden is also there – with its twelve carved thrones. The symbols of the Cearcall litter the hall and garden. They'd have had the knowledge and influence to build both. The hall is huge, far larger than any other manorial structure from that period."

Arkyn frowned. "The stories don't match that. It's written into several histories that the Cearcall observed proceedings in the hall from the Viewing Gallery."

"Histories are written by the victors or, in this case, by the survivors, sir. When the Cearcall were blown to the winds, King Adelard claimed Ceardlann. Who is to say he didn't claim the hall and rewrite part of its history? When the Age of Tyranny came, Onraet was so paranoid that he wouldn't use the King's Hall, after the first few years, and wouldn't have it destroyed. He said that the magic there was unbreakable and malevolent for him."

Arkyn sat forward. "Where did you read that?"

Kensal hesitated. "I heard him say it."

"So, you trying to convince me of something you know is the truth?"

"Your Highness, would I do that?"

"Yes." Arkyn grinned. "Just for the enjoyment of debate. Are you?"

Kensal shrugged. "If I said there are times I can't penetrate in that hall, I wouldn't be lying. What I know is, as far as magic goes, there's more in that hall than you might think. I'm certain what I'm saying is true, but I couldn't tell you that I have proof. But just imagine it, sir. What if that hall was a feasting hall of the Cearcall? The road used to go directly north from the King's Gate. It was Arlis who split it in two after the Fire of Oedran in 777 so he could build the Court following the destruction of the old palace."

Arkyn smiled. "I'm imagining it. Answer this: why did the kings during the Age of Battles hold the grievances in the hall? Why not in the old palace?"

"Possibly because they were using it for great feasts and other ceremonial occasions. It was next to the Justice Hall. The Administrative Quarter wasn't what it is today. You'd have had a ceremonial centre beyond the city walls. It would have felt safe for anyone visiting."

"What does Irvin think about your mad ideas?"

"I haven't mentioned any of this to him. Thought I shouldn't undermine the carefully crafted façade the FitzAlcis built so expertly."

Arkyn laughed out loud. "I should probably say thank you."

"Probably," said Kensal with a grin, "but you're a prince. Thanks are for other libraries. Anyway, that hall has more history to live yet." His face fell. "Not all of it good—"

A thud, a scream, a yell rent the air.

"Men, the coach! Sanders, Halien take the rear. Anyone moves, I want to know about it. Howard, can you see anyone?"

"Not a soul… To your right."

Pandemonium took hold.

* * *

A brief moment of shocked immobility later, Arkyn reached under his seat, retrieving his sword and a crossbow. He loaded the bow in silence. Whoever was attacking his entourage wouldn't find him undefended.

Kensal reached for his sword, unsheathing his weapon. "Let your guards deal with it, sir."

"No. Get out of my way."

"Not on your life, Your Highness." Kensal twisted and leaned over blocking the door. "If you think I'm going to let you put yourself in danger, you're in the wrong library."

Arkyn couldn't help but grin. "If I'm in a bloody library at all I've taken the wrong turning! Get out of my way. That's an order."

Kensal got up, pushing his friend into his seat. "No!" He fell forward, his whole body shuddering.

Arkyn caught him, trying and failing to pull out the crossbow bolt. He turned Kensal over. The young lord's features said it all.

"Don't you dare die on me, my friend. We've more to debate."

Kensal grimaced. "You can't… order life. Trust your brother's library… He holds the keys."

The light died in his eyes. Furious, Arkyn laid him down and opened the coach door a crack, two splintering thuds later he closed it, trapped. If he tried to join the skirmish that way, he'd die. He looked at Kensal's corpse and cursed. A trapdoor caught his eye.

"There is another way out, Kensal. I'll just have to move you.'

Without showing his head above the level of the bottom of the coach window, he moved the young lord's body onto the seat and pulled up the trapdoor by its ring. Thanking providence for the necessities of long journeys, Arkyn leaned down and failed to see what was happening. Reaching for his weapons, he lowered himself through the hatch with careful movements to minimise rocking the coach and giving away his actions. Lying low, in the shadows under the coach, he watched through the spokes of the coach's large wheels. His guards were all engaged with the bandits. Several corpses littered the area, some his own men. All the activity was on the right-hand side of the coach. The side where the copse was. He snaked his way out of the other side. Using the coach as cover, he shouldered his crossbow and fired. The bandit attacking his administrator fell. He reloaded. Three bandits still alive. Surrounded and fighting viciously.

"SURRENDER BEFORE MY MEN KILL YOU!"

Nothing changed. Shouldering the bow again, he took another shot, missing everyone. The breeze wasn't helping now.

A voice at his shoulder said, "Thank you, sir."

"It's lucky you're good with a pen, Edward; you're bloody useless with a sword," remarked Arkyn, watching the fight for an opening.

"So I've been told, sir. Might I request you get back in the coach?"

"You can request it until the sun sets, but I'm not going to. Hold these. We don't have much time before they realise where we are."

Edward took the quiver. "Isn't it a bit dangerous, sir?"

"Remind me to rewrite the advice for bandit attacks to include the information," observed Arkyn dryly. "Pass me a bolt."

Instead, he was shoved unceremoniously aside, banging hard into the rear wheel. As swords clanged above him, he lunged upwards with his own. The blade slipped under the heavy set, scarred bandit's ribcage. He fell.

Heart racing, Arkyn rolled aside, pulling his sword free as the clash of weapons stopped.

"Sorry, sir," apologised Edward.

Arkyn winced. "Don't be. I'll live."

A voice on the other side of the coach was shouting orders. Arkyn peered around carefully before walking around the rear of the coach.

Sergeant Smithers saluted. "Thank you for your help, Your Highness. You caused a welcome distraction that forced them off guard."

Arkyn glanced at him, passing the crossbow to one of his guards, and his sword to another with the words, "Clean that, Halien. Casualties?" he asked, trying to avoid examining the surrounding carnage.

Smithers held his gaze. "Captain Marsh, Masters Thomas and Alan, sir. If you hadn't intervened Administrator Edward would have joined them. As for the bandits, two taken and eight dead."

"Nine dead. There's one on the other side of the coach. Oh, and…" He took a steadying breath. "Lord Kensal didn't make it."

Smithers whitened. "He was with Your Highness, I thought—"

"He saved my life. Put the captain, Thomas and Alan carefully in my coach. I'll ride the rest of the way. Sling the bodies of the bandits in the spare cart and their captured companions I want blindfolded and brought with us by the roughest way you can devise. Mark the site well and I'll deal with everything else at Lord Faran's."

Smithers nodded. "We're already on His Lordship's land, sir."

Arkyn grimaced considering what to do next. Should he continue to Faran's or divert to the closest fort? The fort would be better, but, if he did that, Faran might conceal evidence by the time investigators arrived.

Arkyn cursed. "I hope he has a good lawyer. Get to it."

As the Prince turned away, the inactivity ended. Someone was in a messenger link. He watched the bodies being moved and the prisoners being more firmly bound with an odd dissociation. His guards were all busy, Edward and his secretary were making sure the carts hadn't been damaged and nothing would be left behind. His groom was calming the horses and for a couple of minutes Arkyn felt useless, a spare part; everyone had a job apart from him but, as Halien handed him his sword, he shook himself from the feeling of inadequacy. He had to decide how to deal with what came next. He nodded his thanks before viewing the open road. His manservant was eyeing him, concerned.

"Is there anything you need, Your Highness?"

Arkyn bit back the retorts he considered in the heat of the moment. "A bit of philosophy, I think."

Kadeem smiled sadly. "A bandit in the hand is worth four in the cart, sir... I'm afraid my normal skill has departed me."

Arkyn sighed. "I'm not surprised. Are you all right?"

"I've survived, sir. Will you come and sit down?"

"No. I wish to be moving." He gazed at the road ahead. Like before there was nothing of concern in the scene. How had the day turned to tragedy so swiftly? He blinked. He couldn't dwell on events.

A few minutes later, Smithers said, "Your Highness, we're ready."

Moments later, Arkyn was settled in the saddle and his entourage swung into mode with a modification he tried to object to.

"Smithers—"

"Sir, your guards will be flanking you until we reach Lord Faran's; it's their duty and mine to see that Your Highness is safe."

Arkyn gave in. "Of course, Sergeant, do berate me if I interfere in you doing your job."

Chapter 4

OEDRAN

Early Afternoon

Palace of Oedran – King's Chambers – Inner Office

"THERE'S BEEN A BANDIT ATTACK, sir, in Lufian..."

Adeone sprang to his feet, the words ripping through him, stripping him of all mental support as his world instantaneously crashed down around him. The richly furnished office became a haze. Arkyn couldn't be dead...? Scanlon couldn't have succeeded, could he? Arms were supporting him and he was lowered into his chair. Quietly, gently, almost coaxingly his manservant said,

"Arkyn's unhurt, Adeone. It's all right."

His world began to coalesce. As his vision cleared, his long-standing friend, Judge James Tancred, passed him a glass of whiskey. He took it and drank it straight down. Tancred retrieved the glass and refilled it. Adeone sipped the amber liquid, enjoying the taste. His companions were waiting for him to speak but he couldn't find any words. The shock still coursed through his veins. He took a deep steadying breath and realised how worried his manservant must have been. He couldn't remember Simkins ever using his name before.

Eventually, he managed to ask, "Where was the attack?"

Simkins knew what the news would do. "On Lord Faran's land, sir. They're making their way to His Lordship's house now."

"How do you know what's occurred?" enquired Adeone tersely, trying to keep his emotions hidden. Friends could betray as well as enemies.

"Kadeem informed me, Sire. I think he was wondering if they should continue to His Lordship's."

"Yes. I trust Faran," replied Adeone, thinking, *'Alcis, I trusted him until... No, he can't have done this. He'd have made damned sure it happened elsewhere. Wouldn't he?'* He said, "Get me Major Wynfeld, Simkins." He eyed the judge. "Any advice, James?"

Tancred smiled. "Wait for the facts, Sire, but I rather suspect you will anyway."

"The Major told me that they'd cleared that region."

"Bandits are, by their nature, nomadic, sir. It is never possible to rid the empire of them and, if I am right in suspecting the ultimate source of this attack, the term bandits must be applied in the most general of senses."

Adeone sighed; Tancred was a good friend and confidant. "What you mean is my brother ordered the attack."

"Yes, Your Majesty. I am sorry, but I do."

"Well, even if Scanlon did, and I could prove it, until my younger son is twenty, and replaces him as full Justiciar, I can't arrest him." Cradling the whiskey, he whispered, "Maybe it's time to change the law."

Tancred hesitated. He might be the King's friend, but they were straying into territory that made him wary. "If Your Majesty has discounted all other options, you could try, sir, by sealed orders, but I doubt the Etanes would enact it; there are too many of His Lordship's friends there."

Adeone got up exasperated. "Don't I know it. Sicla. I put laws forward and the Etanes debates for months; my brother puts them forward and they're passed within weeks. What am I doing wrong, Judge?"

Tancred smiled. "You are trying to be a good man as well as a king, Sire. Many people thank you for it. It is only those of hereditary power with a love of traditional autocracy who object, but they are few."

"They are numerous enough to block my work! The Lords of Oedran are split and, due to a couple of chance circumstances, my brother's supporters are more numerous in the Etanes. They also buy the cisan members through fear; is that justice?"

"No, it is not, but, in time, I trust Your Majesty's regime will flourish."

Adeone cursed. "It's nearly nine years since I became King, James. I had hoped for more immediate effects."

Judge Tancred crossed to him, laying a supporting hand on his shoulder. "Adeone, your work has benefitted many people. Do not begin to doubt yourself. If the Etanes are not co-operative, hunt elsewhere for support. The Lords of Oedran are only the traditional guardians of law making. By-laws, decrees and proclamations do not need reference to them. If you are careful, they can be bypassed."

Adeone studied the elderly judge. "I never thought you'd give me such advice, James, and yet I'm not surprised you have. Why?"

"Possibly because Your Majesty recognises that I have, over my life, spent much time circumventing convention."

Adeone snorted. "I suppose you have... Come. Ah. Richardson. Wynfeld is due here soon and there will be some mayhem – rearrange what you can."

"I'm sure I'll cope, sir." The administrator left but was barely in the Outer Office before he turned on his heel to announce the Major of Oedran.

Wynfeld saluted, saw the judge was present and relaxed; the recent revelations about Tancred's family history hadn't permanently damaged the King's trust in him then. That was fortunate.

Adeone moved to his desk. The judge seated him and remained standing at his right hand.

"What could have made my day the worst for years, Major?"

Wynfeld frowned. "I would have hoped nothing, Your Majesty, but I see I must be mistaken." It had to be significant; the King had had many days in recent years which could be termed 'bad'. The death of his father, uncle, daughter and wife, numerous attempts on his life, including resulting dagger wounds, his sons' lives being attacked, his friends discredited – the list was long. His King was saying,

"Your Prince has been attacked by bandits." Adeone considered the Major. "He's survived. Sit down. James, can you pass him a drink, please?"

Two moments later, Wynfeld managed to say, "Where?"

"On Lord Faran's land. I'll be needing answers from the Major of the

Northern Empire."

Wynfeld pulled himself together. There was no point dwelling on what could have happened. "You'll be getting them or his resignation, Sire. Sicla!" He ran his hand over his head. "We'd been informed that area was safe. How many, do we know?"

"No, not yet. Prince Arkyn is still travelling to Lord Faran's—"

"Is Your Majesty convinced of his loyalty?"

Adeone regarded the Major carefully. "I've never had reason not to be. Check where your intelligence came from."

"Do we know—?" Wynfeld broke off as Richardson entered.

Seeing his administrator had news, Adeone motioned for him to speak.

"Secretary Gunn says there were four casualties in His Highness' entourage: Lord Kensal, Captain Marsh, Masters Thomas and Alan, sir. Nine bandits died and two were captured. They're not far from Faran House. Gunn mentioned Smithers has men riding at close protection stations and His Highness seems calm."

"Thank you, Richardson. We'll wait until Prince Arkyn gets in touch to discover other details." When the door closed, the King swore. "He'll feel that loss."

Neither of his companions had to ask for clarification. Kensal had been a close friend and confidant, Marsh had protected the FitzAlcis for years, and the other two casualties had been high ranking in Arkyn's household. Adeone filed away his own feelings on Marsh's death. Their history had been unusual, but there had been a stronger bond than many knew.

The judge murmured, "May their ancestors greet them with smiles."

"May the people they've left wish them well," replied Adeone.

"And may their memory be forever honoured," added Wynfeld.

The King refocused. "The investigation is in your hands, Wynfeld. Inform the General and make sure he doesn't overreact."

Wynfeld rose. "It's not primarily his reaction I'm concerned about, Your Majesty; it is my own." He saluted and left before Adeone could reply.

"There goes one man whose loyalty you need never question, Sire," observed Tancred.

"Yes, but I sometimes wonder who he serves in his mind," admitted Adeone. "He was carrying my wife when she died and I rather suspect it's her memory that keeps him loyal." He saw Tancred's confusion. "He worked for Ira's family until he enlisted. I rather think he still does."

"Your Majesty, Major Wynfeld serves the living first and foremost. Is not that the important fact?"

* * *

Major Wynfeld left the Inner Office cursing roundly. He strode through the Outer Office and Audience Chamber without a sideways glance. By the time he reached the barracks, he was fuming. All the preparations and planning and still his Prince had been attacked. He told his corporal-clerk he'd need a word with Beaver before striding to the General's office where he unapologetically ignored the clerk, knocked and entered without waiting to discover if Paturn was engaged.

The Commander of Oedran took one look at the Major's face, glanced at the General and left.

Paturn pursed his lips. "You better have an excellent explanation."

Wynfeld obliged and watched Paturn sink onto his chair. The fact their Prince had been attacked was bad enough, the fact his entourage had lost so many was devastating.

"What did you know?" demanded Paturn.

Wynfeld shrugged. "I don't think we knew anything, sir. I'll give it a short time before contacting Smithers. He'll have a lot to arrange."

"Yes. I'll contact the Northern Major and see about security. You see about intelligence. Tell the commander our business can wait."

* * *

Major Axton answered General Paturn's messenger without concern. By the end of the explanation, he was white and cursing.

"Do more than curse!" snapped Paturn. "Closest fort to His Highness?"

"Erm, Skylabrae, sir."

"Get men from there to Lord Faran's. I want our presence protecting Prince Arkyn. His guards will be exhausted."

"Understood, sir."

"Then get yourself to Faran's and sort out the mess. I'll be in contact."

* * *

Ignoring his clerk's confusion, Paturn strode to Wynfeld's office, interrupting the meeting with Beaver. On hearing there'd been no forewarning he swore and set off for the Palace. Even if the King hadn't sent for him, he would still make a report.

Adeone looked up at his entry. "I presume Wynfeld's told you."

"Yes, Sire. Any orders? I've a unit of men en route to Lord Faran's to take over guarding duty whilst the Prince's Guard gets some rest."

"Thank you. I want to know the rest of His Highness' time in Lufian is safe and I want answers. Axton is to report to His Highness and deal with the consequences."

"I'll see he does, sir, and prepares a report for Your Majesty."

Adeone pulled a face. "He'll report to Prince Arkyn, completely. My son is my Representative and a senior officer of my army, Paturn. I hope

33

I don't need to state the obvious."

Paturn inclined his head fractionally. "As you wish, sir."

* * *

Axton blinked on hearing the orders. "Sir, I know His Highness—"

"No, you don't," replied Paturn, "but you're going to. You have your orders. I presume Wynfeld's also been in contact."

"Yes, sir. I'm not appreciating his interference."

Paturn crooked an eyebrow.

"Either I am dealing with it or I'm not, sir. He's been rather forthright in requesting I investigate who the bandits are, as though that thought didn't occur to me."

Paturn smiled. "A lot of people will require answers. Get yourself to Lord Faran's as quickly as you can."

"Sir, shouldn't we be moving His Highness elsewhere?"

Paturn snorted. "Axton, His Highness is my superior officer. He and the King trust Lord Faran. *You* do not question that. You make sure His Highness is safe."

"Sir, I can't do that at Lord Faran's. He is surely under suspicion!"

Paturn crooked an eyebrow. "You seem to have forgotten Lord Faran's history as a ward of the FitzAlcis and friend of the King, not to mention a powerful player in Lufian politics. Until the King or Prince say otherwise, we do not interfere. You need to determine how to ensure His Highness' travels and stay in Lufian can be safely continued."

Chapter 5

LORD FARAN'S

Late Afternoon
Lufian – Lord Faran's House

ALERTED TO the approaching cavalcade as soon as they were sighted from his gatehouse, Lord Faran walked outside to wait for them, glad that the weather had been kind. It was no fun travelling in rain and Lufian was better seen in sun. His eyes swept over the approach to his house. The gardeners had done a good job. He hoped the rest of his household had been as industrious inside and his steward had been thorough in his checks.

As his eyes swept over the approaching visitors, his mind weighed up what he saw. The guards' positions were unusually protective. What were the bundles on two of the horses? They couldn't be men. Yet a niggling worry surfaced: something was wrong.

As the party drew closer, Faran recognised Prince Arkyn, not only from the young man's attire but also his resemblance to the King. The child he had met years before had grown into a young man in features and bearing. As the Prince reined in, Faran stepped forward but a guard politely barred his way.

The sergeant riding next to the Prince dismounted and strode forward requesting his weapons in hushed but resolute tones.

Faran looked to the Prince, who raised an eyebrow in emphasis of the request. With a courtier's blank face, Faran handed over his sword and dagger. As Arkyn approached him, he bowed with a languid ease.

"Your Highness, it is my pleasure to welcome you to my home. Might I enquire why a sergeant has disarmed me? I understood Your Highness travelled with a captain." He took in the disordered, stained and dusty tunic a moment too late. What *had* happened? It surely wasn't blood spattering the Prince's white tunic.

Arkyn eyed him. "Are you complaining about being disarmed or the rank of the man who did it?"

"I hope I am not complaining at all, Your Highness, merely asking for an explanation."

Arkyn's lips twitched, but to smile or frown Lord Faran didn't know. The Prince caught Smithers' eye. "For the moment you're Acting Captain, thereby allaying part of Lord Faran's confusion. Your Lordship, we will talk inside. Her Ladyship and your daughters will have to excuse the lack of normal courtesies – today has not been normal."

Faran said carefully, "Her Ladyship is unavoidably engaged elsewhere, sir. She sends her sincerest apologies."

"They are accepted. Your study?"

Faran led the way, confused by the Prince's manner. Everything he'd ever heard or seen of him had suggested a more courteous approach, not this rather brusque style. It obviously hid something. Being disarmed suggested circumstances he didn't want to contemplate, but the fact no guard followed them into the privacy of his study reassured him slightly. Though he didn't miss the tread of boots outside as a guard followed them to the door.

Once that door closed on the rest of the house, Arkyn said, "An hour and a half ago we were attacked by bandits on your land. Nine were killed and two captured. Four of my entourage met their end, including Lord Kensal Parchi of Anapara and Captain Marsh. Because of this, your affairs are now under official examination."

Understanding flooded Lord Faran's mind. He replied, dismissively, "Examine my affairs," before continuing, "Is Your Highness hurt? There is a doctor here—"

"That is unimportant."

"I doubt His Majesty would think so, sir."

Arkyn frowned. "When His Majesty asks me, I shall tell him! I am obviously aware of Your Lordship's close association with my father and that you were once a ward of the FitzAlcis; so, the measures I am ordering are not easy and the King may well overrule me. I will say that if I find you've been falsely implicated, I shall pursue the proof."

Faran nodded. "Thank you, Your Highness, the assurance is much appreciated. Can I not, at least, send for some refreshment in return?"

"I doubt, with Kadeem here, Your Lordship needs to send for anything. What delayed Lady Faran?" enquired Arkyn.

"The birthing of our child, sir: the arrival was heralded a couple of hours ago."

"Then go to her. What remains of my household will see to my needs."

"Your Highness, my conscience won't allow—"

Arkyn shook his head. "Go! I'm able to stand my own company."

Faran bowed and left but, on the threshold, he turned and smiled. "Thank you." He was gone.

Sinking onto a chair by the door, Arkyn reached for the decanters on the table next to him, pouring himself a whiskey as pain relief. Sipping it, he gazed blankly at the room. Gradually, its arrangement began to intrigue him. His nearfather's study contained a desk and comfortable chairs; it was a place of retreat. Faran's study contained his desk and a long oval table of dark oak, which could seat eight people. This room wasn't a retreat. It spoke of influence rather than privacy. Arkyn pursed his lips. He had ordered an investigation into one of the most powerful lords in the empire. As days went, it matched his arrival in Tera. Antagonising the situation wouldn't be wise, but he'd already done that by having Faran disarmed. He put his head in his hands. Would his father overrule him? Had he overreacted? He winced and straightened up, cursing, as his side complained about his slumped posture. He'd had no choice. Lords had a responsibility to make sure no bandit operated on their land. Sicla, Merchant Fullerton in Bayan had been arrested in 1210 just because bandits were caught on what had been his land, and they hadn't attacked the FitzAlcis and killed a future Lord of Anapara.

A few minutes later, the guard on the door opened it for Kadeem, who entered with a laden tray. He put the tray down as the door closed.

Arkyn smiled half-heartedly at him. "I told Lord Faran he didn't need to send for anything."

Kadeem smiled grimly back. "I'm intrigued there weren't refreshments prepared, Your Highness."

"His mind was elsewhere, Kadeem; Her Ladyship is in labour."

Kadeem nodded. "That might explain it then, sir. I've some camomile tea and a sweet-cake if Your Highness would like it?"

Gingerly, Arkyn pushed himself to his feet and crossed to the long table before sitting down. Noticing Kadeem's face, he said, "Your eyes are sometimes so sharp you'll blind yourself. I'm perfectly fine and that's an end of it."

The anxiety didn't leave Kadeem's features. "Your Highness, you once promised me in Terasia that you'd never be, to use your own words, 'So stubborn headed again'. Let's see what damage has been done. Please. Edward did mention you'd had a fall."

Half amused, Arkyn pushed himself to his feet. "You know it's not really fair, using my own words back to me."

"I'm sorry, Your Highness, I shall try to forget that."

Arkyn drew a sharp breath as he pulled his tunic over his head. "Don't you mean 'remember that'?"

Grimly, Kadeem took the tunic, shaking it out. "No, sir, I don't. For that would be hypocritical. Your Highness, when you said you'd pulled a muscle, is it meant to be purple and black?"

Arkyn glanced down at his side. "Maybe I should have added 'bruised' as well, for completeness' sake—"

"I'll request Lord Faran's doctor attends on Your Highness. He should be able to give you some pain relief that isn't whiskey for a start."

"How…?"

"I'm trained to spot empty glasses, Your Highness."

"Trained to perfection, it would seem. Annoying perfection, I might add. Very well, Kadeem, I'll eat before accepting the doctor's ministrations – in whichever rooms Lord Faran has put aside for my use. In the meantime, though, for the pain, pour me another whiskey: a large one. If it offends your sensibilities, turn away whilst I drink it."

* * *

Once Arkyn had eaten, he tried to summon the strength to contact his father. He wanted reassurance but didn't want the palaver that would follow his father discovering what had happened. In those moments, he wished magical messengers didn't exist, that a letter would have to be dispatched and it would take days for the King to hear he had been attacked; however, such times were long in the past for when Ull had appeared and brought magic to Erinna he had also brought messengers. They had many uses, from simply carrying a verbal message to forming private face-to-face links, no matter how far distant the parties involved were. The links put the participants at a comfortable speaking distance; outside of the link,

37

observers would see an opaque heat-haze-like disturbance.

His messenger was a red dragon called Fafnir – small enough to nestle in his palm, with a steady character. Arkyn called him, trying to smile as the link formed with his father.

Adeone said simply, "I know."

"Sire?"

The King sighed. "Why, when something has happened and you need support, are you formal? There's no shame in it."

"I… It's a weakness though."

"Nonsense. Maybe you shouldn't let everyone see it but, Arkyn, I'm your father! Are you unharmed?"

"I've some bruised ribs. I'll get them seen to. Kensal, Marsh—"

"I know," admitted Adeone. "I'm sorry for it as well. Kadeem contacted Simkins. I had to be told, and I suspect Kadeem was seeking reassurance on whether you should have continued to Faran's. I'm pleased you did."

Arkyn shrugged. "I can't believe he's had anything to do with this. I trust Wynfeld's reports that said this region was clear of bandits; therefore, they must be here for a specific reason. Or, at least, they must have been here for one. I don't think we missed any. We've captured two—"

"Good. The Northern Major is en route from Lufia to report to you. Until then, the Chief Captain of Skylabrae fort has specific instructions. One of his units should be with you shortly. If Marsh is dead—"

"I've made Smithers Acting Captain."

"Promote him fully," stated Adeone. "He was going to be Tain's captain in a couple of years. Now, do you need to talk?"

"I think I do, my head's… I don't know…" Gradually Arkyn explained the events. Including the one piece of information the captured men had revealed, their leader had been the man Arkyn killed at the coach.

By the end of the recitation, Adeone was grave. "Several aspects of that were interesting. Well done in ignoring every bit of common sense in the book. Your guards are there to deal with such attacks, but I'm proud that you didn't just sit in the coach and wait for it to be over. As for Edward, he's getting another dose of training – for his own safety… I'm truly sorry Kensal died, Arkyn."

"I'll contact his family."

"Let me do that. His body should be returned to them."

"Father, if Kensal's funeral is to be at his home, I won't be able to attend, and I want to show what I feel."

"I can understand that, but his family should send him to his ancestors."

"Marsh, Thomas and Alan though—"

"Marsh was a guard, Thomas and Alan were part of your official household; their ashes will be returned to their families, but they knew, if they died whilst abroad, their funerals would be abroad. Lord Kensal had taken no oaths; his family can afford to have his body returned to them."

Arkyn murmured, "I will bear that cost, father. I would also ask a favour: can you persuade the Dean of the Advisors' School to permit Irvin some leave from his studies? I'd like him to represent me at Kensal's funeral."

"He'll be there. I'll deal with the immediate consequences of this attack and let you know tomorrow what's been done. The Northern Major won't arrive by then. Wealsman might have managed it but Axton doesn't have his skills. Now, you need to get some rest. Faran will have to excuse the niceties," said Adeone with finality.

"Lady Faran's in labour, so I told His Lordship to go to her, sir."

"Good. That removes one complication. About Faran—"

Arkyn hesitated. "I've ordered that his affairs be examined, but realise you might rescind that."

Adeone shook his head. "I'll not do that. For one thing, it should hopefully exonerate him. I'll send an apposer, with his staff. If Edward can see to the initial securing of papers, that's all I ask of him."

Arkyn smiled. "He and Smithers should already be doing so, sir. I'm sorry for all the trouble this is causing."

"Me too, but none of it is your fault and there's nothing to feel guilty about. Go and put your feet up; you look, if I may say so, atrocious."

Arkyn sighed. "Thank you, father. I always appreciate honesty."

Chapter 6
RUFFLED FEATHERS
Late Afternoon
Lufia

AXTON CURSED when the link with the General broke. How was he meant to ensure the safety of Prince Arkyn when he'd put himself at risk by staying with Lord Faran? He called for his clerk, requesting his batman, maps of Faran's estate and the information they had on the Prince's entourage. When the last arrived, Axton said simply they were leaving for Faran's at dawn. They needed the hours between to set other aspects in motion. He pulled the maps of Faran's estate towards him. Where had the attack been? He checked the list by his hand and tried to contact Captain Marsh. When the link couldn't be made, he blanched. At least he'd known Marsh. He glanced down the list again and contacted Kadeem.

"I'm sorry to trouble you, Master Kadeem. I wondered who was heading

His Highness' guards."

"Acting Captain Smithers, Major Axton."

"About—"

"Speak to Smithers, Major. I'm needed elsewhere."

"Sir." Axton broke the link. Menservants were all the same. Their job and only their job. When the next link formed, he said, "Smithers, I need your side of what happened."

Smithers explained, filling in several gaps, including the location, deaths and captures.

Axton swore. "His Highness?"

"Isn't your concern, sir," replied Smithers.

"Are you satisfied Lord Faran's is safe?"

"I have no reason not to be. Amongst other things, a birthing is currently underway and the household rather preoccupied by it. His Highness is content, His Majesty is content, I am content. Is that all?"

"I'll be attending on His Highness as soon as possible. It's a few days' hard ride."

"Very good, sir. I shall see His Highness is informed after he's rested."

Axton closed the link. Would he even be allowed to see the Prince when he arrived at Lord Faran's? Too many men were in the way. He found the mile marker that Smithers had mentioned on the plan as the closest to the attack and looked between it and the next for any clue as to where the attack had occurred. There was only one copse marked that could have hidden the men. He'd have to visit the site. A cairn had been built, Smithers said, so at least it would be marked. Well, that and the bloodstains would mark it if it didn't rain first.

He contacted the Chief Captain at Skylabrae and ordered a unit of men to Lord Faran's. If everyone was happy, he didn't see the necessity of sending more. They needed a day's worth of shift changes.

By the time Wynfeld was in contact, he thought he'd got everything sorted. He explained to Wynfeld what Smithers had said, what had been ordered and what he'd done.

Wynfeld eyed him. "You don't think you've missed anything?"

"Not that I can see, Wynfeld, and please remember—"

"Axton, His Highness will tear apart your work without a second's thought. You need patrols from Shinglis to Lufia, you need to make them frequent and you need to ensure there are no more ambushes waiting for His Highness when he leaves Lord Faran's. I suggest you station men in every copse and woodland close to the road until His Highness has returned to Oedran. For his return journey, don't forget Tradere, and I will attend to those in Anapara. You search every building before His Highness passes.

We will provide you with our information for each host. His Highness is likely to dismiss the threats, but that doesn't mean we don't check for them."

"I think I know what I'm doing, Wynfeld."

"Think again. I've dealt with His Highness through treasonous attacks. I've travelled with our Prince and King and handled their safety on the road. They are not prone to unconditional second chances."

Axton snorted. "You disprove that. How often have they been attacked on your watch?"

Wynfeld's eyes narrowed. "Obviously not enough to hinder my career. Maybe what you should be asking is how many times my actions have saved their lives. I didn't do that by being complacent."

"Weren't you a sergeant in 1209?"

Wynfeld smiled. "Yes, in Garth. I learned quite a lot about you then. Now, do I have to order you or will you maintain the fiction of our rank?"

Axton broke the link, irate. Of all the jumped up, cisan spawn, Wynfeld had to be the most diabolical. A foundling with ideas of command. He contacted the General to complain about the interference.

"Let me get this straight, Axton. You are objecting to someone of higher rank, with more experience, advising you of the best way to avoid resignation?"

"I… Hadn't seen it in that light, sir."

"And I never want to have to point it out again. Now, report to His Highness. I hope I don't need to instruct you in other subtleties such as reporting to the Sagamore as well. Dismissed."

* * *

Once out of the link, Axton bit back several frustrations. He called for his clerk, demanded a strip map of the road between Lufia and the Anaparian border, snapped that he knew it also went through Tradere and strode out of his office. He fumed all the way to the Pala, where he obtained an audience with the Sagamore with only a short wait.

"How can I help, Major?"

Taking a breath to calm down, Axton said, "Your Excellency, His Highness' entourage was attacked by bandits not two hours ago on Lord Faran's land. I'm informing you I've been ordered to have patrols on the road, and properties and woodland searched until His Highness has returned to Oedran following the review."

Lord Eames raised an eyebrow. "That will be extremely inconvenient for our citizens."

"It's not particularly convenient for me, Your Excellency!"

"Nor, I suspect, His Highness. Was he hurt?"

"I have not been informed that he was, sir. I have been informed that

Lord Kensal, Captain Marsh and two footmen in the Prince's household were killed. The entourage and guards killed all but two of the bandits, who are being questioned. I've men en route to protect the Prince at Faran's."

"His Highness is still staying with Faran?"

"Yes, Your Excellency. Everyone seems satisfied he isn't responsible. I am setting off at dawn to report to the Prince."

Eames nodded. "Do we know if this will delay His Highness' arrival and the review?"

"I don't, sir. I think you would be best to contact the Prince's staff, but avoid his manservant."

Eames raised a discreet eyebrow. "Is all well, Axton?"

"It has been a frustrating day, Your Excellency. I will inform you if I hear anything that will affect the review. Other than, of course, His Highness being attacked on his way to do it. If Faran isn't blamed, I expect we will be!"

"I don't recall His Highness taking his frustration out on anyone in Terasia for events there."

"No, but Wynfeld was in Tera at the time and Wynfeld is their golden boy, apparently."

"I think you need to calm down, Major. I do not know what has happened, but Major Wynfeld can only act with the King's authority behind him. You are not, therefore, in a position to question it, in the circumstances."

Axton bit back another retort. "Of course, Your Excellency. Is there anything you wish me to say to the Prince?"

"Assure him of my loyalty, please. That's all for now, Major."

Axton saluted and left. He returned to the fort, contemplating the fact that no-one seemed minded to censure Wynfeld. What had that man got that had made him rise so high, so quickly? His clerk informed him there had been no further messages, so he left for his quarters where his batman said all was ready for them to leave at dawn. Axton hesitated, considering. There was nothing he could do in Lufia now and he needed to regain favour with everyone senior.

"Get everyone in the saddle. We leave immediately."

* * *

Axton's party, consisting of himself, his batman, clerk and three guards, had barely left Lufia when Lord Scanlon was informed that the bandit attack had failed. The man informing him seemed unconcerned by the Justiciar's rage. He sat with legs akimbo, watching the younger man rail against the situation.

"Adri did say that all wasn't lost. Seems our other targets may have met their end."

"It will get them examining affairs in Lufia!"

"You wanted to risk it, Greatness. You were very definite about the merits of your plan."

"And you told me your man was up to it!" snapped Scanlon. "Is he dead or captured?"

"I don't yet know. If he's dead, there will be fewer issues. If he's alive, he won't be for long. Our contact at Faran's will see to that."

Scanlon pursed his lips. "I should hope so. If he's dead, do you have a deputy for him?"

His companion smiled. "Oh, I do. He's champing at the bit of promotion."

"I want to watch his scarring."

"Oh, the promotion is much more than that. He needs to prove he will do anything I order. I have to know there are no other ties."

Scanlon raised an eyebrow. "Bind him and wipe his memory."

"Ah, but there are rumours such bindings can be broken. He has no parents, only a brother and four sisters. Or he did have, if he wants to be my right hand."

Scanlon crooked an eyebrow. "Killing good stock now?"

The man shrugged. "Someone would need to break their spirit."

"And your point is? Round them up and hand them to Syri. He can distribute the sisters. You can decide what to do with the brother."

"Are you deciding what happens to my tenants, Greatness?"

"Is that a problem?"

"Of course not, sir," said his companion silkily.

Scanlon's eyes narrowed. "Good. I will still witness the scarring and then we find a new plan. Events in Oedran will soon swing in our favour, though the King won't know it. And, withdraw everyone we can from Lufia. Prince Arkyn cannot suspect anyone there. I trust Adri but everyone else needs to keep their heads down. No letters leave. I will discover if any messengers are being watched. We must withdraw for a time."

"Being strategic, Greatness? I never thought I'd see the day."

Scanlon glared at his guest. "There are repercussions for such comments."

The man smiled back. "Call your guards then. Have me flogged. Have me flayed. Have me tortured. You'll lose my silence and, if I die, there is no guarantee of your safety. I made sure of that many moons ago." He pushed Scanlon further. "My room is in the attic, isn't it?"

"No. One maid, that's all! There's sure to be one misbehaving."

"Thank you, Greatness. Your secrets are safe with me. I'll bring you a treat next time I visit."

Scanlon's eyes narrowed as he watched the man leave. He'd need to check his guest had followed orders. Those sisters would be valuable. He just hoped Syri would have the sense to split them up. He didn't care what happened to them after that. They would enrich his coffers and that was all that bothered him. They could work for their lives. He needed gold more than ever.

Chapter 7
ADJUSTMENT
Late Afternoon
Lord Faran's

BY THE TIME Arkyn was ensconced in his private rooms with Faran's doctor ministering to his bruises, Faran's secretary had given Edward several chests and he was ready to tackle the study with two of his clerks. With all their hands full, they entered the study without knocking, a mistake. Lord Faran was sitting at the end of the long table furthest from his desk with his head in his hands.

Edward hesitated. "My apologies, Lord Faran."

Faran glanced over. "You have your job to do, Administrator. Don't mind me. The women threw me out. Waiting is the worst part."

Edward hesitated. "Is the birth—?"

"Progressing? Yes. Over? No. Is the Prince settled?"

"He is, my lord. Thank you."

They eyed each other. Edward more nervous than he expected. The situation had thrown all the careful hierarchies into disarray.

"I hope my staff haven't hindered you," said Faran.

"They have been remarkably helpful, my lord."

"I am pleased. If there is anything His Highness needs, just ask. The house is his whilst he stays here. I will see that preparations for dinner haven't been disrupted. I thought His Highness might like to dine privately before events overtook us all. Will a private meal still be best?"

Edward hesitated. "Yes, my lord, but it is His Highness' wish not to disturb Your Lordship with trivial concerns. Master Kadeem will see to such arrangements."

Faran never hesitated. "Of course. I understand—" He broke off as a golden, winged wolf appeared in a flash of green light. He closed his eyes for a moment and glanced at Edward. "Will you excuse me, Administrator? It appears His Excellency wishes for a word."

"In the circumstances, it would be best if I joined the link, my lord."

"Of course. Lahama, please ask Lord Eames to include Administrator Edward in the link."

44

The wolf-messenger inclined his head and two moments later three people glanced at each other in the plain surrounds of a messenger link. Lord Eames eyed Faran first but spoke to Edward.

"Might I ask why you wished to be included, Administrator?"

"His Highness would expect me to be, Your Excellency." Edward watched the non-answer rile the governor of Lufian and wondered if Prince Arkyn would have anything to say about the liberty he'd taken, but letting the two most powerful men in a province speak privately after the attack was probably best avoided. No-one knew who was responsible.

Faran's lips twitched. "I have no concerns about the administrator's presence, Your Excellency. How may I help? His Highness has arrived and is settled."

The Sagamore reddened. "But you can't say 'arrived safely', Faran! As far as travesties go, this is monumental. How dare you not act to remove bandits from your land? You have brought the entire province into disrepute."

"Your Excellency, do you believe I would not have acted if I had known they were there?"

"His Highness has been attacked on your land and you are claiming complete ignorance? That is your defence?"

Faran crooked an eyebrow. "It is not only my defence but the truth, Eames. Your Excellency is more than aware that I have had the FitzAlcis visit before and am therefore fully informed of expectations and requirements. Without wishing to be flippant, having bandits on my land has never been part of those requirements."

Eames coloured. "If you are trying to defend yourself with such trite remarks, I recommend you save your breath. You're under house arrest until investigations are concluded to my satisfaction."

Faran didn't look at Edward. "I am already under house arrest, Lord Eames. Oh, no-one has been so impolite as to call it that, but it is a fact."

"Good. I'll send an apposer to interview you."

"Your Excellency, His Highness and His Majesty have the matter in hand," said Edward carefully.

"Administrator, I want answers."

"I will inform His Highness of that wish, Your Excellency, but given the attack's target and victims, it is the King's Apposer who will investigate."

"I am His Majesty's Representative, Administrator."

"You are, Your Excellency, but so is His Highness."

Faran's lips twitched again. "That's called being out-ranked, Eames."

The Sagamore glared at Faran. "Do not make your position any more precarious than it already is. His Highness' presence at your house does not make you untouchable."

"No, it doesn't," agreed Faran. "The investigation currently occurring is certainly proving that point. It does, however, set strict lines as to who is in charge. I am sure that the matters surrounding the review will take up most of your time, anyway."

Edward hid his wince. The two men obviously had a history and the manoeuvrings for ascendency were blatant. All Faran's careful manner had disappeared.

Eames took a deep breath. "I'll still have time to devote elsewhere. I'll be keeping a careful eye on you, Faran."

"You mean you haven't been before? I am surprised. Your Excellency, His Majesty and His Highness have done me a great courtesy today, I would hope that you could take your lead from them, especially as His Majesty's Representative. I will be mindful of events, of the investigation and of the doubts swirling around me. I shall abide by any injunctions from the FitzAlcis or their staff and act only as befits a man under such suspicion. I realise Your Lordship is concerned for both the province and His Highness and understand that this display of mistrust and ire is not Your Excellency's normal manner."

Eames eyes narrowed. "Then there's nothing more to be said, Faran. I shall see you soon, Administrator."

"You shall, Your Excellency. I will inform you should any plans change."

"Thank you for the consideration. Lahama, please close the link."

When faced once more with his study, Faran let out a long breath and momentarily put his head in his hands, before crossing to a window and gazing over the gardens at the front of his house.

"Thank you, Administrator."

"Do I need to inform His Highness of the antagonism between Your Lordship and His Excellency?"

Faran turned back to the room. "It is a personal matter and will not jeopardise His Highness. Lord Eames likes being Sagamore far too much to risk his position, especially as he wasn't always destined to be Sagamore."

Edward filed that away under *interesting*. "Thank you, my lord. If His Excellency contacts you again, it would be better for you to refuse the link, at least until the investigations are over, likewise any other messenger links. The obvious exceptions being those investigating events, the FitzAlcis and their staff."

Faran relaxed. "Thank you for that, Administrator. I can see several of my fellow lords being inquisitive under the guise of making sure I'm well. Oddly, I do not wish to talk to any of them."

"May I continue securing papers, my lord?"

"Of course. Though, could we be private for a moment?"

Edward nodded at the clerks to leave.

Once alone, Faran relaxed, crossed to a panel in the wall behind his desk, moved a portion of beading aside and opened the panel.

"You will need all of these as well, Administrator. I would be grateful if you would keep the knowledge of this space secret."

Edward eyed the hidden alcove. Three shelves, fingertip-to-elbow deep, held piles of scrolls and papers. "What do these contain, my lord?"

"Personal correspondence and some accounts, marriage agreements and family papers." He closed the alcove. "I would prefer it if *you* would decide whether the correspondence there is investigated. You will recognise the King's seal on many of the letters, and Queen Ira's on several. Until you tell me I may, I will not re-enter this room."

Edward swallowed. "Thank you for trusting me, my lord. I shall take advice and let Your Lordship know the decision as soon as I may."

"Then I shall leave you to your work, Administrator."

Edward watched him leave with an odd feeling. He *wanted* to trust Faran, but that might be exactly why the Lord of Lufian had shown him the safe area. He doubted that the lord's secretary even knew about it. What had hung in the air between them had been a test, unspoken but of great magnitude. Edward had taken oaths to keep personal correspondence private, yet he'd been told to secure *all* papers. He called the clerks back in. He'd contact Richardson at the day's end and ask his advice. He suspected it would be to leave the FitzAlcis correspondence alone. The King's letters were private, he wouldn't need an apposer to tell him what they contained.

Chapter 8

SUPPORT

Early Evening

Inner Office

Aᴅᴇᴏɴᴇ ʜᴀᴅ ʙᴀʀᴇʟʏ ᴇxɪᴛᴇᴅ from the link with Arkyn when Lord Landis entered his office. They exchanged a solemn glance.

As the door shut, Landis said, "Close one."

"Far too close. Thank you for coming, my friend."

"I have to have my uses," replied Landis satirically. "Defender of your life, your Chief Advisor, a Lord of Oedran with far too much responsibility for two other lordships…" His tone changed to a more serious one, "But most importantly to me, your friend and nearfather to your children. The rest can wait until we've had a drink and you've explained what's happened. All I know is that Arkyn's survived a bandit attack."

Adeone pointed at the decanters. "Help yourself. Who told you and whom have you told?"

Landis crossed to the sideboard. "Richardson informed me, and I admit I went and told Lady Amara and Lady Rhian on my way here."

Adeone frowned. "Why? Aunt Amara I understand but my cousin?"

Landis passed him a whiskey. "She happened to be there, Sire. I didn't think you'd mind."

Adeone took the glass. "I don't particularly. I just wondered if you had an ulterior motive."

"No, but now you mention it, she was *very* concerned…"

"Festus!"

Landis chuckled. "Sorry. So, this attack?"

As Adeone explained, his mind cleared. Stress would never change what had occurred. He had to accept it and make sure his orders dealt with the incident without anyone becoming overly aggrieved.

Landis watched his friend's face relaxing. He wasn't as calm and, when he left the Inner Office, certain people would find out just how deep his anger went. They'd been assured the area was safe and although he trusted Major Wynfeld, for the most part, he didn't trust all Wynfeld's men and informants. He'd have to ensure that units of the army always travelled with the King and Princes when they were on progress.

* * *

A short time after Landis left, Adeone was trying to concentrate and failing miserably. A knock at the door brought a welcome distraction from the mundanity of everyday business.

Richardson entered. "Lady Rhian, Your Majesty."

As his cousin entered the office, Adeone motioned for Richardson to leave. Getting up, he moved around his desk. "Rhian, how are you?"

Rising from her curtsy, Rhian eyed him. "How I am is secondary to how you are. Your son's just been attacked again, lost one of his closest friends, and you're stuck here where you feel like you can't give him the support he needs. You're feeling useless…"

Adeone swallowed, watching her face.

"…How close am I?"

He smiled sadly. "Spot on. However, Landis didn't know Kensal had died when he told you what had happened."

"I have my methods, Your Majesty. So does mother, come to that, and hers are more direct."

Adeone paled. "Please tell me she hasn't contacted Arkyn?"

Rhian put a steadying hand on his arm. "No, she hasn't. She spoke to Major Wynfeld. Do you need to talk?"

"I've done so much talking. I'm not sure more will help."

"Then go and see Tain. If you stay here there'll be questions to answer. Get away from it all."

Adeone sighed. "I've still that to sort out." He motioned at his desk.

Rhian gave him a piercing glance and then raised her voice to request Richardson's presence.

The administrator entered the office and took in the tableau. Lady Rhian was facing the exhausted King, searching his face. In their features was their lineage. For the first time, in his mind, he acknowledged Lady Rhian as the King's *immediate* family. Her hair colour was almost identical to his, just the slightest hint of the Fairson blonde coming through but, from where Richardson was standing, the thing that struck him most was their noses were the same straight shape.

The King was watching his cousin with an edge of defeat. Did Adeone realise how close he'd become to Rhian? He was accepting her support both physically and mentally. He was letting her care for and about him, as he hadn't let anyone in recent years. What would happen when the King realised? It wasn't his place to interfere, or outwardly interfere anyway. Helping things along was different.

"Sire?"

"Lady Rhian is giving orders. She's taken lessons off Lady Amara."

Rhian's gaze searched Adeone's face. She let her hand drop from under his elbow as he nodded. "His Majesty's going to see Prince Tain, Richardson, and that lot," she pointed to the desk, "urgent or not, will wait until His Majesty's return."

Adeone saw Richardson's face twitch. "I can still be contacted and could always give a verbal order."

"Of course, Sire," replied Richardson, "but I agree with Her Ladyship and will not be disturbing Your Majesty under any circumstances."

Adeone glanced between them. "I sense a conspiracy…"

"Is one needed, sir?" enquired Rhian.

Adeone flicked his eyes in dismissal at Richardson and, as the door closed, his drained gaze turned on his cousin with no words needed, but still he thanked her.

She shook her head in amused admonishment. "I'm family." She pulled him into a hug and felt him relax.

"How's Neassa?"

"Coping," replied Rhian quietly. "Court has been easier than expected.

Banning Rufus certainly helped. Rathgar's tried whispering there was more to the divorce but no-one is listening to him. They see it as sour grapes. Especially as Peaga hasn't shunned his mother. The lawyers are still talking but that's what they get paid for."

Adeone's tired gaze met hers. "Will you both come to dinner soon?"

"Yes, if you go to Ceardlann tonight and let the valley take care of your troubles. Or let Tain chase them away."

Adeone nodded. Being in the valley's embrace sounded like just what he needed.

* * *

Adeone rode to the Rex Dallin considering, as he had on many another ride, how fortunate he and his ancestors had been in the existence of the valley. If you were not born there or granted entry by the King you were debarred from the valley's bounds, and to transgress that was treason. A magic set up in the distant past, by the ancient and now extinct Cearcall, protected that ideal: without the right token, arrest was a foregone conclusion and death the normal consequence. Within the valley, just over a mile from the northern boundary – marked by encircling cliffs, a river and the Pillars of Alcis (two standing stones either side of the road) – was the FitzAlcis' house, Ceardlann, a retreat from officialdom, the calm in the storm of an empire. The very mention of its name brought a smile to the lips of all who knew it and, when away from it, a longing to be within its soft, appealing embrace.

When Adeone arrived, he told Prince Tain, Lady Elantha and Tain's friend Calumiel Galdwin of the attack. Tain took the news solemnly, accepting all implications of the bandit attack.

"Father, Arkyn will be all right, won't he?"

"Yes. He's got a few bruised ribs but that's all. He was fortunate."

Tain shook his head. "No, that would suggest luck and, with our guards, luck isn't a factor. They're excellent. I'm glad Smithers went. I didn't want him to, but Arkyn said he should get experience travelling."

Adeone smiled. He hadn't known that. "Arkyn was right. He's going to promote Smithers to captain. Can you cope with that?"

Tain nodded. "Yes, but it's really Arkyn's decision. The Princes' Guard answers to him first, for all Smithers is normally my guard. When will he be home?"

"Arkyn? A few weeks yet."

"Pity. Can I go with him next year?"

Adeone shook his head. "Not until you're a few years older." He put a reassuring arm around his son. "When are you next seeing James Tancred?"

Tain grinned. "Tomorrow. I'll ask him about banditry laws. It's apt,

50

at least… Arkyn'll miss Kensal, won't he? I wish I could do something. I feel so useless here."

Adeone ruffled his hair. "You're doing more than you realise."

Cal, who'd been writing, said softly, "There's nothing to say you have to be with someone to help them, Your Highness."

Tain looked over at him. "Thanks, Cal. Any suggestions?"

"Plenty, but I'm not sure His Majesty would appreciate them."

Adeone laughed. "I think I'd give you a run for your money, young Cal. Who's your next poor victim for a practical joke?"

"I haven't got a target in mind, Your Majesty. Would you have any suggestions?"

Elantha glanced up from her painting. "Please don't give them any ideas, Uncle Adeone; they're bad enough without them."

Adeone chortled. "Sorry, lads, but the lady has spoken." He crossed to his niece, asking, "What are you painting, little flower?"

"The Wishing Tree. I sketched it a couple of days ago, early in the morning, and the colours have stayed in my mind…"

It was only as he was falling to sleep that Adeone realised Cal had skilfully changed the subject on purpose and with more tact than expected.

*　*　*

In the small hours, Adeone started tossing and turning. His mind painting pictures and these were the most vivid yet. He was riding through Oedran. Blackness engulfed him. It wasn't absence of a dream, this was part of the dream. The enveloping void held him fast. Voices echoed in his mind; he wouldn't recall their words, but the fact of the voices remained. He tried to recognise them. Chapa, Landis and Arkyn were all discernible.

He awoke to reality with a start. Shaking, he got up and put a wrap around his shoulders. Retrieving a decanter and glass, he poured himself a whiskey and sat watching the stars. His ancestors, wife and daughter were amongst them. Were they sending him these dreams? He didn't know how long he sat collecting his thoughts, but eventually he started yawning and rolled into bed, having pulled the covers straight.

In the morning, Simkins entered and removed the decanter and glass wondering what had made the King seek for them in the first place. Realising Adeone hadn't slept well, he left the room again, delayed breakfast and contacted Richardson to put back the King's arrival in Oedran by an hour. Half an hour later, he woke the King and was perplexed by Adeone's first question.

"Do we know where Laioril is at the moment, Simkins?"

After collecting his thoughts, Simkins said, "I'm not sure we do, sir. He's not in the immediate vicinity."

Adeone sighed. "He never is when he could help."

"I suppose, Your Majesty, that is a consequence of being the Chief of a nomadic tribe."

"I'm not sure that was helpful either. Is my bath ready?"

Simkins hid his smile at the change to more practical matters as he replied with a simple affirmative.

Chapter 9
COLLAPSE
Imperadai, Week 4 – 25th Cearal, 4th Middis 1213
Messenger Link

BEFORE BREAKFAST, Adeone called up Dragoris and obtained a link with Faran, intending to get the lord's version of events. Faran's drawn face and distressed eyes told a thousand tales.

"What's happened?"

"I've been up all night, Sire, and have another daughter, but that's not the point—"

"Congratulations. You should get some rest."

"I was going to, sir, but I don't quite know how to put this..."

Adeone's eyes narrowed. "What is it?"

"It's His Highness. He's not been to bed and won't stop pacing around his room. Master Kadeem's worried and—"

"Right. Don't worry. Get yourself breakfast. I'll see if he'll talk to me."

He wouldn't.

Adeone swore to himself. Shock could be many things, but he didn't think this was shock. Arkyn had always felt things deeply and would exhaust himself through feelings alone if he wasn't careful.

Adeone contacted Kadeem. "When did the Prince start acting like this?"

Kadeem took a steadying breath. "Last night, Your Majesty. I don't know what to do. Something's seriously worrying him. The doctor can't do anything, and His Highness won't even have a drink."

"No, he'll know you'll put something in it. Sicla. I wish I was there, or Landis or Wealsman come to that, even Wynfeld. Just one of us. Right. You've got to get my son to stop walking. Dragoris, ask Smithers to join us, please." Adeone sighed as Smithers appeared and saluted. "Yes, time for that later. Listen to me, both of you. Kadeem, you're going to try to get His Highness to stop walking. Smithers, you're going to remove every bit of steel or military attire you're carrying or have on. I mean that. Every single bit, down to the daggers in your boots. I'd say your boots but you're a guard and I don't think it would be a good idea. You're to go into the room with Kadeem and – I can't believe I'm ordering this – you're to restrain His Highness if Kadeem's brand of persuasion fails. Just get hold of him. He'll probably fight for a couple of minutes. Keep him secure and stop him from hurting himself. When he collapses, as I'm sure he will, carry him to bed. Then you forget *any* of that happened. Is that clear?" (They both nodded.) "Good. When he's asleep, let me know how it went."

* * *

Kadeem entered the sitting room. "Sir, is there anything I can do?"

"Yes: go away," muttered Arkyn.

"You know I won't do that, sir. Please, sit down. I know you won't accept a drink or any food for fear we've tampered with it, but you've got to sit down before you fall. Please, His Majesty's worried—"

"Who told him?"

"I didn't and nor did Edward or Smithers, sir."

"Talking of Smithers… What are you doing here?" enquired Arkyn glaring at him.

Smithers said quietly, "I'm charged with protecting Your Highness from mishap. Unfortunately, this might be classed as a mishap."

"You're hardly dressed for it!"

"A softer approach was needed, sir." He took a step closer to Arkyn. The Prince snapped, "Stay there!"

"No, sir." Smithers took another step.

"Stay there!"

"Do you think I'm disobeying Your Highness through choice, sir?"

Arkyn didn't answer and continued to pace.

Smithers intercepted him and held him tightly, carefully avoiding Arkyn's bruised area as much as possible. "Sir, stop struggling. Please stop. We're following His Majesty's wishes and, frankly, someone's got to do something."

Arkyn struggled weakly for a few more seconds. He closed his eyes for a long moment and sagged.

"Call if you need me, Master Kadeem," whispered Smithers letting the manservant take Arkyn's weight.

Arkyn heard the door close. "I'll have him on a charge for that…"

"No, you won't, sir, for His Majesty would override it."

"My guard. Marsh is dead. For me! We shouldn't take lives that should

53

be ours." He slid further down onto the floor. Opening his eyes, the world was blurred. Silent tears wetted his cheeks.

Kadeem looked at him kindly. So that was it; the guilt of survival, of having seen others sacrificed. He picked Arkyn up. "They'll watch over us all, sir, from their seats in the heavens. It is no sacrifice when it is made through love."

"Philos… ophy is…n't always 'propriate, Kad…eem…"

Kadeem smiled. "No, sir, it's not; you're right, I'm a fool."

Arkyn relaxed into warmed sheets with heavy covers pulled over him. "Not fool, just not…" he hadn't got the energy to finish the sentence.

* * *

Kadeem sat by him until he was sure he was asleep and then contacted the King. "He's safely in bed, Sire."

"Thank you, Kadeem. Did it take Smithers' interference?"

"Yes, sir, but I don't think it would have been long before he'd have collapsed anyway. He's… Forgive me, Sire, I probably shouldn't…"

Adeone watched Kadeem's face. "Tell me. I need to know what has had this effect on my son; it's not an order but it will be in confidence."

Kadeem paused, torn between different loyalties: technically, he answered to the King until Arkyn was twenty, but the Prince had to be able to trust his discretion as well. He weighed up how to not answer. "Sire, I think it would be better for me not to. I'm sorry, but, I suppose, it isn't surprising when you consider the bandit attack."

About to tell Kadeem to stop messing around, Adeone paused. "He's feeling guilty that others died for him, isn't he?" He read the truth of it in Kadeem's face. "It's *not* surprising, but it could be devastating. Thank you for keeping my son's confidence, but someone is going to have to talk it out of him and I can't see it being Wynfeld this time. Don't you try it. I don't think he'll appreciate even gentle encouragement from you after what happened. I'll speak to Lord Faran."

Chapter 10

LECTURE AND SURPRISE

Mid Afternoon

Lord Faran's House – Prince Arkyn's Bedchamber

KADEEM SAT BY ARKYN until the Prince awoke in the afternoon. He passed his master a drink without a word. Arkyn drank thirstily. Taking back the glass, Kadeem refilled it. Arkyn emptied it again.

"I must see Smithers. His actions were rather drastic. I'd only been thinking for a couple of hours."

Kadeem replaced the glass on the bedside table with deliberation. "Forgive me, but I feel I must intercede. I'm afraid to say Your Highness had been pacing for much longer than that. In fact, you'd not stopped since dinner last night. It was breakfast time when Smithers intervened. His Majesty insisted we got you to bed."

Arkyn rubbed at his splitting head. "Oh. Right. Well, thank you. I *did* say in Terasia that I wouldn't be stubborn headed again when you requested something of me. I made you a promise and I've broken it. You care for me so well that I must be nothing but trouble to you. I wreck everything you try to do and all without meaning to. I'm very sorry, Kadeem."

"Sir, it really doesn't matter to me. I wouldn't get paid so well if the job were easy," replied Kadeem, appreciating the apology nonetheless.

"True, all too true. Do you happen to have a headache remedy?"

"Yes, sir, it's called food and rest. You're not to get up today. Doctor Chapa's orders…"

"Ah. I shall be good and stay in bed. I don't think all the miles between here and Oedran would stop the doc berating me. Tell me, is Lady Faran safely delivered?"

"Yes, sir, of a baby girl. I believe they are to name her Samara. If you'll excuse me, I'll go and order a meal for you."

Arkyn nodded and closed his eyes once more. When he opened them, a couple of minutes later, he found Faran at the foot of his bed, wearing a simple plain tunic without adornment on his belt. The Lord of Lufian bowed and waited as Arkyn glanced at the door and noted Smithers was also present.

"Congratulations on the birth of Samara, my lord."

"Thank you, Your Highness. I thought I owed enough to the FitzAlcis, so I've named her in your family's honour." Seeing Arkyn didn't know what to say, Lord Faran added, "I've spoken to the King, sir, and would like to ask you something."

"What's that, my lord?"

"I wondered if… That is, would you be Samara's nearfather?"

"Lord Faran, you hardly know me. Surely, if you wish for such a protector for your daughter, my father would be better?"

"I have discussed this with the King, sir. There is a tradition in this province that a guest of the house at the birth of a child is part of the family of that child for all the years they both grace the mortal world. It's why a lot of births are private here."

Arkyn studied Faran's face. "What does Lady Faran say?"

"She's certainly not opposed to the idea, sir."

"Then I would be honoured to accept, my lord. Honoured but stunned. Thank you."

Lord Faran smiled. "Other than that, how are you feeling?"

"I was thinking things over all night, so rather exhausted, my lord," replied Arkyn. "My manservant is overly cautious and has suggested I would be better remaining in bed."

"I can believe that. Simkins' caution often frustrates the King. I'm sorry if our activities kept you from your rest."

"I hardly noticed them. I was thinking of yesterday's events."

Faran watched a shadow pass over Arkyn's face. "Yes, I rather think quite a lot of people will be thinking on those. Some who thought all was well here. Myself included. There's quite a lot of activity occurring because of it... I understand Your Highness was injured in the attack."

"Not badly. I simply bruised my ribs. Others lost their lives..." He sighed, whispering the words he hadn't said before, "It's my fault."

"Why?"

Arkyn raised an eloquent eyebrow. "Your daughter should be thankful that she is not truly of my family."

"Being born of the FitzAlcis does not mean that you are culpable for the actions of those who disagree with the empire."

"We have created the empire. Surely that means that I am, in some measure, responsible for it and, therefore, for the lives of the men who serve it, whether that is in the army, a guard or a household. Their lives are given into our keeping and we have failed if we lose them."

"No, sir, you have failed if through bad decisions you lose lives but when attacked as you were yesterday it was through no decision of yours," protested Faran.

"If you believe that, maybe you are not as astute as many think," observed Arkyn, frustrated. "I have got a reputation that precedes me. You, yourself, were hesitant in meeting me yesterday and it wasn't all because you wanted to be with Her Ladyship. That reputation might well have caused the attack."

"No, sir. I suspect your uncle's greed and psychopathic tendencies caused the attack. His orders, not your actions."

Acknowledging that the lord was close to his father, Arkyn hadn't got the energy to object to Faran's blatant disparagement of his family. "Then could my actions have dissuaded his orders? Could I have done something differently to change his opinions?"

Faran considered. "You could have ignored the situation in Terasia, drunk the poison, died there and you would not have been attacked but your father would have died of a broken heart and your brother would have been murdered. You could have ignored the incompetency of the former Domini and not replaced him, but the people of Anapara would have become more dissatisfied, and rebellion might have resulted; that might have led to the destruction of the empire and triumph for your uncle, whilst your immediate family suffered and even died in the ensuing battles. So, sir, you might have changed yesterday's events but, I expect, if you could talk to any who lost their lives in the attack, they would say that they would rather have died there than have lived through the alternative. Your actions do have consequences but, sometimes, not taking action may have more devastating results."

"I'm not sure if that's made me feel any happier or not. My head's in even more of a muddle than it was last night."

"I apologise, Your Highness. Maybe it wasn't a good speech and my decision to make it awry."

With a touch of his normal humour, Arkyn observed, "It might have resulted in a more devastating consequence by not being said though. Who can tell?"

"Time, sir, time and experience. I ought to leave you to eat. Is Kadeem always so silent when entering a room?"

"Only when he wants to make sure I'm behaving myself. Thank you, my lord, for the talk."

"Your Highness, the pleasure was mine."

As the door closed, Arkyn murmured, "Yes, because I received a lecture and a shock. Never a good thing." More loudly, he said, "Smithers, you realise you don't hear anything when in private, don't you?"

Smithers' lips twitched. "I do, sir. I'm remarkably blind also."

"Good. Thank you for earlier. That's all for now. What have you decided I can eat, Kadeem?"

The manservant lifted the cloche. Tomato and herb aromas wafted from the plate. A chicken breast sat covered in the sauce with cheese melting on top. It was both simple and indulgent.

Arkyn inhaled. "I'm impressed already." He picked up the cutlery. "Sit down. Lord Faran steered the conversation very deftly. How much did you tell my father?"

"Precisely, nothing, sir."

"How about imprecisely? Ah. Look, Kadeem, I know you can't refuse to answer questions, I know you'll never willingly betray my thoughts and feelings but can't you lie?"

"To His Majesty, Your Highness?" enquired Kadeem.

"Well, no, obviously not, but I don't know... do something?"

"I did, sir. It didn't make any difference... His Majesty only asks when he's seriously worried."

Arkyn considered that. "Then I suppose the trick is not to let him get worried. Who contacted him?"

"I don't know, sir. I suspect His Majesty might have contacted Lord Faran this morning, for His Lordship was refusing to get breakfast until he knew you were tended and then he did just that."

"Ah. He acted like he didn't know anything about my stupidity."

"Maybe he didn't believe it *was* stupidity, sir," suggested Kadeem.

"I never thought you'd stoop to pedantry, Kadeem."

The manservant smiled. "The future is always uncertain, sir."

Chapter 11
ON BANDITRY

JUDGE TANCRED primarily taught Prince Tain in a room, above an inn, a mile from the bounds of the Rex Dallin. It had been decided it was the best solution as the judge, although he held permission to enter the valley, had voluntarily promised Prince Lachlan many years before that he would not re-enter the Rex Dallin after scattering his ashes there. Lachlan had tried to object, but Tancred had been adamant for reasons he could never explain. With Scanlon's plans to kill Adeone, Arkyn and Tain, it was considered too dangerous for Tain to be in Oedran often, therefore the inn was a good compromise. An old soldier, guard and friend of the King's ran the inn, so Adeone had no doubt that Tain would be as safe there as anywhere.

Tain grinned as he entered the room. "Morning, Judge."

"Good morning, Your Highness. I hope the ride was pleasant."

"Very, thank you." He went and curled into his favourite chair.

Tancred eased himself into the one opposite. "I see Your Highness has some documents with you. Is there anything I can help with?"

Tain pulled the satchel onto his lap and rifled through the pages. Half his notes skittered across the bare floorboards before he found what he wanted. Tancred reached to retrieve them, attempting to get them in order.

"I'd give up, Judge…"

Tancred smiled. "It is surely not that hard a challenge, sir?"

Tain gave him a look that plainly said, 'Don't be so sure'.

Tancred placed the papers on a table by Tain's hand. "Then may I help with something else?"

Tain grinned. "It's this: you said yesterday that the two surviving bandits are being questioned by the army but come under the jurisdiction of the Justiciar. That is civil law not military."

The judge nodded. "Yes, Your Highness. Can you determine why?"

"No, Judge, that's what I am asking," replied Tain, exasperated.

Tancred smiled. "Where did the attack happen?"

"On Lord Faran's land; everyone knows that. Or they will."

"Maybe there was a clue in the question, sir, to answer the puzzle."

Tain took a breath, focused his mind and frowned. "Sicla, it can't be that simple, can it? There's no true civil enforcement outside of the cities. The army investigates severe criminal activity. The culprits are handed over to the judges only for their trial. Crimes such as thievery may be investigated by village elders."

Tancred smiled. "Correct, sir. You will make a lawyer."

Tain grinned and carried on thinking. If the place determined the people doing the questioning, what else was there to consider? The manner of attack, the people attacked, the victims and the survivors.

"Arkyn is currently a King's Representative… so, even if he hadn't been father's heir, it would be treason to attack him."

"What is the conclusion of that fact, sir?"

"Treason has to be investigated until the ultimate source is known. There are actions taken that might not be taken in other circumstances."

"Can you name some, sir?" (Tain swallowed.) "They may not be pleasant to contemplate, Your Highness, but it is unwise to pretend such actions do not exist."

Tain sighed. "Torture, Judge."

"Correct. Is there a point at which it is unacceptable?"

Tain looked him in the eye. "Most of the time."

"I cannot argue with that, but I was referring to our laws, sir."

"Torture is unacceptable when information can be obtained from other methods. It is a last resort and information gleaned is unreliable. It should never be continued after information has been obtained."

Tancred nodded. "Very good, Your Highness. What if you discover the torture has continued?"

Tain said, "Arrest those responsible whilst investigations take place."

"Would there ever be a reason not to follow that action?"

Tain thought. "Not that I can envisage, Judge. If it was in a military camp, I would have no jurisdiction but I could request an investigation from the chief officer of the fort as a prince – and, therefore, technically an officer senior to the General – but that would be dependent on His Majesty naming me as such an officer and as Justiciar it isn't always deemed appropriate."

"You will make a judge one day, sir."

Tain grinned. "I can't be content with that, so there's something else to find with this. Bandits, torture, treason…"

He was obviously talking to himself. Tancred smiled.

It took a couple of minutes before Tain said, "The army are investigating because the bandits were outside of a town or city, the methods are determined because it was Arkyn attacked, but who will try the men?"

"Will there be a trial, Your Highness?" enquired Tancred. "There is no doubt that they are guilty."

Tain frowned. "Surely there has to be, Judge."

"Not if the treason has been admitted by the traitor in the presence of the King or His Majesty's Advocates – which includes the King's heir and Representatives along with any Defenders. As His Highness witnessed events, there is only one line of defence they could take. Can you work it out, Your Highness?"

After several moments, Tain frowned. "It's only treason to attack Arkyn, not his entourage. They could claim that they never intended Arkyn harm and that their target was someone else."

Tancred smiled. "Would that defence work?"

"With a good lawyer, the right judge and a blind jury, probably."

Tancred laughed. "There is certainly a justiciar in you, Your Highness. Cynicism like that will be an invaluable skill. Do you think these bandits will ever get to trial?"

Tain shook his head. "No, Judge, I don't. It would be far too dangerous, but that doesn't mean that their deaths will be hidden, because that would also be dangerous. It is obvious Arkyn was the target: Kensal died in the coach and the leader attacked him as well. The other bandits must have known the target, as they gave no warning and were fighting to reach the coach. The act of drawing a sword sealed their fate."

Tancred nodded. "I agree with Your Highness, but I would recommend that, if you sit on judgement in a trial, not to conclude so quickly but—"

"Listen to all the evidence impartially."

Tancred smiled. "Just so, sir. Now, may I see your notes?"

The judge spent several minutes deducing the right order for the notes and marking them to make Tain's life easier next time. As he finished, he asked, "Have you ever been taught how to order notes?"

"Not exactly, Judge. Advisor Spellen simply expects me to make them."

Tancred smiled and started to explain different methods to help with sorting and retrieval. Tain listened to him keenly. Tancred appreciated the enthusiasm but was intrigued by it.

He concluded with, "It will not only make Your Highness' life easier, but your administrator, in future years, might well appreciate it."

"I pity the man that takes on the job of trying to keep me organised."

Tancred laughed. "I cannot imagine why, sir. Now, do you mind if I make a suggestion about the way you take the actual notes? It might be seen as controversial though. Start truncating words, for example use 'circs' for circumstances, 'rep' for report, maybe a capital 'L' for law and so on."

"Like scribes do?"

"Similar, Your Highness. Scribes use a completely different writing system known as scribes-hand, clerks-hand or, more commonly, shorthand, but it is not considered proper that a prince of the FitzAlcis knows it."

"Why? If it could help, surely it doesn't matter. It would only be for personal notes, wouldn't it?"

"It does take some time to learn properly."

Tain bit his lip. "If it saves me time in the end, Judge, surely it would be worth it and I can't get into any more of a mess than I'm already in."

"Then I shall suggest it to His Majesty when I find an appropriate moment, Your Highness."

* * *

After lunch, Tancred changed his planned lesson. Tain's questions of the morning had given him the opening to tackle an important subject.

"Treason, Your Highness: understand the motives before you judge the actions."

"Rather controversial, Judge. If the person has plotted against us, they should take the consequences." He saw the glint in Tancred's eye. "Fine. This is a challenge I can't refuse. Treason is anything that works against the King. It can be the murder of one of his Representatives or the planned assassination of himself."

"It can also be as simple as starting a rumour, sir. The complexities are such that many people do not realise how diverse the treason laws are. Some are centuries old and considered obsolete, or only relevant in times of crisis; however, they have never been repealed. I will devise some studies for Your Highness. This, though, impacts on our discussion about understanding reasons."

Tain nodded. "If treason is so diverse, the reasons for committing it must also be diverse. Some people may not know that they've committed treason until too late."

"You would make a lawyer, sir. This morning's discussion does influence this afternoon's topic."

Tain sank into thought. The judge obviously thought it important.

After several minutes, he mused, "Some people will know what they've done but claim ignorance. Ignorance won't prevent the sentence, but care is needed to stop accusations of tyranny. In more obvious cases, ignorance is unlikely to be supportable."

"Very good, sir. I might advise that, if the law is ancient and rarely referenced, care should be taken and action weighed against the impact of the treason. Lord Daioch was aware of this when he offered a life-bind. His action was courageous and likely designed to circumvent the Justiciar's potential involvement. Pick the right law and the decision rests solely in the King's hands; however, Lord Daioch was not and is not a traitor. Others, sadly, are."

Tain frowned. Was there something else? They were looking at *reasons* someone might commit treason. He needed to stop listening to distractions. Moments later, he saw the answer. "In obtaining proof, reasons are pivotal. If you cannot understand why someone acted the way they did, then you cannot prove ignorance or knowledge. It is possible that mercy may be shown, in some cases; therefore, reasons could be important for determining that. Reasons underpin actions, sentencing is based on actions; therefore, reasons may determine sentence. If you understand the character of the traitor and the reasons they took action, sentencing may be fairer – and that doesn't just apply to treason."

Tancred smiled. "I think you might have jumped straight to Justiciar, Your Highness."

Tain grinned. "That's the purpose of your teaching, Your Honour."

Chapter 12
SKETCH
Hexadai, Week 4 – 27th Cearal, 6th Middis 1213
Lord Faran's House – Prince Arkyn's Sitting Room

HAVING SPENT PENTADAI RESTING, Arkyn looked up as Edward entered his sitting room on Hexadai. Everyone had felt the stress of the last few days, his household and staff included. Some were adept at hiding it. He smiled in welcome and, getting up, crossed to his decanters. Pouring two good measures of whiskey, he passed one to Edward.

"Sir?"

"We both need it, Edward."

Edward swallowed. "I'm fine, Your Highness."

"Then you're the only one of us who is. Sit down and tell me what's on your mind."

Edward hesitated before sitting down. "I'm not sure there's anything on my mind, sir."

Arkyn raised an eyebrow. "Don't give me an opening like that. It's far too tempting. What is bothering you?"

Edward sipped his whiskey. "You don't need my burdens also, sir."

"I asked for a reason. It might have been the selfish one that I need your mind on your job."

"That's just it! I'm a bloody useless fighter. I'm never going to be good protection for you—"

"Do I employ you as a guard?"

"No, Your Highness. I'm not sure that was the point though."

Arkyn said seriously, "Maybe not yours but it was mine. Edward, I don't expect you to put yourself in danger for me. That's what my guards get paid for; it's also why they follow me around everywhere – much to my private chagrin."

Edward tried to smile and failed. "I should still be prepared, sir."

Arkyn sighed, half exasperated, but realised exasperation wouldn't help. "Will you try to believe what I tell you?"

"Of course, sir."

"Thank you. Your swordsmanship is pretty bad – you won't mind me saying it as you know it yourself – but, whatever the empire thinks, I never expect you to put yourself in danger for me. I employ you as my administrator and it's those skills I respect and value in you. I will be sending you for further weapons training when we return to Oedran but for one reason only: your own defence. Selfishly, I want you to be able to defend yourself as I need you. I appreciate and respect your feelings and thoughts but please accept that your job does not include putting yourself in danger for me. Worry about all the traitors who put you in danger instead."

Edward said, "Exactly, Your Highness."

"No, I meant that you should consider your own safety, for traitors will come after you as well."

Edward finished his whiskey. "I know, sir. I'm sorry that I've been preoccupied..."

Arkyn shook his head. "Nonsense. Don't be sorry for your feelings. Just work them out until they no longer control you; it's the only way."

Edward, who'd been studying his glass, caught Arkyn's eye and gave a nod of acknowledgement, recognising experience in the Prince's voice.

Arkyn continued, "Take the rest of the day off. If I need anything, it can wait. Go for a walk and find a quiet spot to clear your head."

"Thank you, sir, but I'm perfectly able to carry on working."

"That I don't doubt but take the time, Edward. Lord Faran won't object to you taking a walk around his grounds."

Edward said, in his normal competent manner, "Very good, sir."

Arkyn smiled. "Now, before you go, why did you come to see me?"

Edward frowned, trying to remember. "We're dealing with the bodies of the bandits tomorrow; is there anything Your Highness wishes done?"

Arkyn frowned, thinking. "Yes, have two sketches of each face taken. We'll send one by secure routes to Major Wynfeld and keep one with your files, again securely. The two prisoners do likewise. I want to know if they're known to the Major."

Edward nodded and made a note on the wax tablet he carried at his waist. "I'll have them done this afternoon, sir. Do you want to see them before they're sent on?"

"Yes, please. Ask Lord Faran if he knows of an artist."

"Smithers should manage, sir. He's not bad, all things considered."

"Smithers is an artist?" enquired Arkyn, intrigued.

"I'd say he can draw, sir."

Arkyn grinned. "I look forward to the results of his endeavours. Let Smithers know, then you have the day off."

"Very good, sir." He got up and bowed before turning to leave.

When his administrator was on the threshold, Arkyn said, "I'll check you've not been working, Edward; I just thought I'd clarify that."

Edward turned and smiled, almost caught out. "Of course, sir."

Chapter 13
FORMAL DINNER
Alunadai, Week 5 – 1st Tradal, 8th Middis 1213
Lord Faran's House – Drawing Room

ON ALUNADAI, Faran entered the south-facing drawing room, with its pale silks and large windows, where his eldest daughters were ensconced with Arkyn. He bowed to the Prince, who met his gaze with apparent equanimity. On seeing her father, Faran's eldest daughter asked if they could visit Oedran.

"One day, Lucille," replied her father, "but not for a few years. I wouldn't do that to the city."

Arkyn chuckled. "I'm sure Oedran could stand a bit more liveliness, my lord, especially for the pleasure of welcoming your family."

Faran gave a noncommittal smile; he was still under suspicion, so why was Arkyn behaving as though nothing was wrong? The previous few days had been uncomfortable. Arkyn hadn't been hostile, far from it, but there had been more tension between them than there should have been. The unit of the army had arranged watches around the grounds and he'd been politely steered away from disturbing the Prince on several occasions by Kadeem, Edward and Smithers. After such close association with Adeone, it was particularly unnerving.

Seeing Faran's unease, Arkyn enquired after Lady Faran and Samara.

Faran shook himself; whatever else had happened, Arkyn was nearfather to his youngest daughter; he had every right, therefore, to be relaxed in his home. "My wife is recovering from the birth, Your Highness. I hope she'll be about before long. Samara is making her presence known, as all my children have." A pensive mood overtook him.

Arkyn recalled a few years before there had been a son who'd died. "Lucille tells me that there's a formal dinner this evening."

Faran sighed, exasperated. "I'd arranged one so that you could meet the lords of the area and then, with one thing and another, I've forgotten to cancel it. If Your Highness feels you'd rather—"

Arkyn lifted a finger. "My lord, turning your guests away is unthinkable. I will merely need to change into my formal wear, as will Your Lordship, I presume. Therefore, what is there to be concerned about? Your neighbours will, I hesitate to mention, be exceptionally curious about my inauspicious arrival. Let's not disappoint them."

"As Your Highness wishes, sir."

* * *

In his private rooms, Arkyn cursed himself for a fool. He *really* didn't want an official evening, but everything he'd said to Faran was true, and he needed to meet as many lords as possible. Kadeem noticed his mood.

"Sir, what are a few hours for a lifetime's endeavour?"

Arkyn glared at him. "Are voicing my feelings part of your duties?"

"If it helps Your Highness fulfil yours, I believe it could be," replied Kadeem with a small smile. "Are you wishing for your mantle, sir?"

"Yes, and don't change the subject so smoothly, it can be very annoying. Why did I agree to, in fact order, this madcap scheme?"

"Because, maybe, subconsciously, you need the diversion, sir?"

"Maybe. Have the bandits talked yet?"

"Not to admit they know anything significant. The Major of the Northern Empire is expected imminently."

"Thank you. Who are the guests this evening?"

"Lords PenWarden, Toral and Monamy, sir. Their lands all border Lord Faran's. We'll potentially be staying with Lord Monamy on our return trip."

Halfway through dinner, Kadeem discreetly advised Arkyn that Major Axton had arrived. Arkyn hesitated. Should he excuse himself to talk with the Major or ask him to wait? The first would indicate scant regard for Faran's hospitality or a rare dedication to duty. The second would show respect for his host or contempt for his duties.

"Lord Faran, Major Axton has arrived. He's had a hard journey. Would there be any chance of a meal for him? I can then see him when he's suitably refreshed."

Lord Faran nodded. "Of course, sir."

"Do men of the army actually need to eat?" joked Lord Toral.

"I believe more than some lords," snapped Arkyn. "They do a vital job, and deserve the same courtesies I extend to every other man who works hard and circumstances have forced into unlooked for hardships."

"Forgive me, sir, it must be the potency of the drink—"

"That is easily remedied," replied Arkyn. "You shall be served water for the rest of the evening. I would hate to think overindulgence should lead to unwise utterances. Lord Faran, I was wondering if I might look round your library; His Majesty tells me it is exceptional."

Faran smiled. "Of course you may, Your Highness."

Arkyn fell silent. Even the word library brought forth memories of Kensal. A few minutes later, he rose abruptly and left the room.

"Was it something we said?" enquired Toral.

Faran snapped, "Not 'we', Toral, you! Do you realise what Prince Arkyn went through on the way here?"

"Well, yes, but I don't see—"

"Of course *you* don't! He lost one of his closest friends: a man whose perusal of libraries was renowned in Oedran and Paras. How could... Oh, never mind. Excuse me, gentlemen."

Faran found Arkyn in the library as he'd somehow known he would. The cloaking safety of the room, isolated as it was from the noisy bustle of the house, was an island of calm within the tempest. He ignored Kadeem's attempt to steer him away at the door. Though he didn't miss the fact that the manservant didn't close it fully behind him.

Once in apparent privacy with Arkyn, he kept a careful distance between them. "Sir, Toral's a fool!"

"It wasn't his fault."

"Yes, it was. I'm not making excuses for him and I doubt you want to in your heart. Don't spare my feelings as your host."

"It's engrained into me," admitted Arkyn.

"In my house it's unnecessary, Your Highness, and always will be – my conscience told me so."

Arkyn smiled sadly in acknowledgement. "Lord Faran, I think I need to be on my way to Lufia. I'm too emotional here. I need work to take my mind off... everything."

"It is not unexpected, sir. When?"

"A couple of days. I wouldn't like anyone to assume that I left because I disliked your hospitality. Kadeem's pointed out that I can run from memories as long as I remember to turn and face them when I'm able to."

"Your manservant is right, sir, and has sense beyond his age."

"He says a philosophical outlook was the result of living in Landis House for his formative years."

Lord Faran laughed. "Knowing Lord Landis, I can imagine it was, Your Highness."

"I shall rejoin you shortly, my lord."

* * *

Toral had gone when Arkyn returned to the table, but at whose instigation he didn't know and didn't care.

Faran said, conversationally, "Lord PenWarden was wondering if Your Highness will visit Faral during your stay."

Arkyn smiled. "I have heard your second city is beautiful."

PenWarden said, "Ah, but not as beautiful as our capital, sir. She's something else entirely."

Arkyn accepted a glass of water from Kadeem and listened for six minutes as everyone talked around him. Half an hour later, the party ended and Lord Faran ushered his companions to their coaches with relief whilst Arkyn went in hunt of the Northern Major.

* * *

"Your Highness, it is a pleasure to meet you."

Arkyn eyed the greying, sunken eyed Major. "Would it were under better circumstances, Axton. I won't keep you from your rest for long. I simply wished to greet you. Given the hour and your ride, we'll speak tomorrow about what happened. Lord Faran has organised a room for you here. Any men with you can find accommodation in the paddock. Presumably, you have tents and rations with you."

"We've one field tent, sir, and some rations, yes. I believe my men are settling in."

"Good. Everything else can wait. I'll send for you in the morning to go through the deployment of your men and my expectations."

The Major left with a salute and slight bow. Arkyn's frown followed

67

him when the door was closed. One tent didn't sound to him like Axton had brought men north. Field tent suggested they'd travelled light. The tent would house six men at most.

Arkyn gave the Major a few moments to be clear of the entrance hall before leaving the library for his bed. He walked tiredly up the stairs, yawning as he reached the landing. There were settles and sideboards at strategic intervals, and sitting wrapped in a blanket on one was Lucille Faran reading by the light of a candle.

Arkyn smiled to himself. "Shouldn't you be in bed?" he whispered.

She started. "Samara's fretting and I woke up. If I read in the night nursery, I'll wake the others."

Arkyn settled himself on the other end of the settle. "Wouldn't the dark help you sleep though?"

"Not with a baby grizzling. You get used to it."

Arkyn chuckled. "I remember I did with Tain and Ella. I learned to sleep through it too. What are you reading?"

She shrugged. "Just a story. It was lying around." She passed it to him.

Arkyn looked at the title, *The Lady of Lone Island*. "Is it any good?"

"It passes the time, sir. It's too twee for me. Too much moralising and not enough real feeling."

"I remember reading several like that." A soft tread drew his attention. "Lord Faran."

"Your Highness. I hope my daughter isn't bothering you."

"It's precisely the other way around, my lord. I stopped her reading."

"I'm sure she didn't mind, sir, but she should really be in bed."

Lucille explained again, this time more hesitantly. Arkyn found that intriguing. Though he supposed her father probably was more concerning, given he knew she was out of bed when she should have been asleep.

Faran pursed his lips. "Six minutes then." He turned to Arkyn, "Do you require anything else this evening, sir?"

"No, thank you, Faran. Goodnight."

With a smile playing around his lips, Arkyn watched Faran walk off. When the lord had disappeared into his bedchamber, Arkyn whispered,

"What would happen if I kept you longer than the six minutes?"

Lucille giggled. "Can we find out?"

"I wish we could, but if your father doesn't check, I expect Kadeem will appear to see where I am."

"He seems very attentive."

"It's what he gets paid for," said Arkyn with a wink.

Lucille nodded. "I guess so. Sir, I know I shouldn't ask but... Is father in real trouble?"

Arkyn sighed. "He might be, but there's no point anticipating the outcome of the apposer's investigation."

Lucille hesitated. "What would happen if it goes against father?"

"He could lose his lordship, he might lose his life but it would be up to His Majesty, not me, and the King didn't order me to leave here."

"Father's told us not to worry, but I want to know what's happening."

He studied her concerned face. "He's trying to protect you, that's all."

She nodded. "Thank you for being honest, sir. I should get to bed."

He watched her go with an odd feeling of guilt.

Chapter 14
MORNING MEDLEY
Cisadai, Week 5 – 2nd Tradal, 9th Middis 1213
Lord Faran's House – Arkyn's Bedchamber

THE FOLLOWING MORNING, Arkyn woke sluggishly when Kadeem pulled him out of sleep. The day looked to be pleasant, blue skies, billowing clouds and a gentle breeze. Summer was being kind, kinder than his body was to him. Maybe he needed to venture into the gardens and sit soaking up the warmth. It would be his last day of relative freedom until he reached Oedran once more. He dressed thoughtfully. He had several things to do before he could relax. The first was to contact his father and try to explain about the previous evening. The more he studied his actions, the sicker he felt. He was his father's official Representative and he'd probably alienated Lord Toral. He'd certainly shown him up in front of his peers.

When Kadeem had cleared his breakfast, he called Fafnir and obtained a link with the King, explaining the events of the previous evening. There was no hiding from the fact his words had made Toral leave the dinner early. The fact Lord Faran had probably asked him to was an unfortunate complication in the circumstances.

Adeone's only reaction was a snort.

Arkyn swallowed. "I shouldn't have let my angst show, sir."

"What was the word Daia or Kristina taught you? Codswallop."

"I could have undermined you, sir."

"No, what you did was prove you are principled. You didn't ask Toral to leave. As host, Faran was entitled to do so. He might also have considered the words out of order. Talk to Faran. See what happened before you make assumptions on who is or isn't to blame. Toral might have got indigestion."

Arkyn sighed. "Faran isn't truly relaxing around me."

"You were attacked by bandits on his land. However good friends we are, nothing changes the precarious position he's in." Adeone studied Arkyn's conflicted features. "Why is it bothering you so much?"

After several moments' contemplation, Arkyn said, "Your friendship runs deep and I trust your judgement."

"I'm flattered," quipped Adeone. "There is one truth we face that many others don't: friends can betray us. It's an immutable fact proved time and again in history. I admit, I overreacted with Lord Daioch. You have not done that. If you hadn't known Faran's history, what would you have done?"

Arkyn considered. "I'd have diverted to Skylabrae. Or possibly seen where one of the contingency stops was and made for that."

"So you've already shown more faith in Faran than he can expect. That faith has protected his future if he's innocent. Apposer Nallvir should be with you shortly. He had specific instructions to ride ahead of his team."

"I'm leaving for Lufia tomorrow, Sire. I need to be busy."

Adeone's eyes softened. "Do what you need to. I'm sure Lord Eames will cope if you arrive early."

Arkyn hesitated before asking, "Should I be aware of your friends who are spies this time, father? Any wards who seem innocuous but have hidden skills?"

Adeone chuckled as much to himself as at Arkyn. "Why wouldn't I have told you?" He sobered. "One, and you're currently staying with him."

Arkyn blanched. "Is that *why* Uncle Scanlon—?"

"It's possible. There was evidence coming to light that Faran is a target of your uncle's, but, equally, we have no evidence yet that Faran *wasn't* behind the attack. I will await my apposer's findings before I take action. Having overreacted with Ifor, I never want to do it again."

"The lack of reaction may be unnerving Lord Faran."

"Considering events, his detachment is not calming my night now."

"He is very detached. Last night's dinner was the first time I'd really spent with him since my arrival."

Adeone pulled a face. "That's because your retinue has strict instructions to manage interaction with suspected traitors. Let them do their jobs in this, please. We might not believe it, but we can't risk it either."

Arkyn swallowed. "Of course, sir."

"What are your plans for the rest of today?"

"Talking with Axton and then soaking up some of the sunshine in the gardens, if I can."

When the link broke, Arkyn let out a long breath. Talking with Faran probably was wise, but considering everything his father had said, distance was probably wiser. Feeling somewhat on the wrong side of uncomfortable, he rang for Kadeem and asked him to send Edward to see if he could borrow Lord Faran's study for the morning. The room had the right ambience he needed for a talk with Major Axton.

* * *

Edward received the message from Kadeem with a nod before asking, "Will Smithers be needed as well?"

"Probably a good idea. Someone messed up and Axton is in charge of the army hereabouts. If it wasn't Faran, the army didn't do their jobs."

Edward pulled a face. "Possibly. How is His Highness this morning?"

"Conflicted over last night, I think. He's spoken to His Majesty and wasn't relaxed when requesting the link."

"Do you know what's bothering him about it?"

Kadeem hesitated. "Probably the events with Lord Toral. He left the room for several minutes shortly after. I couldn't prevent Lord Faran speaking to the Prince, but I rather suspect that turned out best in the end. Toral wasn't there when we returned to the dining room."

Edward cursed. "The Prince will blame himself for that."

Kadeem chuckled. "Well, maybe Toral didn't like being told he had to drink water for the rest of the evening." Seeing Edward's confusion, he explained in more detail what had occurred.

"Ah. Well, I'd better tell Faran the Prince is borrowing his study."

Kadeem snorted. "I'm sure His Highness said 'ask'."

"And I shall, but Lord Faran won't see it as a request."

* * *

Edward knocked and entered Lord Faran's study two minutes later to find the Lord of Lufia cursing quietly, opening and closing desk drawers, obviously hunting for something.

"His Highness wonders if he could borrow your study for a time, Lord Faran. He needs to talk with Major Axton."

"Then it's his. I'm not getting much done."

Edward crooked a discreet eyebrow. "Is there anything in particular you need from your papers?"

"My estate book for the last month would be a start."

"I shall ask one of my clerks to copy it for you, my lord. Might I ask Your Lordship why Lord Toral left early last night?"

"I asked him to. I say ask, I mean told. My conscience won't permit anyone to dine at my table who upsets other guests as his comments upset Prince Arkyn. It's as simple as that. His Highness is a guest in my house and my daughter's nearfather. *His* comfort is the most important to me. You seem perplexed. I am under suspicion of treason, but my daughter is not. I wish to introduce Samara to the Prince properly. Am I able to?"

"My lord, that is up to His Highness."

"No not, Administrator. I'm more than aware of the protocols yourself, Master Kadeem and Captain Smithers are operating under. No matter how careful you are being to make me think it's at His Highness' request. You are right to do so. I do not dispute the methods. If I may make a suggestion that my children's nurse brings Samara to His Highness, would that be permitted? I would prefer to be there, but I do understand that you are protecting him and don't wish to interfere with that."

"I will check, sir." Edward saw resignation on Faran's face. "I *will* check and not make a unilateral decision. It might be that Smithers will also need to be present. I can't imagine that His Highness will not wish to meet his neardaughter."

"Thank you. I shall go to my library for a time. Please let me know any of His Highness' decisions."

Edward watched the lord leave feeling oddly conflicted. Were they being played for fools, or was Faran honestly trying to make the best of the situation? Either way, he needed to clear the lord's desk and gather everyone.

He glanced without thinking at Faran's papers. One was a sketch floor plan of the house with a potential extension. Was Lord Faran planning building work when he was under such suspicion? It was either a sign of delusion or optimism. The other papers were scribbled accounts or at least estimates. No wonder he needed his estate book. The visit was costing him in victuals. By the looks of things, he'd taken on the task of feeding the army unit. Edward carefully put the papers away in the top left drawer of the desk. He opened the top right drawer and retrieved some fresh paper. If nothing else, he'd learned his way around Faran's desk when securing everything on the day of their arrival.

Leaving the room, he went down the backstairs and poked his head into the servants' sitting room, that the Prince's retinue had taken over.

"Gunn, Lord Faran needs the last month of his estate book copying out and I'll be with His Highness. Can you see to it, please? Keep your eyes out for anything odd whilst you're doing it. Scott, can you inform Major Axton the Prince would like to see him then hang about outside the study in case you're needed? Smithers, you'll need to be there too."

* * *

A knock at the door broke Arkyn's contemplation of the gardens. He quietly requested the knocker to enter and wasn't surprised to see Edward's calm visage or practical bow.

"Good morning, Your Highness. Lord Faran has said you're more than welcome to use his study and has confirmed he asked Lord Toral to leave last night."

"Did he offer the information?" enquired Arkyn, shrewdly.

"When I asked why Lord Toral left, sir, yes."

Arkyn snorted. "Why did you ask him?"

"It seemed opportune, sir. If Lord Toral left because of any affront to him, there are other considerations for your staff. As Lord Faran asked him to leave, it makes things easier."

"Then thank you. I should see Axton."

"I've let him know you wish to, sir. Lord Faran also wonders if Your Highness would like to meet Mistress Samara? He has offered to absent himself from the meeting if that is easier in the circumstances."

Arkyn swallowed. "I'd like very much to meet her. Lord Faran need not absent himself, but it might be an idea if Smithers is there."

"Very good, sir."

* * *

Arkyn made his way to Faran's study thoughtfully. In the time it had taken Edward to arrange the loan, he'd informed Kadeem that they'd be leaving in the morning. For once, he didn't care about the chaos he'd caused. He needed to be elsewhere. Faran's considerations were making things almost uncomfortable. He needed to harden up. The Lord of Lufian was acting properly. The short time they'd spent together without others present had made him realise he liked Faran and that was dangerous when suspicion hung over him. If Faran was a spy, it explained why the attack had happened where it had. The problem came in the guessing and double guessing of every little fact. He needed to leave it to people who weren't as invested in the situation.

As he drew close to the study door, Smithers saluted. Arkyn nodded at him. The new captain was bearing his elevation with stoicism and also, Arkyn thought, a slight trace of irony.

"Come in, Smithers. How are you?"

"Fine, sir. Thank you."

"Good. After I've spoken with Axton, I'm going to sit out in the gardens whilst Kadeem packs. We're leaving for Lufia tomorrow. His Lordship wishes me to meet Samara. I'd like you to be there when he brings her. A caution I expect he'll understand. Come in."

A minute later, Edward announced Axton and settled himself at the long desk to take notes.

Arkyn nodded in acknowledgement of the Major's salute. "I trust

73

you're rested, Axton."

"Very much so, sir. Lord Faran is an attentive host."

"Yes. Please take a seat. I'll be leaving for Lufia first thing in the morning; so, if you need to interview any of my staff, you'll have to bear that in mind. I realise you'll wish to see the site of the attack. One of my guards, Halien, will go with you to show you the way. How many men did you bring with you?"

"None, sir. I thought it best to get here as quickly as possible. I'll use the men from Skylabrae or summon more if necessary. Lord Landis was in touch during my journey. He's asked I supply a unit of men to accompany you to Lufia. If Your Highness is leaving tomorrow, I'll need to request them from Skylabrae as soon as possible."

Listening, Arkyn privately cursed his nearfather's caution. It might be well placed after the attack but arriving in Lufia with a unit of the army wasn't the image he wished to portray. He'd have to warn Lord Eames.

"I am grateful for Lord Landis' concern. The men who were sent on the day of my arrival have been efficient and discreet. I would be grateful if that discretion continues after my departure. The King is sending an apposer to investigate the situation here. Although he is under suspicion, Lord Faran is not under arrest. I expect whoever is stationed here to abide by the normal courtesies."

"Your Highness, I understand that His Lordship is an influential man but bandits have been found on his land."

"No-one is in doubt of that. It doesn't mean he was *harbouring* them," replied Arkyn. "Merchant Fullerton in Bayan was cleared of similar charges in 1210. I will not anticipate the outcome of any investigation, and neither will His Majesty. The captured bandits have been unremarkably recalcitrant. I expect they know nothing and won't have any useful information but don't stop trying. Now, were there any reports of bandits before my arrival?"

"None that I know of, sir, but no-one is beyond my investigations. If there were reports, and we failed to investigate, there will be repercussions for those involved."

"So there will. What was done here to ensure my route was safe?"

"I'll ask the Commander of Lufian and the captain at Skylabrae at the earliest opportunity."

"I hope your oversight will be more diligent in the future." Seeing the Major's annoyance, Arkyn continued, "There are lots of people involved in this debacle, Major, but you are in charge of the army in the Northern Empire and I was attacked on your watch. I, therefore, hope your endeavours in discovering what happened match that responsibility."

Smithers winced. He hadn't often witnessed Arkyn's temper, but the

Prince's anger was slicing through the room like an ice knife. Edward's studied blankness as he made notes was revealing. Either the administrator was immune to the cuts or he thought the Major deserved them.

Arkyn continued. "As to the attack, tell me what you've ordered to avoid a repetition, please."

The Major did so. He had men patrolling the road between Shinglis and Lufia, with search parties deployed for its entire length and for five miles on either side.

Arkyn eventually said, "Good. The two bandits captured will be handed into your care, and you'll be personally accountable if they escape. I shall expect a briefing of your findings and a copy of any report you propose sending to Major Wynfeld. Your report to the King will be confidential."

"His Majesty's wish is that, in this, I report directly to Your Highness."

Arkyn paused. "Then your report to me will be confidential, apart from the copy you will send to His Majesty. So, Axton, anything I should be warned about in Lufian politics currently?"

The Major never hesitated. "No, sir. Lord Eames was most exercised by the attack and wishes to assure Your Highness of his loyalty. I can only expect his diligence in ensuring Your Highness' safety and comfort will match expectations."

"Nothing about the Sagamore's Court?"

"I do not attend, sir, so am uninvolved in its politics."

Arkyn started weighing up what Axton was revealing. He hadn't had oversight of ensuring his safety, was almost dismissive of the fact and didn't attend Court. The last was intriguing, if nothing else. General Paturn and Major Wynfeld might attend Court seldomly but they attended and knew about its politics, mainly as those politics impacted on the empire's stability. Annoyed though he was, it was a minor aggravation compared to the larger one of the Major's lack of oversight of his route. That incompetence had lost lives.

"If anything does come to mind, let me know. I should allow you to continue. Before I leave, I'll need an update on arrangements for my trip to Lufia. That's all, Major. Thank you." Once the door had closed on the Major's retreating back, he swore and glanced at Smithers. "About those sketches: send Halien to Oedran with them. They mustn't go astray."

"Sir, you'll be two guards down."

"I'm sure Lord Landis will have much to say on the matter, but this is my decision. Thank you, Captain." After the new captain saluted and left, Arkyn said, "Let Lord Faran know I'll sitting in his gardens. I feel like I need sunshine."

Edward pushed himself to his feet, gathering his notes together. "Of course, sir. Is there anything else you require?"

Arkyn smiled sadly. "No, thank you, Edward."

* * *

Arkyn entered Faran's gardens, glad to stretch his legs. The sunlight stole through his senses as he ambled aimlessly around the grounds for several minutes, trying to ignore the guards and soldiers strategically located on paths. Scents of herbs in the warm sun reminded him of Ceardlann and he allowed himself several moments soaking up the ambience. The fragrance of roses was heady in the flower garden and it was there he found the older Faran sisters chasing each other, completely carefree. Lucille spotted him first and gave a more polished curtsy than he expected. He grinned at her.

"Did you sleep well?"

She chuckled. "Very, sir, thank you. Did you?"

"Yes. I was full of good food. What's your excuse?"

"Clear mind, sir. Would you like to join us?"

His eyes narrowed. "Am I safe if I do?"

She chuckled. "I think so. We were just about to stop for a drink."

He settled himself on a patch of lawn and listened as the sisters chatted. Lucille seemed to realise he didn't want to be the centre of attention and so didn't try too hard to draw him into the conversation. Glancing around the garden, he realised he should have brought something with him to read. He certainly didn't want to go back inside for a while. After a time, he asked Lucille if there was somewhere to sit and read in the shade. She pointed along a path.

"There's a covered seat down there, sir, but you've no book with you."

"Don't worry. Kadeem will be lurking somewhere ready to be helpful."

Nine-year-old Caitlin grinned. "I'll find him for you, sir." She ran off before he could protest that it was fine.

Lucille laughed at the look on his face. "We like to be helpful too."

"I've noticed," replied Arkyn with a wink. "I'll leave you to your games. I've absolutely no doubt now that my manservant will miraculously appear with reading materials, a cushion and a drink for me. If I'm lucky, it won't be the review briefing he brings as my reading matter."

* * *

Half an hour later, Arkyn was once more gazing at the gardens, watching the pollinators at work. A cat, likely from the stables, was curled up in a patch of sunlight. Somewhere a dog barked. The guards were changing shifts with muffled conversation, which he was sure was muffled for his benefit, drifting on the slight breeze. He spotted Faran walking towards him with

76

a nurse carrying a swaddled baby. Discreetly following them were Kadeem and Smithers. Arkyn pushed himself to his feet, smiling in welcome.

"Your Highness, might I introduce your neardaughter?" asked Faran.

Arkyn nodded, held out his hands and supporting Samara's head sat back down, cradling his neardaughter carefully. He glanced down at her. She was blinking awake and felt so delicate in his hands. His heart melted. He'd missed doing this with Adeona and Vian Wealsman and the loss became acute in that moment. Faran settled himself on the bench next to him, whispering,

"She favours her mother."

"Life's never that simple," whispered Arkyn in return. "I look like father but I inherited a lot from mother."

"Yes. Your mother had one of the kindest hearts I've ever known. She liked her fun though."

Arkyn swallowed. "Yes. Samara's beautiful."

"That's why I think she favours her mother," quipped Faran. "My conscience convinces me it's the path to peace."

Arkyn laughed. "What do you think Samara would like as a blessing gift, my lord?"

"Something her nearfather thinks is appropriate."

Arkyn sighed. "There was me thinking a little bit of help wouldn't go amiss, Samara, and your father proves he's a courtier at heart."

Faran snorted. "It was engrained into me by your grandfather, sir, and, much as your father has tried to relieve me of the consideration, it's stuck like butter at the bottom of a churn."

"I'm more of my father's mould than my grandfather's."

"And I'm still under suspicion, sir. No, I do not mind. I would rather an investigation cleared me than it was supposed your father or yourself just decided not to act. I will not put the King through the necessity of a second life-bind unless there is no other option. Ifor's situation was hard on all concerned. I cannot see your father put in that position again."

They were still talking in hushed tones but Arkyn's skin tingled for other reasons. If Faran wanted reassurances from him, he was going to be sadly disappointed.

"I'm sure Apposer Nallvir will be diligent in his investigation."

"I hope so, sir. He's just arrived."

Arkyn glanced up and caught Kadeem's eye. A slight inclination of his manservant's head told him it was true.

"Kadeem, give the apposer my greetings but say I have decided it would be better if we didn't talk ahead of his investigation. If he wishes to interview anyone in my retinue, he is not to delay our departure."

Kadeem left on purposeful feet.

Faran murmured, "The apposer will be sorry he rode so hard, sir."

Arkyn snorted. "Would you prefer conjectures about our discussion?"

"Definitely not, sir. I've also spoken with Kadeem. I'm lending you my two senior footmen for your journey. Your retinue will need help, and they are discreet men."

"There is no need, my lord."

"There's every need, sir. Wynfeld cleared them before you came to stay, if that helps calm your mind. They were going to be in the house, and Major Wynfeld is extremely diligent."

Arkyn merely pursed his lips. It was one thing for Faran to maintain a diplomatic distance but to send his staff with Arkyn's entourage was something else entirely.

"Yves and Simmons will take any oath you need them to, sir."

"I'll consider the proposition, my lord." He shushed Samara as she started gurgling. Six minutes later, he handed his neardaughter back to her nurse and watched as they and Lord Faran left. Smithers stayed at a look from Arkyn.

"What's this about the footmen, Smithers?"

"Exactly what Lord Faran said, sir. They do seem like discreet men. His Lordship hasn't had private conversations with any of his staff since our arrival. I, or another of your guards, have always been present. I consulted with Major Wynfeld and Captain Beaver; they are both happy with the situation. Kadeem will keep them all in their places. He manages it with the rest of us."

"Me included," muttered Arkyn with a smile. "All right, I'll talk with Kadeem. He'll need the help, won't he?"

"Yes, sir, and probably better that it's men who have been checked before your arrival."

"You have a point. I'll read for a time. There's no need to wear your feet out watching over me, Captain."

Smithers saluted and left. Arkyn let the peace of the gardens steal back into his senses.

* * *

That evening, double guessing himself, he contacted his father asking advice about the offer of footmen from Lord Faran.

"Would you accept, sir?"

"Yes. Look, your household needs the help. I've met Yves, he's good. I don't know Simmons, but Wynfeld is happy. I'm more concerned you didn't want to speak with Nallvir."

"I was in effective privacy with Faran when he arrived and didn't think it would be wise."

"Admirable caution, but you weren't completely in private. It might be as well just to have a neutral meeting with him. He has clear instructions from me. There's no need to give him any."

Arkyn nodded. "I'll see to it in the morning, Sire."

* * *

The following morning, Arkyn decided to see Nallvir as they were all leaving. There would be plenty of witnesses and little that could be conjectured about that meeting.

As he left the house to mount, he glanced at the assembled men. Axton and Nallvir were standing together on one side, with Lord Faran opposite. He turned to the officials first.

"Axton, any news?"

"Everything's ready for your journey, sir. The men have orders to answer to Captain Smithers."

"Thank you. Apposer Nallvir, it's a pleasure to meet you."

"Likewise, sir. Is there anything you'd like me to see to in particular?"

"I believe your remit is clear. I look forward to your report. Please observe the normal courtesies." He turned to Faran. "Thank you for your hospitality and courtesy, my lord."

"Your Highness, the pleasure was truly mine."

With that, Arkyn nodded to his entourage, who all swung into their saddles with a jangling and collective sigh. Arkyn mounted Ponder and urged him forward, oddly torn. He hadn't expected to relax at Lord Faran's after the attack, but he had found a sort of peace.

Chapter 15
LUFIA
Hexadai, Week 6 – 13th Tradal, 20th Middis 1213
Lufian – Lufia

LUFIAN WAS A GREEN, rolling country. Cotton fields stretched for miles and sheep grazed on higher pastures. Vines grew on sunny slopes and the weather was warm and pleasant. The hours spent riding weren't arduous, and Arkyn enjoyed the scents and colours of the journey. Most evenings and nights were spent at manors with hosts who filled a spectrum of attitudes: subservient, sycophantic, quiet, confident, blunt, formal or informal. The differences made Arkyn smile. His host's manner dictated much of his mood and few realised it. He tried to be consistent in his dealings but, on one occasion, he asked Kadeem if that night's host understood how his manner might affect his standing. Kadeem replied if His Lordship didn't then he soon would. Arkyn had merely nodded; even if he didn't say anything to the Sagamore, the Governor of Lufian would still be informed. To patronise a King's Representative, even if he hadn't been a prince who would become a king, was political suicide. One thing Lord Wealsman, Margrave of Terasia, knew was Arkyn would tolerate most things but patronisation, unjust remarks, blind prejudice and political backstabbing were best avoided if the Prince's respect was sought and without that respect, one's career was on shaky ground. Arkyn wouldn't always move against someone personally but others would notice and that was all it would take.

* * *

They reached Lufia mid-morning and, riding towards the city gates, Arkyn was pleased to see a welcoming committee. He was even happier to note the Sagamore was part of it. For the first year in the last three, the welcome was correct for the arrival of a prince. Either events meant Lord Eames was being extra careful or else he had actually checked what was expected and not made assumptions.

Strewn along the route to the Pala were bunting and flowers, with rose bushes in full bloom lending a heady aroma to the scene of brick-paved streets swept clean and cheering residents. It was, as Arkyn wrote to Tain, spectacular and welcoming.

At the Pala, Arkyn dismounted, aching. He handed Ponder's reins to Simon before walking with the Sagamore into the impressive brick building, to walk almost straight out again into a lawned quadrangle. In the centre stood a sculpture of the province's emblem, a golden flower and a silver snowflake.

The Sagamore said, "Some say it's too extravagant, Your Highness."

"They are wrong, I think. It is beautiful."

"So I think, Your Highness, but then I might be biased."

"I doubt it, Your Excellency. This quadrangle appears a peaceful place."

"It is, sir. Your father spent many hours here when he visited us twelve years ago. If you'd care to follow me, I'll show you to your private rooms."

Arkyn nodded. "Thank you. Is anything formal planned for this evening?"

"Nothing at all, sir. The view was that you'd had a long journey and would wish to rest."

"The thought is appreciated, Your Excellency." Arkyn's gaze took in the cloistered walks around the edges of the quadrangle. It said much about Lufian weather than the more enclosed palaces elsewhere mirrored. Lufian was about warmth and sunshine, not blistering heat like Denshire, or rains like Terasia, or cooler winters like Anapara and Bayan. What the

80

arched windows lacked in glass they made up for in beautiful curvilinear tracery, with snowflakes and flowers worked skilfully into the smaller openings or carved into the stones and bricks.

Eames was explaining the layout; quiet competence emanated from him. The Sagamore's Court was on their right, including the great hall from a much earlier palace. Arkyn swallowed. Kensal would have found that fascinating and the Sagamore wouldn't have been able to continue with the explanation that the FitzAlcis Chambers were just beyond the great hall in what historians supposed was the remains of the private apartments of the Lufian kings.

"And the rest of the Pala?" asked Arkyn, wanting to get the Sagamore away from talking of the history. He was interested, but it tore open wounds that had barely stopped bleeding. Libraries and history, neither would ever be the same again. The Sagamore finished explaining the rough layout of the Pala as they entered the cloistered walk at the top right corner of the quadrangle. The dim cool of the passage helped Arkyn relax as the Sagamore led the way to a spiral staircase with guards at the bottom. He opened a door to the left and entered a small outer office before leading the way into a spacious inner office, with the normal arrangement of desk, chairs, comfortable seating and sideboard.

"This is Your Highness' office. I hope it suits. If anything requires alteration, please don't hesitate to say and it will be done. There's a room for officials to wait on the other side of the outer office."

"Thank you. Edward?"

The Prince's Administrator moved forward. "It's perfectly acceptable, from what I can see, sir. Shall I make a start?"

Arkyn smiled. "After lunch should be fine. Thank you. Don't forget there's all tomorrow untouched."

"Of course, Your Highness."

Intrigued by Arkyn's underlying order that Edward should take some time to recuperate after the journey, Eames kept his thoughts to himself and, at a nod from Arkyn, led the way back to the corridor and up the spiral staircase to the Prince's private chambers. The antechamber was neither bare nor opulent. There were no seats, but a tapestry showed a scene of summer harvests. It made a change from feasts or hunting.

"Intriguing subject matter, Your Excellency."

Eames glanced at the tapestry. "Never thought about it, sir. It's always hung here, from what I know. I can have it changed, if you wish."

"Not at all. I find it oddly pleasing."

Arkyn continued looking at the tapestry. It didn't challenge him as some might. In fact, it reminded him of Ceardlann and the Rex Dallin.

There was a peace emanating from it that drew him in. He reached for the wall to ground himself. Kensal, Kensal would have known the history, would have fathomed out the mystery, and here he was idling in thought. Kadeem took his arm, steadying him whilst Eames watched, perplexed. He had to rescue the situation.

"Thank you, Kadeem. I'm all right. Probably just dehydrated from the ride and talking too much." He straightened up as Kadeem motioned for Eames to continue. He doubted he'd fooled his manservant, but hopefully the Sagamore wouldn't question it too much. He entered his sitting room. Sunlight soaked into every corner through large windows that were in the same style as those in the cloisters, but these three had panes of glass. At the top, the glass was stained sapphire blue, the colour of Lufian. An inglenook fireplace on his right had seating around it. A door opposite the fireplace led to a bedchamber with equally vast windows. Arkyn caught Kadeem's eye. The curtains weren't the thick drapes he was used to, but there were hangings around the four-poster bed, so hopefully he'd still get darkness.

Kadeem said, "Lord Eames, are there thicker curtains?"

"There are winter curtains in storage, Master Kadeem. Those are much heavier. I'll ask our chamberlain to see them changed as soon as possible."

"Thank you, Your Excellency," said Arkyn. "I won't expect them to be changed for this evening."

"That's most considerate, Your Highness. Thank you. Your dressing room, bathroom and Master Kadeem's room are all off a small corridor through this door."

Arkyn nodded. "Do you have time to sit and take a drink with me, Lord Eames?"

"I'm am Your Highness' to command."

Arkyn's eyes narrowed. "I'll take that as a yes but please understand my questions are just that in private, not hidden requests or orders."

As they returned to the sitting room, Smithers said, "Your Excellency, can I just ask that your sword and dagger wait for you in the antechamber? Lord Landis has asked that until investigations into the attack are completed, no-one is armed in His Highness' presence when in private."

Lord Eames smiled. "Of course. I'll just go and remove them."

When the door closed behind him, Arkyn raised an eyebrow at Smithers.

"His Lordship's been busy with such orders, sir," replied Smithers.

Arkyn snorted. "You can brief me on those later, Captain. I might have something to say about them."

Smithers lips twitched. "I'm sure His Majesty's Defender will appreciate the response, sir. Shall I wear my feet out in the antechamber?"

"Probably best. Thank you." As he left, Arkyn turned to Kadeem, "Just unpack the Denshire trunk for now. Everything else can wait for tomorrow when I'm elsewhere. I expect at the end of that small corridor is a second staircase. If there is, make sure my guards are on it as well."

Kadeem had barely opened his mouth to reply when Eames re-entered. Not only had he removed his weapons, he'd removed their sheaths as well. Arkyn nodded at Kadeem to say they'd finished their conversation. Waving Eames to a chair, Arkyn sat down with his back to the windows.

Taking his seat, Lord Eames said, "I hope the remainder of your trip was pleasant, sir."

"Well, no other bandits attacked my entourage, so that was good," answered Arkyn, trying to make light of it. "I'm hoping for my stay here to be just as peaceful."

"So are we all, sir. I cannot apologise enough for the events that greeted your arrival in our province. My clerks have been checking all records but we had no forewarning of bandits in that area. I've asked the Merchant Guild as well, and there was nothing reported. I cannot believe it of Lord Faran and he was adamant there was no warning of trouble."

"Edward mentioned you contacted His Lordship." remarked Arkyn.

"Given events, Your Highness' safety is now my first concern whilst you are in Lufian, sir. I needed an explanation."

Arkyn crooked his eyebrow. "Had you checked with Axton about arrangements prior to the attack?"

"I had and was assured all was in hand. There are certain matters the army deals with that don't come under my remit as King's Representative. Matters directly surrounding the safety of the FitzAlcis is the main one. Unless I have substantiated doubts, which I did not."

"Very well. Then let us leave the subject there. I presume an itinerary has been drawn up for my stay and the review."

"Yes, sir. My officers are all expecting their summons. Their reports are ready for Your Highness and your advisors to look over. If you wish it, we can move everything forward to match your early arrival. I've moved the welcome feast already."

Arkyn chuckled. "I won't concern your officials. We shall stick to the interviews as you had them planned but maybe I could have sight of the reports. I can then read them more at my leisure, so to speak. What do you expect from the review?"

"Nothing devastating, sir. We don't have missing tax for a start and I would hope my sinecure is acceptable. I am not planning on requesting retirement, nor am I anticipating being murdered by my deputy."

Arkyn snorted. "Do you mean I might actually do a review that goes according to plan?”

"I am very much hoping that now you're here in our city, sir, that it will do just that."

"I look forward to the unusual experience. Maybe you could explain everything about your officials that they wouldn't want me to know."

PART 2

Chapter 16

PETER

PETER SELTH LOOKED AT the cooling corpse that had so recently been his pa. The pain had left the features, smoothed out by his mother and eldest sister as they washed and tended the body. He blinked back his feelings. His brother and sisters were sleeping. Their mother had shepherded them away six minutes past. His own body ached for sleep, for rest, for release from the emotions he had been denying. He wasn't just mourning his pa, he was mourning his lost future, his family's lost chances. He drew the sheet carefully over his pa's face. How he wanted to believe the last promise he'd made, that he wouldn't give up his studies, his fight to better the family. He'd managed to keep from his pa how close to ruin, how precarious their situation was. Had it been fair? No, but his pa had died happier believing the lie.

He tiptoed from the room as though his pa was sleeping. The three rooms they rented weren't small but the living room was practical. His fees had taken anything spare. Now the burden would fall on him to provide enough to keep the five of them. His mother had closed the shutters the previous evening and, even though the sun had risen, they remained pulled to. The street would know there'd been a death. Half of him wished they'd knock, ask, be inquisitive, but it wasn't the way. They would be left to mourn as best they could. Only the closest of friends and relatives would disturb their peace. His mother was sitting by the fireplace, its embers still glowing. He put a bundle of rag scraps and straw on to keep the glow and, finding a blanket, tucked it around her slumbering form. She stirred, long habit keeping half an ear open even in sleep.

"Go to bed. Nothing we can do now."

He squeezed her shoulder gently. "I'm off to the alcium. Do you need anything picking up whilst I'm out?"

"No. It'll all wait. I should let the judge know."

"I'll see to it, ma. You get what sleep you can."

He left the house, pulling the door to until he heard the latch click. His neighbours were stirring, or roused already, some trudging off to a craftsman's house or a merchant's shop, others slinking away to more dubious pursuits, the rest settling down to what work they could in the house or street. A ragman picking over yesterday's crop, a laundress off with a bucket to draw water from the well, a pieman with a bucket of vegetables and meat scrapings off to the bake-square, whistling. As he passed Peter closing the door, he squeezed his shoulder.

"Gone?"

Peter nodded. "A couple of hours back."

"Aye, 'tis hard. He was a good man. The ancestors will've greeted him."

"Thanks, Larry. Need a hand?"

The pie-man shook his head. "You look after yourself now. My best to your ma."

He was gone. His silent form vanishing around the corner as Peter pondered on his words, touched he hadn't started whistling again.

Peter glanced around and received a couple of solemn nods and sad smiles. He nodded back. Confirmation another life had been given to the ancestor's keeping. He wanted away. The early morning always teased his senses before assaulting them later. Oedran was never quiet, it never truly slept, but the early morning had a contemplation of its own.

A minute later, he turned down the alley to the alcium. Always there for if someone needed peace or solitude. The heavy wooden door creaked faintly as he entered. They needed a bit of tallow on the hinge, his hindbrain thought. The entrance was empty, no alcia waiting to welcome him. That was fine. He needed this time, this space for himself, even for a moment. He'd been blessed here, as had his siblings. His parents had married under the ancestors' dome. It was a place of community and family as much as contemplation.

He ran his hand along the plain stone pillar. The colonnade around the edge of the alcium itself was dark still, but the glimmerings of day were weeping through the four high windows to be swallowed by the vast space.

He sat contentedly at the edge, on one of the stone benches that surrounded the alcium in an almost unbroken circle. A lady was seated on the right, bedraggled and careworn. She looked hastily away as he caught her eye. Had she too lost someone in the small hours? Had she tended the body? Or was she here for somewhere to think away from the mayhem of family life? Her feet were bare, her dress tattered, her face too thin. He made himself look elsewhere. Maybe she was just here because it was out of the cold night. He hoped the alcia had a porridge on the go and she would accept a bowl. Sometimes the small things meant life itself within the city.

He gazed unseeingly at the centre of the alcium. The black tiles held no secrets to him. Their muted tones calmed his mind. His pa's presence was as much with him here as at home. The sun was higher now. How long had he been sitting contemplating the space, his mind blank of everything? Had he fallen asleep? No, he was still upright. He glanced to his right. The woman had gone. Had he imagined her? He didn't think so.

He should push himself to his feet, go in search of the senior alcia. It was surely after his rising time, his breakfast. Though, Peter admitted to himself, he didn't know where Adelard lived. There were others but he hoped it was him.

The sun was between the east and south windows when the senior alcia finally entered the alcium. Noticing Peter with a start, he apologised. He hadn't thought anyone was present.

Peter finally pushed himself to his feet. "Don't apologise, Adelard. I needed time."

The alcia nodded. "Aye. I heard your pa is dying."

"He's... That is, last night..."

"May our ancestors welcome him."

Peter tried to smile but couldn't. His ancestors weren't lonely, so why did they need one more soul within their stars? He wanted to yell that, demand an answer from the depths to the deeps but couldn't even speak.

Adelard crossed to him. "I know the details. You wait here. I'll tell you when I need you to sign the roll."

Peter shook his head. "I'll be all right but thank you."

He followed the alcia to his left and into a small, comfortably furnished office. Soft carpet under his feet spoke of extravagance after the bleak tiles. This room, though, was made for comfort, not contemplation. The contrast was marked because it was intended.

Adelard pulled out the death scroll for the year. It was already long and would soon need new parchment stitching onto it. Peter watched as Adelard recorded the basic facts and turned it for him to sign. Taking the polished walnut pen holder Peter dipped the metal nib into the silver inkpot. He couldn't help but compare the riches to the destitution elsewhere. It was to honour the ancestors, that was accepted, but the woman haunted his thoughts. When the bland formality was completed, and the funeral set, he mentioned her to Adelard.

The alcia pursed his lips. "Sounds like Mabel. Her husband's probably been too free with his fists, his drink or his whores again."

Peter frowned. "Can't you break the binding if he's abusing her?"

Adelard shrugged. "She won't have it. I can understand. What would she do? Where would she go? There's enough in this city goes hungry with work and a roof over their heads and she's got three little ones and another growing. We'll find her and make sure she's got a meal for tonight at least. If she'll accept it, o' course."

"Yes, there's that. Wish I could do something more."

"Hey, lad, you're studying to be a lawyer. That'll help more than you know. You won't fix everything, but at least you know what it's like for them not born high."

Peter left Adelard and strolled back through the alcium. A junior alcia was now in the entrance, his white robes pristine. Peter inclined his head slightly in passing and exited to bright sunshine that made his eyes water. Cursing, he dried them, blinking to adjust his sight.

By his reckoning, it was now mid-morning. Should he return home, reassure his mother and siblings? No, he wouldn't be able to wheedle his way out again. His mother would make him rest and, much as he needed to, he needed dreamless sleep.

* * *

By the time he reached the Courthouse numbness had washed over him. Was it grief or exhaustion? He didn't know, but it was all-encompassing. He hesitated outside the building. The imposing structure awed many, but for him it was now a lost dream, at least as a lawyer. So many years of work and hope had died in the small hours. Was it wrong to regret that as well as mourn the man who'd raised him? He hoped his ancestors would understand if they saw his angst.

He knew the corridors, the route to the judge's domain so well he thought he could do it blindfold. He'd run errands here since he was seven. Had found his pa and eaten his lunch in the judge's small outer office. Sat and chatted with the judge as much as his pa during those stolen moments. The judge should have reported him for slacking on more than one occasion but when he'd been asked, all he'd say was 'I needed young Selth to sort some things for me,' and that had been that. No more questions or objections. Peter had loved him for it. Their debates had convinced him to train as a lawyer. If Judge James Tancred thought he'd got it in him, he must have.

The door stood ajar. There was no hiding, no turning back. He entered the once so familiar room expecting his pa to smile in welcome. Ryder merely raised an eyebrow.

"I've come to see the judge."

"His Honour to you."

Peter swallowed. "He's been the judge since I was a bump. Is he free?"

"What name is it?" On hearing the reply, Ryder's eyes narrowed. "Oh. Sorry. How's your pa?"

Peter shook his head, biting his lip. The man's eyes glinted and Peter hated him in that moment. His pa's death had made this man secure. He could continue as Judge Tancred's scribe indefinitely now. In that moment, part of Peter wanted to tell the judge exactly what he'd seen in Ryder's eyes but that would likely get the man dismissed and there was no reason for that simply for a moment's weakness.

He hadn't considered how he'd appear to the judge. He felt paper thin, and the judge's evaluating gaze missed nothing. It was why he was so well respected.

"When, Peter?"

He collapsed onto a chair. "Last night, Your Honour. We'd have sent to you sooner but—"

"I am not the highest priority at such times; I only employed your father…"

"Don't say that. It's not true and even if it was…" He tailed off, then continued, "…You are still you, Your Honour, and pa would have wanted you to know as soon as possible."

Peter sat silently for a long time. The judge returned to reading case papers, apparently completely oblivious of his guest. Peter knew that one of old. The judge never probed, was never inquisitive. If he were to leave, the judge would accept it, but the years of shared experience and memories meant he didn't want to go.

"I'm going to have to give up my studies, Judge. There's just not the money to support me through them and my family also.

"We will sort something out."

"I can't accept charity, sir, and pa wouldn't have wanted me to." Even as the words left his mouth, he thought of Mabel and how he'd effectively requested charity for her at the alcium. The circumstances might have been different but had he just snubbed the judge? He blushed, catching the judge's eye.

Tancred held his gaze. "Be assured, I was not offering it. Having paid my way through the school, I know what it is like; if anyone had offered me a helping hand, with gratitude expected, I would have refused. Anything we work out will be mutually agreed; however, I will speak to Lord Ryson and get the school to hold back on demanding the fees. You do not need to face their demands as well as your grief and familial responsibility."

Peter hesitated. "Judge, I'm never going to be a spectacular lawyer. I'll be a better scribe. I know the job, shorthand and my way around the Courthouse."

The judge settled back in his chair. Peter recognised the posture. A nugget of wisdom was heading his way.

"Never make such a decision with little sleep, great emotion and a friend at hand to dissuade you. Will you accept my help or, if not my help, my advice?" (Peter nodded.) "Then, if I may say so, you need to go home and sleep."

Peter rose. "I think you're right, Judge." It wasn't the advice he'd expected, but it was certainly pertinent.

"If you will accept my company, I shall walk with you and pay my respects to your mother and family."

Peter swallowed. "Of course, but we're all in a muddle."

"I am sure I can cope."

* * *

They left the Courthouse in companionable silence, heading down the tree-lined avenue between the Palace and the King's Gate. The trees gave welcome shade but penetrable shadows. They were barely halfway to the gate when a voice hailed the judge. Peter tried to make himself smaller as the judge greeted Prince Tain. He didn't feel ready to face anyone, let alone the next Justiciar of Oedran. The judge was explaining where they were headed. Peter wished they could just continue, but one didn't snub a prince.

"My condolences to you and your family, Master Selth," said Tain. "Your father will be missed; I have no doubt. Every time I met him, I liked him. I shall not intrude any further."

Peter caught his haunted eye and blinked. He hadn't expected emotion in the Prince's gaze. "T…thank you, Your Highness."

"Peter, do you mind if His Highness accompanies us?" enquired Tancred quietly.

"No, Judge…" He'd replied without thought. Why? He didn't want their grief interrupted. Yet Tain's gaze spoke of something beyond prurient curiosity.

By the time they continued down The Pike, they had four guards dogging their footsteps, the other two had been handed a tangle of reins and instructions to see the horses stabled. The guards unnerved Peter but his unease was settled by the way the Prince and judge ignored their presence. The sergeant had a man before them, two behind and he himself was walking on the inside closest to the buildings, next to the Prince. Peter was between the Prince and judge. Tancred squeezed his shoulder. In understanding? Maybe. They reached the King's Gate into the Lower City and there was no need to wait, or to dodge through the crowd the bottleneck created. Prince Tain's presence ensured their easy passage. The Alcium Plaza was far busier than it had been. The city was truly into its day. The Prince wasn't saying much. He seemed unusually quiet for a lad of thirteen. By the time they crossed the plaza and had entered the

92

warren of alleys and streets that made up the Macarian Lordship, Peter had forgotten the guards. In the narrow streets, the sergeant could no longer easily flank the Prince, who was glancing around curiously, obviously assessing what he saw. Had he ever been in streets such as these? He lived outside the city, only visiting rarely. Did those visits ever include the wider city? Peter didn't think they would. With a jolt he realised that Prince Tain would one day be his landlord. Quietly, he started explaining to the Prince where they were, where alleys led, where the markets were. He caught a gentle smile on the judge's face. What was he up to? Through the Prince's questions, he began to notice his home area as though for the first time. The buildings with their stone footings, some built completely of stone, others with wooden structures above. Windows, some glass but many simply shuttered, as his home was. As they turned into his narrow street, he was suddenly conscious of details he'd never seen before, the clogged gutters and cracked paving, the narrowness and dilapidated frontages.

"I should warn mother..."

Tain said quietly, "I won't intrude, Master Selth; I and my guards will wait here."

Peter shook his head. "Come in, *please*. No-one will mind..."

The Prince glanced at the judge and Peter remembered the judge was tutoring the prince; they weren't passing acquaintances.

Tancred smiled. "Let Peter warn his family and if his mother wishes to invite you in, it would be kind to accept."

Peter entered the dim living room to find his mother awake and preparing vegetables for a stew. He returned her small smile and, in answer to her question, replied that everything was all right.

"The judge is here. Do you mind?"

She shook her head. He'd been a large part of their lives for the last twenty years.

Peter added quietly, "So's Prince Tain." His mother's astonished, shocked and panicky face said everything. "He's sent his condolences and says he'll wait outside. I think the judge should have been teaching him this morning."

"You can't leave him on the doorstep! Invite him in! Cisluna. I'm all of a mess. It's years since—"

"You're not, ma. He's not... what I expected." He put his head around the door. "Come in."

Tain hung back to let the judge enter first. Peter didn't miss the judge placing his hand reassuringly on the Prince's shoulder before leading the way into the dim stone-flagged interior.

"Judge, it was kind of you to come," said Madam Selth.

"I wished to pay my respects and tell you not to worry; Peter and I are coming to an understanding…"

Her brows furrowed. "What about?"

"I am sure he will explain later," replied Tancred softly. "Might I introduce Prince Tain to you?"

Once the initial introduction had been completed, Tain repeated what he'd initially said to Peter, before adding, "Please, Madam Selth, pretend I'm not here."

"Then sit yourself down, sir… Judge, do you want to see him?"

Peter watched his mother and the judge leave. The Prince was standing next to the chairs by the fire, where his mother had been dozing. He pulled the blanket aside, folding it up. Anything to distract his mind now he was home. His mother had obviously been busy too. The table had been scrubbed, the sideboard tidied from the jumble it had become. Where were his siblings? Probably fast asleep. He glanced at the Prince who was taking an interest in the familiar room. There was something in his eyes that spoke of realisation or loss, which puzzled him. Was it simply seeing a home shuttered against the light? Then some small part of him realised the answer: Tain knew the loss of a parent.

"Do sit down, sir."

"I'm fine on my feet, really. I spend too much time sitting around." Tain watched him. "You're looking tired, that is… I hope you don't mind me saying."

"It's been a bit exhausting recently and no, sir, I don't mind you saying as I can imagine the judge is telling mother I should be in bed."

Tain chuckled. "Probably. He's a kind heart. You must know him well."

Peter collapsed into a high-backed chair; his pa's chair. "He's always been there, as long as I can remember. He persuaded me to train as a lawyer, but that's uncertain now…"

Without guile, the Prince sat down asking him why.

Momentarily, Peter considered brushing over the matter, but there was again something in the Prince's manner that invited honesty. "Someone's got to support my family, sir, and I'm head of it now. It wouldn't do for my younger siblings to support my studies and themselves, and I wouldn't want them to."

"I suppose that's understandable. How far through are you?"

"Final year," he replied feeling the weight of lost hopes pressing heavily on him. Four years wasted, four years and more money than he cared to think about. Years of relative comfort snatched away twice from his family, once for saving and once for a future he'd now never have.

"That must make things doubly hard. Let the judge know if there's anything I can do."

"Thank you, sir, but His Honour is already taking a keen interest in my future."

"I can imagine," replied Tain, wryly.

The Prince seemed to sense that talking about the future and the past wouldn't help, so asked him about the neighbourhood and the people. Peter found some of the despondency left him. They sat talking quietly until the judge reappeared.

Tancred said, "We will leave you together, Peter. Come and see me when you feel up to it, but, for now, try to rest. Words can wait, but sleep is a demanding taskmaster at such times. Your Highness…"

Tain got up nodded to Peter, thanked Madam Selth and left with the judge. Once they were alone, Peter looked at his mother. Her eyes were moist. Crossing to her, he hugged her. Unspoken between them was the acknowledgement that his pa's passing had been easier than watching him in agony. It didn't diminish the loss but it eased the pain.

"Go to bed, Pete. There's nothing more to be done."

He nodded. Wiping his eyes, he snuck into his and his siblings' room. They were all still asleep. He lay down in his spot, closing his eyes, sleep overcoming him without dreams.

Chapter 17

SOMETHING TO HELP

Late Morning
Macarian Lordship

As THE DOOR of the Selth house clicked shut behind them, Tain swallowed back his emotion. The living room had been homely and spoke of family in ways that the separate rooms in the Palace didn't. The stew being prepared, the blanket, the chairs by the fire, there'd been ink pots and quills next to cheap paper on the sideboard, carefully separated from the jugs and bowls. What the Selths had they cared for, and he hadn't missed the fact they didn't have any luxury. A rag rug on the flagged floor by the table gave some relief, but it was practical too.

Tain glanced round. His guards were continuing to be discreet, keeping a greater distance than normal. He was pleased. People passing didn't seem to notice him. There were looks; his clothes spoke of a wealth that was unusual in this part of the city, but he wasn't dressed formally. Several people nodded to the judge, who seemed to know his way.

They were halfway out of the Macarian Lordship when he sniffed. In between the aromas of middens, smoke and people hurrying by was something far pleasanter: a herby stew and hints of fresh bread.

"Something smells good."

Tancred smiled. "We must be close to a bake-square, sir." Seeing Tain's confusion, he continued, "After the Age of Tyranny much of Oedran was destroyed in a fire. It was only a few days after the final battle and was thought to have started from a crude oven in a poor man's house. So your ancestors, when they developed the new city, decreed that there should be 'bake-squares': communal ovens set in the centre of a large gathering square so that if cinders or embers spread by accident, the risk of fire should be minimal. Now they are used more seldom but still exist."

They entered the square. Tain gazed around in interest. There were street stalls and shops along three sides and the large oven in the centre. On the fourth side of the square, washing was drying whilst ladies chatted. It was a scene of ordinary life, and he was fascinated.

"That smell is making me hungry."

The source turned out to be a pie stall and, fishing into his belt pouch for coins, Tancred bought two. He passed one to Tain with a wink, saying, "Do not spoil your dinner."

Tain grinned back. "Doubt I could, Judge, but I'll let father know it was your fault if I manage it. Thank you."

"I am sure you will, sir." Tancred nodded to the pie-man. "Thank you, Andrews."

The pie-man smirked. "Thought you 'adn't recognised me, Judge."

"Light-fingered Larry Andrews. Before me five years ago for—"

"Now, now, your 'onour, I've done me time, slate clean and all that."

With a twinkle in his eye, Tancred said, "Very true. Straight and narrow, is it?"

"Every day, Your 'onour. Catch me twice in prison, I dunna think so. Who's your companion?"

"One of my pupils."

Larry winked at Tain. "You learn all you can from the old judge, lad. He's a warm 'eart and a caring mind. Got the respect of everyone who knows 'im – 'igh 'n' low. Most judges wouldn't and couldn't walk these 'ere streets safely, but there's not one I know as would 'arm Judge James Tancred – and if they did, they'd get more than they ever bargained for from the rest o' us."

Tain grinned. "The judge and I already mutually respect each other, don't we, Judge?"

Tancred smiled. "We certainly do, Your Highness."

Larry paled and ate a pie to calm his nerves as they left.

Once out of hearing, Tain chuckled. "That was rather mean, Judge."

"I was simply observing convention, Your Highness," observed Tancred innocently. "How is the pie?"

"Delicious."

"A lot of street food can be; it's the blood of the city."

Tain finished the pie, licking at his fingers. It had been packed with potatoes, carrots and onion, and small pieces of beef, liver and bacon, flavoured with thyme. The pastry had been almost an afterthought, it seemed, but it wasn't bad. He took the handkerchief the judge held out with a grin.

"Aren't you eating yours, Judge?"

Tancred shook his head, eyes twinkling. "No. I know Larry's pies of old and, nice though they are, my wife will have something to say if I don't eat my dinner."

"Then why did you buy it?" asked Tain, confused.

Tancred merely smiled a small smile, his eyes darting around.

Tain frowned to himself. The judge usually had a reason for everything. It was a cornerstone of their lessons. Maybe he had thought it would be odd to just buy one. Just before they left the Macarian Lordship, Tancred excused himself for a moment, crossed to a shabby door and knocked. A girl pulled it open and stood gaping as Tancred handed the pie over.

"For your ma, Jena."

He crossed back to Tain and winked. They left the Lordship on the Ratharia a few moments later. Tain glanced over his shoulder, back at the closed door.

"Judge, why…?"

Tancred considered carefully. "Jena's father was killed in a brawl a short time ago. I oversaw the case and sentenced his killer. I had no choice. The law is clear, but the fratricide has left the family with very little income. I am not prone to offering charity, but a gift is different."

Tain considered that. "Did you know when you bought the pie, you'd give it to them?"

"There were a few options. Now, I must see Lord Ryson, sir. Would you like to accompany me or shall our walk take us via the Palace?"

"I'd like to accompany you, Judge." Two moments later, he asked, "Will Peter have to stop his training?"

"It is probable, Your Highness, but he would not be the first, nor the last, to lose a profession in such a manner."

"I wish there was something I could do." His lips twitched. "Not as charity but as a gift."

Tancred chuckled. "An understandable wish, sir. I am going to see Lord Ryson because of the same instinct."

They continued their walk back to the Administrative Quarter in companionable silence.

* * *

Tain followed the judge into the Law School. Its wide tiled entrance corridor was utilitarian. Several doors led off it on both sides. He asked where they led.

"Lecture rooms, sir. One for each year. Our… The students use them as study areas outside of their lectures."

Tain bit his lip. "Don't they study at home, Judge?"

"No, sir. Many of the texts they need are here or in the Law Library at the Courthouse. Some are dedicated and come every day. Do they not, Payton?"

A student who'd stood aside for them grinned and winked at Tain. "Obviously, Judge. Dedication all the way."

Tancred's eyes narrowed. "All the way where?"

Payton chuckled. "Wherever the future leads, sir. Your Highness."

Tain placed him. "You played a defendant in the mock trial I attended."

"I did, sir," replied the student. "Surprisingly, I passed as well."

Tain chuckled. "I'm glad. We shouldn't keep you from studying."

"Oh, you can, sir. I'm easy." He saw Tancred's face. "But I shouldn't keep Your Highness and His Honour from more important things." He left with a slight bow, entering a lecture room on their right.

They turned down a second corridor, almost straight into another student. Tancred crooked an eyebrow.

"Sorry, Judge. Wasn't able to see through the wall. Oh. Morning, Your Highness."

Tain grinned. "Morning, Tristan. How are your studies?"

Tristan Richardson shrugged. "My marks are moving me up a year, so I guess they're going well, sir. Father's happy. How about yours?"

"I guess you'll need to ask the Judge."

Tancred smiled. "There is nothing to concern me, sir. Tristan, come and see me at the Courthouse when you get chance. We can look at anything that is proving problematic."

"I… Erm, thank you, Your Honour. I appreciate it."

A few moments later, Tain followed Tancred into the Provost's outer office, where a secretary raised a querying eyebrow, then hastily got to his feet and inclined his head. Tain inwardly sighed. He doubted it was because of Judge Tancred's presence and after Payton and Tristan's easy attitudes it frustrated him still more.

"Is Lord Ryson here by any chance, Unwin?" enquired Tancred.

Two moments later, Tancred and Tain were both ushered through to Lord Ryson's modest office. A trained lawyer, the Lord of Oedran had taken the post of Provost of the Law School to keep himself busy. He bowed formally to Tain.

"Lord Ryson, I'm only here by chance. It's Judge Tancred who needs to talk with you."

Lord Ryson smiled. "That's a shame, Your Highness; I was half expecting an afternoon discussing the finer points of law."

Tain grinned at the flame-haired lord. "Another time maybe?"

Ryson nodded. "I look forward to it, sir. Please feel free to sit down or browse my shelves. Now, Your Honour, what can I do for you?"

Tain crossed to Ryson's bookshelves and listened with half an ear as Tancred explained Peter's change of fortune.

"…He cannot work full time and take his finals. I remember how exhausted I was and I would not wish to put that strain on him. All I can ask, for the moment, is that you use what leeway you can in holding back the request for his fees. If possible, I would appreciate a fortnight's grace."

Ryson pulled a scroll towards him, glancing down a list. "They're already late, James."

"His father has been dying, and he has younger siblings and his mother to support. It is understandable."

Ryson frowned. "I cannot simply change our policies for one student, Judge. If he were to be the next exceptional lawyer maybe leeway would be prudent, but he, although good, is not spectacular; he's no Jenkins."

Tancred eased himself into a chair. "What can I say to persuade you, my lord?"

"It is not a matter of persuasion, Judge. It is the fact, consequences and precedent of your request."

Turning from his perusal of the bookshelves, Tain said, "Send the demand to the judge's office, as though the late Master Selth was to receive it there, Lord Ryson. In the mass of Courthouse mail, it could easily be misplaced and you'll have fulfilled your duties here."

As Tancred chuckled to himself, eyes bright, Ryson's lips twitched. "A neat solution, Your Highness. Thank you."

"Glad I could help. It will also give you chance to investigate what can be done. Now, do you have anything on the laws relating to banditry? It's an apposite subject currently."

As Ryson crossed to him, Tain wondered if his interest in Peter's situation would have any effect on it. Ryson was something of an unknown to him. He knew his father and brother didn't trust him, not like they trusted Lord Landis and Lord Iris, but that didn't mean Lord Ryson would ignore his suggestion, did it? He might not be fifteen, but Advisor Spellen was clear during their lessons that lords didn't ignore princes.

Chapter 18
CONSCIENCE
Afternoon
Palace of Oedran – Privy Wing – Nursery

TANCRED SAW TAIN TO the nursery rooms of the Palace, wondering how long it would be before the Prince had a suite of rooms and a manservant to go with it.

Maria, the Prince's long-suffering nurse, glanced over as the doors opened. "His Majesty was wondering if you've arrived, Your Highness."

Tain turned to Tancred. "Thank you for the walk, Your Honour, I ought to see father."

"It was a pleasure, sir. Give my regards to His Majesty."

Tain was gone on swift feet. Maria looked at Tancred companionably offering him a drink that he accepted.

"How are things?" he enquired, taking the glass of melon juice.

"Better than I expected after the news from Lufian. His Highness cares deeply about Prince Arkyn. I'm only just realising how deeply. I've seen their frustrations for so long that I missed the support."

"That is understandable. All siblings get frustrated when they are growing, but I suspect that, once His Highness is over his adolescence, he and Prince Arkyn will be a force to be reckoned with."

Maria smiled. "Oh, aye, they'll be that, Judge. What as, is the question. Prince Arkyn might have the steadiness of character from his mother, but he hasn't completely escaped his father's mischievous streak. Likewise, Prince Tain might be mischievous but, mark me, when he needs to be he'll have all the sobriety and sense anyone could wish for."

Tancred relaxed. "I am glad you see that also, Maria. He has proved it this afternoon. My long-time scribe died last night; we have just paid our respects to his family."

"His Highness accompanied you?"

"I thought it would help Peter, Selth's son. Prince Tain's already lost someone in his life..."

Maria swallowed. "Yes, I suppose you're right. I often wonder what

Ira would have made of him?"

Tancred put a hand on her shoulder. "Her Grace would be proud of the man His Highness is becoming. You still miss her...?"

"I raised her, Your Honour; she was, is the closest thing I ever had to a daughter of my own. She died too young." Maria collected herself. "She's at peace. That's the important thing and her son and niece need me, but for how long? I know His Majesty is hunting for a manservant for Prince Tain and Prince Lachlan's old rooms are being made ready for him. Once he moves into them, how long will Lord Scanlon leave Lady Elantha in my care? She's only here because she's motherless and Ira persuaded him that setting up two nurseries, for three children, was ridiculous. She was trying to help, but I do sometimes wonder if Lady Elantha's presence kept the memory of Princess Ella too vivid."

Tancred said softly, "It probably gave her more comfort than pain. Lady Aelia had just died also."

"I know. She never got over Ella's death though."

"Princess Ella was three; I doubt any mother would, Maria."

"I felt so inadequate... Why am I telling you all this after so long?"

"It does not matter why. I shall not repeat any of it."

Maria swallowed. "Thank you. You have a simple air which worms confidences out of people before they realise it. I admire that but I'm glad I don't emulate it. Can you imagine what His Highness would confide?"

Tancred chuckled. "Perhaps I can, Maria. So, he is to have my old friend's rooms. They should do him well."

Maria mentally shook herself. "Yes. Didn't you know?"

"It has not been mentioned but I doubt for any reason of premeditated avoidance. Prince Lachlan would have been pleased, I think."

They carried on talking for some time. Drinks in hand, their conversation twisted and turned between discussing the FitzAlcis, the city and their own families. In the end, Prince Tain disturbed them.

"Judge, father says have you got a minute for him?"

Tancred rose. "For His Majesty I have as many minutes as he needs, Your Highness."

Maria looked her charge up and down as the judge left.

"Did you gallop through all the mud you could find, sir? No, on second thoughts, don't answer that. Go and get cleaned up."

Tain left, his wide smile blowing a grin onto Maria's face also.

* * *

Richardson rose as Tancred entered the Outer Office. All too aware the judge held a King's Token, meaning he could demand to see the King immediately. "I wasn't expecting you quite yet, Judge. His Majesty's talking with Advisor Rayburn and Major Wynfeld. Would you like me to check if they've finished?"

Tancred smiled. "I shall wait in the Audience Chamber until His Majesty is free, Administrator. Do not let me disturb your work."

"Your Honour, there is a spare chair here. Please use it. You shall not be disturbing anyone. Can I get you a drink?"

Tancred eased himself into the chair. "No, thank you, Richardson. I am fully refreshed."

Twelve minutes later, Major Wynfeld and Advisor Rayburn left the Inner Office. Seeing Tancred waiting, Wynfeld stopped and apologised.

Tancred pushed himself to his feet and smiled his normal contented smile. "It is of no matter, Major Wynfeld. I have been reminiscing with your aunt; she might appreciate a visit."

Wynfeld smiled. "I should see Aunt Maria more. Was there anything in particular?"

Tancred lowered his voice, so the words didn't carry into the Inner Office. "Queen Ira, Macarian House, general past and future…"

Wynfeld nodded in understanding. "Thank you, Judge."

* * *

Two moments later, Adeone said, "Sorry to have kept you waiting so long, James. Major Wynfeld likes to keep me informed and busy."

"It is of no matter, Sire. Prince Tain mentioned you wished for a word."

Once the door closed on the Outer Office, Adeone crossed to the decanters. Passing Tancred a brandy, he pointed at the comfortable chairs.

Once they were both seated, Adeone crooked an expressive eyebrow. "How did Tain handle the impromptu walk?"

Tancred relaxed. "Very well, sir, and showed a level of maturity that I think Your Majesty would have been proud of. He helped Peter focus on something else for a while and the lad was so tired he needed to."

"I can imagine. When my father died… No. I shall not get maudlin today. Tain's wondering if there's anything we can do to help. I don't want to crush his enthusiasm."

Tancred smiled. "His Highness asked me the same thing. I have been trying to think of something. Peter and Madam Selth will not accept anything that might be construed as charity and I admire them for it."

"So do I. How did Lord Ryson react to Tain's presence?"

Tancred eyed the King. "Perfectly calmly, Sire. Courteous but not sycophantic. There was even a practical note to his voice. I would say that there was no hint of unease on either side. Although, when His Lordship asked after Prince Arkyn, His Highness' reply gave nothing away that could not have already been deduced."

Adeone frowned. "What did he say?"

"That His Highness was getting closer to Lufia, but that was as much as he had heard for a couple of days."

Adeone laughed. "And I was worried because of what he'll say at Court in a couple of years."

"I do not think you need to, Your Majesty, His Highness knows the stakes."

Adeone eyed him. "I know he does, James, but he is young still."

"With a maturity beyond his years, sir. I hear he is to have Prince Lachlan's old chambers."

Adeone forced himself to relax; Tancred had not meant the words to criticise his judgement. "Does it concern you?"

"Not at all, sir," replied Tancred. "I am sure the memories for me will be vivid for a time when I visit His Highness, but they will soon become his chambers. I think he is ready for the step. Maria will feel it though."

Adeone started. "James… Sicla, I'd completely overlooked her feelings. Thank you. I'll have to talk to her. How could I be so blind?"

Tancred retrieved the decanter and topped up the King's glass. "Maybe, Sire, because everyone keeps you so busy that you do not have the time to think and remember everyone. If you did manage to, it would be somewhat surprising."

Adeone raised his glass slightly. "Then my friends should berate my conscience more often."

Tancred resumed his seat. "I meant to do no such thing, Adeone."

"Are you sure?"

Tancred smiled. "Perhaps I may have intended to aid Your Majesty's memory but never would I berate your conscience."

"I'll live with that."

Chapter 19

ON REALISATION AND FEALTIES

Pentadai, Week 9 – 5th Lowal, 19th Tradis 1213

Fitz's Inn - Schoolroom

Almost four weeks later, Arkyn was finding little to concern him in Lufia. Meanwhile, Tancred studied Prince Tain's face.

"Let us leave the rest of this for another day, sir, else you are likely to give yourself a headache. The law shall not be changed overnight."

"Am I working *too* hard again, Judge?"

"Possibly, sir, but I was more concerned that you did not leave here feeling unwell. I realise there are laws which are challenging and you will need to understand them in time but little and often is best."

Tain grinned. "Wouldn't it have been easier to say 'yes', Judge?"

Tancred smiled back. "Maybe so, Your Highness, but, in that case, the answer would have been less informative, would it not?"

"I suppose so, Judge. If I'm not discussing this, what should I be doing?"

"Taking advantage of an old man's compassion and escaping into the fresh air whilst the weather is pleasant, sir?"

"I could get just as much pleasure from listening to you talk."

Tancred said, "There are times when it is abundantly clear His Majesty is Your Highness' father. What shall we talk on?"

Tain thought for a long moment. "Could we look at fealties, Judge? I find them fascinating and yet don't really understand them."

Tancred eyed him balefully. "Certainly we can, sir, but may I ask what brought the subject to mind?"

Tain looked back, biting at his lip. "When Lord Daioch was here, I realised Arkyn will one day be king and will command people's loyalty – which must sound stupid because I've known it for years. Then he keeps getting attacked and Lord Faran's our vassal, but he's not been arrested and I don't know if it's because of the fealty or something else."

"Your Highness may know something without understanding or accepting it, or, in this case, realising its full import. How did you feel when you looked at His Highness in that moment of realisation?"

Tain looked away and then back at the kindly judge. "I don't know. All I do know is that now I've seen a glimpse of the future."

"Did you feel awed? Or maybe isolated?" enquired Tancred, studying Tain's features without judgement.

"No, nothing like that. More… calm. As though things had found their place."

The judge nodded. "Not that it should be for many a year, sir, but how do you think you will feel when His Highness *is* king?"

Tain frowned. "Things will change between us, I realise that, but I think I'll be pleased for him when grief has waned."

Tancred smiled softly. "You would not wish it were you, sir?"

Tain looked at him. "No, Judge, I would not – and surely that is a *very* provocative question!"

"It certainly was, sir; intentionally so, I must add. It may be difficult to comprehend but, once the future on which we speak is here, many men may ask you that question with far more malicious intentions. They may try to set Your Highnesses against each other. They may try even sooner if they can find a reason to do so. Always be wary."

Tain nodded. "I am. If anyone other than yourself or my family had asked me even one of the questions, I'd have refused to discuss it."

"A move wise beyond your years, Your Highness; however, I have to enquire where Master Calumiel sits in the scheme you outlined?"

Tain paused. "I think even as such a good friend he'd have to be on the outside of those who could ask such things, but then I don't think he would ask if I would wish to be king."

Tancred smiled. "Probably not, sir. You are right though. Trust as few people as possible with such things."

"It is not a matter of trust, Judge, it's the principle of what is and isn't discussed – and that is one thing that isn't. Sooner or later, someone would overhear and treason cases could be brought against anyone. It's surely better to refrain than to have to defend for, once you are in the position of defending, you are already at a disadvantage."

Tancred laughed. "Sir, you are right in every part of that. I am truly and duly impressed."

Tain blushed. "Judge!"

"My apologies, sir, but, consider, when we started these lessons, would Your Highness have ever have vocalised your thoughts in such a way?"

Tain considered. "No, but you're in need of the congratulations, in that case. You have taught me well."

"Without your natural abilities, I could not have taught Your Highness much. They are the foundation on which we are building, sir."

Tain eyed him. "Court might condemn with evidence presented."

Tancred said, "Sir, flattery may well be the tool of princes but rarely has it been used so."

"Necessity is the mother of invention, Judge."

"The father also, it seems. Now, sir, I believe you wished to discuss fealties. Those we can talk of very easily; however, the decisions around Lord Faran's arrest, or lack of it, is not for me to comment on. I am not privy to the reasons. Were he not a Lord of Lufia hosting His Highness, circumstances may have precipitated his arrest. Equally, from what is common knowledge, he seems to be under house arrest, where he has the freedom of his house but not the freedom to leave it."

Tain bit his lip. "Didn't you just comment on it, Judge, after you said you wouldn't?"

Tancred chortled. "I suppose I did, sir, but I did not discuss the reasons or speculate about the outcome. I stated facts which are known within the empire. With regards to fealty, there are several kinds..."

* * *

When Tain entered Ceardlann, he ambled along the passage to the Comptroller's organised office. He poked his head round the door and, as the Comptroller looked up, walked in smiling. He half sat, half collapsed into a chair. "I've been talking to the judge about fealties. I understand truth and life-binds, I even understand honour-binds and speech-binds in the right circumstances, but he doesn't know how the valley fealty works."

The Comptroller said, "Ah, that problem. This calls for a drink and some cake to help us through."

Tain grinned. "Won't it spoil my dinner, Comptroller?"

"You *could* refuse, Your Highness."

Tain gave him a withering expression.

The Comptroller laughed. "Maybe not. You should practise that look." Six minutes later, the Comptroller settled back. "The valley-binding is peculiar to here. I don't know why, but many have speculated that the Cearcall are responsible and the early Cearcall at that. Did you know there used to be a place associated with each member of the Cearcall? The Rex Dallin is just one and, in fact, it wasn't called the Rex Dallin when it belonged to them. It was known as Encilla, which means 'retreat', but your ancestors wanted to assert their ownership, I believe."

"That doesn't surprise me, Comptroller," said Tain dryly. "It's a more apt name: Encilla, that is."

"Perhaps. Every person born in the Rex Dallin is bound by the fealty. It is a fealty to place and king. This valley will not let within its bounds anyone who is foresworn. We are bound to the essence of truth, as well as the fact, and to the honour of the valley and its head, currently your father. We are compelled to protect and, in turn, the valley protects us."

Tain frowned slightly. "Yes, that's where it gets complicated, isn't it? It's easy to say something protects but how…? Geography is inanimate. How does it know if one is foresworn?"

The Comptroller smiled. "Your Highness, it is most easily understood as a mixture of all other fealties with a bit of magic to make it work."

Tain frowned, concentrating. "Truth fealty I can see, if you can't be foresworn. Honour fealty also, because you cannot work against the FitzAlcis. Speech-binding, though, is a difficult one; I've not noticed that people can't speak their minds to us."

The Comptroller chuckled. "Very true, sir, but speech-binding can be more subtle; it can control a wish to follow the orders of the one who binds, bound to their spoken command, do you see?"

Tain sighed. "I'm beginning to. How about life-bound?"

"If we commit treason, we may not re-enter the valley and that, for people born here, is a living death. Imagine if you could not return here."

Tain tried to. "I may understand that better later. There's just one thing, Comptroller, two actually, you keep saying 'we'…"

The Comptroller said, "The people of the valley, sir. I am one of them."

Tain nodded and missed the inflexions that might have explained far better than the actual words. "Then, there's the fact that fealties are sworn person to person. No words are spoken; no person takes the oath…"

"Have you never felt a presence in the valley? Or felt protected when you explore?"

"Well, yes, but surely that's just my imagination."

The Comptroller asked simply, "Is it?" Tain opened his mouth, but the Comptroller continued, "Now, sir, I should tell Cook that you'll be ready for dinner at half past seven."

Chapter 20
SOLUTIONS
Pentadai, Week 12 – 26th Lowal, 19th Lowis 1213
Oedran

BY THE TIME OF THE MUNPYRAM and the end of summer, Tain and Cal were fretting to visit Oedran and, in Cal's case, his family. They spent the Pentadai before the feast day with Tancred going over mercantile law, then accompanied the judge back to Oedran. After having diverted to the Galdwins', to see Cal safely home, Prince Tain and Judge Tancred continued to the Palace talking intermittently. As they reached the Alcium Plaza, Tain asked how Peter was.

"Coping, sir. Lord Ryson is looking into the matter from the Law School's side and, from my understanding, Peter has found some work as an evening scribe at the Courthouse picking up oddments that are unfinished or urgent notes for the next day. It is unusual, but it will put food on their table and contribute towards his fees."

Tain nodded. "I'm glad he's found something, Judge."

"I also. His father taught him the skills of a scribe from the moment he could walk. He worked as a scribe from the age of eleven to starting the school when he was fifteen. Before that, he was a runner at the Courthouse. He would take any shift going, even after becoming a scribe, to earn that bit of extra money."

Tain swallowed. "It makes my life look so easy."

"Yours has its own unique challenges, sir. I remember Prince Lachlan working so late he fell asleep at his desk. I am sure my wife used to invite him to dinner to look after him, rather than for any prestige. Whilst he visited us, others would not bother him."

"That was kind of her."

"They enjoyed each other's company as well. We would be honoured if Your Highness would dine with us one evening."

Tain chuckled. "Looking after me, Judge?"

"Only if we need to, sir." His eyes twinkled. "Do we need to?"

"Not this time. Unless you want me to write a long essay or something like that."

Tancred chuckled. "Not at the Munpyram, sir."

"I appreciate it," quipped Tain. "I've too many notes to sort out from today."

Tancred winked as they continued up The Pike towards the Palace in companionable silence. Tain's words had stirred his memory and instead of diverting for home, he entered the Palace with the Prince and walked with him to the Inner Office, where he asked Richardson for an appointment with the King the following day. He would not hasten or interrupt a reunion.

* * *

Peter cursed when he woke on Alunadai. He'd overslept. Working in the evenings scribing was all he could do, but it drained him and he wasn't getting much time to do his Law School assignments. If he failed his finals because he was working to pay his fees, it would be ironic. There was a week before the next instalment was due and he hadn't finished paying the last one yet.

He dressed hastily, half running from the room. The living room was empty. His mother and sisters were obviously still looking for work. It explained why he hadn't been woken. He didn't want Jo or Harriet working yet, but they'd been right. They needed dal and could learn at other times.

He ran most of the way to the Law School, feet pounding the pavements, dodging through crowds and around carts on the main thoroughfares. There was a mizzle in the air and by the time he got to the school, his hair was dripping and his clothes damp through. He needed to oil his cloak, but that, or a new one, would have to wait.

He slipped into the lecture room at that back, earning him a frown from Professor Tancred. Quietly he retrieved his paper from his desk and started taking notes. Not for the first time, he was glad of his shorthand. Where most of his fellows struggled to keep up, his notes flowed from his pencil without much trouble. It had been an investment, but he'd save for each one. Lead points were fine, but their markings needed better light than he had at home. Charcoal could be unpredictable, but was his choice when his pencils were finished. He'd sell the last nub back to the Chapas – what they did with nub ends of graphite he didn't know but there was obviously a good trade in it.

At the end of the lecture, he started tidying away his notes. Shorthand not only made him quicker, it used less paper. Glancing down the sheet, he spotted an obvious mistake and corrected it. He needed to start his essay on the Laws of King Arlis soon. He peered out the window. The rain had worsened. He'd got three more lectures before the day was done and then he was due at the Courthouse. He had to start it today. Seeing the desk next to him was empty, he pulled all his notes from his desk and dropped them on it before closing the lid of his desk and retrieving the notes. Riffling through, he pulled out all his relevant notes and a fresh sheet of paper. He'd do it in shorthand first and then write it out in long.

"Hey, Pete, you coming for a drink?"

Peter looked up. "Not now. Maybe later. I need to start this."

"All work and no play…"

Peter chuckled, watching his friends leave from the corner of his eye.

"Father wants a word with you."

Professor Tancred's voice made him jump. He glanced up. "Do you know what I've done, sir?"

Thomas Tancred eyed him. "Other than being late to my lecture, no. You need to have more regard for your studies."

"Sorry. I overslept. I was working last night, sir."

"Father expects you for dinner tomorrow," with that, the professor left.

Peter sighed. The following day was his only free evening. Still, it would be nice to see the judge. Until then, there was no point worrying about it.

* * *

When Peter knocked on Tancred's front door, questions crowded in his mind. The judge hadn't ever summoned him before, but he had spent the odd evening in his company. The door opened and John, the footman, waved him inside with a grin.

"How's tricks, Pete?"

"Tricky. You?"

"Ah, you know. I was sorry to hear about your pa. Here, let me take your cloak. The judge and mistress are in the drawing room."

"Any idea what I've done?"

John shrugged. "I doubt it's anything. He cares about you."

He swallowed. "I know. I'm touched."

A couple of moments later, Madam Tancred was saying, "Come in, Peter. How are you doing?"

He never hesitated. "N… not too bad for myself, Aunt Bets. We knew it was coming but ma's feeling it a bit. I'm missing him, yet I've so much else to consider that sometimes I feel I don't get time to."

She nodded. "I understand that. Come and sit down. Oh, let me move my sewing…"

Peter smiled and took the chair she'd cleared. He sat facing the judge.

"You are looking well but tired," said Tancred.

"I am a bit, Judge. The evening scribing work for the Keeper has helped, but I am a bit worn out."

"Well, we won't keep you too long today," interrupted Madam Tancred. "I've a couple of bits for your ma put by. I've been tidying out a couple of old boxes from when Thomas was younger. He doesn't want any of it, but there's a few tunics and a cloak to rework. They need a good home and, last I knew, George was growing like a weed."

Peter chuckled. "He is a bit. I seem to have stopped. Thank you. I'm sure ma will be grateful, Aunt Bets. My old tunics are ink stained or patched. If you've anything we can help with, let me know."

She nodded. "Well, you could come round for dinner next week and keep us company. It would be nice to see you all. I've not seen Jo or Harriet for a year or more."

Peter chuckled. "I'm sure they'd love to come. Name your day, and I'll try to corral them for you."

Tancred's eyes glinted. "Lost them already, young Peter?"

"Not very successfully, Judge. Should I ask if you wanted me to come to dinner for a reason, sir?"

"It is an option," remarked Tancred. "I think we should leave business until after we have eaten."

"Put him out of his misery," said Madam Tancred. "I should see where we are with that dinner."

Tancred's eyes followed his wife's retreat until the door closed behind her. He turned his attention to Peter. "His Highness has reached a point in his studies where he has asked to be taught shorthand. This is not my area of expertise, nor is it Advisor Spellen's. I have talked with His Majesty, and the King has been kind enough to suggest I offer you the post of shorthand tutor."

Peter blinked. "But— Why me?" he enquired, baffled.

Tancred considered. "There are questions one does not ask of kings."

"Does that mean you don't know, Judge?"

Tancred chuckled. "No, it does not. His Highness wished to find a way to help you. He may have mentioned it to the King. When I was reminded about the shorthand, I spoke to the King and your name was mooted."

Peter's eyes narrowed. He doubted the King would have recalled his name. "Judge… Did you…?"

"There are times you do not question friends who are trying to help."

"Sorry, Judge."

"Good. His Majesty will retain you on the FitzAlcis staff until His Highness is proficient in shorthand. This comes with a salary that will adequately support your family and pay many of your fees this year. Given His Highness does not reside in Oedran, we will have to devise a timetable for his studies that does not interfere with yours. His Majesty is happy with this arrangement and it is better if there seems to be no pattern to it. Will you accept the post?"

Peter stared at the judge. "Will I accept? *Will*? Judge… I…" He swallowed, glancing around the comfortable room, with its rugs and curtains, well-upholstered chairs and couch, its polished furniture and ornaments. Tancred had grown up like he had – on the margins – everyone knew that. Yet here was a comfortable home. It was also well known that the Judge's fortunes had changed when Prince Lachlan noticed him. He'd be every type of fool to refuse. "Y… Yes, Judge."

"Good lad. I assumed it would take most of the year to teach His Highness, so I have an advance on your wages that should satisfy some of the school's demands and also keep your family. We will need to arrange a time when I can introduce you to His Majesty and show you around the Palace, those parts which will be relevant. I have an agreement with the palace tailors; they will provide you with two tunics for this year and a new cloak. They have many already made, so it was no trouble. You will receive a badge you must wear when in the Palace. The best rule is to mind your own business but be aware of others and you survive."

Peter nodded slowly. "Judge, thank you."

"It is my pleasure. His Highness is not a troublesome pupil and you seemed to find a connection. Your situation saddened him in ways even I did not expect. Now, we should, for the moment, talk of other things."

* * *

Peter left the Tancreds' house after dinner with his mind churning over what he'd just accepted. He was through the King's Gate when he stopped turning it all over. His worries around income were receding. He'd count the advance when he got home and read the scroll detailing the rest. At some point soon, he'd need to sort out a budget that would pay his fees, their rent and upkeep, without leaving them starving. It was a glimmer of hope though.

The basket next to their front door was empty. He took it inside. It had long been a tradition to leave a basket out when grief was rife. People would show their support in small ways, a flower, a loaf, a crescent if they could afford it. They'd contributed to others. Their basket had been out for too long. He didn't want it to seem like they were begging. It had helped in those first days when they didn't want to see people or talk over what had happened. The silent support had been everything then. Now they needed to look to the future.

His ma was still awake but appeared drained. He pecked her cheek before explaining their change in fortune. She watched his face, worried.

"Can you do that, scribe and learn as well, Pete?"

He shrugged. "I'll find out, ma. The judge was trying to help."

"Aye, and His Highness seems to have inherited his mother's heart, but it'll be a lot of work. I wish you'd reconcile yourself to letting Jo find proper work."

Peter sank onto the bench by the table. "She's too young, ma."

"I was maiding at the big house at her age. I was widowed by yours and set to remarry."

"You and pa always said we should learn first."

"And Jo has. She could scribe. They take women. Better to get her place when young than fight for it in a couple of years. She'd likely get a better post with a lawyer or judge if she's been around for a time. Ask the Keeper. She wants to work."

Peter sighed. "Aye, I know, ma. I'd just rather she finished school. That's what pa wanted."

"I know, but she'll end up in the same place anyway. Scribe, maiding or wedded. It's all we've got."

Peter knew it, knew the arguments like the back of his hand. Tiredly, he pulled a rush lamp towards him and lit the taper from his mother's candle. They'd not used the fire in weeks. The dinner at the judge's had been his first hot meal in those weeks. There was a refectory at the school but not having paid all his fees, he felt cheeky using it. The Courthouse kitchen was closed by the time he started work. Larry had left them an unsold pie occasionally, but it was normally cold by the time he got a slice. He pulled a wide bowl towards him and emptied the small pouch the judge had given him into it. Gold glittered. His jaw dropped and he glanced sideways at his ma.

"I think it's soup tomorrow."

She gaped at the tumble of gold, silver and copper coins. Her husband had been paid in silver talence at best, made up with copper crescents or 'res' on occasion. She'd seen the odd gold darl but never this many together. Without speaking, she went and retrieved their cash box from the secret compartment her husband had built into the sideboard.

"Here, lad."

Peter counted out the hundred darl, still speechless. Those would pay his fees. If they started spending gold in their area, the yeomen would come knocking, asking questions. There was the equivalent of fifty darl in silver and copper. Peter frowned to himself. 'An advance' was how the judge had put it. He unrolled the scroll from its ribbon-bound comfort. There, in a clerk's careful hand, was his salary for the year. It seemed the judge had not wished to see his reaction. That was kind because tears streamed down his face. His family was secure until he could find work on graduating. He was being paid three hundred darl to teach one young man how to scribe in shorthand. Oh, he knew it was more complicated than it appeared. He would be at the Prince's beck and call, have to look the part, act the part, be discreet – the wage bought his discretion and free time – but for his family he could easily bear that. He wished his pa could have known, but he'd be watching them.

His mother hugged him. Her eyes also moist. "Do we tell the kids?"

He swallowed. "Something. We'll have to. At least there's talence and res as well as darl, ma. If I pay for my fees with the darl, can you manage on the rest? I'll see Piers personally and pay our rent. I can do that with the darl. That should stop the bailiff asking questions, because I can tell Piers the truth. Apparently, the next payment will be at the Munlumen, then the Munewid for the final one. Can this carry us through until spring?"

"Fifty darl? Oh, I think it can, Pete. We've had less than a darl a week for food for years."

Peter blushed. He should have known that. "Sorry. Oh, Aunt Bets invited us all for dinner next week and she's found some bits that she thinks will fit George with a bit of reworking."

"With that largesse in the bowl, I feel guilty accepting either."

Peter smiled. "I think she likes to see everyone. She was sewing for someone else too and she knows what it's like for us."

"Yes. It was a fortunate day when pa started working for the judge."

"Wasn't it? I'll read the rest of this in daylight." He toyed with scroll. "I don't know how to thank the judge."

"Pass your exams. I'm sure that will be thanks enough. He'll know you appreciate it. As you say, he and Bets know what it's like for us. Get yourself to bed, lad. I'll sort this and send the girls to school in the morning. Do you have lectures?"

He nodded. "And essays to complete. I'll see Piers afterwards. I'll take my fees with me. Night, ma."

Chapter 21

RETURN

A FORTNIGHT INTO AUTUMN, Prince Arkyn entered the Inner Office without waiting for anyone to announce him.

His father didn't even look up. "Yes, Richardson?"

Arkyn grinned, taking off his riding cloak and gloves. "Sorry, Sire, I didn't give him chance to say anything. I've told Edward to leave the report with him, so that will keep them busy."

Adeone laid down his pen, eyes bright. "Couldn't you come home once without bringing me more reports?"

"Only if you stop sending me to undertake Provincial Reviews, sir." He swallowed. "Are you busy?"

Adeone shook his head. "Not now. Let me tell Richardson."

A minute later, they were in the King's private sitting room with its comfortable couches and polished sideboard.

Adeone studied his elder son. "Come here." He pulled Arkyn into a hug. "You've been bottling things up again."

Arkyn collapsed into a chair. "Who could I talk to? Kensal died because of me and my stubbornness. How am I meant to live with that?" he enquired, taking a drink from his father and putting it on the inlaid table by his hand.

Adeone eased himself into a chair. "By getting through one day at a time. He did what he considered right, as you did. He might have saved your life but you saved Edward's. I'm sorry he died, I truly am, but he would never have wanted you to blame yourself. He'd probably have said that blame was for another library."

Arkyn smiled half-heartedly. "He told me to trust Tain's library because he holds the keys. What do you suppose he meant?"

"Alcis only knows."

A few moments later, Arkyn enquired, "Can I ask why you don't order Scanlon's assassination?"

"I will not descend to his level. Any authority we have would be destroyed. Never act in the shadows, Arkyn, not when your enemy lives in the light." Adeone held his son's gaze.

Arkyn nodded. "I had to ask. I lost good men and a good friend in that attack—"

"I've lost good friends also. They died because they were my friends.

We're dangerous men to be acquainted with."

"Then why do men bother?" enquired Arkyn dejectedly.

"Oh, because they can advance their fortunes and I might fool myself but I like to think some enjoy our company."

"Then maybe we're both fools, father. Talking of fools, how's Tain?"

Adeone laughed. "Ask him yourself; you'll see him tomorrow. Get him to tell you about learning shorthand."

For once, Arkyn was nonplussed. "Shorthand?"

"James thinks it might help and so a young student's teaching him."

Arkyn shook his head. "A student, why not a scribe?"

Adeone explained, passing his son his abandoned drink.

"I hope the young man can cope. What other news is there, father?"

"Do you read any of the letters we write to you?"

Arkyn chuckled and took a drink. "Yes, but I always suspect there's something missing, like shorthand. Have you had any luck finding Tain a manservant?"

Adeone paused. "Not I. The Steward came up with a name. One Gab Linnt. Rather unfortunate but true. There's a silent T on his surname, so the spelling's not as unfortunate as the pronunciation. Beaver's checks didn't highlight anything, so he's got the job. He's just started."

Arkyn smiled. "Let's hope he's up to the challenge, father. How about Elantha and Cal? How are they?"

"Elantha's growing up quickly now. Her drawing's getting good—"

"I noticed; she enclosed a sketch of the Ceardlann stables with her last letter. I'm not sure why, but it rather looked like Tain and Cal were up to something in the far corner. A bedraggled Speckles was watching them with the most disgruntled cat face I've ever seen."

Adeone laughed. "She's also getting crafty. Cal seems fine. His skill with weapons has increased with the same rapidity as his height. He's taller than Tain now. How have Kadeem and Edward coped this time?"

"Very well. Yves and Simmons did well standing in for Thomas and Alan. We dropped them back with His Lordship on our way through. I offered Kensal's manservant a job, but he declined. Kadeem will find replacements, I'm sure but... I don't want to get close to them again. I knew Thomas and Alan well, given what happened in Terasia."

Adeone put a hand reassuringly on his son's arm. "I can understand that but at least know who works for you. Kadeem, I'm sure, will make sure that you deal only with him."

"I feel like a coward."

"You're not. See it like this: you have a demanding job, from which there should be no distraction. Your decisions affect many hundreds of thousands of people. If, by insulating yourself against future shocks, you feel you can make better decisions, then insulate yourself, but remember not to cut yourself off completely. Let Kadeem handle your household and Edward your staff but never forget to know your friends."

Arkyn gave a wan smile. "I'll try to remember, sir." He took a sip of his drink and sat quietly for some time.

Adeone watched him, concerned. His son had faced bereavements before, but he'd never faced the same semi-responsibility for them. It might have been a couple of aluna-months since the bandit attack, but he hadn't been able to talk about things properly to anyone. Messenger links certainly weren't the appropriate way and letters could be intercepted.

Simkins interrupted their contemplations. Noting the atmosphere, the manservant bent down to Adeone's ear. "There's a light meal in the triniculum, if Your Majesty or His Highness wish to eat."

Adeone nodded. "Thank you, Simkins. That's an excellent idea. Arkyn, come and get some food. You've been travelling since early this morning."

Arkyn looked up. "I'm all right, Sire."

Adeone dismissed Simkins with a glance. "You're still going to eat something, even if I must spoon-feed you as though you were a babe. You need to keep your strength up."

"I'm not hungry, father, honestly."

Adeone got up. "Shall I ask Chapa to join us, Arkyn?"

Arkyn grinned. "I could call your bluff, Sire. I'm sure the doc would have something to say to *both* of us."

Adeone frowned. "Stop turning my threats round on me, Arkyn. It's not very… fair."

"Fairness exists only to make cynics laugh, father."

Shaking his head, Adeone held out a hand. "Come on. We'll wait on ourselves, but I'm getting you fed."

* * *

Arkyn was busy when Tain arrived in Oedran the following day, but as soon as he was free, he made his way to his brother's new chambers. Entering them, he smiled to himself. When he'd been young and Prince Lachlan had been alive, he'd sometimes found his father hiding in the rooms. He entered the sitting room to find Tain bending over a desk concentrating whilst a young man, around Arkyn's own age, read slowly from a short document.

Smiling at the sight, Arkyn waited until the young man noticed him before saying, "Morning, Tain."

Tain looked up. "Arkyn!"

"Shall I return later?"

116

Tain shook his head. "Peter, do you mind if we finish this another time?"

The young man smiled. "Not at all, Your Highness. I can return after my lectures."

"Please. Oh, sorry, introductions. Prince Arkyn, can I introduce Master Peter Selth to you? He's teaching me shorthand."

Arkyn studied the young man. There was unmasked intelligence in his greenish eyes, brown hair was short and neat and Arkyn put him at about five feet ten inches. His initial feeling was here was a young man who was honourable and dependable and, for some reason, it reassured him.

He said, "I heard from His Majesty. I'm pleased to meet you, Master Selth. I hope my brother is proving to be a good student."

"Arkyn!" exclaimed Tain.

Peter, however, replied smoothly, "I'm pleased to meet Your Highness. His Highness is proving to be everything I could expect."

"Oh dear." Once Peter had gone, Arkyn chuckled. "Shorthand! Your schemes get worse."

"One of us has to be spontaneous. Anyway, this was sort of the judge's idea. How was Lufia?"

"I'm not sure I want to talk about it. The review was all right though. It went to plan for once."

"I'm sorry about Kensal. I liked him a lot. I'm sorry about the others as well…"

Arkyn swallowed. "Me too. Have you and Cal been upsetting Speckles?"

"No… How…?" (Arkyn raised an eyebrow.) "We accidentally knocked a bucket of water over him."

Arkyn's eyes narrowed. "I hope it was an accident. How do you like your new rooms and Linnt?"

"It was. We were trying to rig it up to tip over on one of the grooms." He saw his brother's face and hastily added, "I love my rooms but I don't know about Linnt. He's only started today. Do you fancy going for a ride? Or are you…"

Arkyn smiled. "I might manage one to Wynwood."

"Fine by me. Will I have to put up with a grouchy sergeant now you've promoted Smithers?"

Arkyn frowned. "Who's being grouchy? I sent Halien back with some documents, but he shouldn't be complaining. It was a mark of trust."

Tain sighed. "Not exactly grouchy, but I'd got used to Smithers."

Arkyn eyed him. "All right, he's yours. It's better than you grouching. At least I can tell a sergeant to alter his attitude."

"You can tell me to as well."

"Yes, but, unlike the hypothetical sergeant, you don't listen!"

Tain pouted. "Can't you go travelling again?"

"Father would complain about the reports. Shall I see you at the stables in thirty minutes?"

Twelve minutes later, Tain said, "Where's my riding crop, Linnt?"
"I shall locate it."
Six minutes after that, Tain discovered his guards hadn't been warned he'd be leaving his rooms, necessitating another wait. By the time he reached the stables, he was late and Arkyn was frustrated.

* * *

That evening, Kadeem had a quiet word with Linnt about it.
"What's it to you, Kadeem?"
"Quite simply it's better me saying it than Simkins getting to hear about it, or, for that matter, His Majesty. Smarten up your act, Linnt. They won't stand for incompetence. They shouldn't have to stand for it. If things aren't right by the first time His Majesty enters these chambers, I wouldn't like to be in your shoes. He'll be checking at regular intervals that you're doing your job, whatever popular belief has it."

"I'm sure everything will be fine, Kadeem. Shouldn't you be with Prince Arkyn?"

"He's dining with His Majesty – as is Prince Tain, surely you know that! If you like your job, don't be found wanting and, if you need help, for heaven's sake, ask me…"

Chapter 22
VISITS
Cisadai, Week 15 – 16th Macial, 16th Macis 1213
Inner Office

A FEW DAYS after Arkyn's return, Adeone, Landis and Advisor Rayburn were talking over his report and its consequences when Lady Amara entered without herald. Landis and Rayburn rose and inclined their heads smartly.

Adeone warily got to his feet. "Lady Amara…"

She ignored his remonstration. "Young Festus, take Gilbert outside for six minutes. I want to speak to the King."

Landis didn't argue. Lady Amara had a look in her eye that shouldn't be permitted to reach her mouth. The Lord of Oedran simply bowed to Adeone and gave Rayburn a significant glance.

Once they'd gone, Adeone said mildly, "How are you, aunt?"

"That won't save you, young Adeone. I've a bone to pick with you."

"I rather guessed you had. How do you know Rayburn's first name?"

"I make it my business to know. Now, you'll not distract me. When are you going to let Rhian go home?"

Adeone's brow furrowed. "I've not stopped her—"

"Oh yes you have. She must return home at some point."

"Aunt, I truly haven't stopped her. She could leave whenever she wishes. I thought she was staying to support Neassa."

"Your face says something different. You asked her to stay longer, didn't you?"

"Yes, but not longer than she wished to. I thought she'd be leaving at the end of summer. I haven't pressed her to stay since. She knows that."

Amara shook her head. "Oh, Adeone, haven't you realised yet that a look from a king is better than an order from a lord? Maybe you need to *tell* her! She's fretting to go home. I don't know why, but she is. Are you going to face up to it?"

"Why does everyone assume there is more to our relationship than family ties?"

"I can't imagine. Maybe it's because you danced with her and no-one else since. Maybe it's because you have private dinners with her and *always* smile when you see her? Or maybe it's because everyone at Court is simply gossipy and speculative, but, until my daughter returns home, *neither* of you will get any peace and it's not just you the speculation is aimed at."

"Does it… Never mind, I'll talk to Rhian. Why couldn't she have come to see me, by the way?"

Amara gave him a well-practised look. "She doesn't know I'm here."

Adeone chuckled. "Ah. Would you like me to mention your visit?"

"You know better than to. Now, I'll let you resume your discussion with the two disconcerted fools."

"Rayburn's no fool, aunt."

Amara snorted. "Which says everything one needs to know about young Festus."

Once she'd gone, it was Richardson and not Landis or Rayburn who entered the Inner Office. "Sire?"

"You'd better ask Landis and Rayburn to join me and, Richardson, I'll need to talk to Lady Rhian later."

"Of course, Your Majesty."

"Why 'of course'?"

Richardson smiled gravely. "Forgive me, Sire, but Lady Amara rarely throws everyone out of your office for her own benefit."

Adeone sighed. "True. Remind me why she lives at the Palace."

"Because she's your father's sister, Sire, and it's less far for her to walk to air her views."

"Very diplomatic. I'd almost think you'd had lessons in it."

* * *

That evening, Rhian entered the Inner Office to find her cousin in a pensive mood. She curtsied, smiling, but there was something in Adeone's eyes she'd rarely seen before: control of a deep-seated pain.

He moved out from behind his desk, running his fingers lightly along the polished wood. "Have I ever made you think you couldn't return home, Rhian?"

She hesitated. Adeone sagged, guilt spiralling within him. She was family. Had he really fallen into the trap of being *the King* around her?

She crossed to him. "Adeone, it's nothing you've ever *said*, but if a picture is worth a thousand words..."

He crossed to the couches and sank onto one, his head in his hands. "Why didn't you tell me?"

She poured two glasses of water. "Can I be frank?"

"You're Aunt Amara's daughter; I would have thought frankness was part of your soul."

She passed him the drink. "I'm also my father's daughter, sir, and he was more restrained."

"Uncle Ewart knew how to be frank, or he'd never have won Aunt Amara's heart; however, in answer to the question you meant to ask, you *may* be honest."

"I've stayed because you needed my support. I don't mean that in a bad way. You've needed a confidant with Arkyn's trip to Lufian and one who could listen without feeling they then had to order anything in your name. You've needed the knowledge that you could forget everything for an evening and, maybe, think about yourself. I've never minded being that support and confidant. I don't care what the Court makes of it. I'm your family and that's what families do, isn't it? Be there through the bad times as well as the good."

Adeone was quiet for several long moments. "I just wish there'd been some good times recently."

Rhian sat back. "There have. A good time doesn't need to be a day or a week or a year it needs to be the shortest time, a smile on a cloudy day, a glimpse of sun through the rain. Have there been at least those?"

He looked at her. "I suppose there have."

"No suppose. Either there have or there haven't."

He shook his head. "You are definitely your parents' daughter. There have been those moments."

"I'm glad. Sire, can I ask you something?"

"Of course but do it with my name, cousin."

Rhian smiled. "Might I return home?"

"I thought you were going to use my name."

"I'm saving it."

Adeone sighed. "Of course you can."

"Then remember roads lead in both directions, Adeone. This hasn't been my first visit to Oedran and I doubt it will be my last, but I hadn't planned to spend so long here. I have a simple need to settle my affairs in Tradere."

Adeone held her gentle gaze. "I've been selfish, Rhian, and I'm sorry."

"No, you haven't. Selfishness presupposes a premeditated action."

"You're trying to tell me I haven't been thinking, aren't you?"

Rhian smiled. "Perhaps. You know what I meant. You didn't set out to cause me inconvenience and part of it is due to my own reticence. Shall we say we are equally to blame?"

"When we're not, it's highly unfair to do so. If my family can't be honest with me then I've failed."

Rhian took his hand. "I can be honest with you, Adeone, but bandits had attacked Arkyn. The time wasn't right."

Adeone squeezed her hand. "Thank you. I do appreciate it but I feel guilty. That's all there is to it."

Rhian sighed. "Well, you needn't. I am, as you've said, my mother's daughter. I'd have been frank if the time was right... Talking of mother, when did she visit?"

"Erm... Well—"

"Anyone would think I'm a child!" exclaimed Rhian, exasperated.

"You're definitely not a child. I rather think she wanted to berate me for something; it's been a while. She threw Landis and Rayburn out of a meeting and made me agree not to tell you she'd been."

"That sounds like mother. I hope it wasn't an important meeting," quipped Rhian.

"It had its moments. Provincial Reviews and their complications. Notably at the moment that Landis is responsible for three lordships, all temporally next to each other for official visits ahead of reviews, whilst he's also Ealdorman here. Let alone every other post he holds."

"Can't you send someone else?" asked Rhian.

"This year's visit to Areal should be manageable. I can spare him for a fortnight. He and ReJean can do a lot by messenger ahead of that. I've told him to take young Lord Rale as well. As the one who should have done the visit, he needs to meet ReJean. Next year, well, I found myself agreeing that Julius can represent Landis on the Pale Lands visit as long as Rayburn goes too. As Landis is actually responsible for the Pale Lands' interests here and Julius will inherit that, it makes sense, but I feel like I'm putting too much on him."

Rhian squeezed his wrist. "Your nearson will cope. He needs to be able to if Festus gets himself killed."

Adeone chuckled. "Quite, but don't tempt fate. When would you like to leave?"

"Next Septadai, maybe?"

"At least there's time for a couple of private dinners and a banquet."

"The rumours?"

"The rumour-mongers can go to Sicla's Cavern for all I care. Will Neassa cope without you here?"

"I expect so. She said she might come to visit later in the year. I think she wants to face things out here first."

Adeone nodded. "I'll make sure she sits with me at some of the Court Suppers. That should quieten things nicely. What is it you need to settle in Tradere? No, I'm not trying to get you to stay. I'm interested."

Rhian hesitated. "I'm setting up an orphanage in the area. We had a winter fever rip through several villages. We contained it by being careful, but several families were left without adults. A few of our tenants have been helping with the children that were left and we've a few staying in the house, but it did highlight we've no orphanage. Gerens is happy to fund it. The building work has just been finished and they want me there for an opening. Amongst other things, I'd like to be there to see everyone settled. We might well have children at the house every so often, but it will be nice for them to be together."

Adeone searched her face. "Let me know if there's anything I can do."

"I will, but I can't think of anything. Hopefully, this will keep the youngsters in our area and they can later return to their family homes or be given new tenancies. We'll keep them trained in their family skills or new ones if they'd prefer. It felt like something I could do to help."

"I wish everyone had your heart."

"Adeone, you really don't." She saw the way he was watching her. "I should let you recover from mother's visit."

"That takes longer than an evening," quipped Adeone.

Chapter 23

DEBRIEF

Pentadai, Week 15 – 19th Macial, 19th Macis 1213
Oedran – Administrative Quarter - Barracks

Rᴇᴛᴜʀɴɪɴɢ ᴛᴏ Oᴇᴅʀᴀɴ after a week at Ceardlann, Arkyn saw Ponder stabled, told Kadeem and Edward he'd be back eventually and left on foot for the barracks.

The blustery walk across the Administrative Quarter wasn't unpleasant, but he was glad to reach the barracks' gate. The guards didn't recognise him and he'd sent no warning but, when they asked him for the password, he said simply,

"I didn't read the briefing but this will suffice," and handed over his signet ring to the senior guard who paled on examining it.

Returning the ring, the guard said, "My apologies, Your Highness."

"No apology needed. I did wonder if you'd considered the group of guards with me, all wearing the appropriate uniform for my guard…"

"I was at the Guildhall after Gad infiltrated it in 1210, Your Highness. He wore a guard's tabard too."

"Excellent point. What's your name?"

The guard hesitated. "Jost Lyndon, sir."

With a nod, Arkyn walked through the barracks' portcullised gateway. A sergeant, crossing the sand-strewn parade ground, saluted and moved hastily aside.

"Can I help, sir."

"No, thank you," replied Arkyn.

Leaving the parade ground, Arkyn walked quickly, acknowledging the salutes of the men he passed. He entered the Major's outer office and the corporal-clerk hurriedly rose.

Moments later, the door closing behind his clerk, Wynfeld saluted smartly. "Your Highness, I'm pleased to see that you're safe and whole."

Arkyn sighed. "Thank you, Major. I'm pleased to be back." He looked round Wynfeld's office and acknowledged Captain Beaver's salute. "Do you have time for me to interrupt your conference?"

Wynfeld nodded. "Yes, sir. Please sit down. Would you like a drink?"

Arkyn seated himself. "Not for the moment, thank you. Please be seated, Major. First, so that Beaver can return to his duties, I'd be interested to know if anything came of Smithers' drawings?"

Beaver replied, "Quite a lot, Your Highness."

"All right, Captain, that's all," said Wynfeld. "I'll take it from here, with our Prince's consent." When Beaver had left, the Major enquired conversationally, "Could we borrow Smithers' skill, sir?"

"If he's not required by myself or Prince Tain, yes. What did Beaver mean by 'quite a lot'?"

Wynfeld passed over a file. "My report isn't quite ready, sir, but please feel free to examine this."

Arkyn took it. Why wasn't the Major telling him? He picked the file up, sat back comfortably and flicked open the file. He read each page carefully, there were witness statements, bits of information, lists of men's names, genealogy tables, drawings – some of which Arkyn recognised as Smithers' handiwork but of older origin – there were reports on places and routines. He found he was impressed with the detail and a picture formed.

He closed the file. "Interesting indeed, Major." He flicked his eyes to the door. "Bring this to my office later. I don't have the time to peruse it properly. I am also considering a few ideas following the attack. Edward is sorting out my notes, so it will be easier to talk with those at hand."

* * *

Later that day, Edward announced Wynfeld and Arkyn rose in greeting.

On invitation, the Major sat down. "Thank you for understanding my predicament, sir."

"It is unfortunate that you've lost trust in your corporal because his brother was a traitor."

"In the circumstances, Your Highness, he will not be my corporal tomorrow."

Arkyn nodded. "That, I think, is wise. Now, the other bandits, I noticed you'd traced some of them. How, exactly?"

Wynfeld frowned. "There are ways and means, sir, and we thought we knew the region in which these men originated. Unfortunately, they left some time ago, so no direct links can be made."

"Ten miles from Black Hills is an interesting coincidence. The families?"

"Are being observed as best I can manage it in small communities. There's something odd about that region. It's as though an immense burden is placed on it. My agents, who have got within hail of the area, all report that there are undercurrents which they can't pinpoint, sir."

"Nicely vague enough so that we can't do anything. I was intrigued by Smithers' earlier drawings. When were they made?"

Wynfeld flicked open the file and searched for them. "The first day of 1212, sir. He thought the people in them were watching Prince Tain malevolently."

Arkyn ran a hand through his hair. "I wish he wasn't a target."

"We all do, sir, but then we wish none of you were. What struck Your

Highness about those drawings in particular?"

"The scar in one of them. The leader of the bandits had a similar one. It made me wonder if it's a deliberate mark, a badge of allegiance, maybe, or of rank, even of confusion. If I'm not mistaken, there have been reports of a scarred man involved in dubious enterprises, mostly treason, for a few years. It struck me earlier that there might have been an assumption there was only one man with such a distinctive scar, but if it's deliberate..." he moved his hands to indicate that Wynfeld could conclude the sentence in his head.

"But we know there's more than one, sir," remarked Wynfeld perplexed.

"We do *now*, but did you before the sketches of the bandits arrived?"

Wynfeld swore. "Thank you, sir."

"Don't worry about it, Major. It was a reasonable assumption in the first instance and the sketches revealed the fact probably more quickly than other means. Next, the captain at Skylabrae: what would you recommend?"

Wynfeld pulled himself out of his preoccupation. "He stayed, cleared up the mess and then resigned, sir. It was appropriate."

"His Majesty was satisfied with that?" enquired Arkyn thoughtfully. His father wasn't prone to demanding resignations, preferring officers learned from the mistakes so they would occur less frequently.

Wynfeld said, "I was awaiting the official report from the Northern Major before I explain to His Majesty."

"Aren't we all? I have completed two journeys and a Provincial Review in the same time. I can't say I'm impressed. He was efficient when I was at Faran's, and he reported to me at Lufia, but I want that written report."

"I shall inform him that such delays are unacceptable, Your Highness."

"Inform the General, please."

Wynfeld watched his Prince's implacable face. "Is that quite fair, sir?"

"If you don't, I will."

Wynfeld recognised the tone. "I understand, sir."

"I'm sure you do, Wynfeld. I wish you'd been there."

Wynfeld said lightly, "So do I, sir."

Arkyn simply nodded before saying, "There was one last thing: I came across a man I'd like in my guard today; he was on the barracks' gate: Jost Lyndon. Will you see to it, please?"

Wynfeld frowned slightly. "Of course, sir, but might I ask what drew your attention to him?"

Arkyn explained the events quickly, easily and without rancour.

As he finished, Wynfeld frowned. "My apologies, Your Highness. I shall see you're not placed in the position again."

"Don't apologise. Lyndon was quite correct. Do all the checks and, if he passes, he can head my guard when Prince Tain borrows Smithers. That's everything official. Come and sit in more congenial surroundings and stay for dinner, if you can."

Wynfeld rose as Arkyn did. "Thank you, sir, but I'm still on duty..."

Arkyn chuckled. "You never seem to be off duty, Wynfeld. Does the commander or General know where you are?"

Wynfeld said wryly, "Yes, Your Highness."

"Then that's all that matters. I'd be glad of your company."

* * *

When seated comfortably with a drink in hand, Wynfeld said, "I was glad Your Highness accepted the militia's help for your journeys."

"I did it for my entourage, Major. They don't deserve death. I don't think I've ever felt so guilty before and so utterly useless..."

Wynfeld watched him carefully. "From my understanding, Your Highness saved Edward's life."

Arkyn said, "That wasn't my point."

"No, sir, but self-recriminations, no matter how justified you believe them to be, are unproductive. No-one can change the past; we can only let the past change how we act in the future, my prince."

Arkyn swirled the wine in his goblet. "I wish the knowledge of that could stop the responsibility I feel."

Wynfeld looked closely at him. Compassionately, he asked what had happened in the coach.

Arkyn started explaining. He hadn't even told his father the exact events and he realised he'd been avoiding it.

When Arkyn finished speaking, Wynfeld said, "Lord Kensal was a brave and determined man, sir. We knew that from when he found the merchants who'd been attacked last year and told his protection to go with them instead of accompanying him. If you'd been on horseback, he'd have protected you in the same spirit—"

"I was stubborn and hotheaded, and it got him killed," retorted Arkyn.

"Do not travel that path, my prince. Was Your Highness thinking only of yourself? No. If you had been then you'd have meekly stayed in the coach destroying the respect you gained from your guards. What you did is no different to what Lord Kensal did. You both thought of other people. Would you have wanted him to feel guilty if he hadn't managed to stop you and you'd taken that arrow?"

"No," whispered Arkyn.

"I doubt he'd want you to feel responsible either. Do not belittle what he did by considering it your fault, because that takes away honour from him. He acted as he saw fit and he saw fit to protect you above himself.

You're our Prince, sir. You'll find many men do the same. Your guards, staff, friends, the militia, lords all over the empire and common men will all have the same instinct. Possibly not for the same reasons, but men die every day in your family's service; Your Highness is not responsible or culpable for that, and the men who respect and guard you are masters of their own fate."

Arkyn said so quietly that Wynfeld nearly missed it, "I wish I was."

"Never think that fate is foretold because then life's triumphs become meaningless. In 1208 I thought I'd be sergeant until I saw out my time in the army. I thought that was my fate and now look at me."

Arkyn chuckled. "You enjoy the challenge, Major. Thank you, I think, somehow, your words have helped."

"I'm glad. I don't like to see Your Highness so troubled and I never have."

The memory of the first days he'd met Wynfeld sprung to Arkyn's mind. "You always seem to be there when I need to talk."

"Or do you need to talk because of me?" enquired Wynfeld wryly.

Arkyn chuckled again. "Never that, Wynfeld, but maybe I now talk because you're there."

Wynfeld smiled in return. "I'm glad I can help, sir."

Chapter 24
AXTON AND EDMONDS
Hexadai, Week 15 – 20th Macial, 20th Macis 1213
Barracks – Wynfeld's Quarters

WYNFELD WOKE the following morning with a slight headache. He enjoyed his Prince's company, but he hadn't drunk so much in a while. He hadn't been drunk, but he felt like he needed a decent amount of water and a breakfast to match it. As he dressed, he turned over the revelations from the discussion of the previous evening. As far as he could tell, Axton had met expectations in everything but providing the report. He probably required a nudge but his Prince had been precise in his orders.

A bowl of porridge and an apple later, he went to the General's office. Paturn wasn't a late riser. No officer who valued his commission was. It was drilled into all recruits. There might be duty times, but, unless you were on nights, you woke early. The General's clerk rose and saluted as he entered the small outer office.

"Is he free, Newman?"

"Yes, sir."

Wynfeld knocked on the General's door and entered when bidden. His salute was exact, but the General's gaze was evaluating.

"Nice evening with the Prince?"

"Yes, sir. His Highness sent for me to discuss revelations regarding the bandits where the wrong ears couldn't hear. He then invited me to stay for dinner."

"I hope His Highness was well."

"Very, sir, if a little perturbed by Axton's lack of report."

Paturn sat back, turning his pen over and over in his fingers. "Why are you informing me, Wynfeld?"

"His Highness ordered me to, sir."

Paturn pushed himself to his feet. "Oh. That is unfortunate. I will have to report to the King. I cannot take action against him without the King's agreement."

"Sir, you have Prince Arkyn's—"

"I do and His Highness knows this is what happens. How's Edmonds?"

"Still not good, sir. I think the doc has him sedated."

Paturn hesitated. "Bring him round. It won't help him face what's happened. I know what might. I'm for the Palace."

* * *

Paturn entered the Palace by one of the garden gates. There was no need to fight his way through the early morning bustle on the city's roads. He strode through the grounds, worrying about everything that had happened. Prince Arkyn had to be annoyed to have taken the route he had. He could have spoken to the King himself. He could have dealt with it quietly. Halfway between the gate and the imposing hotchpotch of wings that was the rear of the Palace, Paturn stopped. *Was* this what the Prince had wanted? The King didn't hide matters from his son and he doubted the Prince hid things from the King.

Cursing, he made his way to the Prince's office. There, Edward informed him that Arkyn was still breakfasting. Paturn decided to wait. He would rather check than act in haste.

* * *

Half an hour later, Arkyn settled himself behind the desk and motioned for Paturn to speak.

"Major Wynfeld has informed me of Major Axton's lack of report, sir. Would you like me to recall Axton to give an account of himself?"

Arkyn rang the bell on his desk. "Edward, if Advisor Rayburn isn't with His Majesty, I'd like a word."

"And Advisor Caple, sir?"

"This isn't his area of expertise."

Edward left, his face a picture of misgivings that Arkyn ignored. Caple might be his senior advisor but there were some matters it was better to keep within the expertise and knowledge of the King's Advisors. He didn't think his father would object.

They waited in silence for the couple of minutes it took for Rayburn to arrive. There was little point going over the same ground twice.

Rayburn entered, made a slight bow and nodded to Paturn. "How can I help, Your Highness?"

Arkyn explained the facts. It was better if his views didn't prejudice Rayburn's advice.

Paturn watching found the technique curious. King Altarius would have left his advisors with little doubt about his feelings. King Adeone was likely to offer a solution amongst the explanation, thereby allowing the advisors some direction. Prince Arkyn's bland statement of fact, meant Rayburn had next to no idea how the Prince felt.

At the end of the explanation, Rayburn sighed. "Axton's an idiot. Worst case, he's been suborned. Best case, he's just incompetent, Your Highness. Presumably, Major Wynfeld would have suspicions if it was the former. Are we certain he hasn't sent the report and it's gone missing?"

Arkyn hesitated. "A good point." He called for Edward and put the question to him.

"I checked three days ago, sir, and he hadn't sent it then. I asked him to inform me when he did."

Arkyn nodded in dismissal. "General, what are your thoughts?"

"I will endeavour to ascertain what's happened, sir, and get you that report as quickly as possible. Do you want Axton's resignation?"

"Rayburn?"

The advisor never hesitated. "It wouldn't be unusual in the circumstances, sir. Given Axton's rank, His Majesty will need to be consulted. There is also the concern that if he hasn't been suborned, you might replace him with someone who has. That attack was directed at Your Highness, I have no doubt of that, but it doesn't mean that there weren't other motives as well. His Majesty is still awaiting the report from Apposer Nallvir on Lord Faran's loyalty. Captain Marsh's death was likely pre-decided. Lord Scanlon will know the precarious position the militia is in. The Commander of Lufian has been saved simply because the Major was in the province. The captain at Skylabrae has resigned already. I am minded to recommend that Your Highness treads carefully."

Arkyn nodded. "Thank you. Can you ask Edward to see if His Majesty is free as you pass, please?" Once Rayburn had gone, he continued, "Your thoughts, Paturn?"

"If Axton keeps his commission, sir, it's his final chance, as far as I'm concerned. This is completely unacceptable."

"We'll see what His Majesty says, but I don't disagree with the sentiment."

* * *

Six minutes later, they explained everything to Adeone, who pursed his lips and caught Paturn's eye.

"Court martial."

Even Paturn was surprised. "Sir?"

"He does not get to defy His Highness' orders without repercussions. I accept what Rayburn is saying, but this is far more fundamental. I don't want Axton warned."

Arkyn opened his mouth and then closed it again. His father's face was implacable. Axton would be recalled and face a court martial.

"Who do you want to command in the Northern Empire in the meantime, Sire?" asked Paturn.

"Fachin can take over temporarily. Axton may be reinstated but I'm sending a message. Is there anything else?"

Paturn hesitated. "Edmonds is in a bad way, sir. His Highness' return made it all real."

Adeone sighed. "How bad?"

"The doctor has been keeping him sedated. If it's not too much of an imposition, sir, it may help if Your Majesty sees him."

Adeone pushed himself to his feet. "I'll come now. Arkyn, accompany me, please. You need to understand something."

Rather perplexed, Arkyn followed his father out of the office. They left the Palace the way the General had entered, with Adeone ordering a coach was to meet them at the barracks for their return. When they reached the barracks, the silence that spread around them made the hairs stand up on Arkyn's neck. The men they passed couldn't move aside or salute quickly enough, and even he felt an unnerving power radiating from his father.

They entered the infirmary with its tiled corridors and echoing rooms. The General led the way to a private room that had a less clinical feel. Edmonds, the training captain of the barracks, was curled up, shivering, facing away from the door.

"General, please leave us," murmured Adeone, watching Edmonds' back.

Arkyn waited for the click of the door, before saying, "Sir, what—?"

Adeone silenced him with a swift look before crossing to Edmonds, sitting on the edge of the bed and squeezing his shoulder. "Talk."

The word was soft, harmonious and resonated a command without being harsh or demanding.

130

"I can't," whispered Edmonds. "I was meant to protect him."

"And you did," said Adeone. "You kept him with you until he could look after himself. You risked everything by lying for him."

"He should be here."

"Yes, he should, but he's still with us in spirit. He was everything you hoped he would be. Brave, loyal, dangerous in a fight… Almost had you legless on occasion."

Edmonds gave a snort. "Sir, that's not fair."

Adeone chuckled. "He did you proud, you know. You couldn't have protected him better but he had to make his own way. I would have been lost without him and so would Arkyn."

Arkyn didn't miss the informality. He hadn't realised his father knew Edmonds so well. Who were they talking about? Paturn's words about the timing of Edmonds' collapse suggested it might have been one of his retinue. He realised the answer just as his father said,

"Marsh knew the risks. When I asked him to head my guards, he knew what he was doing. He took on the task without a moment's hesitation. Just as he accepted watching over Arkyn without demurral. Your little half-brother never shirked his duty. There's been justice for him."

Tears streaked down Edmonds' face. "He shouldn't have been in the army. He shouldn't have been here. I shouldn't have lied."

Adeone moved his hand slightly, so that his fingers rested on Edmonds' pulse point. "Be easy and free from guilt. Let dreams take you and, when you waken, come and see me."

Watching, Arkyn would have sworn he saw the faintest gold shimmer around his father's hand. Edmonds' shaking stopped as his breathing deepened. Had the captain fallen asleep on command?

Adeone pushed himself to his feet and drew a blanket over Edmonds. He collected Arkyn with a glance. This wasn't the place to explain. They found both Paturn and Wynfeld waiting.

Adeone didn't even acknowledge Wynfeld. "He's sleeping, Paturn. Keep him busy when he's fit to get up. Don't let him dwell on events. I think it will have helped but I can't swear to it. Don't sedate him again. I've told him to come and see me when he wakes. Please don't prevent him, but give me warning he's on his way. Your Highness, we should return to the Palace."

* * *

Once in the corridors of the Privy Wing, Adeone said, "Can we use your chambers and not be disturbed?"

Arkyn nodded. The day was more perplexing by the minute. When they entered his sitting room, his father collapsed onto the couch and Arkyn felt the years roll away. These had been his father's chambers until his grandfather's death. For the first time in those years, he expected to see his mother enter to greet them.

His father sat slumped forward. His head in his hands. For several moments Arkyn wondered if he was crying, but it seemed not.

After those moments, Adeone said heavily, "Edmonds is Marsh's half-brother. I should have realised sooner there'd be a reaction."

"How do you know, sir?"

"It's a long story. Suffice it to say, I know. There's lots of events tangled together from the time I found out. Marsh was too young for the army when I found them. Edmonds had lied about their ages. Father wasn't happy with my solution, but it kept them safe. When Ella died, Marsh found me in a worse state than Edmonds just was. He kept my collapse private and all he'd say when I tried to thank him was, 'What collapse? Grief is different.' Your mother suggested I promoted him. He'd worked with Fitz, knew the threats, wanted to be helpful. I saw no harm. I made him your captain because I knew he wasn't ever going to give your uncle a moment's thought. Edmonds is right; he shouldn't have died. Still, that's not what I wanted to talk to you about. Do you know what I did for Edmonds?"

"Not exactly, sir."

"Father told me he'd explained something of the King's Aura to you."

Arkyn swallowed. "He said it's a dangerous power that comes unbidden."

"It is and it can, but it may also be controlled. I used it walking through the barracks. It manifests at your coronation. I don't think anyone understands it completely, but the oaths men swear in our service play a part. Fealty is strong. Laioril once told me that there is strength passed from vassal to liege on taking an oath, but whether that is true, I do not know. If it is, our ancestors have used the knowledge. It's in our bloodline but like most things, the aura has a second side. It's known as the King's Blessing and is all part of the same power, but one sounds so much nicer than the other. It boils down to the same thing: we can make men forget, we can control their emotions and bring them peace, we can compel them to obey. Edmonds will be compelled to come and see me. When he does, he'll seal the blessing by acknowledging me as his liege. The obeisances, the taking of our hand is powerful. Never rely on the aura, but there are moments, like today, when it is kinder to use the blessing to help someone find a peace. Edmonds will never lose that feeling of loss. I'm just hoping he forgives me for removing his guilt."

Arkyn hesitated. "I can't see why he wouldn't, father."

"People do get upset when you mess with their emotions."

"It was for a good reason, sir."

Adeone rubbed at his face. "Yes. I suppose it was. Arkyn, will you promise me, whatever the future brings, use the power only to help others?"

Arkyn hesitated. "I can't promise that, father. Not because I don't want to," he added hastily, "I truly wish I could, but we don't know what will come. I will promise that I will only use it in direst need or to help. Though, if it comes with my coronation, I have years to work out what to do."

Adeone sighed. "I shall content myself with that." His gaze searched his son's face. "You never cease to surprise me."

Arkyn chuckled. "I could say the same, father. Are you really going to court martial, Axton?"

Adeone pursed his lips. "Do you think it is a bad idea?"

"His actions make no sense; however, he can't be the only officer in history to have messed up."

"No, and the rest were court-martialled or resigned," said Adeone.

"Wynfeld?"

"He didn't mess up in this way." Adeone saw Arkyn's crooked eyebrow. "All right. I ended up attacked because of his mistake, but no-one died. Marsh, Thomas, Alan, *Kensal*, died because of the army's mistakes and Axton can't even get you a report on the matter."

"Might I make a suggestion, Sire?"

"Is this going to be one of your infamous compromises?"

Arkyn chuckled. "Yes. Let the General tell Axton he's going to be court-martialled for failing to follow orders. I expect the shock of that will mean I get a report on my desk within days. I also expect it was just ready to send as the General informed him."

Adeone's eyes narrowed. "Then what?"

"I'll persuade Your Majesty that he should be let off with a reprimand and we watch him carefully. If he puts another toe out of line, we replace him. We have given other officers second chances."

"If that report isn't on your desk within a week, I'll court martial him."

"Thank you, Sire. I shall inform the General of the change of plan."

Adeone's eyes glinted. "You don't need the King's Aura; you do know that, don't you?"

Arkyn chuckled. "I can only be what you have taught me to be, father."

"I wouldn't be so sure of that if I were you." Adeone leaned back, looking up at the ceiling. "I should return to my office before Richardson sends out a search party. Knowing where I am won't stop him. I'm dining with Rhian tonight, but you're welcome to join us."

Arkyn shook his head. "Thank you, father, but I've invited Irvin and Julius. We'll probably be at Court later."

"I won't be." Adeone hesitated, his father's words crossing the years. "Get to know everyone in your generation at Court, Arkyn, as far as is prudent. They'll be with you throughout your life. If you're inviting Julius, it might be an idea to start including Finian. He is a Lord of Oedran, even in his minority, and he is also our ward officially, not Landis'."

Arkyn nodded. "I shall do so." He watched his father leave with a hundred thoughts chasing through his mind: Axton, the King's Aura, the King's Blessing, Finian, hidden connections between people like Edmonds and Marsh, events of the bandit attack. He swallowed back his own emotion over that, half wishing his father had used the blessing on him. Though maybe it wouldn't work the same. He had never sworn fealty.

Chapter 25
RHIAN AND REASON
Septadai, Week 15 – 21st Macial, 21st Macis 1213
Arkyn's Office

ARKYN GLANCED UP as Paturn entered his office the following morning. He waved to a chair. "You have His Majesty's revised instructions?"

"Yes, sir. I have informed Major Axton. He went rather pale and admitted there isn't much to put into a report. They did what was expected but the bandits obviously knew what they'd do."

"And I want all of that in a report, General. I want every bit of information Axton has gleaned, whether that says the army did what they could or that the army did nothing at all."

"He is concerned that in saying everything was done, he won't be believed, sir."

"General, we need an honest report. Facts should never be falsified to suit what we are expected to think. If I ever get wind that's happened, court martial will be least of the officer's worries and I believe His Majesty is in agreement with me on that."

"His Majesty has always been very clear that he requires the truth, sir."

Arkyn gave a short nod. "How long would Axton's report take to arrive?"

"He's still at Skylabrae, sir. So three days with a quick courier. Can I offer him any reassurance?"

"No. We cannot let this pass. If Axton had needed clarification, he could have requested it. He had access to the area, my staff, Skylabrae and Faran's household. The captured bandits weren't immediately executed to give him time to question them. The attack was twelve weeks ago. I am disappointed you are even asking the question."

"That does put a different perspective on it, sir. I will take action even if the King doesn't wish for a court martial."

Arkyn gave a short nod. "Thank you, General. Then that's all that needs to be said on the matter."

* * *

After the General had left, Arkyn waited long enough for him to be clear of the Palace before making his way to the Inner Office, where he found his father and Lady Rhian quietly talking. He gave the obligatory bow and waited.

Adeone broke off his conversation. "Should I be worried?"

Hearing the click of the door as Richardson left, Arkyn shrugged. "Not really, Sire. I've just been talking with the General about the missing report."

"Ah. Come and sit down and tell me."

Rather self-consciously, Arkyn did so, then added his own thoughts.

Adeone frowned. "So you now think we should court martial him?"

"No. I don't know. I think *something* needs to happen. *What* is more difficult. Anything up to commander, yes, court martial. Maybe I should have been clearer. Maybe it rests as much with me as with him."

"Did you tell him you wanted a report, sir?" asked Lady Rhian.

"Yes, and mentioned His Majesty would need a copy, so it was clear it would have to be written."

"Why are you therefore blaming yourself?"

Adeone snorted. "It's what he does, cousin. He looks for the compromise. I admire it."

"So do I," she replied whilst watching Arkyn's face and the worry lines etched on it.

Adeone said, "Do you want me to deal with this?"

Arkyn met his gaze for an instant then glanced away. "Not exactly. The more I consider it, the more annoyed I am, but then I also wonder if I'm irrationally annoyed. We know, or think we know the source of the attack, so why is having it confirmed in writing that the army couldn't anticipate it so important?"

"Because they should have anticipated it, sir," said Rhian quietly. "Even were your uncle not the threat he is, attacks on kings and princes when they travel have been common. One of the Lufian kings was murdered on a journey. Saying they couldn't have anticipated it is an excuse, not a reason for not acting to prevent it."

Adeone watched her face. "What would you do, Rhian?"

"Read his report and let him know he's on his last chance. It's still a reasonable action. Uncle would have demanded his resignation, but we're living in a different time. If you believe Axton is loyal, why remove him?

135

I understand you can't be seen to let incompetence pass, but you could order him to report here and give him a dressing down."

"If we did that, why not a court martial?" asked Arkyn.

"Subtlety," replied Rhian. "Granted, not much, but you don't then risk being forced to dismiss him, or have Arkyn have to explain his orders."

"Given Arkyn would have to be one of the judges…"

Rhian sighed. "There might be a slight conflict of interest there. If you really think about it, I'm sure you'll see that Scanlon will just twist it all. You'll be dismissing someone for personal reasons."

Adeone swore. "Thank you, cousin. What am I going to do when you're not here?"

She smiled. "Listen to your son's voice of compromise. It'll keep you both safe. There's too much emotion flying around with this situation. Now, I'm going to let you two talk and see mother."

"You don't have to go," said Arkyn watching his father carefully.

"Mother likes me to be prompt." She chuckled at the look on their faces. "I'll tell her I walked out on the King, shall I?"

Adeone laughed. "Probably better not to."

Once she'd gone, Arkyn sighed. "I hope I didn't interrupt anything important, sir."

"Not at all. Are you happy with the compromise?"

"Yes. Would uncle twist it?"

"More than likely. You see, dismissing or demoting someone because they've been negligent is all well and good, but it would be because he'd annoyed you. At any other time, that would be acceptable and right; however, in this situation, Scanlon would capitalise on it. He probably already plans to, especially if he was behind it. Or if it was the idea of one of his accomplices." Adeone saw his son's face. "He can't be acting alone, Arkyn. There have to be others helping, aiding and abetting him. We talk of traitors, but he can't be coercing all of them. I'm certain there's at least one other, possibly more, acting with him."

Arkyn sighed. "If we can't act as we normally would, he's hobbling us as well as attacking us."

"Yes, and that's when your brain becomes the greatest weapon you have. Scanlon doesn't always use his. He rushes headlong and thinks his position means he'll succeed. Though, sadly, he might be learning not to."

"So, shall I order Axton back to Oedran, Sire?"

His father gave him a sideways look. "I think that was the conclusion. We could do it over messenger link but I don't…" He trailed off. "Sicla, even recalling Axton to Oedran would cause issues."

"He's got the Northern Empire in his remit. That includes Eyllyn, sir."

Adeone looked at Arkyn, dumbfounded. "You're not suggesting Ifor does our dirty work for us, are you?"

"I'm suggesting that getting someone who is life-bound to you and knows your thoughts, to give an officer – who could legitimately visit his city – a polite but discreet rebuke, might be an idea, Your Majesty."

"I'll tell Ifor. You can tell Paturn. He can send Axton to Eyllyn, after you have the report."

Half an hour later, Adeone watched Arkyn leave with a mixture of emotions. His son had definitely left his childhood behind. Three provincial reviews and the work from the Petitionals had certainly hardened him.

* * *

Three days later, Arkyn glanced up as Edward entered his office with a scroll tube in hand. Having accidentally overheard snippets, and having put requests, questions and visits together, the administrator thought he knew what the report was. So, lips twitching, he mentioned he'd also arranged time for Arkyn to talk it over with the King.

Taking the report, Arkyn snorted. "In which case, Edward, can you please let General Paturn know this has been delivered?"

"Very good, Your Highness. Shall I clear the other papers away?"

"Will you be returning them to my desk later?"

"More than likely, sir."

"In which case, save yourself a job."

After his administrator left, Arkyn broke the seal, cut the ties and slid the rolled parchment from its casing. Unrolling it and then rolling it back on itself, he eyed the four pieces of parchment. As reports went, he'd seen more substantial ones. Reminding himself that quantity didn't equal quality, he started reading. It didn't give any indication to events beyond whether the army had done their jobs. Nothing about the wider situation. There was a list of patrol dates and times, there were lists of men on those patrols, and reassurance that travellers had been asked their business from Shinglis to Lufia in the days before he arrived in the province. He had no reason to doubt the report or its contents. The only conclusion that Axton had drawn was that the army couldn't have done anything else other than accompany Arkyn every step of the way, and that hadn't been requested and so would have overstepped the bounds.

Arkyn had to admit that, in that, Axton was right.

He called for Edward and asked him to check whether the King was in counsel. On hearing he was ensconced with his justice advisor and lawyers, Arkyn returned to his other papers. It would all wait.

An hour later, informed his father was free, he wandered to the Outer Office and crooked an eyebrow at Richardson.

"Lord Landis is with His Majesty, sir."

Arkyn merely nodded and waited for Richardson to announce him. If nothing else, it would tease his nearfather, who rarely waited to be announced.

Bowing, Arkyn saw his father's expression, inwardly he cursed.

"You still think we shouldn't have Axton court-martialled?"

"I think we've been over it multiple times, Sire, and concluded it would be counterproductive. Axton should be on his way to Eyllyn tonight. I don't suggest we give him another chance after this one. If they did everything they say they did, then they had met expectations. I doubt very much the bandits were camped out saying, *'Please arrest us; we're here to kill Prince Arkyn.'*"

Landis snorted. "He's got a point, Sire."

"Fine. I'll let Ifor handle it. He has a way with words. You do realise this report could firmly lay the blame at Faran's feet, don't you?"

Arkyn hesitated. The thought hadn't occurred to him and it should have done. "It may, sir, and I'm sorry if it does, truly. I like Lord Faran, but nobody should ever be made a scapegoat."

"All right. I'll wait for Nallvir's report. He's had more than enough time as well. Though, admittedly, he had a lot more ground to cover with all the interviews he had to conduct and the documents he had to examine. I want this whole thing over and done with."

Arkyn blinked, reminding himself that his father hadn't been there, hadn't seen the victims die. Personally, he wanted the truth, whatever that truth was. He wanted to know that when he saw Kensal in the heavens, however far in his future that might be, he could look his friend in the eye and say that everything possible was done, that justice was achieved.

Landis saw the brief emotion. "Sire, I'm sure everyone wishes the events hadn't happened."

Adeone nodded. "Give us two minutes, Festus." Once Landis had gone, he continued, "I do care, Arkyn. I'm tired of the discussions keeping the wound open."

"I understand, sir."

Shaking his head, Adeone crossed to his son and wrapped him in a hug. "When Rhian's left for Tradere, you're due time at Ceardlann."

Arkyn relaxed. "That would be nice, father."

Chapter 26

FARAN AND CAMLYN

AFTER MILITARY COUNSEL the following day, Adeone was intrigued when Wynfeld requested a private word. He was more intrigued when the Major of Oedran said quietly that Prince Arkyn might also like to hear the report.

Once everyone was settled, Adeone said, "What's happened, Wynfeld? Bearing in mind, I have Palace Counsel this afternoon."

Wynfeld smiled. "I really hope it doesn't take that long, Sire. I've had word from Lord Faran's estate."

Arkyn stilled and glanced at his father's set face. "I hope it's good news, Wynfeld."

"In the essential fact of His Lordship's innocence, it is, sir."

Adeone got up and turned to the windows. His relief was almost palpable. Arkyn and Wynfeld also rose and waited for Adeone to collect his thoughts, which he did more slowly than normal.

Wynfeld opened his mouth to elaborate, but Arkyn silenced him with a look; there were times to carry on with reports, but this wasn't one of them.

Eventually, Adeone let out a long breath. "Wynfeld, wait outside, please."

The Major saluted and left without a word.

"Can I do anything?" asked Arkyn, seeing the stark emotion in his father's eyes as he turned back to the room.

Adeone shook his head. "Do you think Wynfeld realises what he's done?"

Arkyn smiled sadly. "I doubt it, sir. I'm glad Faran's innocent."

Adeone rubbed at his head. "Alcis, so am I, Arkyn. I could never have asked for an investigation when Ella died. I was too wrapped up in grief to act in haste, and then the time was gone."

"Did the apposer know—"

"I told him to investigate Faran's loyalty, not simply the bandit attack."

"Why *didn't* you summon him to Oedran once I'd left, sir?"

"Faran? I'd overreacted with Ifor. That's most of it, but it would have caused more problems than it solved whilst setting an unhealthy precedent. One which he understood, for he could have offered a fealty test and didn't. I was worried at that point, but not everyone has Daioch's resolve."

"He told me he wouldn't put you through another life-bind unless there was no other option. It wasn't for himself he let the investigation happen."

"Why tell me now?" asked Adeone, perplexed.

"Because now you're more likely to believe and appreciate it, father."

Adeone sank back onto his chair. "Thank you. Faran is one of the men closest to me. Landis, Wealsman, Faran and Daioch. Only Wealsman hasn't been targeted by your uncle and only because we kept our friendship secret. He's lost that protection but… I'm sorry. This isn't about my troubles. Faran is innocent of harbouring the bandits that attacked you. The army did all they could. It's another dead end."

"Yes. I expected nothing less, Sire. I expect they went into Bayan, possibly by the Oaks Ridge road, then made their way to the coast and crossed the Faral Sound, before hiking to the ambush spot. After they left the main highway, they wouldn't have encountered the army patrols. It's too much ground for an investigation to cover."

"True. We'll never known now. Let's get Wynfeld back." A moment later, he acknowledged the Major's salute. "Sit back down, Wynfeld, and explain the rest of your report, including how you know the outcome of my apposer's report before I do."

Wynfeld said, "By being Chief of Intelligence, sir."

Adeone pursed his lips. "Is there nothing you haven't infiltrated?"

"Plenty, Sire, but I did get a man onto the apposer's team as a guarantee, you might say. I thought it was safer to make sure."

"Probably right. So, what was the unessential part of your report?"

"It's not so much unessential, Sire, more subsequent findings. Everything points to Lord Scanlon having carefully orchestrated Lord Faran's part in this, or it is supposed it is Lord Scanlon."

"We'd worked that out but why?"

Wynfeld paused. "It is known His Lordship, that is the Justiciar, is far lower on funds than he was. There are several rich lords, with daughters only, who have found themselves in precarious legal positions. As though they are being, for want of a better phrase, set up, Sire, so that their daughters become wards of the Justiciar and they themselves are discredited or even executed. We have prevented all manipulations thus far. The situation regarding Lord Faran must have been planned far more carefully because we never saw it coming and I must apologise for that."

Adeone steepled his fingers against his mouth. "You didn't think it wise to tell me of this before?"

"We weren't certain before, Sire. There was just circumstantial evidence and coincidence."

"You are now, though?" enquired Arkyn.

"Yes, Your Highness. We suspect Lord Camlyn of Bayan is next, Sire. He has an only daughter, Mellonia. She's still young, but he is elderly and ailing fast. He's not going to remarry; he's already had three wives. His lands are rich and a lawyer has visited him about discrepancies. That's as much as I know. The meeting with the lawyer was behind closed doors and all our informant heard was the word discrepancies."

Adeone cursed. Camlyn had once been a potential governor for Bayan; to attack him surely showed Scanlon's current mood: either he was desperate or showing he could attack anyone, possibly both.

Adeone held Wynfeld's gaze. "You apparently know the movements of my staff better than I do. Where's my apposer?"

"Compiling his report at Lord Faran's, sir."

"Which fort is closest to Camlyn? I'm meaning a primary or secondary."

Wynfeld thought for a moment before saying, "Primary, His Lordship is about equidistant from Paras, Garth and Rathgar, Sire. Secondary, there is Fort Perivale. I'm not sure if it is within his lands or just outside – for it joins the main highway, which marks the bounds."

"Who's in charge at Perivale?"

"A Chief Captain, sir. I can get you his name if I may step outside for two moments."

When Wynfeld returned, Adeone said, "Well?"

"One, Captain Gervase Ballard, Sire."

"Thank you. Ask Ballard to post men at Lord Camlyn's to secure everything before my apposer gets there. It should prevent him and his daughter becoming victims of my brother's schemes." He saw Wynfeld's face. "Ask him yourself. Don't get Axton to. I'll speak with Camlyn."

* * *

As the messenger link formed, Adeone studied the white-haired lord. "You're stressed, Lord Camlyn. Might I enquire why?"

"It is nothing, Sire, a trifling matter," replied Camlyn, trying to settle his unease.

"Would it be something to do with a visit from a lawyer earlier this week? Ah, I see I'm right. What did he say?"

Lord Camlyn swallowed. "That it had come to the Justiciar's attention that there were criminal activities occurring on my land and that I had a cisluna-month to deal with them."

Adeone said, "He wasn't more specific?"

"No, Your Majesty. I'm sorry if—"

"Camlyn, if there weren't criminal activities occurring I'd be surprised. Your lands are vast; somewhere someone will be doing something that isn't as it ought to be, but that doesn't mean you should be under this pressure. Now, the Exarch has mentioned you've not been in Garth for some time. Is there any reason you've been shunning the Citadel Court?"

Camlyn said, "My health isn't what it was, Sire."

"Very well. Do you swear on your fealty that you'll never divulge our

141

conversation elsewhere?" enquired Adeone matter-of-factly.

Perplexed by the specific request, bound so highly, Camlyn frowned. "As Your Majesty wishes, Sire."

"Now give me your word."

"You have my word that I will not divulge this conversation, Sire. Can I just enquire—?"

"Why? Yes. Did you know that my brother is out to murder myself, your Princes and anyone else who might stand in his way in attaining the empire, which he then plans, or seems to plan, to destroy? Ah, I take it not. Well, he is. He is, however, short of funds. Your lands are rich, my lord, and you don't have a son. Your daughter is young and you are in ill health. It's a tempting proposition for him."

Camlyn blanched. "Your Majesty, the Justiciar would never abuse—"

"Do you think I'd be blackening his name to you if he wouldn't?" snapped Adeone. "I've just received word that he's tried the same with Lord Faran and several others. The bandits who attacked Prince Arkyn were nothing to do with Faran. They weren't even local to the area and yet they happened to stumble across my son on my friend's land. The odds against are quite long, I think you'll agree. Now, my lord, will you let me help in your predicament?"

Pale, Camlyn said, "Of course, Sire. How can I ever refuse Your Majesty?"

Adeone wryly considered what Arkyn would have said to that. "Thank you. Do you know Captain Ballard?"

"He has introduced himself, Sire."

"Good. He's sending a posse of men to secure your papers and estate, as far as possible. The apposer who has been dealing with the incidents at Lord Faran's will be with you in a week, two at the outside. He will deal with the accusations in such a manner that there will never be any reprisals. You must, however, do one thing as soon as this link breaks: add a codicil to your requests and bequests stating that you want the guardianship of your daughter placed in my hands should anything happen to you. It is the only way to make sure Lord Scanlon can *never* claim it. Do you understand?"

Still white, Camlyn nodded. "Aye, Sire, I do. Her nearparents will be mystified though."

"Make sure their names are included in the codicil as potential local guardians and, should anything happen, they will still get their dues. You have my word."

"Thank you, Sire."

"Small comfort, I suspect," admitted Adeone. "Camlyn, I'm sorry he's chasing you and for the upheaval this will cause. If you have any questions, please contact me. If, for whatever reason, my apposer oversteps the bounds of his office, I want to know."

* * *

When the link broke, Camlyn looked around his study with a new eye. Shaking, he poured himself a large whiskey. His daughter disturbed his contemplation.

"Father, are you ill?"

He smiled. "I'm not myself, Mellonia. There are some decisions I've had to make. Tell me something, when I pass on… No, young one, listen to me, it will happen… If you've not married, how would you feel if His Majesty was your guardian?"

She stared at him. "Why, father? I don't know how I'd feel. I don't want to think of you not being here."

He put an arm around her. "Me neither, but it will happen. I'm elderly, Mellonia. With His Majesty as your guardian, these lands would be protected for your future."

"Then I… It would be best but, father, it won't happen because you'll live until I'm old and married."

He wrapped her in a hug. "I'm sure I shall, but we must be aware of what's around us, mustn't we?"

She nodded. "Can I see the stone? Please, father."

He considered for a long minute. She was thirteen, bright, intelligent and responsible. Taking a key from his drawer, he crossed to a secret panel, unlocking the box within the void. He drew out a worn orange velvet bag stitched with black thread portraying a bird in flight. He passed it to his daughter with a gentle smile.

Grinning, she carefully removed the stone from the fragile bag. The orange star stone glittered in the sunlight. Entranced, she sat by the fireplace for six minutes, turning it this way and that in the light, watching the white star in the middle of the stone as the perspective changed. She knew it could be worn as a pendant or a brooch. Idly she turned it over. The silver setting had tendrils of design etched around it. Tactile, warm in her hand, she reluctantly put it back in the bag and held it out to her father.

"It's yours, young one. There's little point locking it up until you're twenty. Take it with you but guard it well."

She hesitated. "I… Are you sure, father?"

"Aye, I am, but don't talk about it openly. Now, why did you come hunting for me?"

"I… Well, I was going to ask if I could have a kitten? But it doesn't matter now."

He eyed her. "A kitten grows into a cat. Will you want a cat?"

143

"Yes, but I'd like to see the kitten grow into that cat."

"You'll turn my house into a menagerie."

She giggled. "Only with a bit more practice. Anyway, the doves are so pretty. Is there any chance of a falcon as well, father?"

He sighed. "You'll be the ruin of my sanity, young one. Go on with you, I've work to do."

Mellonia left smiling; her father was never annoyed with her when he called her young one.

Camlyn watched her go humming to himself. A kitten and a falcon shouldn't be too difficult to acquire. She'd guard the star stone well. It was worth more than all their estates being a source of magic and one of only twelve in all of Erinna. The legendary Cearcall had drawn their power from the stones, but they were currently dormant and the rebirth of the Cearcall was a myth. No-one, least of all him, believed it could happen.

Chapter 27
ON INHERITANCE
Pentadai, Week 16 – 26th Macial, 5th Easis 1213
Dellwood – Fitz's Inn - Schoolroom

On PENTADAI, Judge Tancred rose and bowed as Tain entered the schoolroom at Fitz's. He might be his tutor and mentor but Tain was still a prince of the FitzAlcis and there were modes of behaviour expected.

After an initial conversation, Tancred studied his charge thoughtfully. "Has anyone ever explained what your inheritance is and what the significance is, Your Highness?"

"Not in so many words, Judge. I know I'm to become the Justiciar of the Empire, that I have no choice in that…"

Tancred smiled. "You have a choice, sir. Shall we go back to the beginning? Feel free to tell me if I reiterate too often what you already know."

"Please, Judge. It might fill in gaps I'm not yet aware of."

Tancred inclined his head. "An interesting observation, sir; you would make a judge with thoughts like that. Firstly, you need to understand the difference between cisan-age and alunan-age…"

"I think I do, Judge."

"If you would explain your comprehension, we can check, Your Highness."

Tain grinned. "There are two sections of society, cisan and alunan – cisan the poorer, alunan the richer – the age at which a person becomes an adult differs for the two sections. Cisan come of age at fifteen, they become adults then, can claim inheritances, trade in their own name and so on. Alunan come of age at twenty and only at that point can they claim inheritances, trade and so on; therefore, there are many laws dependant on age and social position. There's a slight confusion for the alunan still mark cisan-age, as they enter their adolescence at that point and can be given more responsibility, for instance being allowed at the King's Court."

Tancred nodded. "That is all perfectly true, Your Highness. Adolescence as a term is normally reserved to the alunan section of society. Cisan are either child or adult. Do you know why adolescence is important for the alunan?"

Tain thought for some time. "Is it so we learn to be responsible, Judge? I presume there is less damage to be done by a cisan who is irresponsible than by an alunan, especially if they are to inherit anything when they are of age."

Judge Tancred looked at Tain levelly. "I am impressed, Your Highness. That is the main reason. You might be interested to know that there are exactly the same number of cisluna-months for cisan-age, as there are aluna-months for alunan-age. Two hundred and forty, to be precise. Cisan take their dates and measure their life by the cisluna calendar, alunan by the aluna calendar. It is why sentencing in court is based on the felon's rank in society. It is also worth noting that for the alunan sentences are actually longer as an aluna-month is four weeks and a cisluna-month is three. So although sentenced in months, the alunan serve longer in prison."

"It seems unfair, Judge."

Tancred said, "Cisan are not required to be educated, alunan are; therefore, it was thought that the alunan should know better and so receive sentences dependent on that. It is worth noting, however, that the laws under which defendants are tried are the same for both sections of society. Let us resume examining Your Highness' situation. Most people know that the second son of a king becomes a justiciar. The roots of this lie far in our history. The true beginning of this system of government is older even than our reckoning of years. King Anaparus dealt with the security of Anapara, before the country was ever called Anapara after him. There was a Justa, a justice king, who ruled alongside King Anaparus dealing with the law whilst the latter was off fighting. His existence is told in the Legends of Ull but we know little, if anything, about him. The coming of the Cearcall and peace removed the need for a justa: if a king wasn't at war, why leave someone to deal with the law…"

Tain nodded. "There was quite a long gap, wasn't there? When the Anaparian Kings dealt with law and justice directly."

"Over three hundred years, Your Highness. Some of our law is a result of that time – and it is the basis of much more than many people realise; however, that is a subject for another day. Those years of true monarchical government were broken when King Aelfmar had twin sons: Alden and Emlyn. Alden would become king as he was born first but King Aelfmar considered that fate had been unkind to Emlyn and decided that, when he came of age, he should inherit the right to oversee the law and used the precedent from Anaparus' rule to make the amendment. Prince Emlyn worked hard and became well respected. At that time, Paras was the capital of Anapara. The strong, forbidding castle had been required for centuries to keep the peace, but Prince Emlyn pointed out to his father that times had changed and that with the Cearcall maintaining order between the lands the strength of a castle was becoming less important. Oedran was the most important settlement, other than Paras, and Emlyn suggested to his father that he oversaw the law from there. To that end, the Justice Hall, an ancient hall even then, was rebuilt in stone; Oedran would become the true centre of law and Paras would stay as the centre of other government. The Cearcall personified Truth and Justice, as I am sure Your Highness is aware, and bound them to the Justice Hall with one of their star stones—"

"Is it true that the personifications are still trapped unseen in the Justice Hall?"

"As far as we are aware, yes, sir; however, it is hard to prove as they *are* unseen. Prince Emlyn moved permanently to Oedran once the Justice Hall was completed in 350. He'd been overseeing the law for ten years by that time and had become well respected. His father, King Aelfmar, died in 352 and the brothers found they needed each other's support for a time. King Alden pointed out that he could rule from anywhere, but Oedran and justice had become synonymous. So, temporarily, he moved the seat of government to Oedran. It never completely moved back to Paras but the King's Representative there, the Domini, oversees certain governmental matters for Anapara still. He is not a governor, in the pure sense, but being a King's Representative he has many similar responsibilities and therein lies the confusion. In law, he is not a governor, but it would be treason to attack him. The Provincial Review for Anapara is undertaken from Paras because it was the historical capital of Anapara; however, I am wandering off the point of the explanation."

Tain grinned. "I don't mind; I find it all fascinating."

"Thank you, sir. We should, however, resume the purpose of this discussion. Oedran became the capital city of Anapara. The King's Advisors approached King Alden in 359 and pointed out that although everyone knew Prince Emlyn was in charge of the law he had no relevant title, and asked what would happen when he had died, though I believe they did not put it so bluntly. King Alden started thinking. His father had not looked at the consequences of the initial decision and King Alden recognised that his life was easier because his brother oversaw the law. He realised that the system worked and decided that it might be worth continuing. He talked to Prince Emlyn, who agreed and also agreed that one of the King's sons could quite well assume his duties in turn. It was decided that the second son would always assume the duties with his coming of age. After a bit more thought, Prince Emlyn went to see his brother and pointed out that the princes who would assume the role would need to be taught the law as their primary discipline. King Alden agreed, but his second son was getting near twenty and time was short. Prince Emlyn suggested that his nephew shadowed him for a time. At the same time, the King's Advisors asked that the King grant the title Justa to Prince Emlyn. The King agreed to consider it. Prince Emlyn returned to discuss his nephew's education with the King, to find him deep in thought. As twins, they had an instinctive understanding of each other. Prince Emlyn apparently said that the title Justa was not appropriate, for it suggested two kings, and he wasn't and would never be a king."

Tain nodded. "I understand that, but didn't he end up with the title?"

Tancred smiled. "He did, sir. As you know, every judge must take an oath, and that oath is taken in a place of law. The would-be judge swears to serve truth and justice and when the oath is taken in the Justice Hall, it becomes all the more poignant as the personifications, the deities if you will, live within its walls. The supplicant effectively becomes their vassal, as a lord becomes the vassal of a king when swearing to serve him."

Tain became thoughtful and his mind was so obviously pondering the revelation, that the judge was silent for many minutes.

Eventually, the Prince said, "So what happened and why did Emlyn accept the title Justa?"

Tancred smiled. "Because Truth and Justice bestowed it on him themselves. I wish I had been there to see it. It had been decided that Prince Emlyn's nephew, Prince Kushal, would take a judge's oath on his twentieth birthday; therefore, on that day, King Alden took Prince Kushal's oath. There had been many debates of the title that the Prince should hold after that oath and the most appropriate that anyone created was Lord of Justice. As the new Lord of Justice rose after taking the oath, Truth and Justice appeared in the Justice Hall. They turned to Prince Emlyn and Truth said, 'Are you to leave us?' Prince Emlyn is reported to have said that his time was ended and that his nephew would serve them well. Justice replied, 'We would not be so strong without your hand. Your judgements strengthen us, your compassion and wisdom we should honour.' He turned to his new vassal, 'Do you object to your uncle continuing?' Prince Kushal knelt to his liege, 'If it is your wish he continues, it is my pleasure to work with him.' Justice simply raised and thanked him. He turned to Truth and between them shimmered into existence some robes, which then flowed over Prince Emlyn's shoulders. 'These robes are our present to you, Justa Emlyn; they are clear for truth should be transparent, they can be seen because justice should be seen and are woven of Mercy's strands. They will be seen when needed.' With that, it is said, they disappeared. They used to appear to Emlyn regularly, highlighting when defendants or witnesses were lying but since Prince Emlyn's death have rarely been seen. If you are interested in the magical aspects of the Justice Hall, I shall find some relevant texts."

Tain absorbed the history with obvious enthusiasm and interest. "I'd like that, Judge. Did Emlyn continue in charge of the law?"

"Yes, for many years. King Alden recognised the title Justa and had a coronation ceremony for him; the regalia from it are mostly lost. Justa Emlyn and his nephew worked closely together. When Emlyn's great-nephew was born he and Kushal looked at the decrees that had given them their power and positions. They had them converted into law but insisted that the law included the fact that a king could reclaim the power if it was deemed necessary..."

"So father could strip Uncle Scanlon of his power?"

Tancred said softly, "There is the option, sir, but I do not believe His Majesty would ever consider it viable until someone can replace him; when that occurs, the fact that he could strip Lord Scanlon of power becomes redundant. The King does not believe that absolute power, of the kind he would hold, is beneficial to anyone."

Tain frowned. "It might be less stressful because he wouldn't be constantly fighting Uncle Scanlon."

"He might also be considering the dangerous precedent it would set, Your Highness."

Tain considered that. "I suppose it could be a dangerous precedent, Judge, but surely any king could do the same."

"Yes, Your Highness, but I do not believe that all kings have known the option is there. They are not taught law as you are."

Tain nodded. "I think Arkyn's glad about that. So how does father know?"

Tancred said softly, "It came up in conversation one day with Prince Lachlan. I have, however, found the whys and wherefores of our friends and acquaintances are sometimes better left to mystery, Your Highness."

Tain grinned. "So, what happened after the decrees became law?"

"Justa Emlyn and Prince Kushal reviewed the education the new prince would need to assume the role of a Lord of Justice. It was decided that his training should start as soon as possible and that by the time he was fifteen, he should be ready to take the oath. He could then shadow the courts and, under careful observation and instruction, sit in judgement. Whilst the system was only in use in Anapara, it worked well and, when his great-nephew turned twenty, the Justa retired from the public eye. When he died, Prince Kushal refused to accept the title Justa saying that it had been his uncle's and his uncle's alone and that he did not want to trivialise it with overuse. The title Justa has never been resurrected. The title of Lord of Justice evolved into Justiciar and the original meaning, that of a vassal of Justice waned. As the post of Justiciar evolved, the concept of the King's Justiciar was born. It is subtly different from the post of Justiciar. At any one time, the King's Justiciar is the King's brother. It is thought that, as brothers, there are fewer inhibitions when disputes arise. A nephew, son or uncle may not be as free with their thoughts as a brother. The King's Justiciar has rights over treason, whether or not he is Justiciar of the province where it is committed. That is, he can demand the trial occurs in his jurisdiction, he can insist on seeing reports regarding treason and he can advise on petitions relating to justice matters. Not only that, it is his duty to crown his brother, whenever possible, forgoing his rights to the crown at the same time. I am, however, digressing from our history lesson. Over the centuries following Justa Emlyn and Prince Kushal's tenures, whilst the Cearcall kept the peace, the system devised by them continued to work down the generations. The younger prince learning all he could and taking responsibility at the age of twenty for the law, between fifteen and twenty, sitting on the courts only with his uncle at his side."

"What changed that, Judge?"

Tancred said, "The Fall of the Cearcall in 600 and the birth of the Oedranian Empire in the following years, Your Highness. As Anaparian influence spread over the lands, the work of the Justiciar became more problematic. He travelled far and wide and it was discovered that he could not always be there to supervise his nephew's education and so a mentor was appointed in Anapara, until the prince was twenty, and the young prince would follow him. Over the years, it became clear that by handing the young Justiciar complete responsibility for small areas, he became better prepared for his whole inheritance at aged twenty; therefore, as the empire grew, he was handed a province a year to look after until he was looking after them all and his uncle retired, still there to be called on, if necessary, but having relinquished the majority of his power."

Gloomily Tain muttered, "I think I finally understand why I am to be given full responsibility for Oedran when I'm fifteen. It's because some bright ancestor thought we'd always be able to cope. I wish I could meet him…"

Tancred chuckled. "Have faith in yourself, sir. The system has worked for hundreds of years."

"Has it? I'm not convinced."

"No, sir, you are nervous."

"Wouldn't you be?" challenged Tain. "I have responsibility for Oedran when I'm fifteen. Anapara is added when I'm sixteen, Areal when I'm seventeen, then the rest of the Northern Empire at eighteen, the Southern Empire at nineteen and the Eastern Empire when I'm twenty and become full Justiciar…"

Judge Tancred considered how to approach Tain's despondency. There had always been reluctance within his charge, but he began to understand it was more than that. "Your Highness, please have faith in yourself. There is time yet to build your confidence, but you need to stop fearing the future – fearing it will not change it."

Tain said, half brokenly, "I can't seem to, Judge."

"What primarily worries you, sir?"

Tain hesitated. "That I won't succeed. That I'll fail in stopping Uncle Scanlon and the destruction of the empire will result."

"There is more to becoming justiciar than that, sir. No, I do not rebuke you, I cannot, but consider this, if all you see your future as is the destruction of one man's mistaken aims then the empire has lost the potential of a great justiciar and I will have failed you, your father and the empire. Your Highness needs to learn how to be a justiciar before the application of that knowledge can be brought to bear on the empire's problems."

Tain swallowed. "Am I being selfish?"

Tancred said gently, "No, sir. You have identified a primary purpose that has overwhelmed the longer-term responsibilities of your inheritance. When Lord Scanlon's influence is gone – however that is achieved – you will still have duties to the empire and its citizens."

"I fear those duties, Judge."

"I am not surprised, sir. No, truly I am not. All I can do is to try to help but Your Highness might like to consider that fear will only hinder our endeavours. Be apprehensive but do not fear, for fear is destructive."

Tain swallowed. "Judge, how can I just put aside fear?"

"With a lot of courage, sir. I have seen you have that. I will try and help all I can but please try not to close your mind."

Tain nodded. "I can try, Judge, but I can't promise success. You mentioned

I have a choice about becoming Justiciar."

Tancred said, "No-one can force the words of the oath from you, sir, not if you really do not want to speak them. I would suggest that you complete your studies before you decide."

Tain bit his lip. "Father wouldn't be happy."

"No, sir, but it is Your Highness' life. There could be solutions found. There was a second son who did not become Justiciar, his younger brother assumed the duties."

"Oh… Judge, I don't have a younger brother to take the responsibility. If I did, he'd be the next Lord Macaria anyway."

Tancred smiled. "So he would, sir, instead you will have the protectorship of that lordship once you are of age."

"More responsibility. Though I suppose Lord Landis looks after a lot of it and Lord Julius will, until any son I have is of age."

Tancred smiled. "Can you explain why, sir?"

Tain grinned. "It's because a king or justiciar can't sit in the Etanes and decide laws, so Grandfather Macaria asked Lord Landis to oversee those responsibilities until either my parents had a third son, which they never did, or until my first son is of age."

"Why your son, sir? Why not the direct line?"

"Because that could go on for generations if no king has three sons. Whereas if it passes through my line the most is a two generation gap: my mother's and mine."

Judge Tancred nodded. "I am pleased you understand that part of your inheritance, sir."

Tain grinned. "I feel sorry for Lord Landis over it. He gets all the hard work and being Finian's wed-uncle he has to look after the Rale lordship as well until Finian is twenty."

"I am sure your nearfather relishes the challenge, sir."

Tain laughed. "I think he simply got lumbered, Judge."

Chapter 28
FEASTING FRIENDS
Hexadai, Week 16 – 27th Macial, 6th Easis 1213
Palace of Oedran – Court

THE FEAST FOR THE FINAL NIGHT of Rhian's stay in Oedran came around more quickly than Adeone wished. She was returning to Tradere for all the right reasons but he'd become used to her company, whether over dinner, during the day or at Court in the evening. Since she'd said she was going home, he'd made a concerted effort to see more of her.

When the feast had been announced, there had been speculative murmurings, soon stopped by those close to him. Lady Rhian's surname was not FitzAlcis, she didn't hold the title of 'Princess' but she was the granddaughter of a king and without a husband to control her status, Adeone did so. He wanted people to recognise his cousin as such, though he couldn't work out why it had become so important to him. Was it because he hardly ever saw her and, when he did, he enjoyed her company? Why should it only be his male relatives who were honoured?

They dined early as a family before Court. He, Arkyn, Tain, Elantha, Amara, Rhian, Neassa and Neassa's son Peaga. He hadn't advertised the fact they would but as they ate, he once again realised how dangerous such evenings were. If Scanlon had anyone working in the kitchens, it would be so easy to poison them all in one go. He'd sworn to himself years before not to let all the family be together in such situations until Scanlon had been dealt with. He was getting too careless. So, when Tain asked if he could attend Court, Adeone said no. Tain sulked but his safety was more important to Adeone in that moment.

Feeling oddly self-conscious, he entered Court with everyone but Tain and Elantha in tow. They rarely all entered at once and he noticed a few puzzled glances and discreetly raised eyebrows. The evening had included a full Court summons, so everyone in Oedran eligible to attend, who had attended in the last year, was expected to be present.

Lord Para greeted him as he entered Court. He appeared somewhat disconcerted by the crowd. Adeone saw his eyes narrow at Neassa, who stiffened slightly. Para and her former husband were friends. She had no reason to worry about bumping into Rufus Rathgar though, his yearlong ban on attending Court was barely into its stride.

After Para had greeted them, Lady Amara waited long enough for the point to be made that this was an evening for the FitzAlcis before excusing herself and her daughters to make sure all the ladies were behaving. Adeone had little doubt they would when they knew she was on her way.

He glanced at Arkyn and Peaga. "I'm more than content if you want to find your friends."

Peaga glanced at Arkyn, who said, "If you're sure, Your Majesty. Can I ask anyone to join you?"

"Seeing Lord Landis prowling in my direction, I doubt you need to, Your Highness."

Arkyn bowed and moved off with Peaga, who soon left him to find Kenelm Para and Chander Teran. Arkyn wandered in search of Irvin Iris and Julius Landis. That said many things about the difference between them. Though, in his mind, Arkyn reminded himself that Peaga had grown up at Rathgar House and probably considered himself a Rathgar, even though he was technically part of the King's family. A little niggle surfaced in his mind. What did Peaga know about the family situation and what did he reveal to those friends whose fathers supported Lord Scanlon. He hoped his second cousin was sensible but there was no guarantee. He glanced around. His father was in conversation with his nearfather. There would be other days to mention his unease and, if he was honest with himself, Court really wasn't the place.

* * *

Adeone saw Arkyn glance over and wondered what his son had realised for there was a set to him that suggested something had come to mind. When Arkyn turned back to Irvin and Julius, he decided not to disturb them. His son didn't get much time with his friends. He and Landis left the Denshire Room with its doors out to the gardens and entered the Low Plains Room. Here, murals of woodlands and lakes adorned the walls. It was calming after the desert scenes in the Denshire Room but the thing that caught Adeone's attention was Judge Tancred bowing. He strode to his friend, smiling.

"Judge, I didn't expect to see you this evening."

Tancred inclined his head slightly. "I was sent a summons, Sire."

Adeone frowned. "Why?"

Landis murmured, "When you issue a full summons, sir, token holders are included if they're in Oedran."

"Of course. I'm sorry, James. I should have thought."

Tancred's lips twitched. "It does me good to have a change of scene occasionally, Sire. I am very pleased to be here."

Adeone's eyes narrowed, but he didn't read dishonesty in the judge's face, only amusement. "In which case, shall we tell Lord Landis to play elsewhere and confuse everyone?"

"I am Your Majesty's to command," replied Tancred.

Landis sighed. "If Your Majesty will excuse me then, Sire, I might see if Lady Amara needs anything."

Adeone winked at him. "I'm sure she'll have much to say." Once his Defender had left, he turned back to Tancred. "It is good to see you, James. How's Bets?"

"She is very well, sir, and hopes Your Majesty can spare time to come to dinner soon."

"I'll ask Richardson to arrange it. How's Peter coping?"

"Very well, sir. The lack of worry has done him more good than anything else. He is growing in confidence too, which is extremely pleasing. His

153

stutter is becoming less pronounced. I hope it will help, for he has a good mind and dedication.”

“Tain seems to have enjoyed their lessons so far. I understand they spent some hours together earlier. I’m hoping that’s why he seemed tired this evening.”

Tancred hesitated. “I expect our lessons tired him yesterday also, Sire, for which I must apologise.”

Adeone crooked an eyebrow. “Must you indeed? The enthusiasm you’ve engendered in my son is nothing to apologise for.”

Tancred gave a slight bow.

Adeone glanced sideways at him, caught the eye of an usher and motioned to a private room. A moment later, Lord Rathgar and Lord Lux left it rather frustrated. Adeone crossed to it with Tancred. After they had drinks, the server stationed in the room left to wait outside.

Tancred smiled as Adeone sat down and waved to the seat opposite. “Will this not cause rumours, Sire.”

“Fiddlesticks to them. What aren’t you saying about Tain?”

Tancred hesitated. In private at Court was not the same as in private elsewhere. “His Highness’ energy is often limited by his enthusiasm, sir.”

“I thought we’d sorted that one out,” muttered Adeone.

“All lessons bear repeating at least once, sir.”

“I’ll have a word. Did you really wish to come tonight?”

Tancred quiet smile gained an ironic twist. “Did I have an option, Sire?” He chuckled. “I have not attended in many years. Maybe the time was right. I do not care for the politics, as you are aware, but sometimes it is best to take opportunities as they present themselves.”

Adeone deciphered that. “You needed to talk to me and didn’t want to disturb my day.”

“Or maybe your son’s sense of humour has had an effect, Sire.”

Adeone groaned. “My courtiers are meant to cheer me up.”

“Am I one, sir?”

“No, definitely not. Your friendship is worth far more. Though talking of my son’s sense of humour, shall we continue to confuse courtiers?”

Tancred inclined his head, his eyes twinkling. “I am Your Majesty’s to command.”

Back in the hubbub of Court, Adeone and Tancred wandered aimlessly for several minutes. In the Terasia Room with its storm laden murals, Adeone caught Lord Ryson’s eye. The Lord of Oedran crossed to them with an unusual wariness. Adeone’s face never betrayed his thoughts. Was the Lord of Oedran wary of him or the judge? In many ways, Adeone thought it was likely Tancred. After a few moments polite conversation, Adeone left Tancred with Ryson and an instruction that the judge was to be seated on the dais, before crossing to his mother's cousin. Merchant Chapa welcomed him with smiles and a knowing grin.

"It's nice to see the judge here, Sire," remarked Henry Chapa. "How did you persuade him?"

"I didn't realise he needed persuading, cousin. I have far too much respect for him to ask him to act against his wishes."

Henry Chapa inclined his head slightly. "Of course, sir."

"How's the family?" asked Adeone, deftly changing the subject.

* * *

By the time the feast was served, Adeone was ready to take the weight off his feet. He seated himself and looked at the spread before him. Maybe the early dinner had been a bad idea, for all it had been simple soup and a spiced pudding for dessert. The pies, gravies, roast meats and preserved fruits laid out tantalised his tastebuds before he'd even taken a bite. There was a tureen of soup, cheeses and different breads as well. Sugar-paste confections modelled into flowers were dotted throughout the spread. Adeone idly wondered who had made them. Someone with skill, he reasoned. As the hall filled, he watched courtiers and servers alike. Rhian took her place next to him.

"You know, I quite like my waistline," she whispered as she sat down.

Adeone chuckled. "You quite like indulging once in a way as well."

"This is true, sir. It will set me up for the journey. I probably won't need to eat again until Amphi."

Adeone laughed. "Two days… Shall I ask ReJean to organise a feast for you there as well?"

Her lips twitched. "You mean you haven't, sir? How very remiss of Your Majesty. I'm sure Governor ReJean will have anticipated my arrival with his normal aptitude."

"No doubt," replied Adeone. "Shall I make a speech?"

"Don't you dare," said Rhian.

He chuckled. "Just for you then, I won't." He nodded to the Steward who opened the feast.

The swell of noise gradually diminished as people finished passing dishes around and started eating. Then it rose once more and fell again. Adeone talked quietly to Rhian on his left and Arkyn on his right. He half wished Tancred could have been seated higher but with all his family present, let alone Para as presiding lord and Landis as Defender, the judge was further down than he wished.

Rhian saw him glancing along the dais. "Shall I swap places, Sire?"

155

He took her hand. "No." As Simkins moved to clear his plate, he released her hand self-consciously, pulling his attention back to his companions and the hall in general. Most of the Court had a contented look from being well fed. The servers were all clearing plates and refilling goblets. Soon they put out bowls of nuts and small confections. Adeone looked at his and smiled. The aroma of peppermint stole into his senses, soon followed by the sweet taste of the sugar creams.

The music swelled and professional dancers and acrobats entered as the evening's entertainment. Everyone relaxed, either watching them or holding whispered conversations with their neighbours, sometimes both.

By the time the entertainment finished, Adeone was attempting not to yawn. Good food, good company and good conversation and all he wanted to do was sleep.

Rhian chuckled. "Retire, Sire. I won't be offended."

"I'm fine, really."

"I never thought anything else, sir."

Adeone snorted.

An hour later, he admitted defeat. The dancing between courtiers had long since started and many eyes were watching the dancers. He whispered he was retiring, but no-one was to make a fuss. Rhian squeezed his hand.

"Thank you for this evening."

He smiled. "It was a pleasure."

Chapter 29
AN ENDING
Septadai, Week 16 – 28th Macial, 7th Easis 1213
King's Sitting Room

THE FOLLOWING MORNING, happily ensconced in his sitting room, Adeone turned from perusing the view when Simkins announced Arkyn, Tain and Elantha.

"You're all looking far too bright-eyed."

Arkyn chuckled. "Shall I ask Doctor Chapa to bring a remedy, Sire?"

"No." Adeone rubbed his head. "How much did I drink last night?"

Tain grinned. "Too much, apparently."

Adeone eyed him. "Just step this way... Thank you. It's so much easier to tickle you from there."

Tain wriggled away. "Father!"

"Don't be cheeky then. Now, how have you found Linnt?"

Tain bit his lip. "He takes some getting used to. Arkyn thinks he could be doing his job better, but I know I used to drive Maria to distraction, so I rather think it's my fault."

The King sighed. "It could be, I suppose. After all, you are a little terror at times…"

"Only at times? I'll have to improve that. Father, are you coming to Ceardlann with us?"

"Why?"

"Because I wanted a good reason to change the subject, and it's a while since you've been."

Lips twitching, Arkyn said, "I think it's a good idea."

Adeone sighed. "Then I suppose I am. When were you going?"

"After lunch," replied Tain, "but we can make it sooner."

"What would the Comptroller say if we descended unheralded?"

"Probably, 'Not again!'" muttered Arkyn with a wide grin.

"True. Just ring for Simkins, will you? One of you, not both. How old are you both again? Children, who needs them."

"Well, you do for one and Arkyn will…" observed Tain.

"Try a bit of diplomacy for a change," grumbled Arkyn.

"Why? Have I ruffled your feathers?"

"Last time I looked I'd only got skin."

Adeone simply listened to them until his manservant entered. "Boys, quieten it down a bit. Simkins, I'm going Ceardlann and, believe it or not, we're leaving as soon as you can say the guards are ready and our horses saddled. Fortunately for my hearing, that means these three will have to go and change straight away. Everyone and everything else can follow us when they were meant to. Oh, and don't bother warning the Comptroller, I like to give him opportunities to berate me."

* * *

Everyone was gathered the in the Inner Office again and Adeone was swinging his cloak around his shoulders when Richardson knocked and announced the General without asking if the King would see him. Adeone frowned slightly, then recollected himself. The General could insist on seeing him and, looking at Paturn's face, he'd done just that.

Adeone glanced at Arkyn, Tain and Elantha. "Wait in my sitting room."

Tain pouted but a nudge from Arkyn persuaded him to move. Elantha smiled at Paturn before leaving with her cousins. Adeone watched them until the door closed behind them. Arkyn would ensure Tain didn't listen at the door. It wasn't that he distrusted his younger son's motives but he didn't think it was good news.

"Thank you, Richardson. What can I do to help, Paturn?"

The General swallowed. "Axton's dead, sir. Took his own life."

157

Adeone grasped his desk for support. "Get Arkyn."

Paturn hesitated.

"Bedchamber, turn left."

The General left. Adeone moved to sit on the comfortable seats. The shock still coursing through him. Had he been right to get Arkyn to join them? There'd be no keeping it from his son, but should he have told him at Ceardlann?

Arkyn entered self-consciously. He saw his father's white face and turned to the General. "What's happened, Paturn?"

Paturn glanced at Adeone, who motioned for him to explain.

"Lord Daioch contacted me, sir. He did as requested and spoke with Major Axton. It seems the discussion didn't surprise the Major. Lord Daioch mentioned Axton's hands shook. He knew how bad the situation was—"

"Knew?" interrupted Arkyn, glancing at his father.

"He was found dead this morning, sir. His wrists slit three times."

Arkyn sank into the chair opposite his father. "We never suggested... He wasn't a coward, General!"

"No, sir. He wasn't. Lord Daioch never suggested it either. His Lordship explained to Major Axton that requests from superior officers should be fulfilled as quickly as possible. He mentioned how disappointed yourself and His Majesty were by the delay. He said Axton took the reprimand and sent his apologies. There was no hint that he would do this."

Adeone took a breath. "Are we certain he did it?"

"Lord Daioch never told anyone why he was sending for Axton, sir. I didn't mention the troubles to anyone, Wynfeld wouldn't. I doubt Lord Aldwy as Tuchlin was aware of them either. Unless Your Majesty or His Highness told him."

"We didn't," said Adeone. "Sicla. How many people know?"

"Too many, sir. His batman found him. There's no containing the manner of death."

Arkyn swallowed. "I did this. No, Sire, I did it. I told Wynfeld to inform the General of Axton's missing report. I started this and it's ended his life. Paturn, did Axton leave a note, something, anything to say it was his own hand that took his life?"

Paturn nodded. "Yes, sir. Lord Daioch read out his letter to me. Axton wrote his career was over and he had no future outside the army. That he would have resigned but had nowhere to go."

Adeone cursed. "His body isn't to be treated as that of a coward, Paturn. See he's sent to the ancestors as befits his rank."

"Sir. What about command in the Northern Empire?"

"Fachin – at least temporarily. No. Sicla. I need to make a decision now.

Let it be Fachin. He's in Garth, isn't he?"

"Yes, sir. I'll have him report to Oedran to take the oath."

"No. Princess Lilith can take it." Adeone saw Paturn's face. "It can't be Lord Tyler. Princess Lilith is my father's cousin. She can take the oath. She's indisputably FitzAlcis. Dragoris."

Adeone's red dragon messenger appeared with a flash of green light. It glided onto Adeone's outstretched palm, looking helpful. He requested a link with Lilith. When it formed, his father's cousin was eyeing him with a slightly wry expression.

"How may I help, Sire?" She took in his appearance. "What's happened?"

With a few pauses, he explained the whole sorry mess to her. They'd met in person once, when he'd been younger than Arkyn. Beyond the blood tie, Ira had lived with Lilith for a year and had considered her a good friend and mentor. They had kept in contact, even when Adeone had been distracted. Since Ira's death, he'd spoken to her several times but never about something like this. She listened patiently.

"Axton's choices aren't your responsibility, Adeone."

"We forced him into a corner."

She shook her head. "No. You did just the opposite. You allowed him a way of keeping his reputation. Is it possible that there was more to his decision than you know? More than he was able to state in a letter? Your little brother visited us in 1210 and Axton was in his company more than perhaps should have been normal."

"What?" asked Adeone. "Are you suggesting…? Sicla. He was loyal."

"Speaking from experience, there's no guarantee of that. We thought we'd quietened the Bayan lords before 1169. Only one of those kept his lordship. Well, only one son managed to inherit it and he had to swear an honour-binding fealty and betray his father. As far as politics go, Bayan has some of the most intricate. If Axton had been drawn into the web, realised he was failing, it may be one reason he ended his life. There's no surviving Lord Scanlon's displeasure, apparently."

"When he comes for me, watch over Arkyn," said Adeone bleakly.

"How are the boys?"

"Arkyn's shocked. Tain makes me smile. James Tancred's working wonders with him, but there's still fun. Though he's working too hard."

"You all do when you realise what's at stake, Sire," said Lilith sadly. "When you came to Garth, you came a boy and left a man."

Adeone swallowed. "Your doing, Cousin Lilith."

"Not completely, sir. How's young Elantha as well? Is she learning anything from Cousin Amara?"

"I hope not everything Aunt Amara knows. She's fine. Growing beautiful and quite the artist. I need to find her a mare soon. They're all growing up."

"Children do that." She studied his strained face. "What do you need of me, Sire?"

"Can you take Fachin's oath as our new Major of the Northern Empire, please? I don't want to recall him to Oedran or draw attention to what's happened. It could be unfortunate."

"Sire, when was the last time a FitzAlcis Princess took a military oath?"

"1169 and you did it. So, maybe it's time to remind people you can."

She smiled. "You've been talking to Cousin Amara too much. Very well, Your Majesty. I shall send for Commander Fachin. Will he be informed of his promotion beforehand?"

"I'll do it immediately. Thank you, cousin. I'm sorry for the trouble."

She held his gaze. "I have had far worse, Sire. Now, how are you?"

"Hungover. We had a banquet to wish Rhian well last night. I think I drank more than I should have done. She's gone back to Tradere."

"You'll miss her." It wasn't a question. "Get yourself a remedy, sir. There's no point suffering if you don't have to."

Adeone chuckled. "Of course. I should see that Arkyn's all right and inform Fachin. Thank you, cousin."

"It is my pleasure, Your Majesty."

When the link broke, Adeone noted the General and Arkyn were in discussion. He recalled Dragoris and informed Fachin of his promotion. Refocusing on the Inner Office, he realised he was still pale when Paturn tried to pass him a drink."

"No, thank you, General. Can you ask Richardson to send for Chapa. I may need one of his remedies after last night."

Paturn nodded. "Is there anything else, sir? I understand I delayed your departure."

"I have no complaints about that, General. That's all for now. I will need names for promotion to Commander of Bayan when I return."

"Sir." Paturn saluted and left.

Adeone put his head back and exhaled. "Cousin Lilith wonders if Axton had become enmeshed in Scanlon's plans."

"It's possible, sir. It would explain a lot."

"Yes. I just wonder if we're seeing his shadow when we shouldn't."

Arkyn hesitated. "Again, it's possible, but when you can't trust anyone, the shadow will darken everything. I hope Axton's at peace now. I won't forget this tragedy."

"Arkyn, listen to me, it wasn't your fault. No. It wasn't. It is sad and yes, it's a tragedy, but it wasn't anyone's fault. You are not responsible for Axton's actions. You're not. On any level. Requesting a report is perfectly acceptable. Especially given the attack on your life and the deaths of your entourage and friend."

Arkyn swallowed, nodding.

They sat talking quietly for a few minutes until a knock preceded Chapa, who entered, took one look at the scene and hmphed.

"Who has the hangover?"

Adeone's eyes flashed. "Not the day for levity, Chapa."

"Sorry, Sire." He fished into his bag, took out a vial and crossed to the sideboard. He mixed the smooth herbal concoction with water in a glass and passed it to Adeone. "Sip it slowly, Your Majesty." He knelt by Adeone, studying the King's face. "Shock as well?"

"It's been one of those days, doc," whispered Arkyn. "We're going to Ceardlann though."

Chapa nodded. "The remedy I would have advised. May be best to take a coach."

Arkyn swallowed. "I want to ride. Get some fresh air and exercise. Don't you usually advise that?"

Adeone burst out laughing. "He's got you there, cousin."

Chapa chuckled. "Very true, sir. Is there anything else?"

Adeone shook his head. "I think we're fine, doc. Thank you."

Once the doctor had gone, Adeone finished the remedy before saying, "I'm not going to investigate Axton any further. I'm going to let him rest in peace. The events in Lufian are... concluded. The loss will never leave you, but we have nothing left to pursue. Can you accept that?"

Arkyn considered. "I think I must, Sire. The bandits are all dead, Faran is innocent, Axton proved the army did what it could. I just wish we had something else. Oh, Wynfeld knows where the bandits originated but, at the moment, there's no lead in that either. I have to accept this is over."

Adeone squeezed his wrist. "There is no must. If you want Wynfeld to pursue his lead, he can."

"I think he'll follow it until we tell him not to, and there's an option that he'd keep an ear out even then."

Adeone decided not to push any further. His son would take his own time to settle his mind. He rose. "Let's find your brother and cousin. Are we collecting Cal on our way through Oedran?"

"Yes, sir. He's enjoyed being home a bit more but I think he appreciates the peace at Ceardlann as well."

"With five siblings, I imagine he does."

Chapter 30
CEARDLANN
Late Morning
Ceardlann

WHEN THEY REACHED CEARDLANN, the Comptroller walked out to greet them, a smile playing around his lips.

"I wasn't expecting you, Sire."

Tongue in cheek, Adeone said, "Surprise is good for the blood."

"So I've heard Your Majesty say before, sir, but if I was of Lord Landis' mindset I might point out that it could mean—"

"Please don't. I left Festus in Oedran and I rather hoped I'd left his observations there as well." Noticing that Arkyn dismounted more heavily than normal, he crossed to his son and pulled him into a hug. "Take some time for yourself if you need to." His son nodded briefly and walked indoors. Adeone ruffled Tain's hair before saying to the Comptroller, "I'll come and annoy you for twelve minutes so that I can spend the rest of the day hiding." Once in the privacy of the Comptroller's office Adeone said, "Were you going to say something about a 'bloody nuisance' outside, Comptroller?"

"Not with Lady Elantha and Prince Tain in hearing, Sire. I rather thought you caught the train of thought without me voicing it."

"Yes. How's the Rex Dallin?"

"It's fine, sir. Not even the Wanda to make the gamekeeper wary."

"I get the feeling you're trying to hide something."

"No, Sire. I'm trying to make sure Your Majesty relaxes – a completely different matter," admitted the Comptroller. He studied Adeone's features. "What's happened, sir? Prince Arkyn looks as drawn as you do."

Adeone explained. He realised he needed to talk about it, about the shock he'd felt. His mind went back to the conversation with Paturn. The General had been far more careful in how he broke the news to Arkyn and that made him wonder why. Was it that he thought Adeone could cope better or that he'd had time to think?

At the end of the recitation, the Comptroller said, "I'm truly sorry, sir. How long are you staying?"

"Just tonight. Tain twisted my arm. It didn't take much. Given events, I can't spare any more time. Though Arkyn will be staying for a few days. Do you think Cook will manage to provide a lunch of some description?"

The Comptroller smiled grimly. "I expect so, sir, but maybe you'd like to forgo the description."

Adeone caught his eye. "How is the irascible one?"

"Still cooking. He might be glad to see you."

"Then I might see him, if he promises not to throw me out of the kitchen… Comptroller, how much is Tain working at the moment?"

The Comptroller hesitated. "Far too much, I suspect." Seeing dejection on Adeone's face, he added, "I'll pick up the pieces, but he's got to learn this for himself. You all must."

"If I hadn't told him about Scanlon, he'd never have…"

The Comptroller squeezed his wrist. "In future years, we may all be glad he's working so hard now. He knows how to relax, and I'll see he does, but maybe things are happening for a reason."

"Maybe. Thank you. There's a lot on your shoulders these days."

"No more than I can cope with."

"If there was you wouldn't tell me. Thinking about Tain, it's about time he got used to giving orders. When Arkyn and I are elsewhere, chivvy them out of him."

"Of course, Sire. Do they have to be sensible orders? Because that might be more difficult."

* * *

Arkyn walked heavily to his room. He didn't want to get caught up in Tain or Cal's chatter. Even Elantha's quiet support would be intrusive. He closed the door on the rest of the house and sank onto his window seat, just watching the view across the valley, over the river to the cliffs. It calmed him in a way he didn't consciously notice. The sun was out, but its summer warmth was long gone. He pulled his cloak around him. No-one had expected him to use his room so early; the fire was unlit and he couldn't move to remedy the situation. He didn't want to move. Could he have done something differently? Something that would have saved Axton? That wouldn't have made him despair? He swallowed, tears pricking at his eyes. After Kensal, after everything, it was the last straw. He cursed as a quiet rap sounded on the door. He didn't want to answer it, but it was probably Kadeem with refreshments.

"Come in."

Cal entered, hesitantly. "Are you all right, sir?"

Arkyn shook his head but turned back to the view. He heard the door close. That was fine. He wanted time alone, to think. A flint struck and soon the scent of the fire stole through him. Cal hadn't left.

He glanced round. "Cal?"

"Being cold won't help, sir. Do you want to talk?"

Arkyn swallowed. "No. I don't know. I gave an order and now someone is dead." He saw Cal's face and explained more carefully.

Cal listened, without interrupting, until Arkyn had talked himself out.

"Did Axton ever contact you to apologise, sir?"

"No. He didn't. Why?"

"Well, pa always says if you annoy someone, apologise in person. If Axton had, I'm sure you'd have reassured him. It's who you are, sir. He didn't do anything to help himself. Nothing. He could have talked to you about the report, he didn't. He could have contacted you to apologise, he didn't. He never even wrote you an apology, did he? And yet you're carrying all the guilt because you expected someone to follow an order, someone who is oath-bound to do so. I understand why you're distressed, but, maybe, you're not as much at fault as you seem to think."

Arkyn watched him. "You're not just saying that because it's what you think I need to hear, are you?"

Cal looked puzzled. "Is that an option?" He smiled. "I'm saying what I see, sir. Don't let this distress you. Please."

Arkyn swallowed. "Sometimes I can't help it."

"I know. I wish I could help more."

Arkyn stared at him. "You don't realise how much support you give us, do you?" Seeing Cal fidget, he sighed. "Fine. Just know we appreciate any and all of the support you offer. Where are Tain and El?"

Cal hesitated. "Not completely sure. I snuck out. I expect His Highness is somewhere with His Majesty and Her Ladyship is drawing. She went to get her sketch box the moment we returned."

"You know, you don't have to use the honorifics in private."

Cal shrugged. "It's something I feel I should do, sir. Shall I run and ask Cook for some biscuits?"

Arkyn chuckled. "If you're brave enough. I think he'll be cursing father for not sending warning."

"He enjoys His Majesty's visits though. They often talk late at night."

Arkyn's eyes narrowed. "How do you know that?"

Cal grinned. "I know. Apparently, I get hungry because I'm growing, sir."

Arkyn laughed. "Yes. You are, aren't you? How was home? How's your family?"

"It's growing too. Ma's carrying again. There's already six of us."

"*Do* you miss them?"

"Sometimes, Your Highness. I don't miss Haltern so much. He's just annoying. Lou and Cris, I do. Ma's going to find it tough later. I guess Hal and Lou are old enough to help more now. I just remember how tired she got with Tabitha and Elsie." He sat on Arkyn's bed, running his hand over the candlewick throw. "I'll just have to write. How was the feast last night?"

* * *

Adeone was idling around the gardens when Tain found him. Without a word, they took a different path and started a longer walk towards the trout stream where they sat companionably on the bank, watching the water burble past, taking with it small bits of flotsam. Grinning, Adeone moved to the stream; lying on his front, he started guddling trout until he had four large fish on the bank. After gutting them, he washed his hands in the stream. Tain sat watching his father with a small smile on his face.

Adeone eventually said, "You're quiet. It's not like you."

Tain smiled. "I thought you were concentrating, father."

"Why break the habit of a lifetime? Talking of habits of a lifetime, some birds have been telling me you're working too hard."

Tain chewed his lip. "People wanted me to be more serious…"

Adeone ruffled his hair. "No, they wanted the practical jokes aimed elsewhere."

Grinning sheepishly, Tain said, "But I've got to become the Justiciar in less than two years' time. I can't be so childish, can I, father?"

"You'll only be the Justiciar for Oedran, Tain, not the whole empire; you can still have fun."

Tain sighed. "I know, but I don't want to be seen as a child when I start, because that will only help Uncle Scanlon."

In the privacy of his head, Adeone cursed Scanlon for making their lives harder. Out loud, he said, "Tain, listen to me…"

Tain glanced at his father; his tone had been soft, almost cajoling.

"…Don't lose who you are because your uncle is misguided. Remember to be yourself and everything else will sort itself out. I don't like to see you stressed and neither does anyone else."

Tain rested his head on his knees. "There's so much to learn."

"Yes, and remember, like how to relax. You're taking a few days off before you collapse again."

Tain looked away. "Right."

"Do you remember how Arkyn got after Ella died and your mother was ill?"

Tain swallowed. "Yes."

"Have you ever thought that, in your own way, you're getting to be the same? You've become quiet, and that, with your personality, is worrying."

Still watching the far bank, Tain said, "Oh."

Adeone put an arm around his son. "You don't have to manage everything alone."

Tain was shaking, and Adeone kept his arm around him.

Part of Tain wished he'd move it, allowing him to run off and be alone with his thoughts. He hadn't expected the discussion, and his heart sank.

He'd known he'd lost something of his spontaneity and it had begun to concern him, but he hadn't realised other people had also noticed.

"I'm sorry," he whispered into the breeze.

Ignoring his son's reluctance, Adeone pulled him into a hug. "There's nothing, Tain, nothing, to be sorry about."

Tain was silent as tears fell and kept falling. He didn't know what to say, how to explain himself, but maybe he didn't have to.

Twelve minutes later, Adeone smiled wryly at his son. "Shall we go and have lunch? We can drop the trout off in the kitchen."

Tain simply nodded, still feeling numb.

"So, what plans have you got?"

Tain looked away. "Not many, now."

Adeone wrapped an arm round his shoulders. "We'll soon sort that."

Tain grinned and, seeing it, Adeone's heart lifted.

* * *

Cook glanced over as they entered the kitchens. "Lunch will be ready shortly, sir."

Adeone nodded. "I didn't come to disturb you yet, Cook. Just to add to the larder. I shall take myself and this terror out of your way before he empties the aforesaid larder."

With a grin and a small flourish, Cook said, "I'm most grateful, sir."

"Come on, Tain, let's find your brother and cousin."

Tain grinned and picked up a pastry in passing.

Adeone eyed him tolerantly. "You'll spoil your lunch."

"Apparently it's better to eat little and often, father."

"I really am going to take your books away from you."

Tain sighed. "Can I do anything right, father?"

Adeone realised he was entering a battlefield as he said, "Almost everything. It's just your enthusiasm getting the better of everyone else."

"Enthusiasm is good."

"Wearing yourself out isn't but, if you want to be enthusiastic about something, Arkyn was trying to compile a definitive list of our treasures here, and date them. See it as a hobby."

Tain grinned. "You know you can tell when I'm changing the subject?"

Adeone sighed. "Yes."

"I can when you are, but I'll give it a go."

* * *

That evening, when Tain, Cal and Elantha had gone to bed, Arkyn excused himself for an early night. Adeone watched him go, hoping that the sleep would help settle his mind. He poured himself a drink and settled back, watching the fire. It wasn't too late but the house was almost silent. Most of the servants had left, and the others weren't going to disturb him. He eyed the decanter, picked it up and wandered to the kitchen. They wouldn't interrupt him, but he could be a law unto himself. Two candles, on the long central table, lit the faces of the Comptroller and Cook. Or he supposed they would be lighting Cook's face, for he had his back to the door. The Comptroller pushed himself to his feet.

"Sire?"

Adeone shook his head slightly. "Sit back down, Comptroller. I come offering whiskey. The children have all gone to bed. Are you going to throw me out, Cook?"

Cook snorted. "Not when you've brought whiskey." He caught Adeone's eye. "You're looking strained."

Adeone sighed as he sank onto the bench, pouring Cook a drink. "It was a long day before I arrived. Still, it's dealt with and your dinner definitely helped. Sorry for the surprise visit."

"Ah. It's what we're for, Sire. With the Princes in Oedran more, I don't get as much chance to cook large meals."

"Believe that and you'll believe anything, sir," said the Comptroller sagely. "Especially from the rogue," he added, tipping his beaker at Cook.

Adeone chuckled. "Yes. How's everything here, Cook?"

"Oh, much the same as ever, sir. Joe's looking after His Highness far more successfully than David is young Calumiel. Completely forgot to wake the lad on his first morning on duty. We found it funny, and young Master Calumiel didn't seem to mind, but David won't live it down."

"You mean you won't let him," said Adeone, chortling. "Who reminded him?"

"Maria. Who else? She's keeping them all in line. Will say, it seems very quiet when Prince Tain and Master Calumiel go to Oedran."

"I know. Landis thinks I should keep Tain here more, but he needs to be seen if he's to be a successful Justiciar in a couple of years."

"Well, it's not just him we miss," said Cook, getting up to throw another log on the dying fire.

Adeone frowned. "It's not been that…" He tailed off. "When did I last visit? I can't think."

"After the attack on His Highness," replied the Comptroller.

"Sicla." Adeone rubbed his head. "I need to escape Richardson's clutches more often. It's been a little busy one way or another." He topped up his glass. "Definitely need to escape more," he continued as Cook put some oat biscuits in front of him.

The Comptroller chuckled, a warm laugh full of memory. "How many evenings have you spent in this kitchen over the years?"

"Far more than my father would have liked to know about," said Adeone with a grin. "Aided and abetted by you, I might add. It all started when Susan was working here the first time."

Cook chuckled. "Aye, it did. You just can't get the kings around here. Coming chatting to the servants, it will never do."

Adeone's lips twitched. "Is that what you are? You missed a few lessons and the Comptroller is the Comptroller. Our rock."

Leaning over, the Comptroller took his glass and sniffed at it. "Just checking." He passed it back. "Talking of servants, how is Prince Tain coping with Master Linnt."

Adeone groaned. "I'm not sure, but it's not Tain, I suspect. Linnt seems rather haphazard. I'm glad I haven't given him permission for the Rex Dallin yet."

"He won't be a manservant to a king, there's no reason to ever give him permission. Are Simkins and Kadeem just too good at their jobs, sir, and everyone else pales by comparison? Have Prince Tain and Linnt had time to get to know each other yet?"

Adeone eyed him, taking a biscuit. "If it were one of them, I might be able to accept that. I've already had to speak to Linnt. I thought it was Tain being tardy, but it turns out Linnt didn't know where Tain's riding things were. Linnt was recommended as knowing his job, but that event didn't reassure me." He swirled the whiskey in his glass. "As for time, no, I don't suppose there has been. I doubt they've had a week together in total yet." He glanced at the moving liquid. "It's so difficult to know if things are really wrong or if it's just misunderstandings."

The Comptroller nodded. "Give it time and you'll find out which. It might be better not to act in haste. Generally people find their own level when they've settled down."

Adeone nodded. "Quite. Why am I hungry suddenly? I could just eat a bacon sandwich."

Cook pushed himself to his feet. "Midnight snacks won't do you any good, sir…"

"It's not midnight," replied Adeone, gazing vacantly into the distance.

"I knew you'd say that. Comptroller? Bacon sandwich?"

"Why not, Cook. I'm sure His Majesty won't mind."

"He's not here," muttered Adeone pointedly. "He wouldn't be sitting in the kitchen. He'd be tucked away in the snug, behaving himself far better than I am. He'd be being normal."

"As Doctor Chapa would say, sir, what is normality?"

Adeone eyed him ruefully. "I think I'll find a different doctor to visit us here. It might be better for my arguments."

They continued teasing and talking for another hour before Adeone found he was yawning. Good food, good company and good whiskey worked their magic again. Excusing himself, he made his way to bed to find Simkins waiting for him.

"I'll sort myself, Simkins. Get yourself to bed. I'm sorry I didn't think to let you know earlier."

"Don't worry, Sire, thank you, but as I'm here, I'll continue as normal, if you don't mind?"

Adeone simply nodded. Twelve minutes later, he was sound asleep.

Chapter 31
RATHARIA
Septadai, Week 18 – 14th Meithal, 21st Easis 1213
Palace of Oedran – Prince Arkyn's Office

A FORTNIGHT LATER, Landis entered Prince Arkyn's office as he tended to enter the King's: without herald. Talking with Advisor Caple, Arkyn noted something in his nearfather's face he couldn't name. He dismissed Caple with a quick word as his heart sank. His nearfather wasn't often in his office and even less often looking so grave.

After the door closed, Landis said, "Sir, your father's been knocked out. He's still unconscious."

Arkyn paled. "How? Where?"

"By a ball flying out of a window about half an hour ago on the Ratharia. I should mention that Doctor Chapa didn't want me to tell you, sir."

Without saying a word, Arkyn hastened to his father's rooms. On entering the bedchamber, he looked at his father. Why hadn't he been taken to the closest house? As the thought occurred, Landis said quietly,

"Sergeant Hillbeck thought best to bring him back here, sir. Safer for everyone, given the uncertain situation."

"Right. Chapa?"

"His Majesty should wake up soon, sir," replied Chapa. "The rest is probably doing him good. Maybe we should try it more often."

Arkyn bit back the rising rebuke seeing in his grandmother's cousin's eyes something that was far from flippant. "I'm not sure father would thank you for it, doc."

"I'm sure he wouldn't, Your Highness, but then being thanked for doing my job is a rare sensation."

Landis chuckled. "Yet, therefore, all the more poignant when you are thanked. Do you intend to berate His Highness' conscience anymore?"

"I don't only attend on the FitzAlcis, my lord."

"Or mine?"

Chapa gave a grave smile. "Probably, Lord Landis, more than likely I'd say. Your Highness, I can let you know when His Majesty has woken if you have things to do."

Arkyn said quietly, "I have nothing more important than being here, doc. If someone needs to issue orders, I'm sure Lord Landis... I'm not of age."

"I'm not currently a King's Representative, sir," stated Landis.

"You're his Defender, Chief Advisor and Ealdorman!"

"It doesn't mean I can interfere today, Your Highness." When Arkyn sagged, Landis put a hand on his shoulder. "At least Scanlon's not here, it precludes him."

"There's always Lady Amara," observed Chapa, tongue in cheek.

"No!" exclaimed Landis and Arkyn in unison.

Arkyn added, "She'd cause havoc for her own amusement."

"I don't think she would, Your Highness," replied Landis. "I think she'd just seem to.

Chapa chuckled. "Often they are the same thing, my lord."

"I'd be caught up in it; you wouldn't do that to me, doc."

"He would!" muttered Arkyn.

Chapa eyed them both. "You'll give me a bad name, you know."

Adeone said, "Let me. Did you all forget I was here?"

"How could we do that, Sire?" enquired Landis, catching his eye.

Arkyn watched his father's face with silent relief.

"Nice to see you're back with us, Your Majesty," remarked Chapa. "How are you feeling?"

"Aggrieved and with a blinding headache. What happened?"

Checking for concussion, Chapa quipped, "Oh, someone thought they'd balls up your day, Sire."

"A ball flying from a window knocked you out, Sire," explained Landis.

"Right. Arkyn, why are you here?" asked Adeone scrutinising his son.

"I thought he should be, Sire," admitted Landis.

"Thinking never was good for you. Wait outside. You too, Chapa."

Once alone, Arkyn said, "Don't blame Uncle Festus; he was acting for the best."

Adeone held out an arm. "I'm not angry, just winding them up. Stop looking so worried. The assassins will never get me. Have faith. Come and give me a hug. Did Landis say you'd have to start issuing orders?"

"We were discussing the fact when you came round, sir. I said I couldn't. I'm not of age and I'm not a Representative unless I'm on reviews. We'd just started mentioning Lady Amara..."

Adeone chuckled. "Oh dear." His eyes didn't leave his son's face. "It's a good point though. Are you up to facing that incorrigible pair again?"

Arkyn swallowed and nodded. When Landis and Chapa were back in the room, Adeone said,

"Landis, next time I'm incapacitated unexpectedly, take your orders from Arkyn. He might not be of age but he is my heir and I trust his judgement. Chapa, you'd better be solicitous and then you can find yourself elsewhere..."

Half an hour later, alone with Adeone, Landis said, "What happens if His Highness is elsewhere? I admit he's often in Oedran now but he does still return to the Rex Dallin."

Adeone shook his head. "It's not that far away and in that instance, yes, Lady Amara should be consulted, much as I hesitate to say it for everyone's sanity. Does Richardson know I'm not returning to my desk today?"

"Yes, Sire. He's reorganised and not cancelled everything."

"You *could* have saved that depressing news for another day."

"Why? You're already having a bad one."

"You're not meant to make it worse," grumbled Adeone.

Landis smiled. "I'm here for the bad times as well as the good."

"Have you been saving that up for an appropriate moment?"

"Of course. Whiskey?"

When he was finally on his own, Adeone became pensive. He didn't hear Simkins enter, nor his manservant ask a question then leave realising he wouldn't get a response. To Adeone there was something disturbingly familiar about the day's events.

Chapter 32

CONVINCED OR NOT

Alunadai, Week 19 – 15th Meithal, 1st Meithis 1213
Inner Office

THE FOLLOWING MORNING, Wynfeld confirmed the incident as an accident. The ball had been thrown by children playing. Their mother worked as a legal scribe and their father had been elsewhere, his profession unstated. The children had been in the care of an elderly neighbour who had been oblivious of the ball.

"Would you like any action taking, Sire?" enquired Wynfeld.

Still feeling sore, Adeone considered for several moments. "What can I possibly do, Wynfeld, against children being children?"

"That would be your decision, sir."

"Very helpful. I can't take any action in all conscience, not if you are satisfied that the whole thing was a genuine accident. Maybe the children have already learnt their lesson."

Wynfeld smiled. "They may well have done, sir. Their mother was not impressed when she returned home, as well as being rather white."

"What of their father?"

"I'm not sure he's actually home much at all, Your Majesty. I get the feeling that the mother is supporting the family."

Adeone nodded. "Then I most certainly will not be taking any action. Thank you, Wynfeld, for all you've done in this. Thank your men as well. That's all for now. I've more than my normal workload today, yesterday I seemed to take things very easy."

After Wynfeld left, Adeone sat toying with his pen. The Major constantly proved his worth. If he thought it a genuine accident, there was no reason to doubt him. Yet, there was a niggle in Adeone's mind. His dream had been vivid even in its blackness and events mirrored it. Did his brother truly have nothing to do with the attack? Adeone shook himself mentally. It would have been an exceptionally accurate throw. A simple accident was, ironically, more likely.

* * *

An hour later, Major Wynfeld rose as Landis entered his office. The visit wasn't unexpected given events. Waving to a chair, Wynfeld scrutinised the Lord of Oedran's relaxed face; it didn't fool him.

Landis smiled. "Morning, Major. I'd like to talk to you about yesterday"

"Is there any aspect of my report that concerns Your Lordship?"

"Not so much concern, more I'd like to make sure of facts."

"The facts are simple, my lord..." Wynfeld carried on explaining, saying nothing that wasn't in his report for it had been comprehensive and designed to stop an interrogation.

Landis nodded as Wynfeld reached the end of his recitation. "Thank you. Please send me the address that was involved."

Wynfeld said placidly, "It's in my report, my lord. I thought you'd have noted it."

"I came here straight from seeing His Majesty, Major. I will be reading your actual report later."

"Are you troubled by His Majesty's decision, Defender?" asked Wynfeld filing the revelation away. The Lord of Oedran didn't appear troubled; he was sitting quite still, no slight frown, no tapping fingers, no narrowed eyes, but the Major didn't trust that. If there was one man who could act his way out of trouble, it was Lord Landis.

'Clever. Use the right title and I can't object to the question. You've come a long way.' Landis shrugged. "Not if the incident was a genuine accident and not simply a decision to call it such because children are involved. Fortunately, with your determined reassurance I am happier that it was."

Wynfeld thought, *'Am I meant to be flattered?'* He said, "Thank you, my lord, I simply do my job."

"Exceptionally well. I shall see you soon, Major."

With that Landis was gone, leaving an atmospheric whisper that he wasn't as convinced as he seemed.

* * *

Entering his house, Landis smiled. Somewhere his children were getting on each other's nerves. Their wrangling was a reminder that not everything was life or death. Opening the study door, a pleasant warmth washed over him. With autumn into its stride, a low fire crackled in the grate. That was fortunate in more ways than one. He closed some lightweight curtains that let in light but kept out prying eyes. When the draper had remarked they were unusual, Landis had simply stated the fact he was a King's Defender and the questions and observations melted away like snow in the desert. From a cupboard, he retrieved a small cauldron that could sit happily on the hearth. Filling it with water from a jug on the sideboard, he set it to heat in the middle of the embers. The fewer questions from his staff as to why he needed hot water the better. With the water warming, he unlocked a secret drawer in an innocuous box and took out the slim obsidian mirror. Holding it to the light, its translucence was mesmerising. How many other scryers had used it? He'd obtained it when its previous owner met an abrupt end. Had it passed down generations with blood spilt or was it simply sold and bought through contacts? He put it carefully on his desk. From the sideboard by the hall door, he retrieved a decorative gold bowl, the sort that might contain nuts rather than fruit. The obsidian mirror fitted the bottom perfectly. He searched Wynfeld's report; there, in the careful clerk's script, recognisable as formal writing, was the address he sought. He retrieved the cauldron, pouring its contents carefully into the bowl, before setting the cauldron aside on the hearth. Sitting down with the gold bowl of steaming water in front of him, he cleared his mind, blocking out the sounds of family life. He stared at the steam, then through it, the mirror at the bottom of the bowl focusing his mind.

Ethereal, there in mind but not in body, he stood on the Ratharia with blurred shapes hurrying by. Buildings appeared with crisp clarity. Neither the Rathgar nor the Macarian lords had tried for uniformity, so each side of the wide thoroughfare was a hotchpotch of architecture from centuries of change. Stone built merchant shops, spoke of grandeur but between them squeezed brick-built houses or narrow alleys. Some alleys had been built over, their dark passages twisting from street to street; transactions no doubt occurred unheeded and unseen in their depths. The door Landis hunted for came off one of these passages. It was battered wood, barely able to plug the hole. Should he enter the house? If other magic wielders were present, it was risky, but he had to know, had to be sure.

He pushed his mind through the door. The house wasn't a slum, but it was home to many families, each with one or two rooms. He made his way up well-kept stairs. On the first floor, doors stood ajar, blurry figures in one resolved into an elderly lady and two young children. They were teasing each other and he smiled. Family life was family life. The young boy, though, had a black eye. How had that happened? He doubted it was Wynfeld's men; it looked days old. The girl knocked the boy's hand down as he tried to touch the bruising. They glanced at the elderly lady. He lipread the request to open the shutters. She shook her head. They had done enough damage the day before. They wanted to watch the street. They should be concentrating on their letters instead. They should never have been playing the day before. Their parents would tan their hides if anything happened again. The boy swallowed, tears welling. He hadn't meant... his sister, Maud, should have caught the ball. He hadn't meant it to fly out the window. Would his father beat him for it? The lady shook her head. No-one would tell him. They didn't even know where he was.

Landis pulled his mind back, satisfied. Part of him relieved and part of him wondering what Scanlon would be thinking.

Chapter 33
SCANLON

Cisadai, Week 19 – 16th Meithal, 2nd Meithis 1213
Anapara – Paras Castle

UNDERTAKING A LAW REVIEW in Paras, Scanlon was trying not to think about what had been happening in Oedran. His outward aim was simple: attain the crown. He had no friends but many acquaintances. It suited him that way; friends expected confidences, confidences which were beyond dangerous. Para's actions in telling his son too much had proved the danger. Years before, he'd decided his course of action and then revised it as things went wrong, revision after revision to achieve his aims, but each revision ended unexpectedly. Fate had given him a helping hand, but then the hand had been wont to let go. Loss should have broken Adeone's heart and made him long for the death offered but those of his family still living gave him a purpose. He'd found men willing to poison Arkyn; they had thought the idea was their own, but he had sown the seed, only for the seed to germinate too early and poison the wrong man. An inexperienced Prince had seemed like a mandate from the ancestors when needing to pick a new governor, but illness had meant that Silvano's true nature had been seen, and the result had been a Margrave who was completely incorruptible. There had been the money he needed to quieten those people who could be quietened. He'd had a fortune buried in the hills of Terasia, safely stowed away there for use when needed, the entrances to the stashes carefully hidden and or guarded but sharp eyes and a sharp mind had spotted the discrepancies leaving him with nothing, not a darl or even a talence. He'd tried to strip Adeone of fundamental support, not just his officials but his friends as well by disgracing them with their own well-hidden secrets. It had been a good plan but Adeone had thought more on friendship than tradition and that, that might be used but it didn't solve his immediate problem. Even now, Adeone had apparently read his mind. Camlyn's estate had been his prize, his aim. He'd thought Adeone would have been too concerned about events in Lufian to see what was occurring in Bayan. It had been so carefully orchestrated, a discreet lawyer visiting a lord renowned for keeping problems to himself. Somewhere, someone must have played a wrong note and Scanlon was determined to discover whom. Had it been Axton? That man had proved useful, if unwittingly so. Until he had his answers, he would amuse himself with the idea of what Adeone must have looked like when the ball hit him, it was, in one sense, unfortunate that the accident hadn't proved fatal but on the other hand he wasn't quite ready with his near perfect scheme. The audacity of which would be remembered for many years, many, many years. The date would be pivotal, so close and yet so far. It would go down in the annals of history alongside the Fall of the Cearcall and the Age of Tyranny, heralding a new understanding, a shift of power that only a strong man would control. There was a slight flaw but he had time to discover a way around that. This endeavour was for the long game. He'd visit Oedran for the Mundimri and his birthday and remind a few people of their obligations.

PART 3

Chapter 34
ON THREATS
Imperadai, Week 19 – 18th Meithal, 4th Meithis 1213
Fitz's Inn - Schoolroom

THREE DAYS LATER, Judge Tancred stood as his charge entered their usual classroom at Fitz's. As he bowed, the Prince returned his smile. They looked at each other for a moment and it struck the judge how much the Prince was growing. Tain sat in his usual chair and reached for the drink on the table. Then he hesitated.

"Judge, did you pour this?"

"What makes Your Highness ask, sir?"

Tain hesitated. "You'll think me rude, but there's a look in your eye. One that I feel is a test."

"What do you think the test is of, sir?"

Tain frowned, thinking. "Assumptions, Judge."

"Is that all, sir?"

"So I was right. Recklessness?"

"Getting there, sir. You might make a lawyer."

Tain grinned, and glanced at the glass. "Predictability?"

"Now you might make a judge, sir."

Still grinning, Tain said, "Stupidity?"

"Surely, Your Highness, answers should not in themselves be questions in such times. Be definite about your views."

"Definitely stupidity."

Having rung the bell, Tancred finally took his place. "Now, you'll make a justiciar. Ah, Fitz, could you bring His Highness some refreshment he can trust please?"

The former captain chuckled. "Certainly, Judge. What's wrong with that stuff then, Your Highness?"

Tain grinned at his old guard. "It was a test by the judge, Fitz. Seems I passed."

Fitz smiled back. "Ah, but then, does a prince ever fail, sir?" he asked, removing the tray.

"With Judge Tancred involved, yes, Fitz. Thank you."

After the former captain left, Tancred looked at the Prince. "Why was it prudent not to drink that, Your Highness?"

Tain looked back. "It wasn't a case of distrusting Your Honour. It was because there was no second glass. I hadn't asked for the drink and it was in a room that has been unguarded. Elsewhere, there was a chance it could have been poisoned but here I suspected it was more of a test than a threat."

"Is not every threat a test of character?"

Tain put his head slightly on one side. "I suppose it is, Judge, but what was the underlying point?"

Tancred's lips curved in a slight smile. "Your Highness, if I were to hand you every answer as your manservant hands you items, where would be the lesson in that?"

"Linnt rarely hands me anything, but I take your point. If every threat is a test of character then every time something untoward happens I'm being watched and evaluated?"

"That is a logical progression of thought, sir. Can you take it no further?"

"If I'm constantly being observed, should I act consistently or should I vary my behaviour?" enquired Tain.

"Surely that would be a prince's decision, sir."

"Very funny, Judge. If I act consistently, there are more opportunities for traitors to take advantage, surely."

Tancred said, "You are in essence correct, Your Highness, but might I ask if you are considering the law courts or the King's Court?"

"I thought we were considering threats as tests of character?"

"Is a threat only to be found in certain situations, sir?"

"Some situations more than others, I think."

"They are not, however, exclusive to them. Your Highness, might I suggest that you consider the issue in a different way?"

"Certainly, Judge. Is there any hope that you'll point me in the direction you mean?" asked Tain.

Tancred shook his head slightly. "Your Highness should do well at Court; you will charm everyone."

"With a bit of practice, Judge, and Your Honour gives me enough."

Tancred's lips twitched. "I am unsure whether that was a compliment or not so I shall return to the problem in hand. I do not mean to concern Your Highness but is there any place where you should feel safe?"

Tain thought hard. "I suppose not, but Ceardlann is probably the safest."

Tancred nodded and looked over as the door opened. "Come in, Fitz. Maybe you would like to join us for a moment?"

Watching the judge, Tain failed to see a small glint of puzzlement in Fitz's features.

"Of course, Judge. How may I help?"

"We were considering the rather distressing subject of threats against His Highness' life."

Tain explained, "I'd just said that the only place I'd ever feel safe is Ceardlann."

"Aye, sir, sensible but maybe not as sensible as you suppose; every traitor from here to the mountains knows the fact," pointed out Fitz. "I'm not saying there's a traitor at Ceardlann, but it ain't impossible. The guards there aren't just for show."

Tain leaned forward. "All right, I'll accept that but, Fitz, they're not really evident."

Fitz chuckled mirthlessly. "Not as evident as they have been, but there's still the same amount. Your grandfather had 'em greet him every time he entered the valley. Your father's more relaxed, mainly as there are times he doesn't let anyone know he's arriving. The Comptroller once asked him how he could greet him appropriately if there was no notice of his coming. As far as I recall, His Majesty's reply was typical; it went something along the line of when he wanted greeting in a traditional manner he'd let the Comptroller know but he wouldn't be chaperoned to his own home."

Tain laughed. "That sounds like father. Fitz, if I'm constantly under threat, what can I do, practically, to dissuade attacks?"

"Be yourself, sir."

Tancred however said, "Your Highness, Fitz is in essence correct, but currently you have little public persona. It is not what you can do now, as such that is important, but what you should do once you're fifteen."

Tain looked at him. "Should I change my personality when I'm fifteen?"

"Your Highness, not even a lawyer would ask that. Think what your duties will entail."

Tain picked at the hem of his tunic. "Why can't people just tell me what they think?"

"Because, sir, there are more lessons to be learned than answers to be given. By thinking through your answer, you are learning to evaluate what you see and hear and to comprehend it as a whole picture instead of fragments of knowledge."

Fitz watched the exchange with interest. He'd only ever helped to teach the FitzAlcis how to fight; it was interesting, therefore, for him to see how the minds of the empire's first family were forged.

Tain frowned. "Very well, Judge. Threats exist for many reasons and come in many disguises. Occasionally, like with father's accident, they're not malicious. That much is all common knowledge. It is never possible to dissuade threats completely; I know that for a fact as well. Currently, I'm under threat simply because I was born, but once I'm fifteen I am, in a manner of phrasing, forging the assassin's knife myself. My actions will determine the amount of threats."

Fitz nodded. "Aye, Your Highness."

Tancred watched his charge. "You're making a passable lawyer, sir."

Tain grinned distractedly. "Right. There's the issue of consistency versus unpredictability as well rolled into this. If I can't stop the threats completely, then I might as well be consistent… But in consistency is predictability and predictability is fuel for the threats, or at least the manner in which they manifest themselves…" Tain took a drink and paused looking at the goblet. "I'm getting this all tangled. I have two or three different threads and yet I've more ends. Hang on… when I'm fifteen, I'll also be an official, which I'm not at the moment, well not as much. So maybe there are two different ways of looking at this."

Judge Tancred topped up the Prince's goblet. "You might just make a judge if you continue with that thought, Your Highness."

"My official decisions need to be consistent and they need to be fair and in line with the law. My private actions need to be respectable but by no means predictable. I shouldn't confine myself to a particular routine outside of my duties, as that would only help traitors."

"Should Your Highness break engagements?"

Tain frowned. "No, Judge. I shouldn't do anything that might destroy respect. I should only send my apologies as a last resort."

"Are there any exceptions to that?"

Tain frowned. "I suppose not, Judge."

Fitz said, "Far be it for a humble ex-soldier to comment, sir, but it's traditional that the King's orders overrule other commitments."

Judge Tancred looked at his charge's disconsolate face. "We were just getting to that part, were we not, Your Highness?"

Tain grinned. "Eventually. Surely though, Fitz, if I'm the Justiciar then the King would understand?"

"Your Highness, it isn't the place of a king to understand. If you'll forgive me commenting on Your Highness' family, there have been more ructions caused by Lord Scanlon considering he can do what he wants than by anything else over the last few years."

Tain bit his lip. "Fitz, I wasn't planning on being quite so… so… contrariwise as my uncle is. I understand the King's orders are everything; my point was that if I should be somewhere as his official and I explain that then the King is likely to understand."

Fitz inclined his head slightly. "More than likely, sir, it's just the frequency of the explanation that has to be carefully managed."

Tancred broke in softly, "That is another discussion altogether, sir. We were talking about the mitigation of threats against Your Highness' life."

Tain sighed. "So we were, Judge. I think I was concluding that my professional persona should be consistent but my private one can be unpredictable as long as it's still respectable – or at least not unrespectable."

The judge smiled. "A distinction with enough of a difference for me. With a conclusion such as that, I expect your brain is hungry."

Fitz got up. "I'll take a hint and be back soon."

Once on their own, Tancred said, "A soldier's perspective is always different from a civilian's, Your Highness. They are often in harm's way."

Tain chewed at his lip. "Aren't all vassals simply soldiers in waiting?"

"They certainly can be viewed in that light, Your Highness, but it is a little-known fact that princes of the FitzAlcis are never *required* to swear fealty. It is their personal choice."

Tain frowned. "Oh. Right. What should I do, I wonder?"

"I think, Your Highness, that is one decision that must be completely of your own making. Those princes, who have, over the years, sworn fealty, have tended to do so at coronations; therefore, I would suggest that you wait until such a time as that."

Tain nodded. "I suppose that makes sense. So, did I pass, Judge?"

"Do you think you deserved to, Your Highness?"

Exasperated the Prince said, "That's why I asked, Your Honour!"

"Because you do not think you did, sir?"

"No, because I didn't know and it should be a simple yes or no answer."

The judge said calmly, "My apologies, sir, I had not considered how much the discussion had tired you. Your Highness passed quite spectacularly; I should even say you will make a justiciar for the empire to be proud of."

Tain sagged. "Sorry, Judge."

"Your Highness need not apologise, sir. I have challenged for far too much this morning."

"It's your job, Judge."

"Yet I should perhaps be more aware of nuances on occasion, sir."

"Perhaps and *only* perhaps."

They smiled at each other before Tancred asked, "Might I enquire how your endeavours at Ceardlann are? I am meaning more light-hearted endeavours than studying…"

As Tain talked, stress and frustration slunk away. The lesson had given him much to think about that he'd never thought about in depth before. Not just for his own safety but for that of others around him. He had a responsibility to himself and them. He began to understand why his brother had been so affected by the bandit attack and by Axton's death. Their actions weren't just about themselves, but they couldn't be crippled by the threats. They still had lives to lead and jobs to do.

Chapter 35

LYNDON

Septadai, Week 19 – 21st Meithal, 7th Meithis 1213
Palace of Oedran – Prince Arkyn's Office

THAT SEPTADAI, Jost Lyndon saluted smartly on entering Arkyn's office and the Prince acknowledged it with a brief word of thanks before telling the sergeant to stand at ease whilst also assessing what he saw – a man who was uneasy, wary but yet still every inch a soldier, watchful, observant and direct. At five foot eleven, he was roughly the same height as Arkyn, but certainly more muscular and far fitter than he had been whilst guarding the barracks' gates.

"Good evening, Sergeant. My administrator mentioned that you are uncertain why you are here."

Lyndon said, "Yes, Your Highness. After my impertinence, I didn't think I'd be meeting you again…"

Arkyn asked mildly, "What did you expect?"

Lyndon considered. "To be on a charge or thrown out of the army altogether. When I discovered Major Wynfeld was taking an interest, I was even more concerned—"

"I've heard his name alarms people. What was your opinion on the extra training you've received?" enquired Arkyn, genuinely intrigued.

"I thought it might be an unusual fatigue, sir."

That revealed much about Wynfeld's thoroughness that Arkyn was pleased to hear. It was one thing to see training schedules or watch men training, it was another to hear it had been so draining as to warrant the term 'fatigue'.

"It was a necessary measure, Sergeant. Now, as you're no doubt aware, during the bandit attack in Lufian, I lost the captain of my guards. After promoting Smithers, I was left with a vacancy for a sergeant that I'm hoping you will fill."

Arkyn watched the surprise and confusion crash over Lyndon. The sergeant's face struggled to remain neutral. Deep in his eyes was the astoundment Arkyn had suspected would be there. This man wasn't as self-effacing as Wynfeld, but he hadn't expected to be trusted, that much was clear.

After a couple of moments, Lyndon said, "I was rude to you, sir…"

"Was that your intention?"

"No, sir."

"I thought not. You did your job and had excellent reasons for not assuming what I claimed was true. I was at the Guildhall when His

Majesty was attacked in 1210 and saw the results of Gad's infiltration first hand. I do not, therefore, consider your actions unjustifiable. Instead, I recognised a directness and attitude that could be utilised. Will you help protect my life and that of Prince Tain in the same manner?"

Lyndon shook his head to dispel lingering incredulity. "Erm, do I have a choice, sir? Or is this the only option open to me?"

Arkyn said seriously, "As your life will be on the line from the moment you accept, you are perfectly at liberty to refuse."

"Thank you, sir. Then I accept."

Arkyn smiled. "With logic like that you'll appreciate Prince Tain's outlook on life; however, when he is in Oedran, Captain Smithers is his guard. At those times you will head mine. Smithers will be your senior officer. Welcome to the Princes' Guard."

Lyndon paused. "Am I really the appropriate person to head your guards, sir? Won't that put the other sergeants' noses out of joint? Will they accept it?"

Arkyn restrained a smile. "It is normal to ask only one question at a time, two at most - that way I get chance to reply… Yes, head my guards. If they'd shown the spirit you had then maybe they'd be in your position. They will accept it as it is my decision, order if you will – tell them the whole story, Lyndon, you'll go up in the notoriety stakes. In answer to your last question, you have qualities which befit you for the job in hand." Arkyn watched the sergeant struggle not to ask what those qualities were.

"Thank you, sir. I'm flattered."

"You won't be when you've got to grips with the job. I'll just introduce you to Smithers." Two minutes later, introductions and brief explanations made, Arkyn said, "Smithers, introduce Lyndon to the men. Lyndon, if you're ever unsure of anything don't hesitate to ask Captain Smithers, Edward or myself. You'll be one of only three of the Princes' Guard currently recruited from the militia, and the highest ranking, but I don't make any distinctions and I don't allow anyone else to. Do your job well, that's all I require."

* * *

Once alone with Smithers, Lyndon let out a long breath. "I wasn't expecting that."

"His Highness obviously thinks you're worth it. What exactly did you say to him?" (Lyndon explained.) "Ah. Keep it up. Just remember, never be too familiar but we're not courtiers: tell them things straight but politely, they'll thank you for it."

"Right, sir. Can I ask… the other sergeants… Am I going to meet prejudice?"

"I doubt it. No-one wants to be the target for the next arrow and you and I are just that. They took Captain Marsh out without warning… I think they hoped to weaken our defence… but we avenged him and the others. We don't talk about the attack as a rule."

"Understandable. Is there anything I should know though?"

Smithers eyed him. "Plenty. What do you think of Lord Scanlon?"

"Not much, sir. I don't think of him, if you follow me."

"You will. He's the reason we have our jobs…"

As Smithers explained, understanding crashed into Lyndon's mind and the feeling of security ebbed out: maybe the army was a safe place after all.

Chapter 36
PERCEPTIONS
Hexadai, Week 21 – 6th Seral, 20th Meithis 1213
Outer Office

UNSURE WHETHER SHE SHOULD, Lady Neassa visited her cousin. It had been years since they'd talked to one another beyond brief pleasantries at Court, but he'd taken her side in a dispute that would have caused political upheaval. She entered the Outer Office and glanced at the secretaries. When the King's Administrator stood up in welcome, she smiled.

"Is His Majesty free?"

Richardson said, "I'm sure he is now, my lady. If you wouldn't mind waiting, I'll just make sure."

Neassa nodded. The response hadn't been what she'd expected, and it struck her that she'd never been in the King's Chambers during what might be called a working day since King Altarius had died. Was Richardson simply being polite, or did he mean what his words implied? How was she to know? The Court knew very little about him that wasn't rumour fabricated. The other secretaries were still standing and she shook her head to clear it.

"I'm sorry, please continue."

The senior of the two smiled. "Thank you, my lady. I'm sure you won't be kept waiting long."

She nodded. To say anything would betray her unease and lack of confidence. How did Rhian manage? Was her sister confidant when faced with the official machine of the empire? Throughout their formative years, their parents had made sure they didn't come into contact with it, unless briefly when King Altarius had insisted on them being in Oedran.

They had been brought up less as FitzAlcis and more as provincial ladies, and part of her still wished for the Traderian countryside.

It took mere moments for Richardson to return. "His Majesty is free, my lady. Would you like announcing?"

Neassa paused; did she need announcing? She considered what she had heard about her cousin's regime. "I think His Majesty and I know each other."

Richardson smiled. "Of course, my lady."

* * *

Adeone had already moved from behind his imposing desk to greet her. She dropped into a well-practised Court curtsy and her cousin rolled his eyes heavenwards.

"Neassa, we're family, and in private. If you must curtsy, attempt to look after your back a bit more."

Neassa smiled uncertainly. "I shall try to remember, Your Majesty."

Adeone nodded. "Let's hope you haven't inherited the FitzAlcis memory; I have to write everything down. How are you? No, before you answer we'll find ourselves a comfortable seat. What would you like to drink?"

"Erm, water if there is any, sir."

Adeone smiled. "Water it is, and if I've already drunk it all I'm sure Simkins can find some more. No, thankfully we don't need him. Here you are. Sit down and tell me how you are. You're looking well."

Neassa sat uncertainly; Adeone's attitude was unexpected. She'd always known he was relaxed but he suddenly felt like family, like her immediate family, as though he was a mischievous younger brother trying to be sensible. It was the first time they'd been truly alone since the evening of her divorce and the mask he maintained around others had gone.

"I'm well, Your Majesty. A weight has been lifted from my shoulders. I can't explain it, but it's as though I'm free to be the woman I want to be. It must sound odd…"

Adeone shook his head. "No, perfectly normal I think – so many of us are constrained by other's perceptions. When those perceptions permeate into one's private life as well as one's public one it is doubly hard."

That explained the change in him from Court. Where had her prejudices come from? As her inward eye opened, Neassa realised her mind had been shut for a long time and annoyance blossomed at the blindness and the dark it must have controlled for so long.

To her own surprise, she said, "I think I owe you an apology, Sire."

"Why?"

"I don't know why, but I know I do. The time since, well, since I left Rufus, I've found out so much about myself and other people, but I think

I've discovered my true family and I'm cursing that I missed it before."

Adeone's face softened. "Don't regret the love you had for Rufus…"

"That's just it, sir, I don't think I ever did love him. I wanted the glamour of Oedran. Everyone in the empire talks of it, of your Court, and yet I, who am the granddaughter of a king, was brought up away from it. In marrying Rufus, I could experience it all. I just didn't realise what a self-serving introvert he was going to be."

Adeone sighed. "Ah. Yet your father must have been convinced that there was love there."

"Probably because I thought there was and I made his life a misery over it. I dread to think what he'd say to me now."

"Uncle Ewart would have accepted you for who you are and your decisions as your own. He would never have stopped loving you because you made, shall we say, a mistake? He came from a large family and I rather suspect understood the wish to experience a different side to life, to make a mark as oneself, not as part of that family. Didn't he have twenty-five siblings?"

Neassa nodded glumly. "Yes, though some died young or were stillborn. Two stepmothers as well. I can't name all my aunts and uncles on that side even now. I can understand why he moved to Tradere."

"Between us, so can I. My father missed his company, and I rather suspect Aunt Amara's, though he'd never say it."

Neassa gave a small chuckle. "I can't imagine why, sir. Is it true she used to yell at him?"

"Probably, I know she does me on occasion," revealed Adeone, lips twitching. "Normally I deserve it. She berates my conscience as a hobby."

"That does sound like my mother, but it keeps her young."

"She started young, that's why. I'd almost have liked to have been there when she told my father she was marrying yours, regardless of what he had to say on the matter. Mind you, she's not exactly ancient. She just pretends to be."

"She's sixty-five, Your Majesty."

"I suppose she is. I'll lay you a bet she makes ninety."

Neassa chuckled again. "You're on. Sir, Rhian's invited me to Tradere and Gerens doesn't have any objection to me cluttering up his estate as well. Do you mind?"

Adeone hesitated. "Why would I mind? No, that's wrong; I'll miss you being around…"

"We've hardly spoken in years before this all happened, sir."

Adeone looked at her. "For your sake, Neassa. I do not mean to make excuses, but, while you were married to Rufus, if I'd confided in you, it would have put us both in danger. Rufus is close to Rathgar, who is close to Scanlon and Scanlon, unfortunately, wants me and my sons dead. How, therefore, could I… Your loyalties would have been torn."

Neassa held his gaze. "No, they wouldn't. My loyalty would always have been to you. Not just because you're my cousin and King but because, quite frankly, Scanlon's a little tow-rag."

Adeone smiled ruefully. "Thank you. I stand by what I said though; I'll miss you greeting me at Court. Even the smallest family is still family."

"Queen Ira once said that to me. I wondered why."

"I couldn't tell you, but it was an expression of hers. She knew about small families being a motherless only child."

"I suppose she did. Do you miss her?" enquired Neassa before she could stop herself.

Adeone swallowed. He never liked being asked that question. "Yes, Neassa, I do, very much."

She touched his hand, a gesture unthinkable before she'd entered the office. "I'm not surprised."

Breaking the spell after a couple of long moments, he said, "Will you carry a letter for me to your sister?"

Neassa smiled. "Of course."

"Then tell me when you plan to leave and I'll write it."

"On Tretaldai, sir. That way, I should make Tradere before the Mundimri celebrations. I don't think I can face them in Oedran. Whispers are insidious and I suspect I'm the subject of them. I think Rnian is planning to be in Byfa for the Mundimri. I'll meet her there and then we'll go to Gerens' estates."

Adeone nodded. "Then maybe you'd convey a letter to the governor for me also. I'd rather trust your luggage than a mail route."

Neassa smiled. "You flatter me, Sire."

"Intentionally and for good reason. If you're leaving then, I'll ask Landis to postpone his visit to Amphi by a couple of days. He can then escort you there. He was due to leave on Alunadai, so I can't imagine it will cause too much confusion."

"That would be kind, sir."

"It's no trouble. I expect Governor ReJean will appreciate a bit more time to prepare. If he doesn't his officials will."

Neassa opened her mouth and then closed it again.

Adeone chuckled. "Landis is undertaking the official visit ahead of the provincial review in 1215. Lord Rale is too young to do it but will be accompanying him to observe. I'm sure Landis won't worry ReJean at all."

"Are you, Sire?" asked Neassa before she could stop herself.

"If I really wanted to worry him, I'd send your mother. How *is* she?"

As the talk turned to and fro, Adeone watched his cousin's face relax as the cares of the last few months rolled off her shoulders, if only for the duration of their conversation. Her features became animated then relaxed then animated once more. As the conversation drew towards its natural end, she still had something on her mind.

"I don't think living under his uncle's roof is doing Peaga any good, sir. Could you find him a posting somewhere in the empire?"

"I shouldn't see that being too difficult, especially not if he voluntarily joins the army, if you catch my drift."

Neassa did. If Peaga joined the army, no-one could say Adeone was punishing him for his father's actions. "I'll talk to him about it, Sire, though I'd prefer it if he wasn't, as it were, in any direct danger."

Adeone smiled. "As part of the army I cannot promise anything; men know what might happen, but I will say that as a cousin of mine, he should be treated with respect."

She nodded. "It need not be for long."

Adeone said, "It is traditionally a twenty-three-year tour, but many lords do not do that. They buy themselves out of the obligation or get a post close by home. I'll see Peaga understands what's expected of him before he joins, Neassa."

"Thank you, Your Majesty. I should let you continue. I'll tell mother you were asking after her."

Chapter 37
GOVERNOR REJEAN
Tretaldai, Week 22 – 10th Seral, 3rd Seris 1213
Inner Office

WHEN TRETALDAI DAWNED, Landis met Neassa at the Palace and they took leave of Adeone at the same time. Landis was presented with last-minute documents whilst she received a hug from the King.

"That just put us both in our place, Lady Neassa," observed Landis.

Her lips twitched. "Mother will be much the same."

"I'll wait outside," said Landis to chuckles from Adeone.

When they reached the stables, Landis said, "Finian and I are happy to ride, if Your Ladyship would prefer solitude."

Neassa eyed him. "Mother wasn't that bad, Lord Landis. Do join me in the coach. I would appreciate your company."

The coach Adeone had leant Neassa for the journey was comfortable by any standards; well-padded sprung seating was upholstered in velvets of a deep red hue. The interior was lined with wool padding to keep out the cold. Heavy curtains hung at the windows with a lamp secured in from the roof for light if they needed to be drawn. Landis mentally made notes. He didn't often use his friend's winter coaches. Even the fur pelts under his feet were keeping out the cold. Autumn was ending and he wasn't complaining at the comfort afforded for the two-day journey to Amphi.

Neassa smiled to herself. "There should be warmed stones at mail lodges for us if it gets cold too."

The coach lurched slightly as they started moving. Righting himself, Landis said, "I hope it doesn't get that cold, Lady Neassa."

She crooked an eyebrow. "We're spending two days in each other's company, Festus. I think you can call me Neassa. I'm sure Lord Rale will keep our secrets."

"Since living with Uncle Festus, I've learned to be deaf, Lady Neassa," said Finian with a smile.

Landis chuckled. "Just watch the scenery, Finian. How are you, Neassa?"

"Glad to be getting away for a time."

"Have things been that bad with Rufus?"

"No. I've not seen him. Adeone's lawyers are dealing with everything for me but it's the whispers and the looks. Even they are better than the alternative though." She watched his face. "I had no choice but to hide it, Festus. Peaga's old enough now to find his own path."

"Adeone and Ira would have had him in the FitzAlcis nursery without a second thought, had you asked."

"Yes, I know, but Peaga's children won't be the King's family legally. It was better he grew up slightly removed from the circus, as father called it. Better for him not to rely on his status, so his children don't expect it. It's why Uncle Altarius didn't insist on us living at the Palace. Much to Rufus' chagrin. Oh, he was so furious when Uncle Altarius made that decision. I think that's what started the whole mess looking back."

"I wish we'd seen what was happening."

"You couldn't see it, not when I didn't show it. I'm just surprised he didn't murder me. Though that would have led to more questions."

Landis snorted. "I'm glad he didn't."

Finian looked over. "Is that why I'm living with you, Uncle Festus?"

"Which part, Finian?"

"The growing up away from the circus?"

Landis nodded. "Partly but mainly as His Majesty thought you'd like to be with your aunt and cousins."

By the time they left Oedran at the Carnford Gate, they'd finished discussing Neassa's recent history. By the time they were halfway to Carnford, they'd exhausted talk about their children and the gossip at Court. Landis watched the passing countryside with a rare ambivalence. They had men of the army with them, both because he was on an official visit and to watch over Neassa as the King's cousin.

"Where will we break the journey?" asked Neassa quietly.

"If you're amenable, I thought Border Lodge. It might be late when we arrive but tomorrow's journey will be shorter. If it gets too late, we can stop at one of the inns."

"As you wish, Lord Landis." Her eyes sparkled. "Just let me stretch my legs a couple of times."

He chuckled. "That is a given, Your Ladyship."

* * *

They arrived in Amphi mid-morning the following day. The military roads between its cities diminished the vastness of the Oedranian Empire. Built for speed and maintained by the army, their sole purpose was to allow swift communication and travel. As the coach rumbled into the stableyard of the Palace of Amphi, Landis caught Neassa's eye.

"Shall we see if ReJean gets it right?"

She chuckled. "I expect he will. He's far too used to us descending."

Alighting from the coach first a few moments later, Landis held out his hand to help Neassa down.

Governor ReJean stepped forward. "Lady Neassa, I'm pleased to welcome you to Amphi once more. It has been too long since you last visited. Might I present my daughter, Phylicia, to you?"

On the sidelines, Landis watched the ladies greeting each other with a slight smile. Phylicia was thirteen and, if not shy, quiet.

Neassa said, "I think you know Lord Landis, Your Excellency, but have yet to meet Lord Rale."

"That's correct, my lady. Welcome to Amphi, Lord Rale, Lord Landis. Would you care to come inside? Lady Neassa, I've had the same rooms prepared as Your Ladyship used to use."

Neassa smiled. "Thank you, Your Excellency, that was most thoughtful. I am looking forward to the view already."

ReJean nodded. "I rather suspected you might. Lord Landis, I've asked them to prepare the Rale Rooms for yourself and Lord Rale. I hope that's acceptable."

"Perfectly, Your Excellency. Thank you," replied Landis, adjusting to

192

the fact that technically ReJean outranked him socially. When it came to official business for his visit, they'd be more equal, but otherwise, unless it pertained to the King's safety, ReJean outranked him and every other lord in the empire thanks to his ancestor Maldwyn ReJean, the Bard, who had helped restore his half-brother King Arlis to the throne in Oedran, thereby ending the Age of Tyranny. Hereditary posts and standing was only a small part of Arlis' thanks to the Bard. With Finian present as well, he might even be said to be a step further removed given that once Finian was of age, he would be representing Areal in Oedran. He smiled to himself again, ReJean had almost got the greeting right. It should have gone Neassa, him and then Finian, given his wed-nephew was underage. All of that was before the complication of the fact he was Adeone's Defender, which was a status set apart from lordships and official posts.

Entering the building, ReJean said, "Do please join me for refreshments whilst your belongings are unpacked. You too, Landis, if you and Rale wish to."

Landis followed ReJean and Neassa with a small smile. His quick eyes were assessing everything from the uniforms of the guards to the well-swept corridors and polished wooden doors. There was so little dust he suspected the staff would be pleased when he left. They must have been working non-stop for days. Even in the best kept houses he'd expect to spot at least one cobweb from an inconsiderate spider with no sense of timing. Phylicia excused herself quietly when they reached the private area of the Palace, marked by more elaborate floor tiles, paintings and tapestries. Landis watched the young girl. There was no sign of any emotion but contentment. If she felt relieved, it never showed. She asked in an unassuming way if Finian would like to join her.

"I do not mind," said Landis when Finian looked at him. He watched them leave together, almost relieved. Finian didn't need all his days filled with the dry adult discussions about the plans for their visit.

Once in ReJean's sitting room, the Governor waved them to seats and motioned for his manservant to serve drinks. Landis took a watered whiskey and once the manservant had left, listened as ReJean said,

"I must admit I've heard what has happened, Lady Neassa. I don't know your own feelings but I hope you've no regrets."

Neassa said, "Only the regret that I was married to him for so long, Leander, though I never had a substantial reason to ask for the binding to be broken. I seem to be so much more content with life now. I jumped at the chance to visit Tradere once again."

"I'm hardly surprised, my lady. It was your home for twenty years. I'm just pleased that your travels bring you here."

Neassa smiled. "Yes, I was wondering something. Why do I, why have we, always stopped for at least two nights here? It's so close to Oedran."

"I rather suspect that your father had business with mine to conclude for your uncle. Whilst you, your mother and sister visited our markets, our fathers would be together discussing business. Lord Ewart was to King Altarius what Lord Landis is to His Majesty."

Neassa sighed. "I suppose he was and maybe a bit more, being a wed-brother as well. His Majesty sent me armed with letters for you. I also have letters from Their Highnesses to Lady Phylicia."

ReJean smiled. "She'll be pleased; before I say whether I am or not, how long was His Majesty's letter?"

Neassa shook her head. "I don't actually know, Your Excellency, but I doubt it's too bad. I shouldn't interrupt your day any longer."

"Lady Neassa, I have nothing to do other than to sit here reminiscing and enjoying your company. If you're itching to do something we could go down to the markets. I'm sure Lord Landis won't mind delaying his meetings with me for that."

Neassa thought about those markets. The city was called Amphi after them. For the cliff face here was like a great amphitheatre and the markets were arranged on the different tiers. They were both famous and infamous. Everyone wished to see them but few to experience them. To navigate them was, or could be, hazardous. Poles stretched from one level to another, Amphians used them to descend quickly from level to level, using a handle that clipped onto the pole. Ladders were set behind the market stalls to help a quick ascent and over the heads of the market stalls a wooden walkway kept pedestrians safe from the carts. Goods went up and down to the harbour at one end, where a pulley system of ropes looked worse than a wrecked ship's rigging. Every so often there were openings into the cliff face, which led to the infamous catacombs. These were the living quarters of the very poorest of Amphi inhabitants and of the criminals who plied their trade throughout the city streets and markets. If you knew what you were looking for in the top city you could see openings into the catacombs and, if you were sensible, they were the roads you never walked in the dark of night.

"Maybe we could visit them tomorrow, Your Excellency. Or, if you are busy with Lord Landis, maybe you'd let me take Phylicia there."

Landis chuckled. "I'm sure His Excellency wouldn't mind delaying out meetings for that, my lady."

ReJean's eyes narrowed. "I was warned about your sense of humour, Landis. Maybe I should have taken more heed."

"I shall thank His Majesty when I return to Oedran. Truly, Your Excellency, our business will wait on Her Ladyship's pleasure." He didn't miss the slight twitch on ReJean's face. Lady Neassa out ranked them both and ReJean wasn't pleased to be reminded of the fact. Landis swirled the whiskey in his glass. Winding ReJean up might not be on his official itinerary but it seemed far too easy to do.

* * *

A week later, Neassa was well on her way to Tradere and Landis and ReJean were closeted in a meeting with Finian unobtrusively listening to their discussions. They'd covered far more than Finian could ever recall. Structure, trade, concerns and contentments had been discussed, dissected and sewn back up. He hadn't been allowed to attend Court but his wed-uncle had talked with most of the lords and officials who made up the Amphi Court. They had three more days to conclude the visit and he could see the strain of the intensity beginning to take its toll on both men. ReJean had been at best courteous but mostly wary.

"About the date of the review, Lord Landis. What is the likelihood of it happening in the first weeks of the year?"

Landis' jaw set. "Might I ask why you'd want it then, Your Excellency?"

"It would suit us better."

"I cannot and will not give a blanket agreement to that. It will have to be worked out with His Majesty. Obviously, Prince Arkyn will be the reviewer and His Majesty will allow him a say in when the review happens."

"That is unusual," observed ReJean.

"Not when you know His Majesty and His Highness," replied Landis keeping a neutral tone.

Finian winced slightly. He knew that tone. It meant his wed-uncle was furious and he wondered why.

"Will you put it to His Majesty if you will not agree to it now?" asked ReJean equally as frustrated.

"Can you be more specific about the *date* when you'd like to see the review start?"

"Within the first week of the year, Landis. It will hopefully not be a protracted review and I would like to entertain Prince Arkyn as well as have him visiting merely for official work."

"I am sure His Highness will appreciate the thought," replied Landis and changed the subject.

* * *

Later, in the privacy of their rooms, Landis threw his notes onto a table and cursed. There was no way that Adeone or Arkyn would agree to that. There was little point mentioning it to them at all. He hadn't promised ReJean that he would; therefore, the issue could wait. ReJean's snobbish attitude was born from centuries of ancestors holding the only hereditary post outside the FitzAlcis, but his line was failing and he knew it. He had no son, no-one to carry on the Bard's line after his daughter, unless the King decided to let it pass down the female line. As far as anyone was aware, ReJean didn't have illegitimate children. Landis snorted. That would have been ironic seeing how the ReJeans started when Queen Orla had an affair and the Bard was the proof of it.

This province could end up like the others: a governor picked from the lords and men governing the province, given a temporary title to emphasise continuity and then, in the end, to politely retire to allow the next man his chance. It would be a shame if that were to happen, and possibly a political folly. Areal bordered more of the empire than any other province; it touched Anapara, the Low Plains, Tradere, Denshire and Terasia. It had a coastline that gave easy access to both the Macian Isles and Serpent Isle and further afield the Pale Lands. To let the governorship fall into the wrong hands could be catastrophic for the empire.

He glanced over as William entered. "What is it?"

"Would you like to eat before Court, my lord?"

"What I'd like is an evening off," muttered Landis.

William smiled. "I shall inform His Excellency that Your Lordship shall not be at Court, sir."

"Sicla. No. Don't do that. Just sort out a bath and a light meal. I'll be all right after that. Finian, are you spending the evening with Phylicia and her friends?"

"No, uncle. I was going to have an evening to myself."

Landis snorted. "You could have lied and cheered me up."

"Sorry. I didn't think it—"

Landis ruffled his hair. "Your father never dissembled either. It's a good thing in private. I'm sure Court will be just what I need."

"You could retire early, uncle."

"True. I'll consider it."

Chapter 38

BYFA

Pentadai, Week 23 – 19th Seral, 12th Seris 1213
Tradere – Byfa – Satrap's Residence

WALKING THROUGH the Satrap's Residence in Byfa, Rhian hummed to herself. Had Neassa really been coping? Outwardly there'd been relief and even contentment, but it was rare for a binding to be broken – not because every marriage was harmonious, but because of the ignominy and shame of the breaking. Only the fact that she was the King's cousin had saved her in Oedran. Compassion wouldn't accompany the gossip. Every morsel would be picked over without a thought for who might get hurt. The speculation and story would be everything. It was one reason why she'd invited Neassa to Tradere. Here they were themselves and years before had been laughingly known as the FairAlcis sisters.

There was the clatter of hooves and rumble of carriage wheels in the forecourt, and Rhian tripped lightly down the staircase. She smiled at the Satrap and together they made their way out to greet Neassa, who alighted from the coach as they stepped beyond the door. Rhian could tell the journey had tired her sister. She returned Neassa's warm smile, trying to hide her concern, watching as Neassa turned to the Governor of Tradere standing beside her.

"Your Excellency, it's nice to see you once again."

The Satrap smiled. "The pleasure is all mine, my lady. Welcome back to Tradere and Byfa in particular. Your company has been sorely missed. How was your journey?"

"It was pleasant. Though I think winter is truly arriving now."

"If you'd like to come in, I have some warm refreshments and a fire."

* * *

An hour later the Satrap left them to talk but passed Neassa a scroll from Adeone that had arrived with the dispatches from Oedran. Taking it, Neassa broke the King's seal and started reading. She stilled.

Rhian noticed. "What's the matter?"

"It's the final settlement that the lawyers have been drawing up. I... Here, read it. I'm not sure I quite believe it."

Rhian took it. "If you're sure." Two moments later, she was smiling. "What is so surprising about Rufus having to pay you compensation? You could have asked for his arrest and trial: he'd assaulted you."

"But the amount!"

"You're the granddaughter of a king. If mother hadn't insisted on taking father's birth rank, we could have been titled princess."

"But she did and we aren't."

Rhian smiled. "I don't think Adeone quite sees it like that."

Neassa sagged. "I think I've just realised. Carry on reading."

Rhian did so and nodded. "Good, I'm pleased. You'll need an allowance."

"But do you get... I've never asked..."

"Yes, I get an allowance from the King. Uncle Altarius and mother arranged it years ago, when I decided not to marry. You were already wed."

"How? Why did I never think...? I didn't expect any of this. I'll have

197

to talk to His Majesty."

Rhian laughed. "He'll not change his mind. This settlement was reached the day before you left Oedran. Unusually, he waited to inform you until he knew you couldn't object face to face."

Neassa shook her head. "I can't accept it though, Rhian. How can I? I've disgraced our name."

"No, you haven't! Just write to Adeone. He was always going to make sure you were provided for; family means an awful lot to him. Aunt Eliza saw to that."

"Yes. Would Scanlon have been the same man if she hadn't died?"

Rhian shook her head. "Probably not, but you have to wonder why his character is so dichotomous when viewed against Adeone's."

"Our common ancestors weren't all pleasant people. Uncle Altarius had a hard streak in him and grandfather wasn't, by all accounts, kind."

Rhian said, "He wasn't a psychopathic lunatic either. He'd been king from the age of four, controlled by the need to keep his power intact. So much could have foundered during his reign and it didn't."

"It was probably his mother's fault. Anyway, there was a rebellion due to his regime, or have you forgotten that? It happened barely a year after he died."

"Yes, Uncle Altarius can't be blamed for the Bayan rebellion and there's been none since. I tend to think if you look back a few generations, you'll find people all too like Scanlon in our family tree. They might, however, have been content with their lot where our little cousin isn't."

Neassa nodded. "True. I've forgotten what it's like to talk about politics. Rufus didn't want to know my opinions or have anyone else hear them."

"Well, sister, you can air them now for all you're worth; as long as they're not treasonous, I can't see Adeone complaining."

Neassa chuckled. "True. Though talking of our cousin, I've heard he's determined enough when he wants answers and reassurances."

"I'd be surprised if he wasn't, but many men like working for him. It's not ingratiating talk. They genuinely like working for him. I suppose it's because he's fair."

Neassa pulled a face. "Perhaps or he can just read people and uses their strengths. You should have heard the uproar at Rathgar's when he promoted Wynfeld again a couple of years ago."

Rhian smiled. "They're probably scared of the Major. The King's appointments are a matter for him and his appointees; it's a pity some lords think otherwise."

Neassa said with feeling, "Some lords only think of their own self-importance. His Majesty hasn't destroyed the lords' power, he only appoints men who can do the job instead of ones who can't. Is that so wrong?"

"No, but I'm glad you see it like that. I was wondering."

"I had to close my mind to so much," admitted Neassa. "It must sound stupid to you, but he controlled me far more than I realised. I've had my eyes opened, or rather I've realised they were closed and am beginning to see for myself. Now I just need some months away from it all to come to terms with everything."

Chapter 39

MUNDIMRI

Pentadai, Week 24 – 26th Seral, 19th Seris 1213
Palace of Oedran – Stableyard

LORD SCANLON DISMOUNTED in the Palace stableyard and glanced around it dismissively. Visiting Oedran was often a necessity but rarely a pleasure. Every visit had a purpose, even if the eyes watching him never gleaned what that purpose was. The chief groom was hurrying over to greet him as a runner sped off. Adeone would know he'd arrived before he, himself, reached the Privy Wing, let alone the Inner Office.

"Lord Scanlon, welcome home. I hope your journey was pleasant."

"Thank you, ReShard. I trust you're well."

"Aye, sir. I'll see your horse cared for personally. His Majesty wished to see you as soon as you arrived."

"Then I shall attend on the King."

Turning on his heel, Scanlon left the stableyard with a relaxed stride. He might not be in Oedran as much as he had been before but he was still FitzAlcis and the Justiciar of the Empire. He acknowledged the salutes of the guards with pursed lips. He needed more men amongst them. Ideally, he needed to remove Captain Pixney and find a way to install a loyal captain in his place, but the Palace Guard Captain was for the King to appoint and Adeone would never listen to his suggestions there. Maybe he should suggest people who were loyal to Adeone and thereby remove them from the list he'd appoint. First, he'd have to do something about Pixney, or eventually he would. He had more important plans for this visit and having men killed whilst he was in Oedran could produce far too much tedious circumstantial evidence if he wasn't careful.

The Privy Wing no longer felt like home to him. Just as the residences and palaces of the wider empire didn't. It wasn't safe or inviting, let alone welcoming or relaxing but staying elsewhere in Oedran wasn't ever going to be an option. He had to enhance his position, not undermine it.

199

He ignored the guards on the Audience Chamber doors. They knew him and, for all their eyes narrowed, their salutes were smart. Adeone hadn't yet told them not to salute him. He was unusually conventional at times. Their ancestors would probably have disowned him long before now, even with the faintest whiff of conspiracy. Still, Adeone had no proof and that was another unexpected side. Maybe he shouldn't be cursing the memory of Lachlan for instilling the principles of truth into Adeone's mind.

"The King is free?" he demanded of Richardson, crossing the threshold of the Outer Office.

"He is, Lord Scanlon. Let me announce Your Lordship."

Entering the Inner Office, Scanlon gave a perfunctory half-bow as a nod to convention and waited as the door closed on Richardson's retreating back. He had no doubt that the guards would be on high alert, even just outside the door within moments.

"How long are you staying?" asked Adeone by way of a greeting.

"Longer than you'd like me to," snapped Scanlon. "Probably just over a week. I need to go home as well. There's a few things demanding my attention at the Courthouse and I want to spend some time at Court. If that's no inconvenience."

"I'm sure someone will appreciate your presence. I've organised your birthday feast. Try to behave."

Scanlon crooked an eyebrow. "If you do likewise, Sire. I'd also like to dine with my friends without your spies around."

"That's been my wish for years, little brother. Feel free to dine with anyone you care to. I can make no promises as I don't know who my spies are. I let others deal with such details and just read their reports. Did the Domini's guards inconvenience you in Paras?"

"They never bothered me. Though I'm sure you had your report."

Adeone snorted. "The law review?"

"Has concluded, sir. Nothing new to report. I'll let Richardson have a copy of the actual report for your lawyers to rip apart."

"Lord Scanlon, did your horse lose a shoe earlier? You seem to be more fractious than normal."

"I'm sure Your Majesty's greeting had nothing to do with that. How are your babies?"

"Grown up. Elantha is growing too. They have plans for the Mundimri at Ceardlann, so won't be joining us."

"I wish to see my daughter, sir."

Adeone's lips pursed. "Every time you see her, she ends up distressed. So, I won't be permitting it this time."

"I'm her father," snarled Scanlon.

"By right but not by endeavour. Take your tantrum elsewhere, little brother. I will expect you at Court this evening."

"Then you'll be disappointed, Sire. I wish to rest after my journey."

Adeone eyed him. "Then do so alone. If you dine with anyone, I will expect you at Court afterwards."

"I am Your Majesty's to command," said Scanlon, sneering as he left.

He ignored the gathering in the Outer Office and made his way to his chambers on the floor below. Should he defy Adeone and invite guests to dine with him and then not attend Court? No. He'd spend the evening planning his stay and issuing invitations. At least Adeone had removed the necessity of seeing Elantha. He could use the fact he wouldn't allow it against the King. That would be more useful than seeing her.

Entering his chambers, he tossed his cloak over the back of the couch and let his gaze sweep around the room. It was flawless, but he rang the bell and, when his manservant answered, said,

"Is there anything I need to speak to the Steward about?"

"No, sir. Everything was most satisfactory."

"Then ask him to join me so I can tell him that." Scanlon watched his manservant leave and cursed the fact that in Oedran they had to be more circumspect. He couldn't do anything about the plain 'sir' but he could remember that his manservant hadn't even used 'lord'.

Twelve minutes later, the Steward was announced. The man's obeisance wasn't quite as exact as it had been in the past but it was better than none.

"My manservant tells me that everything was satisfactory, which is pleasing. Now, do have a seat. I wonder if you could explain the latest news of the Palace and Court to me? Before we get into other topics."

* * *

The following evening, having spent the day at the Courthouse, Scanlon entered Court early. He enjoyed the assembly. Enjoyed the wariness of those like Landis, who had more of an idea of his aims, and the oblivious sycophancy of those who didn't. Those amongst his acquaintance who knew more were the most attentive. There would be repercussions in private if they weren't.

As Lord Iris crossed to greet him, he smiled warmly. Iris would know everything about the situation as the King's Counsellor, but there was a pretence to be maintained, and he didn't need to talk to the old fool for long. The greeting was pleasant and Lord Iris would be honoured if he would dine at Iris House during his stay.

Scanlon politely declined. He had many calls on his time whilst he was in Oedran. He was sure that Lord Iris would understand and Lord Fairson had already extended an invitation, as had several of the other

201

Lords of Oedran.

Of course Lord Iris understood, and Lord Scanlon must do entirely as he pleased. There would be other evenings on other visits.

'Yes, *to avoid you,*' thought Scanlon icily. A few moments later, he excused himself and moved away, wandering through Court until almost accidentally he ended up talking with Lux and Anguis, who welcomed him with apparently honest smiles. Well, they hadn't needed to be coerced or tricked into his service. He'd have to be careful not to spend too much time with them, but there were others too. His gaze swept around the FitzAlcis Chamber. Various younger members of the Court were talking in groups. His eyes rested on each, assessing possibilities.

"If we can present anyone, do let us know, sir," said Lux easily.

"Are any biddable?"

Anguis' lips twitched. "Generally, sir, but less free than our youth. I rather suspect Lady Amara living in Oedran has had something to do with that."

Scanlon crooked an eyebrow. "My aunt has many admirable qualities." In his mind he added, '*For spoiling my fun.*' After a couple of moments, he said, "No Guests of Court?"

"Not since Lord Kensal died so tragically," observed Lux as Merchant Chapa passed behind Scanlon.

Scanlon caught the movement out of his peripheral vision. When Henry Chapa settled himself within hearing, Scanlon motioned that they'd walk to his companions. He didn't want to be overheard by one of Adeone's confidants. Smiling, he greeted lords and merchants he recognised. Beneficent, his presence soon went unremarked. Though he knew there'd be reports – detailing all his movements and conversations – on Adeone's desk first thing in the morning. He'd almost be offended, if it wasn't so predictable and if he didn't use the fact to his advantage.

* * *

Two days later, the Mundimri feast had passed off without incident the night before and Adeone had just given a noncommittal speech to wish him blessings on his birthday. Strangely, he hadn't mentioned long life, health or happiness in it. Not that the Court cared. They were just enjoying the second feast in two days. He soon remembered why he didn't like being in Oedran for his birthday now that he was Justiciar. Sandwiched between Adeone and Amara, there was no chance of pleasant conversation.

"So, young Scanlon, have you grown up yet?" asked Lady Amara.

Scanlon tried not to see the smile twitching at Adeone's lips. "I'm following a family tradition, Aunt Amara."

"Ha. I'm not so sure you are following the right ones. Though, I've not heard of so many tantrums lately. How is the justice system?"

Scanlon blinked at the speed with which she changed tack. "Working to the best it can, aunt."

"With you in charge? I suppose it has little option. Yes, Sire?"

Adeone's eyes twinkled. "I know you enjoy bantering with my brother, Lady Amara, but he's hardly had chance to eat anything yet."

Her lips twitched. "Very true, Sire. My apologies. Food should be more filling than eating words."

Adeone crooked an eyebrow and Lady Amara turned to Lord Iris sitting on her other side.

Scanlon wondered why the King had rescued him. It wasn't as though anyone within hearing would take his side. Though Lord Cearis was two places from Adeone. Landis had exercised his right as Defender to sit on the King's left, so Cearis had been pushed one seat down. If he didn't know why Landis had done that, then he might have been offended. Still, Cearis was a bit of a weakling. He wouldn't stick up for anyone in the King's presence.

His eyes tracked various dancing couples as the feast ended. Several kept his attention, both men and women. There were some excellent dancers amongst the Court. He was sure a few would be flattered by his attentions.

"Don't even think about it, young Scanlon."

"Aunt?"

"His Majesty does like the younger members of his Court to retain their respectability and marriage prospects. Unless, of course, you're looking for a new wife."

His eyes narrowed. "Not today, aunt, but thank you for the reminder."

"You're welcome."

One of these days, he'd have to do something about her, but she knew too much about him. If she died, he doubted he'd be safe. He had to find a different way of limiting her interference.

Chapter 40
APPOSER

Alunadai, Week 31 – 15th Anapal, 1st Anapcis 1213
Outer Office

As a smartly dressed man entered the Outer Office, Richardson rose, putting down the King's diary and his pen carefully in its rest on his desk.

"Welcome back to Oedran, Apposer."

"Thank you. Is His Majesty free? I have several reports for him."

Richardson said simply, "Please leave the reports here, His Majesty will read them as soon as possible and send for you if he has further questions."

"There were several items, not significant enough to enter my reports but which he might want to know."

Richardson eyed him. "You were informed your reports should be exhaustive."

"They are for the matters they relate to, Administrator. I would however still like an immediate audience with His Majesty."

"Very good. Please wait here." With a brief knock Richardson entered the Inner Office and waited for Adeone to finish speaking to Arkyn.

The King glanced over and crooked an eyebrow.

"Your Majesty's Apposer is requesting an audience, sir."

There was something in the way Richardson said it that made Adeone pause. "Please tell him that I'm rather busy but if he leaves his reports with you then I'll read them as soon as I get chance."

Richardson said levelly, "He is being insistent, Your Majesty."

Adeone glanced at his administrator sharply. "Why? Do we know?"

"Something about extra information, Sire."

Adeone sighed, exasperated. "I don't have time today, Richardson. I've far too many counsels and other reports to get through…"

Arkyn asked mildly, "Shall I take the apposer's report, sir?"

"No but if he's still being awkward when you leave you can emphasise my decision… That's all, Richardson."

Once more in the Outer Office, Richardson said, "I am sorry but His Majesty is busy for the rest of today, Apposer. He will read your reports as soon as he can and then send for you."

"Administrator Richardson, I don't think you quite understand—"

Arkyn leaving the Inner Office looked carefully at Apposer Nallvir. He said, "I rather suspect it is the other way around. His Majesty has many calls on his time and unfortunately cannot see everyone at *their* convenience. You have been informed of the King's decision, please abide by it."

The apposer pointedly bowed. "Your Highness, the information I have for the King is important."

"So is the smooth running of the empire, Nallvir. Pass Richardson your reports and wait for the summons. Such persistence is not helping." He turned to his father's administrator. "Can you liaise with Edward about the next Provincial Counsel, please? His Majesty would like me to be present. Thank you. Apposer…"

He motioned with his hand for the apposer to leave the Outer Office. Nallvir handed his reports to Richardson and left. Arkyn caught the administrator's eye, winked and departed.

* * *

The following afternoon the apposer entered the Inner Office and bowed to the King.

Far too mildly, Adeone said, "Do not act in such a manner again when asking to see me, Nallvir. Richardson is never awkward on purpose, if he says I am busy then I am busy. Do you understand?"

The apposer swallowed. "Yes, sir. I simply thought Your Majesty might wish to know my unofficial findings directly."

"After the weeks of investigation, a day is hardly significant. Please sit down. Prince Arkyn, as you see, is to join our discussions. Now, after all those weeks I am surprised at the sparse nature of your reports. A scroll per place is hardly exhaustive I would have thought."

"I tried to keep them concise, Your Majesty, and accurate. At both locations I found little to investigate."

Seeing his father's pursed lips, Arkyn said, "So what *did* you discover that needed investigation?"

Apposer Nallvir adjusted his position slightly to face Arkyn wondering if it was normal for an underage Prince to question the King's officials in the King's presence. "Nothing of significance, Your Highness. I did find that one of Lord Camlyn's staff wasn't being totally honest with his figures but he was simply pilfering for his own advantage. Lord Camlyn replaced him. At Lord Faran's all I discovered was loyalty but there were some oddities, not to do with Their Lordships or their loyalty to Your Majesty, Sire, but niggles. I'm afraid I'm not explaining it well… Let me see… It was mostly feelings, I don't have proof for any of it but take Lord Faran's son who died a few years ago, according to all the staff he was hale and well one minute and the next they checked and he was dead in his cot. The nurse, re-employed for his new daughter, said that sudden death isn't unknown but she'd never seen one like that…"

Adeone frowned. "Are you saying she thought it was murder?"

"Yes, sir, but there's no proof. Once it was brought to my attention I was bound to investigate and spoke with Lord Faran. His Lordship, obviously unhappy to discuss it, said he'd got his suspicions but that he wouldn't divulge them."

Adeone and Arkyn shared a concerned look.

The Prince said, "I hope you didn't pursue it further, Nallvir."

"No, sir. I wasn't there to distress His Lordship. I kept my ears open for other clues but none were forthcoming."

Adeone steepled his fingers against his mouth. "Was that all?"

"No, Sire. Again, I have no proof of this but I think there's treason high in both Lufian and Bayan government. Nothing directly happened on my journeys but I suspected I was being watched and or followed. I travelled around both estates several times and never felt at ease. I was asked if I would be visiting the principal cities, rather too pointedly, and whether my investigations were truly restricted to Lords Faran and Camlyn. I also had the feeling that of my four clerks and advisor there was only one clerk who wasn't reporting to someone else as well as me. I found my papers had been searched on a couple of occasions…" He broke off glancing between the King and Prince. "I would like to know, to put my mind at rest, if anyone was reporting directly here as a safety precaution."

"I am sure you would, Nallvir," remarked Adeone. "I am sure that given similar circumstances everyone would. If I ever discover anyone was reporting directly to my office, I am sure I will feel able to tell you."

"Which clerk didn't you suspect?" enquired Arkyn.

"Winters, sir."

Adeone nodded. "Apposer, you have said you have no proof for any of this. Maybe you should check all your papers and notes again, then write an exhaustive report and include the relevant papers. I am not going to order an enquiry on vague feelings."

The apposer said, "Very good, sir. I wasn't expecting an enquiry…"

"How fortunate," replied Adeone dryly, "I had better not keep you."

The apposer left the Inner Office wondering whether he should have mentioned anything to the King about any of it.

Once the door closed and the footsteps had receded, Adeone swore roundly. "Sicla, death and damnation! Couldn't he have found some damned proof?"

"Obviously not. It was interesting that he didn't think Winters was reporting to anyone. He was Wynfeld's man."

A slow grin spread over Adeone's face. "Oh dear. Shall we enlighten him?"

"I don't think the Major would thank us. The problem is who everyone else was reporting to."

"Maybe. I see the problem as who is high in the government of both those provinces who could be a traitor, and, if we've missed people there, have we serious problems elsewhere? Are you sure there was nothing in Lufia to give you unease?"

"I can double and triple check all my notes, sir. I can pass them to Wynfeld as well and see if he or his eagle-eyed men can see anything I missed. I really hope there isn't anything but I am as fallible as anyone else and I suppose I had other things on my mind…"

Adeone looked at him. "Yes. I'm not going to blame you if anything was missed but Wynfeld's expertise might be helpful. He also has all his own intelligence information to help. I doubt you did miss anything but together you might spot something new."

Arkyn said, "I'll get everything in order, Sire. What about Bayan?"

"I'll speak to the Exarch."

"If it's him?" enquired Arkyn.

Adeone shook his head. "I doubt it very much, Arkyn. There would have been hints before now. He's family."

"So is Uncle Scanlon, father."

"True but, trust me, Tyler Galwood isn't enamoured of your Uncle Scanlon."

Arkyn sighed. "I hope not. I don't mean to add worry to concern but not every traitor has to support Lord Scanlon, Your Majesty."

Adeone nodded. "But they do seem to be rallying to his side."

Chapter 41
ON LOYALTY
Pentadai, Week 31 – 19th Anapal, 5th Anapcis 1213
Palace of Oedran – King's Chambers

JUST OVER A WEEK LATER, Adeone had had a full day; long meetings and an evening at Court had left him drained and tired. Simkins answered the bell and was silent, but no less eloquent for that, as he helped the King change from day clothes into night ones. He stoked the fire, warmed the King's bed and then blowing out the candles left, knowing Adeone was asleep before the door closed behind him.

It was a deep sleep, black-deep. Adeone's mind was blank, there was no artist painting pictures of his mind as the day's fatigue drifted from him. Midnight came and went and the depth of sleep didn't change, it never altered for hours. When he finally awoke, his burning skin was dry. Fearing he was running a temperature, he sent for the doctor.

Chapa's first words were, "Always thought kings had an easy life, sir."

Adeone sighed. "Doc, I'm not in the mood. Do I have a fever?"

"Sorry, Sire. Let's check. Any other symptoms?"

"Very deep sleep and, I rather expect, fatigue. Other than that, I feel fine. I just woke up and it was like my body was burning."

Chapa eyed him. "You've been working far too hard, Your Majesty.

I realise I'm hitting my head against a wall, but you need to take a breath at some point."

"Anyone would think I was ignorant of it, doc."

"Well, if you know it, can't you do something about it?" enquired Chapa with a trace of exasperation tinting his voice.

Adeone sighed. "Not as easily as you wish, cousin, or as I would wish, come to that."

"You need someone to keep you sensible, sir. As your doctor, I'm saying you're not ill but you should take the day off, completely off. Simkins… Order the King's coach to take him to Ceardlann. It's the only place where he won't do any work. Yes, Your Majesty?"

Adeone had given a small cough. "Let me issue the orders, cousin. I've far more practice at them."

Chapa smiled. "As long as the orders look after your health, of course, Sire."

"Simkins, I'm going to Ceardlann for the day, but I'm not up to riding. Can you see to things please? Let Richardson know as a matter of priority. You can both take the day off."

Simkins gave a half bow. "Of course, Sire. Shall I take the doc with me?"

"No, leave him here for a bit. I could do with a laugh." Once Simkins had gone, the King crooked an eyebrow. "Really, cousin?"

"Really, Adeone. I can't see anything wrong. Surprising but true. You're just as overworked as ever. Have a relaxing day at Ceardlann."

"With all the children there?" mused Adeone, a glint in his eye.

Chapa smiled. "All right then, a more relaxing day than you'd have here with Richardson to contend with."

* * *

"Loyalty is an odd thing, Your Highness. It is more to be feared than a flash of deep emotion, whether that is love, hatred or anger."

"Why, Judge? Surely, loyalty is a good thing."

"I never said it was not, Your Highness. I simply said it is to be feared. You can fear good as much as evil. Emotion is normally like a flame of a fire; it burns brightly and quickly but takes some measure of stoking to keep the flame, but loyalty is the embers, it is charcoal – it burns all the hotter. It is what it might make men do which is the danger. Loyalty to the King, Prince Arkyn and Your Highness is seen as a good thing, but that loyalty is no different, in a traitor's eye, to a loyalty held elsewhere. Loyalty is still loyalty; you cannot try someone for that alone, you need intention or an actual crime. Loyalty, in itself, is not a crime; it can simply lead to them."

Watching the judge's face, Tain nodded. "I suppose that makes sense."

"Do you, however, understand it?"

"I think I might… one day. It's like hearing my brother and father talk; I can't understand every little reference but I get the gist of the conversation."

Tancred smiled. "In such ways there is much learning. Loyalty is a strange concept: there is much that drives and motivates men, and women, to it. It is perplexing, is it not, that humans are concerned, primarily, with survival, and yet will become loyal to an ideal or person which puts that survival in jeopardy. Sometimes it might not only put their own lives in jeopardy, but others close to them: their families, friends and acquaintances might all suffer, but not because of their actions. Men, loyal to Your Highness' family might find themselves in situations where they contemplate the edge of the cliff of morality, they might find themselves stepping out into the sea of crime, where, normally, outside of the demands of loyalty, they would step away and not venture into the hazardous places. They might feel that in being loyal they will be excused anything; that, in acting for the FitzAlcis, they are protected against the rigours of the law. Should loyalty be such, sir?"

"No, Judge, but loyalty shouldn't be unrewarded. Should it?"

"Indeed it should not, Your Highness; however, it might be worth noting that there are other ways for loyalty to be expressed than by the breaking of the laws that the FitzAlcis, in the post of justiciar, is meant to protect. If it is permitted for the retainers of the FitzAlcis, king or justiciar, to abuse the laws, can Your Highness deduce the consequences?"

Tain smiled. He now revelled in the judge's habit of giving him all the clues and waiting for him to figure out the answer. He liked the challenge, liked working out the puzzles, so he put his mind firmly on the issue in hand. Emotions burned brightly but loyalty burned slowly and could be more heated; therefore, an action taken in the heat of a moment, because of emotion, was less reprehensible than one thought out over a long time. Was that what the judge wanted to hear? Tain explained his thinking and Tancred smiled in acknowledgement, but it wasn't open, broad and uninhibited; he had only part of the answer. So, onto the next part of the judge's rhetoric. Onto, in fact, the actual question he had asked.

"If retainers break the laws, then people will see that they have broken them and that we seem to condone such a thing; therefore, the law is worthless?"

"To some extent. Is there anything more?"

Tain frowned. "I guess that there is. I don't know what though."

"Yes, you do, sir. You have seen the first consequence. Is there only ever one consequence to such a subject?"

"I can't seem to focus, Judge."

Tancred looked at his charge. "Very well, sir. Close your eyes, forget the room, forget me. Do you have the shape of the problem? You have said that the law becomes worthless, in the first instance. You have observed that considered actions can be more reprehensible than those of the moment. Now, you have two parts to the puzzle. Can you feel the shape of the problem?"

"I think so, Judge," answered Tain, his eyes obediently closed.

"Then think on the problem."

Tain did so and into his head gradually came the shape of an answer. Hesitantly, he tried to put it into words. "If the law becomes worthless... if it only applies to those outside our sphere then it... No, I can't phrase it."

"Yes, you can, sir. Your vocabulary is broader than mine."

Tain sighed, still with his eyes closed. "It is like there would be no true shape to the world, no order and yet order would be enforced on one section of society whilst the other showed no respect for it. It would, that is the law would, become a tool of despots..." Tain opened his eyes and grinned at the judge, "It would become a tool of tyranny."

"Good, Your Highness. Anything else?"

"Tyrants never succeed. The law would, instead of protecting, destroy; therefore, loyalty might be our downfall instead of our saviour and, therefore, it is to be feared as much as upheld. It is, in fact, an irony and in being such is both a laughable and a serious subject to discuss in detail."

Tancred smiled and now the smile was fully manifested. "Congratulations, sir. You will make a lawyer yet."

"Ah, there must be more, for I haven't achieved a judge or justiciar."

Tancred laughed. "Maybe there is, yet work should not be taken without refreshment."

"I'd prefer to work this out and then relax. May we?"

"Who am I to stop my Prince?"

Tain grinned. "I'll not answer that. So, loyalty can destroy, it can destroy kingdoms and empires, it can destroy in fact everything that men try to protect, yet I can't see how we can follow that any further."

"Then might I suggest, sir, you concentrate on your future post and responsibilities?"

Tain frowned. "It can destroy because retainers might break the law. The law I should protect, in breaking it, they undermine both it and me?"

"Getting there."

"In undermining me..."

"Forgive me, sir, you are thinking along one line, one pathway, think of others. What laws are they likely to break?"

"Any or all. Yet, should it matter what they break? It is the effect on the law that matters."

Tancred merely watched Tain's face, without the slightest hint of emotion.

"Judge! Can't you give me a clue?"

"Our lessons have given you many, sir. Do you consider each lesson is independent from another?"

"No, but how do I know the connections?"

"They are often the small things, as much as the obvious ones."

Tain sighed; he tried closing his eyes and only got frustrated. Pushing himself to his feet, he looked out of the window over Fitz's kitchen garden to the trees at the edge of Dellwood. He heard the thud of horses' hooves from the small earthen stable yard and the jingle of harness.

"A crime is a crime, maybe I should be looking at the crimes that might be committed… No… At the number of crimes that a man commits then… No… If a crime is a crime, it shouldn't matter how many a retainer has committed, they are all crimes and the miscreant should be brought to court."

"Good, sir, you will make a judge."

"Right. I will crack this. Crimes are crimes. It doesn't matter how many are committed or by whom."

"Correct." Tancred felt the frustration and melted slightly. "Sir, think of the crime of taking a life. Would there be any legitimate circumstances?"

Tain saw the answer. "There might be, but we would have to authorise the action and only when no other course presented itself. Does that therefore make us murderers?"

Tancred said, "It would depend on the circumstances. A traitor, beyond doubt, who threatens the stability of the empire, of the lives of hundreds, might warrant their own removal, but the move should never be taken flippantly or in the dark spaces."

"If possible, then there should be no ambiguity, no blurred lines. It should be that everyone understands the metaphorical line and sticks to it. Even if someone is loyal beyond doubt and they overstep that line, then action should be taken. Someone's job or position might mean more licence but we should consider no-one immune from the law's reach."

"Good, Your Highness, you will make a justiciar yet. There is no room for indecision when everyone is watching your actions."

* * *

A couple of moments later, the door opened. Tancred rose, smiled and bowed. Tain turned, surprised.

"Afternoon, James. How goes the lesson?" Adeone held out an arm. As Tain got within reach, he ruffled his son's hair.

Tancred said levelly, "Very well, Sire. We have just finished the main

211

part of the lesson and I was about to send for refreshments."

An arm about Tain's shoulders, Adeone moved into the room properly, "Then I'll stay, if I may."

"Of course you may, father! Whyever not?" enquired Tain.

"This is yours and the judge's domain. I am but an intruder," observed Adeone with a wink at Tancred.

"A *welcome* one, sir. Are you coming to Ceardlann?"

"Until the morning, yes. What have you been discussing today?"

Tain shrugged. "The effects of loyalty on the law."

"I'm glad I missed that. Rather weighty, I'd have thought, James."

Tancred smiled. "I have been testing His Highness' mental agility and he has not been found wanting in any respect, Your Majesty."

Adeone looked at Tain, who seemed a touch uncomfortable. "I never thought he would be, James... When he put his mind to any problem, that is. So, do you require the scapegrace this afternoon?"

"I am sure the continuation of today's talk can wait for another day. If His Highness has no objection."

The Prince sighed. "I don't mind but I sense a conspiracy."

Adeone ruffled his hair again. "Not all conspiracies are malicious, Tain. Come... Ah, afternoon, Fitz. Apologies for sneaking up here."

Fitz chuckled. "I'll cope, Your Majesty. I can see you're safe but I hope you're well."

Adeone raised an eyebrow. "Last time I considered the problem, I was. Are you?"

"As ever, Sire, as ever. The odd twinge, you know..."

"That's age, Fitz. There's no remedy for it. You're not bored, I hope?"

"I'm sure I've been busier, but I can't say I've time for boredom, Sire."

"Good. It's nice to know you're relaxing. Join us for lunch if you can."

They settled down to eat an informal lunch with chatter rather than serious talk.

* * *

That night Adeone's sleep was lighter and dreams again flowed. They danced across his mind in glittering formation: bright, vivid, fleeting and transient. The only thing he recalled when he woke was a lingering feeling of uncertainty; was what he'd seen but not remembered the future, or some approximation of it? He had been able to recall his other vivid dreams so were these meant to be forgotten so that he could continue to live or were they simply dreams as most people experienced them? He didn't know and as he prepared to leave for Oedran once again, his thoughts strayed elsewhere.

He was in the main entrance when Tain found him. When his son was close enough, Adeone ruffled his hair.

"Father! Do you know how annoying that is?"

"Yes, but I have to get my own back. What are you doing today?"

"As someone insists I study, lessons with Advisor Spellen."

Adeone smiled. "I can't think who insists on that. Have the day off. I wouldn't like to annoy whoever's giving the orders around here."

Tain grinned. "Thank you. Will you do the same?"

"I had a day off yesterday. I can't hide forever, my son."

"I wasn't meaning forever, father. It's rather a long time. Someone would want something signing."

"Is Spellen teaching you that sort of humour or is your nearfather responsible?"

Tain laughed. "Uncle Festus every time, unless it's you, of course."

"Very amusing. Now, I'd better get going, otherwise a lot of people are going to be worried."

Tain sighed. "Sorry, father, I'm holding you up."

Adeone gave him a hug. "I don't mind. Shall we forget them all and go for a walk?"

"No. You'd better get back to Oedran. I wouldn't like to think of Uncle Festus giving orders for too long."

Adeone saw for the first time the truly responsible adult Tain would be when necessity called. Before it had been a wish and a prediction more than a certainty but, in that moment, he saw what Tancred had been seeing for months. His younger son was becoming a man faster than he'd realised.

Chapter 42
LORD TERAN

ON PENTADAI, Adeone crooked an eyebrow when Richardson mentioned Lord Teran wished for an audience. The King had no love for Teran, whose face seemed to wear a permanent sneer. The Lord of Oedran rarely said a word to him unless he was presiding at Court and couldn't avoid it. Adeone didn't see anything wrong in the arrangement as Teran supported Scanlon, but there was no reason to antagonise the situation.

As Richardson announced the Lord of Oedran responsible for representing Terasia, Adeone tried to appear relaxed. The bow he received was correct but with an undercurrent of insolence.

"Thank you for seeing me, Sire. I am wishing to arrange a marriage for my eldest daughter, Chandra. We try and maintain links with Terasia. So, I've been considering Lord Penrod Silvano, but I understand he's Your Majesty's ward."

Adeone sat back, his fingers steepled against his mouth. He lowered them. "You are not bothered by the fact that his brother was a traitor, my lord? You are aligning yourself with a disgraced family."

Teran shrugged. "I am also aligning myself with the Visir, Your Majesty, as he is Lord Penrod's wed-brother."

"Very true. I shall consider the proposition when I have more time to do it justice, my lord. I shall let you know when I have reached a conclusion."

Lord Teran rose. "Thank you, Sire."

Adeone watched him go and, once the door closed, swore. He didn't want the marriage. Penrod shouldn't be entangled with everything that was happening. He had already suffered enough when his brother committed treason. He and his siblings had been forced into Adeone's guardianship; their father had no say over their lives. Their family had consequently been torn apart. As Landis was presiding at Court, he sent for Rayburn.

Several minutes later, Rayburn entered the Inner Office and bowed. The King was tapping his pen against the desk.

"How are you on provincial matters, Rayburn?"

"I'll do my best, Your Majesty."

"Thank you. Lord Teran has proposed marrying Lady Chandra to Lord Penrod Silvano."

Rayburn's face said it all. "Why would he want *that* association?"

"I wish I knew. He claims that he's also aligning himself with the Visir, which might be true, but in that case, the Visir has sons..."

"Several, sir. The eldest are certainly of age also. Maybe he's been refused. He could approach the Visir directly for preliminary conversations whereas for Lord Penrod he must ask Your Majesty."

Adeone considered that. "True. He says it's to keep links with Terasia."

"The Terans have been diligent in that regard, sir," remarked Rayburn. "Does Lady Chandra want the marriage?"

"I doubt, if she doesn't, that Lord Teran's bothered. I'll talk to her and Penrod when I get the chance."

Rayburn nodded. "A wise course of action, Your Majesty. I get the feeling that Lady Chandra isn't happy, but I don't know why. It's just one of those feelings."

"I hope it isn't because she's being forced into marriage before she wants it. I still sense there's more to this proposition than meets the eye."

"Maybe talk to Captain Beaver or Major Wynfeld, sir."

Adeone nodded. "Thank you, Rayburn."

The advisor bowed and left, pondering on what the King had said. He mentioned to Richardson he'd be at Court for a while.

His amble through Court, drink in hand, took him into several rooms. In one, Lord Teran was speaking determinedly to his eldest daughter. She looked frightened, but Rayburn thought he detected an edge of relief. Something had occurred at Teran's house – why that came to Rayburn he could never say, but once the thought was there, it wouldn't be removed.

Barely having finished his wine, he returned to the Inner Office. When the King could see him, he said, "I think Lady Chandra may want to get away from Oedran, sir, however uncertain she is about marriage."

"What makes you say that?" After hearing Rayburn's explanation, Adeone called for Richardson. "Ask Lady Chandra Teran to come here, please. She may have someone with her but only to wait in the Outer Office."

* * *

When Chandra arrived, she was worried and timid. Adeone walked out from behind his desk. She didn't need the formality it necessitated. He asked if she'd like a drink and she shook her head.

"Do you know that your father's been to speak to me about a marriage for you, my lady?"

"Yes, Sire."

He asked her the question no-one else had, "Do you want to be married, Lady Chandra?"

She swallowed. "I just don't want to be here, Your Majesty."

Adeone took her arm to steer her to the comfortable seats, but she flinched and he dropped his hand, seeing her distress. "What is it, my lady?"

Regaining composure, she said, "It's nothing, Sire. Yes, I'd like to be married."

His eyes softened. "Are you sure? You don't have to say to me what your father would want you to over this. It is your life we're discussing."

"What's Lord Penrod like?"

Adeone smiled. "From what I know of him, he's kind. Terasia is a beautiful province and Tera is a wonderful city. If this marriage happens, I can ask the Margrave's wife to ease you into life there and introduce you to ladies your own age. She'll be more than happy to help." (Chandra's face cleared slightly.) "You'll not be isolated in Terasia, Lady Chandra. I'll make sure of that."

She dropped into a curtsy. "Thank you, sir. Then I would like to marry."

215

Adeone reached down to help her back to her feet. Although she accepted the help, she was obviously uncomfortable.

* * *

That evening, when the main business of the day was over, Adeone called Dragoris and obtained a link with Penrod Silvano. The youth was sixteen and weathering the notoriety of his brother's treason better than Adeone had ever expected, but then Penrod's brother Melek hadn't been particularly well liked in his family or out of it.

"Lord Penrod, I hope I've not disturbed anything."

"No, Your Majesty. I was merely reading a novel."

"Have you considered marriage, my lord?"

Penrod paled. "No, sir. Father was hunting for a bride before the troubles, but I haven't consciously thought about it since."

"Are you averse to the idea? I only ask because someone has approached me proposing a marriage."

Penrod thought hard. "I must marry eventually, Sire. I realise that, but I hadn't thought it would be sooner. I suppose I'm concerned that I couldn't be a good husband at my age."

Adeone smiled. "I can understand that. I married young to set my father's mind at rest. If you can love your wife, everything comes naturally."

"Who would that wife be, Sire?"

"Lady Chandra Teran. She is willing for the match. I might suggest that you contact her and talk to her. I will not pressure either of you into this, nor will I allow anyone else to, but I would like you to consider it. Let me know your decision when you've spoken to Lady Chandra."

* * *

Just over a week later, Lord Penrod contacted Adeone. The young man looked anxious.

Adeone smiled. "So, my lord?"

Penrod hesitated. "I think Lady Chandra needs to get away from Oedran, Sire, but I don't know if she's using the idea of marriage as the only escape she can see."

"Do you know why she wants to leave?" enquired Adeone, concerned.

"No, Your Majesty, but I'd like to invite her to stay for a time. We can see if we could marry after that. I would like to get to know her better, but I don't think we should decide now."

Adeone studied his ward. "I shall mention it, my lord. It's certainly kind of you to suggest it."

Penrod said softly, "I know what it's like to want to escape, Sire."

"I can imagine you do. Have things settled down?"

216

Lord Penrod considered what his family had been through. "Relatively, Sire. It still haunts father, but he's beginning to be back to normal."

"It will take time, Lord Penrod. I realise it's been over a year, but treason tends to stick in people's memory. How are your studies? Are you still trying to become an advisor?"

"I'm trying, sir, but it all gets complicated. Finding time when the house is quiet is a challenge in itself. My siblings are a good crowd but noisy."

Adeone smiled. "Children tend to be. Just out of interest, if you marry, would you like to move out of home?"

Lord Penrod hesitated. "I think that would only be fair on my wife."

"Maybe so. So, what's bothering you about your studies?"

* * *

The following morning Adeone reluctantly asked Richardson to send for Teran. The Lord of Oedran entered the Inner Office and bowed.

Adeone didn't bother with preliminaries. "Lord Penrod has invited Lady Chandra to Tera to stay for a time to see if they could marry."

"I'm not sending her anywhere without a binding agreement, sir."

"My lord, I think a visit is an excellent idea and support the proposition whole-heartedly. I've asked Lord Wealsman if Lady Chandra can stay with him and Lady Wealsman until she decides. They couldn't be happier and will take good care of her. I can understand your feelings but I think a marriage in Tera, if that is truly what you want, will come out of this even if it isn't with Lord Penrod. Lady Chandra is a charming lady; I cannot see it being difficult for her to be married happily."

Teran looked like he'd just sucked a lemon. "Am I being told to send my daughter to a distant province with no certainty that there will be any marriage waiting for her?"

The King said, "I am saying she has been invited, that she will benefit from the experience and that there are good reasons for her to go. Please consider it seriously. Queen Ira stayed in Garth for almost a year when she was a similar age. That was partly to see if there were any marriage prospects for her there. Obviously, I was pleased there weren't, but it does prove such visits are not unknown."

Later that day, Teran returned to the Inner Office and agreed to the idea. It took two days before Chandra was on her way to Tera. The speed intrigued Adeone, especially as it was winter, but he'd spoken with Chandra and knew it was at her instigation. He really wanted to know what had happened but found himself unable to ask. A group of Teran's men escorted her but, once she reached Tera, Wealsman sent them back, much to Chandra's private relief.

Chapter 43

LESSONS AND OBSERVATIONS
Tretaldai, Week 34 – 10th Bayal, 3rd Bayis 1213
Inner Office

THE FOLLOWING WEEK, Adeone looked up as Richardson announced Tancred. He smiled warmly in welcome and waved to a chair.

"James, what can I do for you?"

Tancred smiled. "I simply wished to talk to Your Majesty about Prince Tain's lessons once again."

Adeone said, "I've told you I trust you completely."

"I appreciate Your Majesty's trust, but I believe His Highness may be ready to observe trials soon. He will be fourteen in just over a season."

"So he will. He's far too short a time left as a child. Though, I can't see that being Justiciar of Oedran will completely remove his sense of humour. So, observing trials. When would you suggest?"

"I tend to hear cases on an Alunadai, Your Majesty, and simply thought His Highness could join me. He would obviously need to be in Oedran the evening before – that is Septadai. Most conclude in a day; therefore, His Highness could easily return to the Rex Dallin that evening. I am aware the predictability might put His Highness in danger."

Adeone considered that. The judge had a point but there was time to find a solution. "It might, Judge, but I wouldn't expect him to observe every week for a long time yet."

"Of course, Sire. I was considering that the summer might well be the best time to start the observations."

"I had thought, from the way you spoke, that you were considering this sooner."

Tancred smiled. "There are lessons I need to have with His Highness before he begins, sir; therefore, I am merely trying to plan when to bring the subjects up."

Adeone nodded. "Then I'll leave the decisions up to you; so far, you've worked wonders with my son."

"Thank you, Your Majesty, but he has put the hard work in."

"He has. I'm quite proud of him. Talking about hard work, do you know how the shorthand lessons are progressing? I always forget to ask."

Tancred smiled. "I believe very well, sir. I have seen him using shorthand in our lessons with few mistakes. Peter must be a good teacher."

"Has he managed to continue his own studies?"

"Yes, sir. He is teaching His Highness and helping me with a small matter also. Lord Ryson took a good look at the measures he could take with regards to the fees and, as Peter has shown he is truly trying to work to pay his way as well as support his family, there is a clause that has proved beneficial."

Adeone eyed the judge. For the first time in months, he suspected James was being evasive. "What is that then?"

Tancred said, uncomfortably, "One I had forgotten was added when we set up the scholarships. If a student is financially inconvenienced in his final two years, he can complete them paying only half the fees and then, when he has graduated and is working, he pays the remainder."

Adeone eyed him. "Uncle Lachlan added the clause on your advice, I presume."

Tancred sighed. "Yes, Your Majesty, and I had *forgotten* about it."

Adeone chuckled. "You can't remember everything, James. I'm pleased for Peter. It cannot have been easy for him. How long until his finals?"

"Just under three aluna-months, Sire. They are at the end of Geryal."

Adeone nodded. "He can have the whole of Geryal without teaching His Highness. He'll need the time to study."

Tancred looked surprised. "Thank you, Your Majesty, on his behalf, but being honest, and saying what he cannot, I am not sure his funds would stretch..."

Adeone smiled. "He is retained officially on the FitzAlcis staff. If we insist on him taking time off, he does not lose pay. Please make that clear to him."

"He is rather stubborn, sir."

Adeone enquired innocently, "How long has he known you, James?"

Tancred said simply, but with a hint of resignation, "Your Majesty."

"Let's have a drink and then tell me how your family are."

* * *

Two hours later, Tancred long gone, the door opened to admit Landis. Adeone raised one questioning eyebrow and Landis closed the door. His thoughtful air immediately filled Adeone with suspicion, but his first question was innocuous.

"Have Cal's parents visited him yet at Ceardlann?"

Adeone sighed. "No, and I gave them permission to a while ago now. He has been here more regularly though."

Landis nodded. "I know, but I still tend to think they should. He writes so often it's obvious that he'd like to see them. Whilst Ceardlann remains unknown to him, Master Galdwin's frustrations will be worse."

"I still doubt we did the right thing..." admitted Adeone.

"Cal's happy, he loves Ceardlann but he misses his parents. He's never asked to leave. So, he can't be as miserable as you believe in your moments of self-doubt," replied Landis. "I was going to invite the Galdwins to accompany me on Septadai. I thought I should see the terrors."

Adeone smiled. "Feel free. I might join you but you'll need a coach: Madam Galdwin is pregnant. Was that all?"

Landis frowned. "No. I'm not sure you're going to like the next. When I was at Amphi for my official visit, ReJean asked if the review could occur in the very first weeks of 1215. My initial reaction was there would be no possibility. I have the feeling he'll ask again."

Adeone frowned. "He can ask. It won't change my mind. Arkyn comes of age in the second week. He should be here. There's the Petitionals, Tain's cisan-age birthday and investiture as Justiciar of Oedran… What's ReJean playing at?"

Landis shrugged. "I don't think he's playing at anything. I believe he hadn't considered the Prince's age; however, after incredulity had waned, I began to think about it seriously and the other day Finian asked me if I'd mentioned it to Your Majesty. I realised I hadn't."

"What does young Lord Rale think?"

"I honestly don't know, Sire. There are advantages to humouring ReJean though. He's a snobbish weathervane. Loyal to the FitzAlcis, but can we be certain it's to Your Majesty? He holds the only hereditary post for an official in the empire, bar the Comptroller. He only has a daughter—"

"I've made him enough assurances about that."

"You have, Sire, but I do think that if you can come to terms with Arkyn's alunan-birthday being in Amphi, then there might be rewards to reap. The empire knows His Highness is dedicated to his duties—"

"Festus, I know what you're aiming towards, but you're asking me to send my son elsewhere to celebrate his coming of age without his family and nearfamily. How could I ever do that?"

Landis sighed. "That's what I thought you'd say. I tend to agree but I was trying to see it from ReJean's perspective. We could all travel there… It's only a couple of days."

"Which part of *no* don't you understand, Festus?"

"The part where you begin to alienate your most powerful Representative, Sire. Your feelings as a father I fully comprehend, but I think the King should make the decision."

Adeone's eyes flashed. "Thank you, Landis, that's all."

Landis left. He knew he'd seriously annoyed Adeone. Should he ever have mentioned the matter? Yes. ReJean would ask again, and, if he hadn't mentioned the original request, Adeone's reaction might well have done far more damage.

Chapter 44

GALDWINS

Septadai, Week 34 – 14th Bayal, 7th Bayis 1213
Oedran – Galdwin's Shop

Septadai dawned bright and clear. Lord Landis entered the Galdwin's shop to find Master Galdwin telling off his third son for playing a prank on his sisters.

Landis caught the eye of one of his nursery staff who would look after the Galdwin children. "Have fun. Do you want to escape now, Master Galdwin, whilst you can? Though I'm sure the scapegraces at Ceardlann are up to as much mischief."

Master Galdwin collected his wife before she became embroiled in the mayhem and they made their way out of the house.

Landis said, "There is another addition to our party. I ought to warn you, His Majesty is also coming."

Master Galdwin nodded. Leaving his house, he saw Adeone and bowed.

"We'll be quite a party arriving," observed Adeone. "The Comptroller has always appreciated unannounced visits."

Once they were all in the coach, Landis turned to his friend. Tongue in cheek, he asked, "Surely you warned him, sir?"

"The surprise does him good. Let's go. The sooner we're there, the sooner I'll find out what my second son has destroyed this time."

Listening, Master Galdwin was disconcerted by the King's obviously relaxed manner. Their last meeting had been a strange mixture of argument, compromise and understanding. The journey to Ceardlann provided more opportunity for surprise. Landis and Adeone talked, always including the Galdwins where they could. Once they entered the Rex Dallin, the Galdwins were intrigued to hear Landis drop all obvious formality.

On reaching Ceardlann, they alighted at the front of the house. Adeone steadying Madam Galdwin as she alighted.

Cal came hurtling around the corner of the house and stopped, stunned, before running to his parents. His mother gave him a hug and his father clipped him round the head lightly. Cal took note of the other two men. He bowed apologetically to Adeone, who laughed.

"Well, young Cal, I hesitate to ask where the terrors I call sons and my niece are."

"Prince Arkyn is with the Comptroller, sir, and Prince Tain is just tidying away our lessons. I'm not sure where Lady Elantha is."

"Fair enough. You've not seen me, not till I've seen them anyway."

"Very good, Sire. Can I show my parents Ceardlann?"

Adeone smiled. "I rather think you'd better. They ought to see where you're living. Master Galdwin, I hope you'll all join us for lunch? Oh, don't worry, formalities are few and far between here. If you need anything at all, do not hesitate to ask. Now, I must go and cheer the Comptroller up."

As he left, Landis eyed Cal. "Where did you say Tain was?"

"Clearing away our lessons, my lord."

"Yes, it was the last bit I couldn't quite believe. I thought you avoided them like the plague."

"Yes, but, like the plague, they find unwilling victims, my lord."

Landis laughed and left. He made his way to the Princes' sitting room, on the first-floor, and carefully walked up behind Tain.

"Your Highness, I hear you've actually been learning something. I came to see if you needed Chapa."

Tain whipped round. "Uncle Festus! What brings you here?"

"I thought it was about time I saw how you were. I've brought Cal's parents with me as well. They're being given a tour of Ceardlann."

"Does Arkyn know you're here?"

"I expect so. I was just worried when I heard the word 'lessons'. Are you sure you're feeling all right? I can ask the doc to visit. It wouldn't be any trouble."

Tain grinned. "I'm perfectly fine, now – especially as I've finished them. What's more, with you here, they can't give us any more. How long are you staying?"

"Only today." (Tain sagged.) "I'll begin to think you only want to see me to avoid your studies, and I thought you were finding them more bearable with the judge teaching you."

"Yes, but you know it wouldn't be true that I only want to see you to avoid lessons, that is. Have you seen father recently?"

"Yes. He's well."

Tain frowned. "Have there been any more attempts on his life?"

Landis frowned. "Not recently. So stop worrying."

"I can't. I just keep thinking one day I'll wake up and he won't be there. We'll be alone."

"You wouldn't be. I'd be here. Now, I completely forgot to tell the Comptroller I was coming today. Shall we go and see him?"

Tain nodded, accepting the obvious change of subject. "I'm sure he's found out you're here by now."

"I expect so, but it's only courteous to let him berate me."

They found the Comptroller in the Great Hall. As Tain entered, he spotted his father. Giving the briefest of bows, he ran across the room to be enveloped in a hug. When he was released, he rounded on Landis.

"You never said father had come as well!"

"Sorry, Tain, it must have slipped my mind," replied Landis, beaming.

* * *

Ceardlann wasn't what the Galdwins had expected. Its warm, smiling, homely atmosphere was at odds with their experience of the ostentatious aura of the Palace. The rooms seemed to be a sensible size, the ceilings reachable, if need be.

Knowing that Landis would be hunting out Tain, and the King would be with the Comptroller and Arkyn, Cal concentrated on other rooms first. The drawing room, snug and library. The maids in the snug smiled and left as soon as they entered. A few minutes later, Cal pointed out the door to the King's study and showed them the Cearcall Chamber with its treasures. Having heard Tain greeting Adeone, he took his parents up the stairs near the kitchen and showed them the sitting room. There was what could only be described as clutter with books strewn around, toys abandoned and drawings on every wall. Looking at them, Master Galdwin realised at least one of the FitzAlcis had a real talent. The contrast with his own house, where haste seemed to live in the walls, was discernible. He'd just relaxed into the atmosphere when the door opened and Adeone entered. All the Galdwins made an obeisance and waited.

Adeone smiled. "I hope Master Calumiel has made you feel at home. I was wondering if you'd care to join us for a walk after lunch. We're planning to go up towards the forest."

"Thank you, Sire. We should be pleased to, if you wish it."

Adeone sighed slightly. "Rules of my asking a question here: it is just that, it is a question. Only join us if you'd like to. I mean that. Here, I am without title to my guests; you count as guests."

Master Galdwin didn't know what to say. He found the King to be an enigma. He looked at his wife and son. "Well, thank you, sir, I think we'd be pleased to join you but maybe not all the way for my wife's sake. I'm not sure, however, that I can forget your title."

Adeone eyed him, amused and resigned. "No, not many people can. I hope you'll join us for lunch."

"Thank you, Sire, we'd be honoured to."

"Then I shall send someone to inform you when it's time." He winked at Cal and left.

Master Galdwin said, "I guess we're spending a day in the King's company then."

Cal grinned. "Not to mention Prince Arkyn's and Prince Tain's, Lady Elantha's, Lord Landis' and, in all probability, the Comptroller's. Don't worry, Pa, you'll get used to it."

Master Galdwin looked at his son. "I somehow doubt that, Calumiel, and you shouldn't either. It's not wise to get too close to them. Always be your own man."

"Lord Landis says that."

Perplexed, Master Galdwin fell silent. Someone so close to the King shouldn't be saying things like that, surely? And certainly not where anyone else could hear him. Then again, the King wasn't exactly behaving how he'd have expected. The appearance of informality unnerved him and Master Galdwin was convinced it *was* an appearance. Madam Galdwin wasn't so certain. The house didn't seem to lie to her and she couldn't imagine a master of it who would deceive. He might have to be devious whilst running the empire, but here she could well believe he was as he appeared to be. Holding less prejudice than her husband, she simply found her surroundings a pleasant change. Her son's ease in them had put her at ease. It was where he lived, and, if he was happy, she wasn't worried. He did seem to be happy as well. He wouldn't be able to hide his disquiet if it had been there. Ceardlann wasn't the palace they'd anticipated. They left the sitting room and were shown the night nursery, before Cal showed them his own bedchamber. Where at home he shared with his brother Crispin, here his room was his own and spacious. Clearly it wasn't a guest chamber. His personal items were strewn over a dressing table and by his bedside. A marble topped washstand held an ewer and bowl with a towel hung from one side and a cupboard below. A pair of his shoes were abandoned near a blanket box, his cloak thrown loosely across it. The fireplace was laid, and candles were half burnt down in their sconces. A book lay with a page marker on the bedside stand along with a carafe of water and glass. The bed was made, its blankets pulled straight, its pillows plumped up.

"Suppose someone does that for you," muttered Master Galdwin.

Cal chuckled. "No. I insist I do it myself. David asserts his rights by making up the fire."

His ma ran her hand over the coverlet. "It's a bit different from home."

"Different but never better, ma."

She looked happier as they left and made their way to the antechambers and Great Hall. That almost had Madam Galdwin rethinking. It was a splendid room, high ceilinged and stone flagged. One large window with curvilinear tracery was set in the wall behind the dais. The wooden panelling, though, gave it the same, almost homely, feel as the rest of the house. There were few ornaments on the walls but pleasant cabinets were placed against them.

Master Galdwin, looking round it, said, "Very nice. Some of those chairs need reupholstering though."

A voice from the other side of the room observed, "Maybe you could advise His Majesty on a durable fabric, Master Galdwin – some basic housekeeping will do him the world of good. How do you like the house?"

"It's very pleasant, my lord."

"Yes, it is, isn't it? I don't know anyone who hasn't appreciated its charm. Have you seen all over it or has Cal left out great swathes? Don't miss the chance of seeing the gardens."

"We didn't want to disturb the King and Princes."

"I wouldn't worry too much. They are used to disturbances. I know from experience that my younger nearson is exceptionally fond of them. It is said he takes after his father, but obviously I can't comment on that. Have you been introduced to the Comptroller yet?"

"Not yet, my lord."

"We'll have to do something about that…"

Entering, Arkyn smiled at Cal and the Galdwins but turned to Landis. "Father asks if you're causing trouble again, Uncle Festus?"

"I can't imagine where he gets his ideas from."

"Past experience? I shall tell him you are entertaining our guests, though what consolation that will be to him I don't know…"

"Sometimes, Arkyn, you prove that you are your father's son. I deny all responsibility."

Arkyn grinned. "I shall leave you entertaining, or being entertaining. It's a pity that the two things should be mutually exclusive."

Landis muttered, "On the other hand, your sense of humour *might* have something to do with me."

Winking at Cal, Arkyn welcomed Master and Madam Galdwin to Ceardlann and left. Shortly afterwards, Landis excused himself and Master Galdwin sighed in relief; the day was certainly turning out to be eventful, in an odd way.

* * *

Halfway through lunch, perfectly timed, Tain enquired if he and Cal could have a joint fourteenth birthday celebration.

Adeone said, "I think you should ask Master Galdwin that."

The cloth merchant found himself saying, "If the King doesn't object, it's fine by me, Your Highness."

Tain turned back to his father, who sighed. "All right, Tain, I'll say yes; I must be mad. Where have you planned this for? If I dare ask."

Tain grinned. "Here, father. The Galdwins have permission, as do my nearcousins…"

"What if Cal wants to invite guests who do not?"

Tain sagged, then grinned. "Where would you suggest, father?"

"Let me have a think. You and Cal will have to organise what you want and who you'd like to be there. I'm not doing all the work for you."

Tain and Cal grinned at each other before Tain said, "Thank you, sir, and thank you, Master Galdwin, for agreeing."

Looking at the boys' glowing faces, Master Galdwin lost some of his inhibitions. "That's all right, Your Highness, I'm pleased I could help."

At the end of the meal, Arkyn said, "Will you excuse me, father? I've a few letters I must answer."

As Arkyn left, Cal looked at his father, who simply nodded, and then Cal, Tain and Elantha ran off.

"If you don't mind, Adeone, I'd like a word with the resident guard captain," admitted Landis.

"Don't work too hard."

Landis laughed. "Who said anything about *work*?"

Master Galdwin realised he and his wife were alone with the King. Almost as though it had been planned. Adeone turned shrewd eyes on him.

"I hope you approve of where your son is living. If there is anything you think he needs, let me know. All will be done to accommodate it."

"Thank you, Sire. I appreciate the thought."

"If need be, act on it as well. Cal seems content with his life here, but I need to know you are also happy with it."

Madam Galdwin smiled. "I think we are, sir. It's different from our life and the rest of our children's, but he's happy. Maybe, when everything is considered, that's what matters. We're pleased he's content and thankful Ceardlann and the Rex Dallin are beautiful places. I can see how it might be easy to lose your heart to them."

Adeone smiled. "You're right, Madam Galdwin. Our children's happiness is important. It is the most important thing. Ira knew that. I cannot deny that I've lost my heart to this valley and house. I never feel quite right in Oedran. If home is where the heart is then I am, I think, exceptionally lucky. I can't deny it. It's nice to escape here."

"I expect it must be, sir. When you're used to bustle, a bit of peace and quiet can go a long way to calm your soul."

"Yes, you've put into words what I've felt for years. The peace is insidious here. Even with the children around, it envelops you."

"I must admit, Sire, I feel fully refreshed after this morning."

"Then you must come more often, Madam Galdwin. In fact, if you and Master Galdwin wish, you may come here and stay overnight. I can imagine that time alone must be difficult to obtain. I find it hard enough in Oedran and I can simply tell my manservant and administrator I'm not to be disturbed."

Her husband broke into the conversation. "But we could never impose, sir."

"Nonsense. It would be no imposition," replied Adeone. "Come for a weekend, when my errant sons are elsewhere if it makes you feel more at ease. No-one in Oedran need know, but a break does everyone good."

"Who'd mind the shop, sir? That's the thing, you see."

"Cal and his tutor? I'll happily give him permission to trade on your behalf. My seal on the letter will mean the yeomen won't argue if they're informed."

Master Galdwin laughed. "That they wouldn't, sir."

"What's more, it'll be good practice for Master Calumiel… There's one other thing, next year Prince Tain will be in Oedran more often. There is one thing I would ask and that is that you allow Cal to visit my sons at the Palace, if he wants to. I think after all these years their friendship will not wane and Cal will need to get used to the officialdom of Oedran."

Master Galdwin said, "You know my feelings about the Palace, Sire."

Adeone eyed him. "I do, Master Galdwin. If I were in your position, I might share them, but it is Cal's position we must think about. He is an exceptional boy who does you proud, and I'm not just saying that."

"If he wants to visit Their Highnesses, he'll find a way, whatever we all say," observed Madam Galdwin.

Adeone chuckled. "That is far too true. Maybe we should leave the decisions up to them."

"Aye, maybe we should," admitted Master Galdwin.

Chapter 45
A DIFFERENT PERSPECTIVE
Hexadai, Week 35 – 20th Bayal, 13th Bayis 1213
Prince Tain's Chambers

TAIN VISITED OEDRAN for three days the following week for shorthand lessons. The hours spent with Peter were anything but regular and the haphazard nature suited Tain's temperament perfectly. He was still getting used to the fact he had his own rooms and a manservant. Having observed his brother and Kadeem, Tain was fascinated by how much Linnt left him to do himself. He didn't particularly mind, but there were days when he was in a rush and Linnt seemed not to notice.

The second day, Tain returned to his rooms after a ride. He was late and needed to change. Nodding to Peter, he hurried past aiming for his dressing room. He expected Linnt would have laid everything out ready. He hadn't. Tain cursed as he found a new tunic and freshened up.

He returned to the sitting room. "Sorry, Peter, I was a bit longer than I intended to be."

Peter smiled. "It's of no matter, Your Highness."

"Did Linnt offer you refreshment?"

Peter hesitated. "Not exactly, sir."

Tain rang the bell. After Linnt had been despatched in the hunt for drinks, the Prince glanced at the timepiece.

"We're not going to get much done."

Peter said, "We can always skip the lesson, sir."

"Do you have things you'd rather be doing?"

"Not exactly. My essay can easily wait."

Tain grinned. "What's it on?"

As Peter explained, Tain crossed to a large box and rifled through his scrolls and books. "This might help."

Peter took the scroll with interest. "Thank you, sir."

"How were you going to answer the question? Thank you, Linnt, that's all for now."

Peter grinned. "I was going to point out that the court isn't there to question the evidence merely to act on it."

Tain settled into his favourite chair. "Isn't it? Surely if someone presents evidence that is suspect, it is our duty to question it. A defendant could be convicted on dubious evidence when he's innocent as well as when he's guilty."

"But the yeomen would make sure the evidence presented is verified."

Tain sighed. "It rather depends if they've jumped to any conclusions as to a person's guilt, doesn't it? I'm not saying that they habitually frame people, but it is surely a possibility and, as a possibility, it has to be considered when answering the question on whether evidence in court is questionable."

Peter tilted his head slightly. "Do you think it's a trick question?"

"I would be surprised if it wasn't. You're in your final year. There's more to every question than initially appears. Or so I'm finding. When you graduate, do you want to work as a defence or prosecution lawyer?"

Peter hesitated. "I don't know, sir. I get nervous in court, even if it's a mock one. I had wondered about teaching, or working in the law library... It's not exactly working as a lawyer but..."

"It still has its place. The judge was explaining to me how not all lawyers appear in court. If you don't do what you're comfortable with, you'll never feel like you're good at your job. I know that one all too well."

Peter said carefully, "Are you worried about being Justiciar, sir?"

Tain looked at him. "Not as much as I was, and please be careful what you ask me. It could be dangerous for both of us. How is your family?"

"Coping, I think. My sisters aren't saying much, my brother is varying between playing up and being quiet and my ma's feeling the strain of not having pa around, but I'm doing what I can. My uncles visit and help with anything they can."

Tain smiled sadly, and whispered, "If only all uncles would." More loudly, he said, "Your brother should calm down; if he's young, he won't know how to cope – speaking from experience..."

Peter nodded but wisely didn't comment. He changed the subject. "More than likely, sir, especially as the judge keeps coming to see if we need anything. The support he gives everyone is extraordinary."

"It is. We've both been fortunate in being taken under his wing."

* * *

The following day, Tain and Cal were sitting chatting after a ride. Well refreshed and feeling free, they were startled by the door opening.

Tain hurriedly got to his feet. "Aunt Amara..."

"Hmm, you're growing too much, young Tailan. You do know that?"

Tain grinned. "Yes, but I plan to be taller than Arkyn, so I have to."

"Sibling rivalry, nothing like it. How do you like your chambers?"

"Very much, aunt. I think I've the best in the wing."

Amara sniffed. "Lachy would have agreed with you. Who's this?"

"Sorry. Might I introduce Calumiel Galdwin to you, Lady Amara?"

"I'm pleased to meet you at last, young Calumiel. Now, Tain, do you have a drink for an elderly aunt?"

Tain beamed. "I'm not sure I see an elderly aunt – but I'm sure I can find you a drink."

"Oh, you're trying to be a courtier; don't bother, it doesn't suit you and I don't appreciate it. What's that? What do I want to drink? Hmm. Have you any sweet berry wine?"

Tain chewed his lip. "Alcis only knows. I'll ask Linnt."

Two minutes later, Lady Amara sipped at the wine and looked Tain in the eye. "So, how long does it take a great-nephew to visit his great-aunt?"

Tain grinned. "Obviously longer than it takes for a great-aunt to visit her great-nephew. I rather had the impression, aunt, that you were out carousing every night."

Amara turned to Cal. "Who's responsible for that sense of humour?"

Feeling rather surreal, Cal said, "For once, I don't think I am, my lady."

229

She laughed. "Neatly escaped, young Cal; you'll go far. The problem is, I need to know who to blame for my great-nephew's sense of humour."

Tain grinned. "How about Uncle Festus, or father, or even Laioril."

"Or all three rolled into one with a touch of my late brother to boot. You might not remember Lachlan but you can't have escaped his influence."

"I do just remember him, aunt."

"I'm pleased. I remember watching you run around this room with him chasing you…"

Tain paused. "I don't remember that."

"You were only just walking, or rather running; you kept Lachy on his toes. I rather hope you're planning to continue in that vein as Justiciar."

"As he greeted our ancestors a few years ago, I don't think I'll be able to keep Uncle Lachlan on his toes…"

Amara eyed him. "You know what I mean, young Tain. Don't get clever with me; you'll lose. How's James Tancred?"

"Very well, aunt. Maybe he'd like to see you?"

She laughed. "Not likely. Give him my regards when you see him and tell him he ought to remember you're Lachlan's great-nephew."

"Aunt, I'm not sure he's forgetting that," replied Tain tiredly.

"I bet he isn't but he'll get the message. Now, youngster, you don't need me around if you're trying to catch up with young Cal here, who's remarkably silent… Elantha tells me she can never get a word in."

Tain grinned. "Maybe she doesn't try as hard as you do, aunt."

She eyed him. "That, young Tain, was cheeky. Young Cal, one thing, be careful coming and going from here. I wouldn't like to hear you've come to any harm."

When she'd gone, Tain let out a sigh of relief. "So, you've met Lady Amara and survived the experience…"

A voice from the doorway said, "I heard that, young Tain."

Both boys jumped.

Tain looked round. "Sorry, aunt."

"I doubt it but I'll accept it."

They waited for six minutes before Tain checked the antechamber. Amara winked and finally left.

* * *

Once they were definitely alone, Tain and Cal grinned at each other.

"I'd heard Lady Amara was a character, Your Highness."

"Can't think who told you that… Come on, let's raid the kitchens."

Halfway there, Cal said, "I keep thinking about the Viewing Gallery in the King's Hall, sir…"

"What about it?"

"Well, last year you mentioned the entrance has been lost for centuries. How do you lose an entrance? Was it bricked up?"

"I suppose it could have been. Father thinks there's a secret lever somewhere on the second-floor corridors as that's the level the Viewing Gallery is at."

Cal looked round. "Why don't we find it?"

"It's never been found yet."

"Isn't that part of the fun, sir?" asked Cal with a conspiratorial smile.

Tain grinned. "All right. We'll have a look. It would have to be on this side of the King's Hall because the Viewing Gallery is this side."

Cal shrugged. "If the Cearcall built or used it; will it be that simple?"

"I wonder if there're any old plans of the Palace. I'll ask His Majesty."

* * *

Adeone wasn't surprised to be disturbed by his younger son or by the reason. "I only know of plans of the current Palace. No-one's ever mentioned any others to me. I said I'd get a set drawn up before, and I've forgotten. Ask Richardson to see to it on your way out – that way it'll get done. Do you have a lesson with Peter later?"

Tain hesitated. "Yes, sir, there wasn't one planned, but I was rather late to mine yesterday, so he's coming today."

Adeone eyed his son. "I hesitate to ask why you were late."

Tain grinned. "I went for a ride and got back a few minutes late. By the time I'd found a different tunic and got cleaned up, I really was late but Peter didn't mind and we talked through an essay he's got to do instead."

Adeone chuckled. "I thought *he* was teaching *you*."

"It just happened, sir."

Adeone looked at Cal. "Why do I always hear that?"

"Because it's the best answer, Sire?" offered Cal.

"Probably. Go on with you both…"

They grinned and left, leaving Adeone mulling over what Tain had inadvertently revealed.

He called Dragoris and obtained a link with Arkyn. "Have you dined in Tain's chambers yet?"

"No, father. He always dines here. Why?"

Adeone said distractedly, "I'd be interested in your opinion…"

Arkyn eyed him thoughtfully. "Would you prefer Kadeem's, Sire?"

Adeone laughed. "Is it that obvious?"

"Not particularly. What happened this time?" On hearing his father's explanation, Arkyn said, "Tain is good at being late, father."

Adeone sighed. "I know."

"Tain will sort it out. How long have they actually had together? The time's been fragmented and memory is fallible. Let me talk to Kadeem and he can nudge Linnt in the right direction. He, that is Linnt, might be complacent because he doesn't often see Tain."

"I suppose that's all true. Maybe I just worry about you both too much."

Arkyn smiled. "Most of the time I prefer that to being ignored. Tain's got a way with people; I'm sure everything will be fine."

"He has. Thank you, you're probably right."

Adeone nodded at Dragoris to close the link, happier in his mind.

Chapter 46

CORRESPONDENCE AND DREAMS

Hexadai, Week 36 – 27th Bayal, 20th Bayis 1213
Inner Office

SETTLING INTO HIS DAY, with personal correspondence before business, Adeone felt content. Richardson had handed him letters from his cousins and Wealsman, before placing the letters from the Sagamore, Satrap, Visir, Exarch and ReJean to one side. They more likely held official business. Breaking the seal on Wealsman's letter, Adeone mentioned he'd need to see Wynfeld later before dismissing Richardson. Indulgence, for once, could come first.

Wealsman's letter was full of family news and one bit of it made Adeone smile broadly: Kristina was pregnant again. There was also news on their daughter Adeona, who had passed her first birthday a season before. Wealsman mentioned that he'd written to Arkyn also and that made Adeone smile more broadly. He was pleased his confidant and son considered each other close friends and they must, for Wealsman had asked Arkyn to be Adeona's nearfather. At the end of the letter was the snippet of information that he thought Lord Penrod Silvano and Lady Chandra Teran would end up marrying.

Rhian's and Neassa's letters were full of their news and talk about Tradere. They were happily ensconced on the Fairson estates and not looking to leave anytime soon. The children at the orphanage were thriving, pleasing everyone involved. Although Adeone was happy his cousins were content, he wished them in Oedran.

The letters from the Sagamore, Visir and Satrap were correspondence from governors to a king. They outlined official matters. The Exarch, who was a distant cousin, provided some family news as well, and Adeone smiled as he read it. Tyler Galwood's grandmother, Princess Lilith, seemed to be as indomitable and indefatigable as her cousin, Lady Amara.

The murmurings about her having taken Fachin's oath had made courtiers more wary of her than they had been in years. They'd realised once again that the FitzAlcis family reached into the heart of their country.

Governor ReJean, however, had written to suggest that the Arealian Review of 1215 should take place in the first weeks of the year. Adeone tossed the letter onto his desk in frustration. Why was ReJean even contemplating it? He considered contacting him by messenger to explain exactly why it wouldn't be happening but decided Landis had probably been right and a simple 'no' would alienate ReJean. Someone would have to talk to ReJean and make him see how ridiculous his suggestion was.

* * *

Two hours later, Richardson announced Wynfeld with little fuss. The Major saluted on entering the office, and registered frustration in his King's normally unruffled demeanour.

Adeone glanced up. "Major, come and sit down. If you'll excuse me momentarily, I'll just finish this." Adeone signed the parchment he was perusing and affixed his seal. Putting the document aside, he asked, "How's the elite regiment?"

"Ready to leave, Your Majesty. I thought I'd send them to the Gardian Ridge for a bit. They can make sure it really is free of bandits this time."

Adeone smiled. "It might be an idea. You're happy with the captain?"

Wynfeld said, "I'm happy he knows his job, sir. I served under him just before you promoted me."

"Is there a difference?"

"I think there's the potential to be, yes, Sire."

Adeone smiled. "Isn't there in everything? What have you heard of my brother recently?"

Wynfeld hesitated. "Very little, Your Majesty. It is known that some of the Lords of Oedran have visited him at Black Hills, but then that's nothing particularly unusual. Following His Lordship's Law Review for Anapara from Paras, there was the expectation a mini review would follow in Oedran, as is normal practice, but I cannot find any evidence that His Lordship is planning to undertake one. He set nothing in motion for one when he visited in winter. I suspect he will ask for travel leave for Gerymor for next year to undertake the law review there early in the year. Other than that, His Lordship seems to be keeping to Black Hills."

Adeone nodded. "Are you concerned?"

"I am beginning to be, sir. His Lordship was exceptionally active earlier this year. The attacks on His Highness, Lord Faran and Lord Camlyn were well co-ordinated. I am wondering if he is getting short of funds, but as his funds aren't stored in the treasury here, it's difficult to be certain."

233

"You still don't have anyone in Black Hills, do you?"

Wynfeld weighed up his answer. "No, sir. Five have not lived to return. There is something strange there. Almost as though His Lordship knows – just by looking at someone – that they're loyal to Your Majesty."

"It's not because he knows exactly who works for you?"

"I suppose it could be, but then there's someone very careless in my ranks and when I checked everyone after the bandit attack, nothing was discovered."

"Try a complete unknown, Wynfeld, someone to whom no links can be made."

Wynfeld said, "We've tried three so far and every one has been delivered back to us in a coffin, Your Majesty."

Adeone grimaced. "You've lost eight men?"

"Yes, Sire. I have been trying for some time."

The King sighed. "I'm sorry …"

Wynfeld said softly, "We could just raid the house, sir?"

"No! That would cause more repercussions than you can imagine, or I can imagine. I will not force this empire into civil war. What about getting someone close by Black Hills? There's a village, isn't there?"

"I've lost three men there as well, Your Majesty. The closest I can get is about ten miles away. Nowhere near close enough, I do realise and I keep trying."

Adeone said, "Thank you but do not lose all your best agents."

"If we get the evidence, sir, some sacrifices may well be worth it, but I shall be careful of my men's lives."

"Thank you. Has he targeted you again recently?"

Wynfeld shrugged. "I'm sure he has, sir, but I'm still here."

Adeone eyed him. "When? And don't procrastinate."

"A few weeks ago, sir. He is also losing his good men."

"Be careful. How about Landis?"

"Lord Landis is protected by the heavens, sir; he must be to have survived so long."

Adeone chuckled. "He also has good men looking out for him."

Wynfeld smiled back. "Apparently so, Your Majesty."

* * *

That night Adeone fell into a restless sleep. He tossed and turned, seeing men falling all around him, his friends and companions. He didn't recall all their faces but several stuck in his mind when he awoke and he knew the reason they'd been there was because he'd read their letters or spoken to them, but he couldn't remember how they'd fallen, for each had been different. He'd woken in a sweat, shaking and, as he rubbed his face to clear sleep, he felt the trace of tears. Entering his bathroom, he splashed water on his face and froze. In the mirror was the reflection of his late wife. He turned to face her.

She smiled gravely. "Someone's missing, Adeone, someone who should be here."

"Which here and who?"

She said softly, "Follow your heart, my dear. You have one, but maybe you've forgotten how to recognise it…"

"Ira?"

She reached to lay her hands on his hot head and the next thing he knew was Simkins waking him in the morning. He had no memory of how he'd got back to bed. Had it *all* been a dream?

Chapter 47
FUTURE ARRIVALS
Septadai, Week 41 – 7th Geryal, 14th Souis 1213
Rex Dallin

WHEN THE WARM DAYS of spring brought scents of blossom wafting along the lanes, Adeone rode for Ceardlann, glad to be outside in the warmer weather, glad to be out of his office. Feeling free, he urged Pursuit into a gallop and sped from Oedran to the Pillars of Alcis, marking the northern entry into the Rex Dallin. He glanced behind him and grinned as Hillbeck caught up.

"You're all getting slow."

"I'll make sure Lord Landis doesn't find out, Sire."

Adeone laughed. "Come on. Once you've seen me safely to Ceardlann, you can have the rest of the day to yourself. I'm glad you're on duty."

Hillbeck smiled as they splashed across the ford. "So am I, Sire. There's nothing quite like being home."

Adeone settled back to complete the journey at a gentle pace. "The valley welcomes us with smiles."

"As we do it, sir. I wish my nephew was here."

"How is he?"

"Fine, sir. He's moved to the couriers. I don't know if he'll want to return to the farm. He enjoys life in Oedran."

"Well, it's up to him," said Adeone. "The current tenant knows the situation. Caswal doesn't have to choose until he's ready to. I'm not expecting his decision for a while. Even if he does give it up completely there'll be a cottage for you all somewhere and, if there isn't, we'll build one. Does he come and visit Susan often?"

"Often enough, sir. He misses his mother occasionally, though he'll never say it."

Adeone nodded in understanding. "I think Susan misses him as well, but it was the best decision at the time."

"They know that, sir. I think they were glad you made it for them. They couldn't have managed the farm without my brother. I think they were touched that you'd noticed."

"Arkyn informed me, and I wanted to do what I could. Susan helped me when I was a child more than I can ever explain. Is that the Wanda ahead?"

Hillbeck squinted. "It certainly looks like them, sir."

Adeone groaned theatrically. "I'll warn the kitchens."

Hillbeck laughed. "I'm sure they'll appreciate it, sir."

Twelve minutes later, they reached Ceardlann and Hillbeck was off his horse and holding Pursuit before Adeone could blink.

"Thank you, Hillbeck. I meant it about your time off. I won't tell Landis you fell behind if you don't tell my other sergeants you get to put your feet up."

Hillbeck smiled. "Thank you, Sire. That sounds more than fair."

* * *

Adeone entered Ceardlann and made his way to the Comptroller's Office. "Comptroller, how are you?"

"Very well, Sire, thank you. How long are you staying for? Just so I can warn Cook…"

Adeone grinned like a mischievous boy. "This afternoon, but Cook might like to know that the Wanda have been sighted in the valley."

"I'll let him know, Sire. The Princes, Cal and Lady Elantha are out for a ride."

"Then I shall take a gentle amble to Encampment Field and see Laioril. I shouldn't be long, but I do need a word with the old rogue."

The Comptroller smiled. "Right you are, Sire. Shall I warn the Princes that you're here?"

"Not if they haven't spotted Pursuit."

* * *

Making his way across the King's Meadow, Adeone crossed the bridge over the trout stream. Leaning on a tree, he smiled at the sight of the Wanda setting up camp. The forming circle of carts and tents hid him from view. He turned back to the trout stream and half an hour later entered Encampment Field whistling.

Sayre noticed him.

"Sire, come to give us a hand?"

"Why not? There's four trout for the Chief here. What can I do?"

Sayre laughed. "I was joking, Your Majesty."

"I wasn't. I'll find the Chief, don't worry."

Two minutes later, Laioril said, "Come to cause trouble, lad?"

"Unlike Sayre, I don't think you're joking."

Laioril sighed. "What did *he* say?"

"Asked me if I was here to give a hand. I replied that I would and what could I do? He recovered very well," remarked Adeone. "Four trout for you, Chief."

"Cheers, lad. It'll save 'em a fishing trip. Just caught?"

"Of course. I have my uses. What can I do?"

Laioril's eyes twinkled. "Stay out of trouble?"

"Never managed that one yet. There must be something."

Laioril's sharp gaze swept over his guest. "Sorry, lad, but we're nearly done. Be quicker next time. What can I do for *you*? You normally wait for a day before you disturb us."

Two minutes later, they ambled towards the forest and finding a dry stone sat companionably. Quietly, Adeone explained about the blackness of his dream and the incident on the Ratharia.

Laioril caught his eye. "I've known some of your dreams have been seeing what is for some time, lad."

"This was more of a premonition than 'what is' though."

"Yes. I've said before, times are changing and magic is getting stronger. *Dunna* fight it, lad."

"Is 'dunna' a word to use to kings, Chief?"

"Never stopped me yet. Look, lad, I can't stop you being worried. You need to realise that the future's coming. Magic's here and the future can't be stopped. Live it instead."

"I sometimes wonder if I'll get the chance," whispered Adeone, staring over the valley.

"The future is not some distant point; it encompasses all time in front of us. Embrace it before the idea that it will run out consumes everything good about you."

Adeone's gaze never wavered. "I'm not sure it hasn't already."

Laioril snorted softly. "Then you don't know the wind from the rain. It's no more consumed what you are than the sun has swallowed the moons."

Adeone got up and offered a hand to the Chief. "Thank you. You always set my head straight."

Laioril hoisted himself to his feet. "I don't, lad; you just forget how to recognise a straight line. How are the terrors?"

Adeone laughed. "The same as ever. What drew you here?"

"We're short of a few things, and your gamekeeper can be obligingly blind. Now, if the camp's as it should be, will you stop for a drink?"

"I'd love to, Chief, but I ought to get back to Ceardlann and see if the children have returned; they don't know I'm here."

Laioril's bright eyes shone. "Probably best then."

* * *

On reaching Ceardlann, Adeone barely made it inside when Tain sped along the passage. Adeone grinned and gave him a hug.

"Where's your brother?"

"Getting too old to run, apparently. Father, Cal's worried about something and won't say what."

Adeone frowned. It was revealing that Tain had mentioned it so soon into their conversation.

Two hours later, Adeone and Cal found themselves alone. Adeone said quietly, "What's the matter, young Cal?"

Cal swallowed. "It's nothing, Sire. I'm just being stupid. I've worried His Highness, haven't I?"

"Yes, but it might not be stupidity. Would you like to tell me?"

Cal curled into a chair. "Mother's close to her time, sir. She's tired. She's not said as much, but her writing gives it away. I wish there was something I could do…"

"Would you like to go home for a bit? Until everything is settled."

Cal swallowed. "Yes, but I know I'd be in the way. We used to be packed off to our aunts and uncles until Tabitha was born – but by then I was old enough to know what was happening and to keep my siblings entertained."

Adeone nodded. "Maybe you could be of help then?"

"No, Hal and Louisa will be coping… I think, anyway."

"Shall I check?"

Cal shook his head. "No, Sire, thank you. If mother knows I'm worrying, she'll worry about me and it isn't good for her this close."

Adeone laughed. "You're very practical about this."

"I've five siblings, Sire. You get used to it."

"I can only imagine that you do. I only got used to it much later in life with my own children's births and my nearchildren's come to that." Seeing Cal withdraw into himself, Adeone made the decision. "I'm taking you home later today and that's that. Just so you can reassure

238

yourself that everything is all right. Stay for a couple of nights or however long you want."

Cal looked at him, tears pricking at the corners of his eyes. "Thank you, sir. I just feel a fool."

"Don't..." said Adeone, wrapping the lad in a tight hug.

Chapter 48
WHO'S WHO
Cisadai, Week 42 – 9th Geryal, 16th Souis 1213
Oedran

Two DAYS LATER, a palace courier entered Galdwin's shop with a letter from Adeone to check if everything was well. Reading it, Cal hesitated. He couldn't tell the King the truth. He replied that things were progressing.

As the courier entered the Inner Office with the reply, Adeone crooked an eyebrow. "Thank you, young Hillbeck. Was he all right?"

Sergeant Hillbeck's nephew paused. "*He* was, Sire, but I'm not sure Madam Galdwin is. There were a couple of midwives there and I'm sure I spotted a doctor. Not that it's any of my business..."

"What else?"

"Master Galdwin seemed short-tempered, as though he was worried and trying not to show it."

"Thank you." Adeone waited until the lad had gone before calling Dragoris and obtaining a link with Chapa. "Just drop in on the Galdwins for me, Chapa, and tell me the true state of play. Madam Galdwin's expecting imminently."

Chapa hesitated. "Very well, Sire. Are there any complications?"

"I don't *know*, but I suspect there are. If you think they would be better without the rest of their brood tripping them up, let me know and they can stay at Ceardlann for a few days."

Three quarters of an hour later, Adeone and Chapa were once again talking over a messenger link.

"She's expecting twins, Sire, and the first is breach. It's not good. Master Galdwin is terrified he's going to lose her and the babes. He's agreed to the children going to Ceardlann if it makes life easier for myself and the doctor here. Though young Haltern refuses to go. Cal's persuaded the others that it would be better but Haltern pointed out that they may need someone to run messages. I think he'd be really uncomfortable at Ceardlann."

"Right. Expect my coach shortly and, Chapa, do your best."

"I had planned to, sir," replied the doctor. "I'll let you know the news, but I think it could be a long one."

When the link broke, Adeone called for Richardson.

* * *

More quickly than either Chapa or Cal expected, the coach drew up outside the Galdwins. The children bade their father goodbye and swung into the coach.

They were subdued as the coach made its ponderous way out of the city.

"Why are the yeomen moving people aside?" enquired Crispin peering out the window.

"It's the King's coach, Cris. It happens," replied Cal. "They've not realised His Majesty isn't in it, and I don't think the driver's going to tell them. It makes his life easier."

Louisa squeezed his hand. He caught her eye and nodded. Neither of them wanted to talk.

The coach picked up the pace once outside Oedran and over the river. Cal opened the window and let scents of spring in. He wanted the cold nip, but his sisters didn't. A mile later, he closed it again and simply watched the familiar landscape go by. They passed through Cilford and he gazed blankly at the scene. In passing through Dellwood, though, he raised his hand in acknowledgement of a wave.

Cris said, "Who's that?"

"That's Fitz. A former captain. He used to be in charge of the guards at Ceardlann, then he travelled to Terasia with Prince Arkyn before retiring. He's a good sort. Prince Tain has lessons at his inn with Judge Tancred."

"That's weird."

"Not when you understand the reasons, but I can't remember them."

A few minutes later Louisa said, "We're slowing. Are we there?"

Cal shook his head. "No, there'll be a change of driver waiting. Not all the King's household can enter the Rex Dallin."

Crispin asked, "Why can we then?"

Cal sighed. "Because I live there and His Majesty has granted you permission, but you can't mention it to anyone. It'll put you in danger."

There was such a grave note in his voice that Crispin didn't ask why. The coach lurched forward and splashed into the river.

Once they'd made the slight rise on the other side, Cal said less despondently, "Welcome to the Rex Dallin. It's not far to Ceardlann."

* * *

A short time later, the coach drew to a halt and David opened the door.

Cal scrambled out, "Thank you."

"Are you all right, Master Calumiel?"

Cal swallowed and nodded before helping his four siblings out of the coach. Louisa took her sisters' hands and Crispin simply looked around in interest. Cal glanced up at the driver and was surprised,

"Thank you, Alfred, that's all of us."

Alfred grinned. "Are you sure there's no more hiding under the seats?"

"Positive, thanks."

The chief groom nodded and moved the coach off. Cal turned back to the house. "Come in. Welcome to Ceardlann…"

They'd barely taken a step when Tain's laughing voice said, "I thought that would be my line, Cal."

Cal gave a slight bow. "Had Your Highness been here, I'm sure it would have been."

Tain grinned. "Good point. Come on in. The Comptroller's around somewhere I'll introduce you… but we've refreshments waiting in the Great Hall and there's still some cake…"

Cal said, "I'm surprised, sir. How long has it been there?"

"Er, since you were sighted but that's not the point."

Crispin laughed.

Cal looked at him and his sisters. "Come on, we'll feel better if we eat."

They were merrily tucking into cake and juice when the Comptroller, seemingly absentmindedly, entered the hall.

"Ah, here you are, sir. Cook wants to know what time you would all like dinner? I'd ask Prince Arkyn but I can't find him either."

Tain grinned. "He's gone to see Laioril. Is seven all right, Comptroller?"

"It sounds admirable for you, sir, but what of our younger guests?"

"Half seven then, with a tea at five."

"Very good, sir." He glanced over the Galdwin siblings, all of whom were looking tired or worried. "Welcome to Ceardlann. I hope, although you're obviously concerned, you can feel like you can relax. Ask someone if you want or need anything. Might I enquire who is who?"

Cal smiled and introduced them in order of age: Louisa, ten, Crispin, eight, Tabitha, five, and Elsie, three.

The Comptroller smiled. "Thank you. Master Crispin, you'll be sharing your brother's room so the ladies may all share the nursery. Mistress Louisa, I hope that's all right. Lady Elantha will be there, but you're the same age so I hope you won't feel too uncomfortable."

Louisa shook her head, surprised that he'd even considered it. "I'll be fine, sir, thank you, and my sisters should be as well."

The Comptroller merely nodded. "Your Highness, maybe when you've finished you could introduce everyone to Maria? I need to find Cook."

"Of course, Comptroller. Anything to prolong the time until I have to pick up my lessons again."

"His Majesty mentioned that lessons are temporarily cancelled and if our guests are still here on Imperadai, he'll explain to the judge and your lessons with him will be rescheduled, sir." The Comptroller left with a short bow and a smile.

Tain jumped up when he'd gone. "Come on, I'll introduce you to people. Maria mainly."

Maria smiled at the Galdwins. The youngest two were exhausted. She knelt by them. "Do you want a nap? It's been a long day."

They glanced at Louisa, who said, reassuringly, "You can say yes."

Elsie simply nodded and Maria picked her up confidently. She then slipped her hand around Tabitha's.

"Come on. If there's one thing to be said for Ceardlann, it's comfortable beds. Your sister won't be far. Just next door, in fact. Shall we find where she'll be first?"

Six minutes later, Tain, Cal, Crispin and Louisa were in the Princes' sitting room alone. Crispin glanced around in interest. Louisa went to look at the drawings and paintings.

"Who did these, Cal?"

Cal smiled. "Lady Elantha. Where is she, Your Highness?"

"I guess she went with Arkyn. I was about to see Spellen when father let us know you were on your way, but Arkyn had already left and I guess El went as well as I've not seen her since."

* * *

Twelve minutes later, footsteps echoed in the corridor outside the room. The door opened and Arkyn and Elantha entered.

Arkyn smiled. "Cal, you're back! Good. He's been a misery. What, Tain? Well, you have. Oh, I beg your pardon…"

Tain grinned. "Have you met Crispin and Louisa Galdwin yet, Arkyn? Elsie and Tabitha are currently tucked up in the nursery."

"Not properly. Welcome to Ceardlann…"

Elantha had walked over to her usual table and put her sketching set down. She gazed around uncertainly.

Louisa said, "I've been looking at your paintings, my lady. I wish I could draw so well."

Elantha hesitated. "I don't think they're any good. Everyone keeps telling me that they are but there's only a couple I like… I've just been trying to draw the Chief again but he kept moving too much. I ought to find my governess. I said I would when I got back."

"She can wait, El. It won't harm her," observed Arkyn.

"I should really, Arkyn. I said I would. I'll explain we've guests."

"She'll probably give you a lesson on being a hostess. I'd just say that father has cancelled lessons, if I were you. As Tain's here, and not closeted with Spellen, I guess his have been."

Elantha nodded. "What if Uncle Adeone hasn't?"

Arkyn sighed. "I'll come with you…"

"May I also?" asked Louisa. "I'd like to see more of the house."

"Of course you can. She might believe us then."

Cal said, "Nice to know my sister has her uses, Your Highness."

"Unlike her eldest brother…" retorted Tain.

An hour later, they were less strangers and more friends. Tabitha and Elsie joined them and Arkyn found he was sitting entertaining them quite happily.

Chapter 49
GOOD NEWS

Tretaldai, Week 42 – 10th Geryal, 17th Souis 1213
Ceardlann – Stables

THE FOLLOWING DAY, Caswal Hillbeck rode into the stableyard at Ceardlann and dismounted with familiar ease. A few moments later, the Comptroller took in his appearance with a smile.

"Good news?"

"Yes, sir. Here's the letter."

"You can deliver it yourself, lad. Come on."

They found the Galdwins running around the gardens. Tain glanced over and seeing Caswal with the Comptroller nodded to Cal. Cal half ran, half stumbled over.

Caswal held the message out. "It's good news, sir."

Cal let out a long breath. "Thank you." Collapsing onto the bank, he broke the seal, read the letter, jumped up and ran over to his siblings, grinning. "Boy and girl, Amin and Amina, and mother's fine."

Tain stood aside as the Galdwins ended up in a group hug, their relief palpable. Quietly and unobtrusively, he crossed to the Comptroller.

"What had Cook planned for lunch?"

"I'll tell him to make sure there's a spread, shall I, sir?"

"Please. I think they'll be hungry. They hardly ate anything last night and this morning."

"Not because you're hungry then, Your Highness?"

Tain grinned and lay watching the clouds until Cal and his siblings were ready for his company again.

Cal eventually ran over to him. "Sorry, sir…"

Tain laughed. "I can cope with watching others receive good news."

Cal flopped down next to him. "Father's said we should stay here for a couple of days, if possible, so that mother has chance to recover."

Tain nodded. "Of course you can…"

* * *

The following day the clop of horse's hooves was the only herald to the arrival of Adeone. He dismounted lithely and grinned at Alfred.

"Remind me to look up the meaning of the word warning…"

Alfred smiled. "I'm sure it's in the Comptroller's dictionary, Sire."

"So am I. He keeps telling me I should send some."

He entered the house and winked at the Comptroller. The Comptroller bowed, very correctly, as though in emphasis of something unsaid.

Adeone crooked an amused eyebrow. "Where are they all?"

"In the Princes' sitting room, Sire." His lips twitched. "Should I send warning?"

Adeone chuckled and shook his head.

In the sitting room, Louisa and Elantha were drawing. Tain, Cal and Crispin were talking quietly but the surprising one for Adeone was that Arkyn was happily entertaining the two youngest girls who seemed more than content with his company. Cal glanced over as the door opened and hurriedly got to his feet.

"Thank you."

"I was glad I could help, Cal. How are you all?"

"Fine, thank you, Sire. Better since we heard the news."

Adeone nodded. "I'm not surprised." He sat down. "So, who's going to give me a hug first?"

Elantha beat her cousins.

Adeone smiled. "I meant of all of you. Hello, little flower."

Elantha grinned. "Uncle Adeone, can Louisa visit more often?"

"They can all visit whenever they wish, to see any of you. So, who's up for seeing the Chief?"

Arkyn and Tain got to their feet.

Cal said, "We'll be fine here, sir. We wouldn't want too many to crowd into the Chief's tent."

Adeone grinned. "Good point. El?"

Elantha shook her head. "I'm fine, Uncle Adeone. I'm in the middle of sketching Louisa."

Two hours later, Cal went to his room to retrieve a book, wondering how long the King and Princes would be. They needed time alone, but he wished he was also listening to the Chief's stories. He closed his eyes for a moment, the stress of the last few days overwhelming his senses. He just wanted the security he always felt when with the Chief.

With a rush, he was disorientated, stumbling and falling, clutching at nothingness.

PART 4

Chapter 50
SHIFTING THOUGHTS
Imperadai, Week 42 – 11th Geryal, 18th Souis 1213
Rex Dallin

A VOICE SAID MILDLY, "I wondered how long that would take. Good afternoon, young Cal."

Cal blinked, swallowing back nausea. "But... I was... Chief?"

Laioril ignored Adeone's, Arkyn's and Tain's faces. "I'd sit down, lad, and don't concentrate on anyone for a few moments. You wouldn't want to do any more damage to the lads."

Cal sat pinching himself, shaking his head, again and again and again. Everyone was watching him. Blood rushed to his face. He put his head in his hands, trying to block out everything but think of nothing.

Laioril eyed Adeone. "Looks like there's a shifter in your midst, lad."

Adeone returned the gaze. "So it does."

Tain rubbed his leg where Cal had tripped over it. "He *can't* be..."

Laioril smiled. "I've known he's something for a couple of years, Tain. He's got more energy than even you have. He's more than talented and quick, exceptionally quick, on his feet. What do you think makes him such a good swordsman? It's more than natural skill. He's only thirteen and he'd beat Lord Landis. Cal, lad, were you thinking of these three a second before you stumbled?"

"Yes, Chief," mumbled Cal. "What *happened*?"

Laioril knelt by him. "You hold an Ullian Spirit, Cal: that of a shifter. You can, when you put your mind to it, move between places in the blink of an eye. You were thinking about the lads, you closed your eyes and, I suppose, a part of you wanted to be with us – I should be flattered – that wish triggered your spirit. Why it's happened now, I don't know. Shifters are rare, *very* rare. I'd be surprised if there had been more than one a century over the last six hundred years..."

A steadying hand on Cal's shoulder, Adeone asked, "Chief, what does this mean?"

"Mean, lad? Meanings can be misinterpreted. All I'll say is that the lad needs to keep this private, secret and he needs to practise. I can teach him what I know of the old spirits, but that's not as much as many believe. He must learn to control this. Cal, come back soon, but for now, you need to shift once more. Just once. Think hard on a room at Ceardlann that you know will be empty. Very hard. The last was an accident. This can't be one. Have you got that room in your mind? Can you see it?"

"Yes, Chief."

"Close your eyes and imagine yourself there."

Cal did so and was gone from the tent.

Laioril eyed Adeone. "It's begun, Sire – whether you like it or not. Young Cal will be a great asset to you if you can keep his spirit secret. Not just to you but to your sons. I thought there was something. I never dreamt it was this; at this time and in this place, it is remarkable."

Adeone nodded. "I get the message, Chief. Can you help him?"

"I can try, lad, but I'm not a shifter." He turned to Tain and Arkyn. "You can't prattle about this, Your Highnesses. If you do, you'll endanger your friend more than you realise. If what he is becomes known, even the Rex Dallin won't be able to protect him. I've known of men killed for being affected by a Ullian Hue, let alone the rarest of all twelve spirits. Can you understand that?"

"Yes, Chief," replied Tain, wondering if he could. If the Chief considered it important, it had to be important, even if he didn't understand why.

Arkyn merely nodded, stunned by the revelations but realising more quickly than Tain exactly what the Chief meant.

* * *

When they reached Ceardlann, Adeone summoned Cal to his study and locked the door. "Laioril thinks it's imperative you keep your spirit secret and I agree with him. Can I have your word that you won't mention it to anyone but my sons and myself?"

Cal blinked. "I can promise, Sire, but I'm not sure that I won't accidentally mention it to someone, probably Lady Elantha."

"Cal, I've promised your family I'll protect you. I can't protect you from this and your life is in as much danger as mine and my sons' now. You hold something everyone wishes for. You could be in Tera one minute and Paras the next second. If Lord Scanlon discovers this, you could be killed or coerced into working for him. I cannot permit that to happen. There are a couple of bindings I could put you under, but you're a child and your father should agree to them. Can you not promise me? I trust your word."

Tears sprang to Cal's eyes. "I want to, sir, but I can't when I don't know if I can keep it. I'm… I'm frightened…"

Adeone wrapped him in a hug, knowing what that final admission had cost the lad. In a gentler tone than before, he said, "This isn't something to be afraid of. A spirit can be an asset, but it's the consequences of what it could be that is worrying." He changed his posture slightly, his hand resting on the back of Cal's neck. With an authoritarian lilt, he said,

250

"Master Calumiel Galdwin, will you bind yourself to the promise that you will learn to control this spirit and, once it is under control, only use it when absolutely necessary? Will you bind and swear to me that you shall reveal this matter to no-one but those who already know and Lady Elantha?"

Cal shook, recognising what the King was doing, "I will so bind and swear, Sire."

Holding him tighter, Adeone whispered, "Thank you, Cal. I'm sorry."

Cal wiped his eyes when Adeone's grip relaxed. "I'm not, Sire. Thank you, it was for the best."

Adeone sank onto a chair. "I hope so, young Cal. Probably better not to mention what I did to Tain and Arkyn; I can't see them being so forgiving. You should know that, when I die, the binding won't transfer to Arkyn."

"Thank you, Sire, but I don't want to contemplate your death."

"Very smooth, Cal."

Cal shook his head. "No, sir. I meant that."

There was a knock on the door and Simkins, realising it was locked, said through it, "Dinner is ready to be served, Sire."

Adeone crossed to the door; unlocking it, he invited Simkins in. "You'd better get your meal, young Cal. Tell them I shall be there shortly." Once the boy had gone, Adeone continued, "I'm leaving for Oedran directly after dinner."

Chapter 51
CHIEF REACTION
Evening
Rex Dallin

WHILST ARKYN, Tain and Elantha said goodbye to their father, Cal slipped away. He wanted, needed to be by himself. His siblings would cope for a time without him; he doubted they'd even notice his absence. If they did… Arkyn and Tain would cover for him. Wouldn't they? He skirted the stables and ran down the path. It was his route, his walk, his space. He patted the great oak in passing. How long had it grown there marking the split between the rear lane and forest track? The well-maintained lane turned to a rougher pock-marked track with puddles to avoid, stones to kick and roots to trip on. He slowed his pace. The way became steeper. Enjoying the exercise, he pushed himself until he reached the flat stone. Collapsing onto it, he gazed down over Ceardlann, absorbing the view. In the distance, the King was riding towards the Pillars with Simkins and a couple of guards. Half of his heart wanted to be going that way. He wanted to run home, just for the security of a hug from his ma. He couldn't talk about what had happened with her, but maybe he wouldn't have to. With his siblings at Ceardlann, he couldn't even talk to Tain and Arkyn about it easily. Who could he turn to? Did he want to talk to anyone? Even if he did, would it help? He was alone with this. There was no-one to help, not really. There wasn't another shifter to ask. He'd promised not to use the spirit, but it wouldn't remain secret if he couldn't control it and he'd have risked everyone. Tears streamed down his face. How could he keep his word? How could he even begin to learn control when it had to be such a secret? Soft feet approached and the attached body sat next to him with a sigh.

"I thought I might find you here, lad."

Frustrated, Cal wiped his tears away. "Chief."

"Let the tears flow. It's the best thing you can do."

Cal recalled being nine and homesick. "Is that your standard response to tears, Chief?"

"When appropriate, lad. Do you want a shoulder? I mean, you've two of your own and a third might look silly, but I was meaning to cry on."

Cal chuckled in spite of himself. "Thanks, Chief… I…"

"You don't know how to react, do you? You're worried and pleased all at the same time. Scared and triumphant. You want to see what you can do but don't dare?"

Cal nodded, picking at the wiry grass by his hand.

"Then wait until your siblings have left and you've slept on things. The world always looks different after sleeping. Normally because it's a new day and the weather has altered…"

Cal chuckled again. "Chief, what did you mean by meanings can be misinterpreted?"

Laioril never hesitated. "Alcis only knows, it seemed to work in getting the King to stop asking me questions. I'll have to use it again."

Cal dried his eyes properly and hugged his knees. "I never want to leave Ceardlann. Not really. I feel lost elsewhere."

Laioril said, "There's many the same, lad. The valley's accepted you as one of its own. It's an honour. I'm never sure if it has me."

Thirteen years old, red faced but with piercing blue eyes, Cal murmured, "I think it has, Chief. You are more of this place than any other."

Laioril returned the look with darker but equally piercing blue eyes. "You've not seen me in any other."

Cal snorted and gave a noncommittal jerk of his head. "True. Chief, what would you do in my position?"

"Find a dry handkerchief? I'd wait until peace descends and then face up to it. Learn to control what you have and then learn not to use it."

Cal frowned. "Why learn how not to use something? Surely you just don't use it."

"Temptation can be overwhelming. Learning to control it is key. The more you use your spirit, the more you'll want to and the more chance someone will see and try to kill you. Anyone with an ounce of brain would see that you're no more likely to turn traitor than I am and, in that case, you're a threat, not an asset to be coerced."

Cal nodded. "I could never betray what the King has done for me. Though… He's ridden for Oedran, I think this worried him."

Laioril shook his head. "No, lad, not this exactly. He has other concerns."

Cal pushed himself to his feet. "I wish I could believe that. Would you like a hand up, Chief? I should make sure my siblings are all right."

"I'm fine, lad. Dunna fret about it all. I doubt your friends will mention this until you do; they've that much sense about them."

Chapter 52
RESEARCH
Late Evening
Landis House

RIDING TO OEDRAN, Adeone pondered on events. He could sense Simkins' curiosity because of his changed plans but ignored the unspoken request for an explanation. The new facet of Cal's personality had changed everything, and he was even more pleased than ever that he'd had the lad trained to handle weapons. What it would mean in a few years for their fight against Scanlon, time would tell, but if they could protect Cal, if he kept it secret… Adeone cursed in his head. Cal wasn't a weapon. He was a bright, skilled young man in the making. A confidant of his sons and niece. Cal's future was his own choice, whatever the necessities of the empire.

As they clattered over the Dallin Bridge, the past seeped into Adeone's preoccupations. Rumours, prophecies and tradition all dwelt in his memory and he cursed. Cal's future would need protecting. He might not be his child, ward or nearchild but he was such a part of his family that his safety was paramount.

He turned left along The Strait, making for the Maclan. He needed to check a text that Landis owned.

He'd barely dismounted and handed Ponder's reins to a guard when Landis walked out to greet him.

"Sire, I thought you'd gone to Ceardlann."

253

"I came back. Might I borrow your library, Festus? I want to look something up that I know I read here. I'm not sure how long I'll be."

Landis smiled. "You know your way, Your Majesty. If you're hunting for something in particular, can I help?"

Adeone smiled. "I think I'd rather be on my own, if you don't mind?"

"Not at all. I'll be in my study."

They walked companionably until they reached the library door. Landis held it open and then closed it softly. He turned and raised an eloquent eyebrow at Simkins who simply shrugged.

"I have no more idea than Your Lordship."

"Glad I'm not the only one confused. Thank you, Simkins. Find yourself somewhere comfortable. His Majesty might be some time."

"Strange you should say that, my lord."

Chuckling they parted company.

* * *

In the comfortable library, Adeone ran a hand idly along the edge of the bookshelves. It still felt new but also had the ageless scent of dry paper and old parchment. He crossed to the desk where Landis kept his ledgers, detailing where the scrolls and books were. Finding the entry for *Places of the Cearcall*, he retrieved the leather-bound book and ran his hands over the embossed cover. How many people over the years had handled this book? He didn't know of another copy and that in itself spoke volumes.

He placed it carefully on the inlaid table next to a chair before turning back to the desk and pouring himself a whiskey. Whiskey, books and an evening to himself. There wasn't anything quite like it. His friend and nearfamily wouldn't bother him until he left the room, Simkins would see to that. As evenings went, there were worse ones.

The chair was comfortable, the book an easy read and he read more than he intended. Within the aged pages were answers to more questions than he'd known he had. Cal would be fine. The valley was its own protection. With Laioril to help, Cal would find his way through the maze. His own requests and bequests might need amending, but there was plenty of time to see to that.

An hour and a half later, Adeone entered Landis' study, glass in hand, and eased himself into a chair. "Thank you, Festus. That was much easier than searching at the Palace."

Landis smiled. "Did you find what you were hunting for?"

"Yes. One day, I might even tell you what it was."

"I get the hint, Sire. Please tell me, though, that it isn't something I'll get the blame for as well."

Adeone laughed. "I think you're safe there, Festus. Oh, Laioril mentioned he thought Cal would be able to disarm you…"

"Is that a challenge?"

"I think it was more an observation. They're growing quickly."

Landis nodded. "Yes. I should visit again soon. How have the younger Galdwins coped?"

"Well enough, I think. They'll come home on Septadai. Chapa thinks Madam Galdwin will be strong enough by then. Now, I shouldn't interrupt your evening anymore," he pushed himself to his feet, yawning. "Don't work too long; tomorrow is another day, as you keep telling me."

Landis smiled as he got up. "Stay here, Adeone."

Adeone hesitated. They had allocated him a bedchamber with the rebuild. As inconveniences went, he wouldn't be a large one. He'd planned to stay at Ceardlann, so wasn't expected back at the Palace. "Why not? I'll have to leave early but will that inconvenience you?"

"Not at all." As Adeone reseated himself, Landis rang for his manservant. "William, His Majesty is staying tonight."

William smiled. "Very good, my lord."

Once he'd gone, Adeone said, "So, what's the ulterior motive in getting me to stay?"

"I'll tell you when I've worked it out, Sire. Until then, I think another drink is called for."

Adeone put his head back on the chair. It had been a long and confusing day. Exhausted, he said, "So do I."

Chapter 53
LORD RALE

Pentadai, Week 42 – 12th Geryal, 19th Souis 1213
Landis House – Dining Room

THE FOLLOWING MORNING, Adeone entered the dining room humming to himself. He regarded the other occupant for a second. At fourteen, the lad was old enough to get used to formality. "Good morning, Lord Rale."

Finian jumped to his feet. "Good morning, Your Majesty. I didn't hear the door…"

Adeone smiled, taking a seat. "There's a school of thought that says sitting with your back to the door is a foolish move."

"There's normally quite a lot of competition for a chair at the table, Sire, so we all tend to stick to the same place."

Adeone nodded in thanks to Simkins as his breakfast was placed in front of him. Picking up his cutlery, he said, "With all your cousins, I expect there is. Do sit back down, my lord."

Lord Rale grinned, resuming his seat. "At least I'm never lonely, Sire."

"True. Have you enjoyed living here?"

"Yes, sir. I'm not sure when I'll move back to grandfather's house…"

Adeone swallowed his mouthful of toast. "You'll know when it feels right and it's been *your* house for a couple of years. How's your mother?"

"I think she's all right. Her letters don't say much. Sire, can I ask you something?" (Adeone nodded.) "I've been thinking about my education when I'm fifteen. I'd like to go into law but Aunt Cornelia said that Your Majesty may prefer me not to… I think I understand why, sir, but I'll have five years of training before I qualify and by that time Prince Tain will be Justiciar of Oedran."

Adeone wiped his lips, regarding Finian. "Do you think coercion, manipulation and avarice will only apply once you're of age?"

Finian swallowed. "No, Your Majesty, but I'm not going to turn traitor simply because I'm studying the law and it's surely better that there's someone loyal to Your Majesty in the school to spot if anyone isn't."

"Have you been taking logic lessons off your Uncle Festus?"

Finian grinned. "Probably, Sire, if unknowingly."

"He has a lot to answer for. Very well, Lord Rale. I shall support your decision, but my condition is that you continue to live here until your studies are complete and you've sworn fealty when you come of age."

"Thank you, Your Majesty; you may be assured I shall remain loyal."

Adeone nodded. "With Lord Landis watching over you, I can only imagine you will. How did you find Areal?"

"Interesting, Your Majesty. It was particularly intriguing to see my uncle and Governor ReJean coming to compromises."

"Any in particular?"

"The one that springs to mind is the one they didn't reach, sir."

"Which was? And, before your finer feelings get the better of you, Lord Rale, you mentioned it first."

Finian sighed. "The issue to do with when the review will take place, sir."

"Ah, that one. What do you think yourself?"

Finian took a slice of toast thoughtfully. "I think that, to my knowledge, no-one has asked His Highness, sir. Also, Governor ReJean might have had a point. There needs to be something to stop the political manoeuvrings that are beginning to happen now that people have realised he isn't going to marry again."

Adeone reached for the tea to find Simkins on hand to pour it. "Do you know why he isn't going to marry again, Lord Rale?"

Finian shook his head. "No, sir, but then, is that the important factor?

Sorry, Your Majesty, I didn't mean to question you."

"I'm pleased you didn't." Adeone pursed his lips. "Thank you, Simkins, that's all for now."

Simkins bowed and left, motioning for the footman in the room to do likewise.

When they were alone, Adeone eyed Finian. "It took some years for his previous wife to conceive and the doctors were confident the trouble wasn't on her side. There is no guarantee, therefore, that he would have another child even if he did remarry."

Finian absorbed the information. "In that case, Your Majesty, maybe he's right to think they need something to illustrate the close relationship between the FitzAlcis and ReJeans."

Adeone said, "That does not have to be my son coming of age away from his family!"

"No, Sire."

The King looked at him. "Sorry, Finian. It's rather a raw subject."

The young Lord of Oedran hesitated. "My father died when I was young, sir… I perhaps see things differently."

Adeone nodded. "Perhaps. Thank you. And, Finian, your father would have been very proud of you now. I heartily wish he was here to see you putting me in my place with such aplomb."

Finian paled. "I didn't mean… I never…"

Adeone chuckled. "Lord Rale, finish your breakfast and stop looking so worried." He'd barely stopped chuckling when Landis entered. "Morning, Festus. I've told Finian he can study law as long as he lives here."

Landis shook his head. "I know I say that traditions can be changed and that there's no rest for the wicked, but it *is* only breakfast time, Your Majesty…"

Adeone chuckled. "Are you saying I'm wicked, Landis? On second thoughts, don't answer that. Lord Rale and I have been having a pleasant talk. It's even made me realise a couple of things I should have thought about earlier."

Landis eased himself into his chair. "Now I'm really worried. Finian, am I going to get the blame for anything?"

Lord Rale smiled. "Possibly, Uncle Festus, but I think I'll be sharing it."

"Traditions can be changed then. What have you realised, Sire?"

Adeone pushed himself to his feet. "Primarily that I must return to the Palace. I shall see you soon, Lord Rale."

Landis walked with his friend to the front of the house. "Finian wasn't rude was he, Adeone?"

"He was merely enthusiastic. He'll make a good Lord of Oedran when he's older."

"Are you sure about him being at the Law School?"

Adeone considered as he took Ponder's reins from his friend's chief groom. "He made some valid points and he obviously wants to study law. I can't block his wishes because my influence is limited at the Courthouse."

Landis nodded. "True and one day it might be useful to have another Lord of Oedran who's a lawyer, other than Ryson."

Adeone merely smiled noncommittally and swung into the saddle. "I shall see you soon, Landis."

With that, he left. Finian had indeed been right. No-one had asked Arkyn his feelings on the matter.

* * *

Landis re-entered his house and spotted his wed-nephew trying to slink away. "Finian, a word…"

Lord Rale sighed. "I didn't mean to annoy His Majesty, Uncle Festus."

"That suggests that you did. Let's go to my study."

Finian trailed behind his wed-uncle uncertainly and once in the study became even more uncertain.

"What did you say to His Majesty?"

Finian rubbed his hands together as he explained his comments regarding the Arealian Review.

Landis eyed him. "Anything else?"

Finian swallowed. "I mentioned that, because my father died when I was young, I see things differently. I was trying to explain I didn't mean to criticise, but it might have come out wrong."

Landis frowned at him. "You do realise that your father and His Majesty were close acquaintances, even confidants, don't you?"

"No, I didn't. I'll apologise to His Majesty when I next see him."

"You'll do more than that, Finian Rale, you'll write your apology now and send it to the Palace. You do *not* criticise His Majesty's decisions. You might be a Lord of Oedran but you're still only fourteen."

"He didn't seem angry, Uncle Festus."

"That is not the point, Finian. The point is that he noticed and, in my house, he is not to be annoyed." Adding in his head, *'Unless I do the annoying,'* before saying, "Write your apology and I'll work out how I'll phrase mine to him later."

Finian swallowed. "I didn't mean to let you down, Uncle Festus."

Landis eyed him. "I realise that, Finian. Next time, think before you speak. All right?"

"Yes, sir. I'll try to remember."

Two hours later, Adeone received the apology and sighed. He hadn't wanted it, but he recognised the lesson that Festus was trying to instil in Finian.

Chapter 54
DEPARTURE AND FUTURE
Septadai, Week 42 – 14th Geryal, 21st Souis 1213
Rex Dallin – Ceardlann

SEPTADAI DAWNED and the Ceardlann coach was made ready to take the Galdwin siblings home. There were mixed feelings all round. During their four-day stay, Louisa and Crispin had enjoyed doing whatever they wanted but, as they prepared to leave, they realised it wasn't always like that.

Tain said, "Are you going home for a couple of days as well, Cal?"

"Just tonight, sir," replied Cal. "Merchant Annatto wants to resume my lessons and Advisor Spellen is asking if I've finished the work he set."

"He's asking me the same. I've a lesson with the judge today, but I'll tell Advisor Spellen that unfortunately we can't escape any longer."

Arkyn entered the room saying blithely, "Tain, I thought you were for Fitz's today."

"I'll ride with the coach."

"It looks like we're all leaving together then. I've got a couple of meetings in Oedran. Edward's just kindly informed me. Mistress Louisa, I hope you don't mind if I share the coach with you."

Louisa said, "No, Your Highness, not at all."

Tain glanced at Arkyn. Four guests had taken it out of him. "Arkyn…"

"I'm fine, Tain, it just feels like it might rain," replied his brother.

Glancing out at the bright spring sky, Tain bit his lip. "Right." He'd got his notes into order when Kadeem entered.

"The coach is ready and the horses saddled, Your Highness."

Arkyn nodded. "Thank you, Kadeem. Come on then, everyone, reality awaits us all."

Holding the door, Kadeem said, "Reality is but a dream of a different night, sir."

Arkyn gave him a sideways look, but his manservant's seeming innocence wasn't at all shaken, though there might have been the faintest twitch to his lips.

∗ ∗ ∗

Tain left the small cavalcade at Fitz's with four of the guards and watched the rest continue to Oedran – half wishing he was going as well.

259

In the coach, Arkyn heard them leave and continued watching the passing countryside. Cal, looking over, considered how white he was.

"Your Highness?"

Arkyn shook himself. "Sorry, Cal, I was thinking of another journey."

Cal murmured, "Lufian?"

Arkyn swallowed. "Yes."

Cal smiled sadly and, mindful of his siblings, didn't say anything else.

They rumbled through the gates of Oedran and Arkyn sat back in his seat, aware he must look pale. At the Galdwins, he helped Elsie and Tabitha out of the carriage.

"I won't impose, Cal. I hope everything's well."

"Very good, Your Highness. Thank you. I think I'll be back at Ceardlann tomorrow. I'll confirm it later."

"Whenever you're ready, Cal. Take care."

Cal swallowed and nodded; they each knew what was meant, for all it might have been a common pleasantry.

Arkyn swung back into the coach and drew the curtain as it moved off. He'd hardly been in a coach since Kensal's death. Had he subconsciously been avoiding them?

* * *

Reaching the Palace, Arkyn alighted swiftly. Seeing his administrator waiting patiently for him he asked if he was late.

"Not at all, Your Highness. Your first meeting has been reorganised. His Majesty wondered if you have a moment."

Arkyn said, "Have I?"

Edward chuckled. "That's why I reorganised the meeting, sir."

"I thought you were looking efficient." As they entered the Palace, Arkyn continued, "I'll ride back to Ceardlann…"

"Very good, sir. I'll have Ponder brought to Oedran."

"Thank you. Before I see His Majesty, what is waiting for me on my desk? Just so I know how long to avoid it for."

Edward's lips twitched; it was an empty comment. "There's some correspondence, Your Highness, and the briefing for the Macian Review. It looks quite weighty…"

"Landis was responsible for the visit last year; I expect the Arealian one next year to be equally as bad. I'll thank him another day. Can you send Irvin an invitation to dinner this evening, please?"

Edward nodded. "Certainly, Your Highness." He looked carefully at the Prince. "Shall I clear the whole day, sir?"

"No, I should be all right. It's just been a busy few days."

* * *

Arkyn made his ponderous way to his father's chambers. Entering the Outer Office, he smiled as his father's administrator rose. "Is His Majesty free, Richardson?"

"The General and Major are just discussing the movement of the legions, sir, but I'll inform His Majesty of your arrival."

Arkyn nodded. "I'll wait then. Thank you."

Two minutes later, the General and Major left. Both saluted Arkyn, who apologised for curtailing their meeting.

The General said, "We were drawing to a close anyway, sir."

Wynfeld watched Arkyn. "Did Your Highness have a pleasant ride from Ceardlann?"

"It had its moments, Major," replied Arkyn. "Excuse me, His Majesty is waiting." Wynfeld's gaze followed him into the Inner Office and knew he hadn't convinced him. As the door closed and he rose from his bow, he let out a long sigh.

"Not a good trip?" enquired Adeone.

"Memories, father. I understood you wanted to see me, Sire?"

"Arkyn, I always want to see you, so stop trying to change the subject and tell me..." At the end of the explanation, Adeone nodded. "It was always going to happen eventually and you're drained..."

Arkyn said, "The last few days have been quite busy one way or another."

Adeone nodded. "Yes, they have. How's young Cal?"

"He's not mentioned it. He will when he's ready. The shock didn't help. Of all things... You're not going to send him away, are you, father?"

"What? Why?"

Arkyn shrugged. "You don't let others with magical spirits anywhere near Oedran; Butterworth for one, and he *really* could be useful..."

"I dislike and distrust magic for ruling, and, yes, I would rather as few people around me can wield it as possible," admitted Adeone. "I have my reasons and I do not plan to explain them, but I will not be sending Cal anywhere; his and our lives are too intertwined now."

Arkyn rubbed at his forehead. "Thank you. I wondered when you left Ceardlann so quickly."

"I left because I had things I wanted to check, that was all. Now, I'm going to tell Edward you're to have the day off."

"Your Majesty, I'm perfectly capable—"

"Of doing everything another day, I know. Take some time to look up the old spirits, Arkyn, and familiarise yourself with your friend's."

261

"Is that bribery, for want of a better word, Sire?"

"Yes."

Arkyn smiled. "It might even work. What did you want to see me about?"

Adeone hesitated. "ReJean has requested that the Arealian Review is held in the first weeks of 1215. I know what my reply would be but Lord Rale's right. This has to be your decision."

Arkyn frowned. "Why—?"

"Because ReJean wants something to prove that we still want him as Governor and to stop the political backstabbing."

"No, father, why has Finian made any comment on it?"

"That, Arkyn, is a long story. You'd come of age in Amphi…"

Arkyn said quietly, "I'll consider it, father."

Adeone took him by the shoulders. "You don't have to do this, Arkyn. If you want your celebrations here then that's what'll happen, no matter who says differently."

Arkyn looked him in the eye. "Thank you, father. I would like to celebrate my birthday here but there could be advantages to celebrating it in Amphi. I shall consider it. When would you like to know by?"

"Whenever you're certain."

Chapter 55
ON LEARNING AND POWER
Afternoon
Fitz's Inn – Schoolroom

HALFWAY THROUGH THE AFTERNOON, frustrated, Tain asked, "Why do you always, or nearly always, answer my questions with another question, Your Honour?"

"Can you not work out why yourself, sir?"

"Probably. I was just looking for a straight answer for once."

The judge studied the Prince; his charge was tired. "Very good, sir. It is rather a controversial reason, I believe. I can simply teach you facts, facts and more facts – sentences and procedures, protocol and tradition. I could teach you by traditional methods using textbooks and law scrolls. Yet there is one major flaw in such teaching: Your Highness would not learn how to think, how to assimilate information in such a way as to present a coherent argument. If facts are all I taught you, we would not have a Justiciar at the end of these lessons; there would simply be a prince with a knowledge of the law. A very different matter, I think you will agree."

Tain sat for a moment. "Your Honour does give me facts to learn."

"Yes, Your Highness, but seldom within the time we spend together. Advisor Spellen needs something to do..." There was a glint of amusement in the judge's eye as he replied.

"What you mean, Judge, is that you'll let him do the boring stuff?"

"Just that, sir. The boring and necessary aspects. We have the fun of tearing it apart. Your Highness needs to know the facts but more importantly you need to be able to think. Your future lawyers could give you the facts and law if necessary."

"I think I begin to understand."

"I am pleased, sir. Understanding is always preferable to confusion. Unless confusion is your aim, sir, and, if so, I am presuming it would not be your own confusion at issue."

Tain grinned. "You'll give me a bad name."

"Never intentionally, Your Highness, and only, in that case, if anyone else was present."

Tain sighed. "Very amusing, Judge. Is that an example of pedantry?"

"I suppose it must be, sir."

"I'll have to get used to it if I'm to have lawyers working for me."

"Your Highness will rise to the challenge, I have no doubt."

* * *

Later in the day, talk had turned and Tancred found himself saying, "To use your power is a necessity; to abuse your power is foolishness. Very few will forget how much you hold, but it is ill-advised to remind people too often. To be approachable is often to be loved, to be loved dissuades conspirators."

"Rather idealistic, Judge."

"Maybe, sir, but I have seen power both used and abused. An understatement of power is the most effective. The obvious portrayal is best kept for decisive, fraught or important moments. Such as rebellions, treachery, true displeasure. Yet not for petty reasons. If you dislike someone, never use power to emphasise the fact, it only causes feuds – outspoken or hidden."

"Yet if we never use power—" protested Tain.

"I did not say that, sir. I said to understate it. When, for example, you are cisan-age and enter a room, all but your father and elder brother should rise; it is an emphasis of your power that they do rise. If someone remains seated, who could rise, a look should get them to their feet. If that does not work, a word might. The more formal an occasion, the more authority should be used. At the King's Court, for example, if lords offend you then you are entitled to ban them from Court for a time – the length of which is dependent on your discretion."

Tain frowned. "How will I know how long for?"

"As long as you are consistent and not tyrannical, sir, and if the sentence makes sense, I would not worry. You can always take advice or lookup what your forbears did. All such decisions are kept on a scroll in the Steward's office. Shall I arrange for a copy to be taken for Your Highness?"

Tain became thoughtful. "Yes, please, Your Honour. I feel like I have no idea what would be appropriate. The Court is a whole different world from a court."

"It is, sir; however, it might be best viewed as a challenge. Has anyone talked you through the duties of a younger prince, or Justiciar, there?"

"No, Judge. I think it's believed I shouldn't concern myself yet."

"Or maybe they forget how rapidly Your Highness is growing," observed Tancred. "I shall try to find a copy of the protocols."

"Thank you, Judge, but shouldn't Spellen…"

Tancred smiled. "I think Advisor Spellen may have his hands full soon, sir. Keeping Your Highness' mind on work during the warmer weather is a challenge, or so I have heard."

Tain pouted in mock offence then caught the judge's eye. He grinned. "Well, I prefer to be outside…"

"Then why not take your lessons outside, sir?" suggested Tancred. "Learning benefits from congenial surroundings and thrives on informal atmospheres. I am sure Your Highness can persuade the advisor."

"Would this be another challenge, Judge?"

"It has that appearance, sir."

Tain laughed. "I will try to match it, Your Honour."

"Why the mirth, sir?"

"I was thinking that father is right, you rarely attend Court and yet are a true courtier."

"Thank you, sir. I do my best."

"Why don't you attend Court, Judge?" enquired Tain with genuine interest. Tancred was so well known that his absence from the King's Court was intriguing.

"I once asked my father what occurred at Court and he replied that it was not for the likes of us. At the time, I accepted that and then Prince Lachlan invited me there. After the first few visits, I knew what my father had said was true. I find I am uncomfortable. I am cisan; I have risen through hard work. The intricacies of Court and the politics are smothering to me. It is where great men go to make their name without the knowledge of how to work. It has its place but not in my life."

Tain put his head on one side. "Surely though, Judge, you must have had some involvement in the Court to rise so high."

"No, sir. It is a myth that the Court is everything. I had the stroke of luck of meeting Prince Lachlan. When he offered me a job, I could not refuse. I worked hard, got to know Prince Lachlan quite well and he persuaded me to become a judge. The Court never focused in my life until after that election."

"Oh, but Ewall and Advisor Spellen have taught us that Court is the only way to favour someone or for them to come to our attention."

"That is the long-held belief. Did you believe them?"

"I had no cause not to, Judge, but I have now."

The judge smiled. "It is often wise to question long held practices; not necessarily to change them but rather to understand why they exist. Your Highness, however, should have little trouble asking the questions."

Tain caught the judge's eye, chuckling.

Chapter 56
FATE
Alunadai, Week 43 – 15th Geryal, 1st Geryis 1213
Ceardlann

CAL RETURNED TO CEARDLANN the following day, looking happier than he had for weeks. He and Tain sat talking about the new Galdwin twins. After a while, Cal fell silent.

"I'm good at listening sometimes, you know…" stated Tain.

"Better at talking though," replied Cal. "Sir, what do I do about my problem…?"

Tain frowned. "Problem?"

Cal rolled his eyes. "I was trying to be discreet and it just confuses him!"

Tain grinned. "You confuse me all the time. I'd do what Laioril suggests. He might be a rogue but he's picked up a lot of knowledge wandering the roads. Why don't we go and see him?"

"Because I'm scared, I think. I almost wish it hadn't happened."

Tain stared at him, incredulous. "But it's fantastic—"

"No, sir, it's dangerous. It might be useful, but it's put me and my family in danger and two of them know nothing of life yet."

Tain said softly, "All the more reason to learn to control it."

Cal stared out of the window. "I'll go and see the Chief… And, if you don't mind, sir, I'd rather be on my own."

Tain simply nodded and watched his friend leave the room.

* * *

As Cal entered the Wanda camp, a voice hailed him. He smiled. "Hello,

Miranda. Is the Chief about?"

The wise-woman nodded. "Somewhere, as always. You on your own today?"

"Yes. Prince Arkyn's in Oedran, Lady Elantha is with her governess and Prince Tain wasn't quick enough."

Miranda chuckled. "What you mean is you wanted time on your own. My congratulations to your family on the birth of the twins…"

"Thank you. I'll pass them on at some point."

"You'll confuse your parents, lad, if you tell them I send congratulations. Say they're from the Wanda; they'll understand that."

"I suppose so. Thanks though, Miranda. I'll find the Chief."

Miranda smiled. "I'll find you some food then."

Laioril heard Cal say his name. "Come on in, lad. I've been expecting you to visit."

Cal entered the tent and sat hugging his knees. "What do I do, Chief?"

"You stay there whilst I find you sustenance…" When Miranda had come and gone, Laioril said softly, "Your spirit, in itself, is nothing to be afraid of, Cal. So, to start with, you stop worrying about it, all right?"

Cal looked into the piercing eyes. "I'll try, Chief."

Laioril shook his head. "No, lesson one, you *succeed*. There is no room for half-hearted attempts now. Come and sit in front of me with your back to me. Right, close your eyes and hope that I can remember what I'm doing…"

Chortling, Cal crooked an eyebrow. "Half hearted, Chief?"

"Oh, shut up, lad…" He placed his hands carefully on Cal's shoulders and gently massaged his neck. Cal's eyes began to close.

"Let yourself go, lad."

So Cal did. If the Chief thought he needed to sleep, he would.

Laioril laid him down and placed a fur blanket over him. The lad hadn't slept properly for days – any fool could see that – and he couldn't start to learn control with his mind half asleep.

Cal woke three hours later to the scents of the Chief's tent wafting over him: earth, a vague smoky atmosphere from the brazier and tea brewing, hints of a poacher's meat stew and a comforting scent based on herbs. He rubbed his eyes and yawned.

The Chief looked over, "Feeling better, lad?"

"Yes, Chief. Thank you."

"So I do have my uses, oh good. Come and have some tea and tell me how your family are…"

"But, Chief—"

"Lesson two, make sure you're refreshed. Lesson three, don't try to do too many things at once."

"Is that where I go wrong in life then, Chief?"

"No, that's being friends with Tain…"

Cal laughed. "I'm glad I know you don't mean that, Chief."

"Don't I? Oh."

They sipped their tea with smiles playing about their lips. Cal did feel better and ready for anything, when he put the mug aside.

Laioril watched him. "Right, lad, we're ready to start something at least. I can't teach you how to shift. I can only teach you to be alert. Is that all right?" (Cal nodded.) "Good. These skills may well be of use in other ways as well, but we'll let fate decide that for you. Close your eyes again but don't fall to sleep." He watched the smile on Cal's lips and crossed the tent noiselessly. Whispering so the sound could come from anywhere, he asked, "Where am I?"

Cal turned his head to and fro.

Laioril gently took his shoulders. "Keep your body still and let your senses do the work. Dunna trust your eyes all the time."

"You're here, Chief," said Cal, opening his eyes.

"Very amusing, lad. Though a good point, we really need a couple of people for the whispering game. Every man or woman has a core that magic can detect. You're going to tell me how many people are in this camp. Go into the dark." (Cal closed his eyes.) "Good. Now, push your senses until they seem to be at the edges of the field. You don't need to visualise it, just feel them spread…"

"I think I understand, Chief."

"Good. Now, draw them carefully back to yourself. What do you sense?"

"Black spheres, Chief… Is that right? It sounds stupid and daft."

"Yes, it's right. How many?"

After a few moments Cal said, "Twenty, twenty-one with me."

"Is your core black?"

Cal started. "No, Chief, it's golden."

Laioril smiled. "That's magic, lad. Open your eyes."

Cal did so. "But, Chief, I'm not a sensor."

Laioril smiled. "No, but then this isn't about being able to sense when magic is used. It's about being able to find people so you can go to them. There are ways of hiding oneself from this, or masking oneself, mimicking others, which could be why some legends say that people with magic can't been seen like this. As you get better, you'll find it ain't always as simple as it seems. Some say the hues can't be seen like this. Some say that only spirits are golden. If you ever find where the Skifta's Star Stone is and own it, legends say more is revealed. Personally, I just dunna want you appearing anywhere and giving yourself away. Now, lad, close your eyes again… You're very trusting, aren't you?"

Endarkened, Cal smiled. "I trust you, Chief."

"Oh, right, that's me worried then. Now, stand up. Imagine your sitting room at Ceardlann. Dunna wish yourself there, just imagine it… According to old legends, a thread is now running to there from your mind, send your senses along it…"

Cal said, "There's two people in the room."

Laioril smiled. "Can you tell who they are?"

"No, Chief, but I think I should be able to, if I concentrate."

"*Don't* concentrate, not until you're better prepared. Bring your senses back. Settle them in your mind before opening your eyes."

Cal did so. Blinking as he focused on the tent, he said, "I can tell if a room is occupied?"

"Yes."

"Why didn't you want me to concentrate?"

Laioril grimaced. "Because in all probability you'd have shifted and you didn't know who was there. It could just as easily have been a servant as your friends."

"True. Chief, is there any tea?" enquired Cal, beginning to understand why Laioril had made him rest first. Fatigue was creeping over him. Was using magic really so draining? Tea drunk, cake eaten, Cal found himself standing once again.

Laioril said, "Now, where is Arkyn?"

Cal smiled. "In Oedran, Chief."

"Lad, close your eyes and tell me exactly where he is."

Cal closed his eyes. "I don't know, Chief."

Laioril smiled. "Think about him, his character, his essence. Can you feel the shape of him?"

Cal swallowed. "I think so, Chief, but I don't know if I quite understand."

"I'm always unintelligible. Now, that shape in your mind, send your senses into it…"

Cal frowned. "I can't…"

"Yes, you can. Gently, don't force it…"

Cal stumbled and Laioril caught him.

"I said don't force it, lad."

Cal righted himself. "I'm sorry, Chief."

"Start again. Clear your mind. Now, where is Arkyn?"

Cal swallowed, steadied himself and his mind. He took a breath and let it out slowly as though he was blowing his senses gently over his idea of Arkyn. The amorphous shape metamorphosed into a different inanimate rigidity. He recognised the feeling of the room, rather than the room.

"I think he's in his office, Chief."

"Is anyone else present?"

Cal imagined it and, as his senses filled it, said, "No, Chief, just one person and I think, I'm sure, it's Arkyn."

"Go there."

"What?" Cal was startled.

"Just quickly and then come back." Laioril never seemed to hesitate but he knew, deep down, he had to give Cal the confidence to shift over larger distances.

Cal swallowed and tried to recreate the feelings he'd had when he shifted before. Nothing happened.

Laioril said softly, "Do you want to see your friend?"

"Yes, Chief, but..."

"Relax into the feeling. Before you were overwrought and worried – that triggered your ability, your spirit, now you need to use it instead. It's part of you. Don't force it."

Cal took a deep breath and thought about the office and his friend.

* * *

A small breeze touched Arkyn's cheek and he looked up, expecting the door to have opened. Cal was in front of him, disorientated.

"Cal?" enquired Arkyn as though friends appearing out of thin air was normal.

"Your Highness. Sorry, the Chief is giving me lessons."

Arkyn smiled. "They seem to be working if you can get back. If not, we'll need a lot of fast talking."

Cal chuckled. "Sir. Erm, enjoy reading that..."

"Give the Chief my greetings..."

Cal closed his eyes and thought about the Chief's tent. He relaxed, took a breath and was gone.

"Prince Arkyn sends his greetings, Chief."

"Oh, good. Just return mine and bring something back with you."

"The Chief wants what, Cal?"

"Who knows, sir? He simply told me to take something back."

Arkyn pulled a piece of parchment towards him, wrote a note, folded it and affixed his seal. "Try that."

Laioril read the note and laughed. "He's certainly his father's son."

"Chief?"

"Never you mind. Now, sit down for six minutes. We're done for the day. When you return to Ceardlann, talk to Tain. You're going to need somewhere safe to practise. Don't always move large distances. Learn to shift very small ones as well, corner to corner of a room, for example. I sent you to Oedran to prove you could but, for now, Ceardlann and the Rex Dallin are your training ground. All right?"

Cal sighed. "Yes, Chief."

"Secondly, use what you've learnt today to make sure rooms are empty if you shift to them. We don't want the empire to know, do we?"

"No, Chief. Who would be able to tell?"

"Sensors will know you wield magic and espiens will likely know what you are, depending where their strength lies. If the yellow star stone wasn't lost, and an Espier existed, they would know what you are. I can't teach you everything you need to know, lad, and there's no-one I know who can. You've got to learn a lot yourself. What you've done today is told in the stories, but now you've got to teach yourself. Your greatest asset, lad, is your brain. Use it."

Cal grinned. "I'll try, Chief. It might be a bit rusty though."

"You think you've got problems!"

Chapter 57

RESPONSE TO A PROBLEM

Hexadai, Week 44 – 27th Geryal, 13th Geryis 1213
Prince Tain's Chambers

TOWARDS THE END OF SPRING, Tain realised the Munewid was fast approaching. He spent one Hexadai morning planning the presents he'd give people before tackling his invitations for his and Cal's birthday celebration in the Audience Chamber. He was rushing to get them done before a mid-morning lesson with Peter when Cal arrived, having managed to persuade his father to let him visit.

"Are you up for a ride, Your Highness? I've given pa the slip."

Tain glanced up. "Cal, I can't, really. I've got to write these invitations."

Entering behind Cal, Peter said, "Your Highness, forgive me for interrupting, but I could write a standard invitation for you; your future administrator would do that."

"Would you really?" asked Tain.

"Of course, sir. All you'll have to do is sign them."

270

"I shouldn't let you but thank you..."

Peter simply smiled and inclined his head slightly. "It's no trouble, sir, and our lesson can easily wait."

* * *

An hour later, Judge Tancred disturbed Peter and noted what he was doing. "Tell me, did you qualify as a lawyer last week simply to become a scribe?"

Equally as grave, Peter said, "No, Your Honour, but maybe His Highness needs a secretary. I don't mind, Judge. He needs the fresh air..." He grinned. "So, I did pass my finals then?"

Tancred smiled. "Yes. I perhaps should not have let that slip. I shall see His Highness sometime soon." The judge left the Prince's rooms and considered carefully. He walked through the Privy Wing to the King's Corridor. Entering the Outer Office, he smiled at Richardson. "Can His Majesty spare me some time, Richardson?"

Richardson said, "Yes, Your Honour," before holding the Inner Office door open and announcing him.

Adeone glanced up. "Thank Alcis, an apt interruption. Come in, James. Would you like a drink?"

Tancred smiled. "I would, Your Majesty."

Adeone laid down his pen. "Good. I hope you've come for a chat."

"Difficult day, Sire?"

"Enough to make me long for a break." Adeone pushed himself to his feet. "Yet I think you're here for more than a chat. Let's get it over with."

Tancred inclined his head slightly. "I believe His Highness is of an age to need an administrator. Peter has been helping him occasionally but he is now a lawyer..."

Adeone nodded, pouring two drinks. "I must admit, I was thinking it might be time to find one. What sort of lawyer is Peter likely to make?"

Accepting the brandy, Tancred said, "He can be good, sir, even exceptional, but he suffers from nerves when he is the focus of people's attention. He had a stutter for years, but that seems to have all but disappeared now. It has taken hard work on his part."

Waving to a chair, Adeone sat down thinking. Sometimes answers presented themselves. "It is unfortunate for him that he suffers from nerves – in front of a judge and jury that could be disastrous for his clients; maybe he needs a slight change of direction. Do you think he could, even for a short time, act as Prince Tain's administrator?"

Tancred thought. "He has the skills and is more than competent but he *is* a lawyer, not a scribe."

Adeone nodded. "I realise that, James, but consider the benefits of a trained lawyer also being an administrator to a justiciar. It is a post that needs skills beyond that which a scribe uses."

Tancred did so. "You certainly have a point, sir. I cannot deny that. Peter has the skills of both as well. He needs no further training."

Adeone smiled. "I shall contact my errant son."

* * *

Quarter of an hour later, Tain and Cal entered the Inner Office. Tain noted the judge's presence but, after the smallest of puzzled frowns, grinned at him. Tancred winked.

Without preamble, Adeone said, "James has just told me you need an administrator."

Tain bit his lip. "I was going to write those invitations myself, Your Majesty…"

Cal spoke up, "I'm afraid, Sire, it's mainly my fault. I shouldn't have disturbed His Highness."

"Of course you should!" replied Adeone. "You see us rarely in Oedran. So, please, stop apologising for being a friend." He caught Tain's eye. "How are you finding Peter's help and tutelage?"

"Fine, sir, I'm learning a lot."

"Good, but how do you find working with him? Do you find, for example, that you have an intuitive understanding of each other? Could you see yourself working with him for longer?"

"Yes, father."

"You wouldn't complain if I asked him to be your administrator for a while?"

"No, sir."

Adeone smiled. "Then I shall have checks made. Please don't mention it to him yourself. What are you both doing this afternoon?"

Cal said, "I'm expected home, Your Majesty."

"We can't persuade you to stay? At least for lunch?"

Cal looked torn. "I really ought to go home, sir. I'm sorry."

"I won't confuse your obligations any further. Go on with you."

Cal bowed and made to leave.

"Will you excuse me also, Sire?" enquired Tancred.

Adeone considered him, intrigued. "Of course, James."

* * *

Outside the office, Tancred said, "I shall walk with you, if you do not mind, Master Calumiel." Once away from the curious ears of secretaries and guards, he continued, "I was interested when you refused to stay for lunch. It is unusual to deny a king's whim."

Cal reddened. "I don't do it lightly, Your Honour, but His Majesty is aware of my father's feelings about mine and Prince Tain's friendship. I find it better, on the King's advice, not to antagonise the situation."

"Then I shall say nothing more than this: remember, torn obligations are nothing new and you need to understand when you go which way. Do not do one thing today and a contradictory thing tomorrow. Unless important for the security of that which you hold dear be where you said you would be when you said you would be or at least send your apologies and remember, Cal, your father has a duty to the empire to release you to attend on the FitzAlcis, friend or not. Now, would you be quicker getting home on your own?"

"Possibly, Your Honour, but I like the slower road occasionally."

"You will make a courtier yet. I would not hold you up."

Cal smiled, said, "Thank you, Judge," and took to his heels.

Chapter 58
PICNIC
Tretaldai, Week 47 – 17th Lufial, 10th Lufis 1213
Ceardlann

THREE WEEKS LATER, unsuccessful in his hunt for the Comptroller, Tain mooched into the kitchens at Ceardlann.

Cook looked over. "You've only just had breakfast, Your Highness; I know that; they're still washing up."

Tain grinned. "Is there any chance of a picnic, Cook? You'll get peace and quiet, if there is."

"Is that bribery or appealing to my better side?"

"Both I think. Go on, please."

Cook sighed. "What has the Comptroller said?"

"I've yet to find him. I thought he might be here. I doubt he'll complain. He'll get peace and quiet as well. Elantha's joining me and Cal and I guess there'll be a couple of guards…"

Cook hmphed. "Peace and quiet, was it?"

"Peace *and* quiet, Cook," insisted Tain.

"I could have sworn breakfast wasn't that long ago, Your Highness," observed the Comptroller entering from the gardens.

Tain sighed. "Why does everyone assume I'm here for food – for food to eat now, that is?"

"Experience," replied the Comptroller with a wink at Cook. "What can we do for you, sir?"

Tain grinned. "I'm just persuading Cook to sort us out a picnic, Comptroller. We thought of going up to the pools for the day. It looks like it'll be clear. Elantha can sketch and Cal and I can swim and get a bit of swordplay in."

The Comptroller eyed him tolerantly. "Guards will have to go with you; just in case you hurt yourselves, sir."

Tain nodded. "We realised. Do you mind, Comptroller?"

"Mind? With tranquillity on the horizon? Not at all, but be careful, won't you? Bandit and Darky were already saddled for your morning ride; if Lady Elantha's joining you, I'll have Gem saddled. How long do you plan to be out, sir?"

"Until this afternoon. I'm not sure exactly. We should be back for dinner at seven."

"Very good, sir. Everything should be ready for you in a quarter of an hour. Does that give you enough time, Cook?"

"If I've space to move," grumbled Cook good-humouredly.

Tain and the Comptroller chuckled, before leaving the kitchen in companionable silence. Cook could give lessons in being hard done by, but there was no real annoyance behind the banter.

The Comptroller sent Joe to the stables before saying to Tain, "You know you don't really have to ask my permission to do things now, sir."

Tain looked at him. "I know, Comptroller, but you've a responsibility to see I'm safe, haven't you? And you're far more sensible than I am."

"You mean you'd listen to me, Your Highness?" (Tain nodded emphatically.) "Miracles do happen then. Any preference on the guards?" he asked, rather surprised by Tain's absolute trust.

"Not really…"

* * *

Tain, Cal and Elantha enjoyed every moment of the ride. The blossom winds invigorated them, the petals dancing in the warm breeze brought smiles. Hedges had lost their skeletal winter appearance, the promise of summer was in the air and there were signs of new life in every glance. They chatted together and with the guards, but when they reached their destination, a guard said,

"We'll be over here, sir, obviously having a nap…"

Tain grinned. "Obviously. Cal, do we have a bucket? We might need to wake Silversley up at some point."

Cal shrugged. "No, but I'm sure we could find something to hold water, sir…"

Tain grinned at the guard. "Thank you."

Carlon Silversley chuckled. "Well, you don't need us cramping your

274

style, sir. Just scream if you need us." He and his fellow guard settled themselves far enough away that their presence wouldn't be intrusive, but they would still be close enough to help. For them, as much as their charges, it was a day to relax.

Tain nodded. He and Cal took the saddlebags off Bandit and Darky and found a shaded spot for them. They took the bottles of drink and put them in the pool to keep cold. Leaving the horses saddled, they left them to roam over the small paddock next to the meadow. A farmer came along the lane whistling and seeing the activity stopped to see what was happening. Tain raised his hand in acknowledgement. A wave came back before the farmer carried on up the lane, still whistling; later his wife arrived with some fresh pies for everyone and also some cool ale for the guards.

Twelve minutes after they arrived, Elantha was happily sketching under a tree for shade. Tain and Cal had kitted up and the clang of metal on metal resounded through the meadow.

Cal grinned as he disarmed Tain. "Sorry, sir."

"No, you're not. Let me level the score…" replied Tain, weighing his sword in his hand.

An hour later, Cal had disarmed Tain three times to Tain's disarming of Cal once.

Retrieving his sword for the third time, Tain muttered, "You are too good to be true, Cal."

Cal grinned. "Or you're really bad, sir? If you want to feel better about your swordplay, we could try archery," he teased.

Tain saw a challenge in his friend's eye and decided to meet it another time. "Come on, let's have a drink. I'll beat you again later."

Divesting themselves of swordbelts, swords and daggers, they ran to the pool to retrieve the drinks. Tain grabbed Cal and, wrestling, they fell in with a splash. Tain laughed and struck out for the middle. Cal followed, grinning. Halfway, cramp assailed him. Seeing him in trouble, Tain swam over and pulled him to the side of the pool before shouting Carlon Silversley over. Two moments later, Cal was swearing colourfully on the bank.

Carlon grinned. "Where did you learn such language, Master Calumiel?"

"Listening near your quarters. Alcis, I feel a fool."

Tain grinned. "How nice to feel what you are… Drink?"

Carlon carefully examined both of Cal's legs. "You'll live, Master Calumiel. Only cramp. Take things easy. You shouldn't go swimming straight after swordplay; your muscles are too tired."

Cal said, "I didn't plan to."

Tain whitened. "It was my fault; I sort of tipped Cal into the pool."

"Sort of…" grumbled Cal.

"All right. I did tip Cal into the pool."

Carlon smiled. "Perfectly natural reaction, I'd have thought, watching the pair of you before. You weren't to know, Your Highness. Give it half an hour and you can try drowning each other again."

Tain grinned. "I see you're concerned for my welfare, Silversley."

The guard pushed himself to his feet. "I get paid for it, sir." He saluted and left.

Tain grinned and passed Cal a beaker of cool juice. "Remind me whose mad idea this was…"

Cal sighed. "I suppose it was mine and now I'm soaked as well…"

Tain sank onto the grass beside him, grinning but not rising to the bait. "That's what I thought. It *was* a good idea though."

Chapter 59
LORD RYSON
Evening
Court

THAT EVENING, Lord Cearis greeted Adeone as he entered Court. The Lord of Oedran was slick, courteous and a true courtier. He acted the part so well Adeone was more concerned about what he was hiding. After brief pleasantries, Cearis returned to Anguis and Rathgar. Adeone wondered what their discussion was about for it appeared pointed, if not intense. His amble continued, his eyes sweeping over each room. He wasn't hunting for anyone in particular; Landis hadn't planned to attend, and Arkyn had returned to Ceardlann for a couple of days that afternoon. He smiled at his two eldest nearchildren as they made an obeisance. They were talking with Malandra Para, Emrys Daioch and Irvin Iris. What exactly Malandra Para was discovering made him pause for thought, but neither Julius nor Julia would be unguarded in their talk at Court.

Ryson was the first person to speak to him and Adeone found himself wondering why the lord had initiated the conversation.

"Your Majesty, I hope you're well."

"Very well, thank you, Lord Ryson. How are your endeavours with the law?"

"Quieter now that the students' exams are completed, Your Majesty."

"I was always curious you accepted the post at the school. Surely your life holds enough occupation without such a job."

"I enjoy being busy, Sire, and have no family to take up my time."

Adeone said softly, "There never has been word of your sister since she left Oedran, has there?" (Saddened, Ryson shook his head.) "I am truly sorry. I liked Lady Leila. She had a bold spirit."

"She did what she thought she had to, sir. I hope, wherever she is, she's happy."

Adeone nodded. "So do I. I was thinking about Finn the other day…"

"Another loss of our generation, sir. He would have made a good Lord of Oedran."

"Yes, his son, though, is showing much promise. He is considering becoming a lawyer."

Ryson smiled. "Then I hope he can fulfil that wish, sir. I have never regretted my path. By knowing the law, I can stay on the right side of it."

Adeone chuckled. "A wise move, Lord Ryson."

Ryson bowed slightly and, sensing the end of the conversation, left without fuss.

Advisor Rayburn caught the King's eye and moved over. "May I help, Your Majesty?"

"I don't see Prince Arkyn's junior advisors, Rayburn."

Rayburn smiled. "I'm not sure His Highness wishes them to attend as a right, Sire."

* * *

That night, Adeone undressed in a thoughtful mood. Seeing it, Simkins was quiet and unobtrusive. So much of his position depended on the King's moods that he didn't like to disturb them too much.

When he was alone, Adeone blew out the candle and closed his eyes, expecting sleep to be elusive, but it enveloped him quickly and stealthily. Colours and sounds swamped his mind: red hair, laughter, the thud of wood on wood, Ceardlann with the sun shining, the pools glistening, strains of music he couldn't recognise, the King's Hall at Oedran wreathed for celebrations and then shuddering blackness. He woke, sweating, and went to his bathroom.

A soft voice said, "You only have to ask…"

He turned, but no-one was there.

Climbing back into bed, he shivered. Closing his eyes once more, he allowed sleep to drift over him and this time all but one dream was lost to memory.

Chapter 60

FEELINGS

Imperadai, Week 48 – 25th Lufial, 18th Lufis 1213
Inner Office

REACHING HIS DESK a few days later, Adeone flicked through his correspondence. With the Munewid only a few days away there was a larger pile than normal, but Richardson, efficient as ever, had bundled together the letters he might want to read first. All of which were marked as private, which meant they were more gossip than business. Grinning, Adeone pulled out Wealsman's latest missive and settled back to read of his friend's exploits and Kristina's pregnancy. Wealsman had a separate seal for anything that was official business, and yet another for anything that was covert information. They hoped the duplicity would continue to protect their communications, as it had for years. Adeona was toddling and beginning to talk, keeping the nursery attendants on their toes. Adeone chuckled. He'd have been disappointed if she hadn't. Kristina was doing well, with very little trouble from the pregnancy. Amongst the family news was the information that Wealsman thought it likely that Penrod and Chandra had formed an attachment. She had settled well into Terasian life with its slower pace and less expectation.

Adeone flicked through his correspondence again. There, nestled between letters from Lord Faran and Lord Daioch, was one from Penrod Silvano. He broke the seal, smiling. It confirmed what Wealsman had suspected. In Penrod's sloping script and formal language was the request to marry.

Adeone called up Dragoris and obtained a link with Penrod. Having made sure the young man hadn't changed his mind and understood that the marriage had to be about them and not the politics of the empire, Adeone congratulated him and closed the link before asking for a new one with Chandra, delighting in the difference in the young lady from when she'd left Oedran. She'd regained much of her poise and confidence. She said that Penrod had proposed and that she'd accepted him and she was glad that the King had no objection to make. Adeone smiled at that. How could he object if she was happy?

Once out of the link, he started to consider how he'd felt when Ira had accepted him and how the marriage had salved both their loneliness. Hers due to being a motherless only child and his not very different reasons: for although he had a brother they weren't close and his father seemed distant. As his mind was drawn into the past, he considered the future and wondered if the loneliness he'd rediscovered with Ira's death would ever heal again – the pain had eased at times but he avoided following the thought to its conclusion, purposefully making himself think of other things he finished reading his letters. Neassa had written confirming that she hoped to be back in Oedran for the Munewid. Adeone started when he realised that it was only three days away, so Neassa was due in Oedran in two. Cursing, he asked Richardson to make sure the house on Palace Walk would be ready for her. Time was slipping away from him with increasing regularity. It would be Tain's fourteenth birthday in a matter of days. Only a year until he became Justiciar of Oedran.

* * *

Two days later, Richardson announced Neassa with a ready manner but a warning in his eye that Adeone couldn't account for. He rose.

"How was your journey? Far pleasanter than your journey out, I hope. The weather was so much warmer for a start."

Neassa smiled. "It was different, sir. They were both pleasant in their ways. I thought I ought to look in and let you know I've arrived safely..."

"I couldn't be happier to know it. How was Tradere?"

"Reassuringly unchanged, Sire, in essentials, that is. We didn't visit Byfa much and the peace and quiet of the estate was quite a restorative. I might return soon."

Adeone sighed. "Don't let me lose you again, Neassa. I've only just got both my cousins back, and they're already deserting me."

"Rhian was never lost to you, sir."

"She might as well be in Tradere sometimes. No, you're right I suppose and neither were you, my own reticence kept us all at a distance. When did you arrive exactly?"

"About half an hour ago, sir. Mother greeted us in her normal way..."

Adeone stilled. "Us?"

Neassa smiled. "Ah, yes, sorry, slip of the tongue. I've just remembered I told mother I'd go and talk with her, if you'll excuse me, Sire..."

Adeone got up. "I don't think I will, Lady Neassa, not until the slip of the tongue is explained."

On the threshold, Neassa said simply, "Sorry, Your Majesty," sweeping into a deep curtsy and leaving.

Watching her go, Adeone stilled as another figure entered the Inner Office and closed the door. "Roads lead in two directions, Rhian?"

"I thought I'd prove it, and you might be pleased to know, or you might not, I've taken leave of Tradere for far longer this time."

Adeone moved towards her.

"I could go," she murmured.

"I don't think so," he whispered, a cacophony of feelings rushing over

279

him. There had been no time to prepare to deceive his mind. Had Rhian known her unexpected appearance would destroy the wall? His heart ached. After so long, loving another woman hurt, but he *wanted* the pain. Their lips met and Adeone was hers; he finally broke away.

Rhian touched his face gently in understanding before calmly walking out of the Inner Office.

Adeone collapsed onto his chair, cursing roundly, wanting to run after her, but he didn't. He needed to come to terms with the realisation and what it meant. Words and phrases half heard through drowsiness haunted him as he put his head in his hands...

'Someone's missing; someone who should be here.'

'Follow your heart, my dear. You have one but maybe you've forgotten how to recognise it...'

'You only have to ask...'

Would he face it or would he run from the realisation? How had he never seen his own feelings for what they were? How had he been so blind? How could he now face Rhian? Why did he feel he was betraying Ira? How...? Why...? Her lips, her mind, her care... His foolishness, his blindness, his future.

Chapter 61
FOURTEENTH BIRTHDAY
Alunadai, Week 1 – 1st Cearal, 1st Cearcis 1214
Prince Tain's Chambers

TAIN WOKE on the first day of 1214 grinning. He pushed himself up in bed and rang the bell.

Linnt entered gravely, "Your Highness?"

Tain grinned. "Any chance of a bath, Linnt?"

"Certainly, sir."

That was all, he'd gone and Tain's eyes narrowed. It was too much to expect that his manservant would have remembered it was his birthday. He bathed and dressed quickly before haring along the Palace corridors to his father's rooms, entering the King's bedchamber with nothing more than a perfunctory and perfectly useless knock.

Adeone woke to his bed bouncing and groaned. "Tain, you could wait until I'm awake, you little rascal."

"Morning, father."

"Morning. Happy birthday. Is it really fourteen years since you appeared in my life?"

Tain grinned. "Not quite. There's a few hours yet, but, basically, yes."

Rolling over, Adeone pinned his son down so he could tickle him. "I knew there was a reason I've not felt sane for years."

Tain struggled to get away and then gave up. "Father, it's not just my fault. Arkyn's older than me."

Adeone rolled onto his back. "So he is. He doesn't, however, come bouncing onto my bed first thing in the morning…"

"One of us has to be spontaneous."

"Arkyn's got plenty of spontaneity in him. It's just better hidden. If you want to breakfast with me, I suppose you'll have to let me get up." Adeone rolled over and rang for Simkins. When his side was exposed, Tain tickled him.

When Simkins entered moments later, he found the King cocooning Prince Tain in blankets, laughing merrily. The manservant struggled to keep a straight face.

After a short time, Adeone said, "His Highness will be breakfasting here – if he can get out of that."

Trying and failing to keep the laugh out of his voice, Simkins said, "Very good, Your Majesty. Your bath's ready." As the King left, he continued, "Happy birthday, Your Highness."

Tain struggled to extricate himself. "Thank you, Simkins… Help."

The manservant pulled the blankets apart. "There you are, sir. What had you done?"

Tain laughed. "Tickled father."

Simkins eyed him. "Maybe I should imprison you again…"

"You wouldn't!" (Simkins raised an eyebrow.) "Would you?"

"Probably not, Your Highness, but that's not a promise. What would you like for breakfast?"

"Food. Edible for preference and non-poisonous for definite."

Simkins laughed. "I'll see what I can do, sir. Have you seen His Highness yet?"

"No, I woke father up instead."

"I'll see if he's awake, shall I? To join you and the King?"

Tain bit his lip. "Can you not, Simkins?"

"Want some time alone?" (Tain nodded.) "Then I'm sure I can manage that for you, sir."

"Thank you." Tain collapsed onto his father's pillows with a sigh as Simkins left.

When Adeone entered twelve minutes later, he found Tain's eyes had closed. Perching on the bed, he woke him gently. "Breakfast?" As Tain scrambled up, Adeone slipped an arm round his shoulders, saying conversationally, "I hesitate to ask what plans you've got for today."

Tain looked at him. "Probably wise, father."

* * *

After breakfast, Adeone and Tain made their way to Tain's chambers. Arkyn was there with a grin on his normally controlled features. He passed Tain a small parcel and Tain opened it with enthusiasm.

In it was a beautifully jewelled key. He looked at it with narrowed, suspicious eyes and then glanced at his brother, eyebrow raised. Arkyn stood aside. There at right angles to the far wall was a bureau carved with trees and leaves, the front inlaid with mother of pearl and lighter woods depicting a woodland pool. Tain opened the front. He laughed and turned back to Arkyn, giving him a hug. In the centre of the desk was a beautiful model of Ceardlann. Tain picked it up to look at.

"Who…?"

Adeone said, "It was in the cabinet you destroyed at Ceardlann. We thought you'd like it. Arkyn's been hiding it from your research for months."

Tain laughed. "Thank you, father."

"It's not from me. That and the desk are Arkyn's presents to you."

Tain turned. "But…"

Arkyn smiled. "A table's no good for keeping things personal, is it?"

"I'll have an office."

"I really wouldn't keep personal correspondence there if I were you…"

Adeone rang the bell. "Is the Palace Carpenter waiting, Linnt?"

The carpenter brought in a fair-sized trunk and Tain looked at it, intrigued. Adeone said, "Go on, Tain, open it…"

Tain didn't see him wink at the carpenter, nor did he notice that the carpenter didn't leave.

Tain tried the lid, but it wouldn't open. He looked all over it for any sign of a keyhole and couldn't find one. Sitting on his heels, he watched his father's grinning face.

"Father!"

Adeone smiled. "Do you remember a couple of years ago I said I'd asked the carpenter to come up with something for you that was more inventive than the carved bugs? This is it. Carpenter, maybe you'd like to explain."

The carpenter smiled. "It's a puzzle box, sir, just a rather large one. Only if you know how exactly to open it can you do so. There's a key, but it isn't conventional. May I?" (Tain nodded, excited.) "Feel here and here, sir. These two carvings, yes?"

Tain did. "Yes?"

"Press them gently. Did you hear the click? Good. Now, turn the

282

crescent moon until it looks right. Good. What do you think is next?"

Tain looked at the front of the trunk and bit his lip. "Opening the lid?"

The carpenter laughed. "I didn't expect you to say it, but you're right. Now, the lid and the actual trunk have separate compartments. That means you could put something in the lid, slide the cover over and it will be safe. You just have to release the cover like so." He moved two carvings on a pivot and slid the covering off. "The main trunk covering has a key, here it is, as well as a similar protection to the lid."

Tain fiddled with the trunk and discovered the method of removing the cover by letting down the border carving on the front of the trunk.

He grinned. "I like this. What next?"

The carpenter smiled. "Look in the trunk, sir."

Adeone said, "I thought the trunk was all of it, carpenter?"

"It was going to be, sir, but I thought His Highness wouldn't mind a few more bits. He might have trinkets to keep safe..."

Tain had removed the covering and whistled. "Carpenter..."

The carpenter smiled at him. "There are twelve boxes, Your Highness. All different sizes. I hope you have fun discovering their secrets."

"They're beautiful. Thank you."

Arkyn said conversationally, "You've been busy, carpenter."

"Yes, Your Highness, but I've enjoyed it. I really have."

Adeone smiled. "Good. I think His Highness will appreciate the challenge you've set as well."

The carpenter chuckled. "I hope so, Your Majesty, but if he's ever stuck, he knows his way to my hidey-hole."

Tain grinned. "So I do. Which one would you recommend I start with?"

"Try this one, sir, and think of Anapara."

Tain took it, turning it over and over, immediately lost in the challenge. He hardly noticed the carpenter push himself to his feet and, at a word of thanks from Adeone, bow and leave.

* * *

Two hours later, still puzzling over the box, Prince Tain looked up as Linnt announced Judge Tancred.

Tain jumped up lithely. "Come in, Your Honour."

Tancred rose from his bow. "Thank you, Your Highness. It has been some years since I have been in these rooms properly. My warmest wishes for your birthday."

Tain smiled. "Thank you. Have they changed much? I can't really remember them when Great-uncle Lachlan was alive."

Tancred looked round, a wealth of memories assailing every sense. "Less than you might think, Your Highness. There is still the same general

283

arrangement, and much of the same furniture, I notice."

"I like it all. I love the views as well, so much better than the nursery. Would you like some refreshment?"

"If it is not too much trouble, I would be glad of a cool drink, sir."

Tain rang for Linnt. In the interim before his manservant appeared, he said, "Please, Judge, sit down. I'm forgetting my manners as host."

Judge Tancred smiled. "I do not believe you are, Your Highness. Thank you."

When Linnt entered, Tain said, "Could we have some cool drinks please, Linnt?"

"I'll obtain some," stated the manservant without emphasis.

Tancred frowned slightly, but mindful of the fact it was Tain's birthday didn't comment. "Are you having a pleasant birthday, Your Highness?"

Tain nodded. "Yes, Your Honour."

After Linnt had brought the drinks and departed, Tain showed Judge Tancred the puzzle box. "There're eleven others for me to work out. All I have is the clue to think on Anapara."

Tancred ran his hands over the lid of the box. Then turned it in his hands. It was circular but with a border of small rectangles on the lid. He hummed to himself, trying to push them out. Two finally moved and he smiled. Tain watched him, fascinated, as he turned the concentric circles that made up the centre of the lid. Tain groaned. There on the lid was the flag of Anapara: three crossed arrows.

Tancred handed it over. "I think Your Highness may now be able to open it."

Tain smiled, ruefully, "Thank you, Judge." He lifted the three-part lid to find the box had been lined in violet velvet. There were three inner divisions which Tain discovered could be lifted out, along with a scrap of parchment with a clue for the Areal box.

He smiled. "They really are beautiful craftsmanship."

"They are indeed, Your Highness. Might I make a small suggestion? Do not show anyone else how to open them and be careful who watches you when you do. Keep them for things that are your treasures. Now, I have a small gift for you myself. I hope Your Highness likes it," he reached into a pocket and drew out a silk wrapped package.

Tain took it intrigued and touched. "Thank you, Judge…" He undid the wrapping carefully. A beautiful green leather-bound book lay in his hand with gold embossed title – *The Laws of the Cearcall and Their Effect on the Early Empire*. He laughed. "I never did finish reading it did I?"

"Now you might, sir. I still have my copy but I thought you might like your own."

Tain got up and gave the old judge a hug. "Thank you."

Tancred, surprised, hugged him back. "I do not think I have ever been hugged for passing over a book on law before, Your Highness."

Tain grinned. "This isn't any old book on law, Judge, this is the one you and Great-uncle Lachlan wrote and it was an intriguing read. Thank you."

Tancred nodded. "I hope you enjoy the rest, sir."

"I should. Oh and, Judge, I know it's my birthday, but it's also the Munewid and traditional to give gifts; so, I hope you can accept this…" Tain passed over a long thin parcel.

The judge took it, surprised. "Your Highness?"

"I wanted to give you something. You put up with my moods so well and you've given me such a lot that I just thought… Anyway, I hope you like it."

Tancred unwrapped a beautiful, but practical and unostentatious, walking cane. He held the handle and smiled as his hand met a friend.

Tain saw the smile. "The carpenter said he made it a bit long on purpose, but if you go and see him, he'll adjust it to the right height…"

"Thank you, Your Highness. It is beautiful and just what I have been hunting for, for a while now."

"I'm glad. I didn't have much of an idea, but father thought it would be all right. I didn't want you to feel like I was commenting on frailty or anything…"

"Your Highness, I shall be sixty-six this year. Age makes joints creaky even before the mind wanders further."

Tain grinned. "It must, because I've not noticed your mind wandering anywhere yet."

"Thank you, sir. So, what is planned for the rest of today?"

* * *

The party that evening was a strange mixture of mayhem and sobriety. Cal and Tain welcomed their guests with a smile, but many of Cal's were uncertain. The Galdwin siblings took the experience in their stride; having already spent time at Ceardlann, all but Haltern were relaxed in Tain and Elantha's company. Arkyn, being older than most of them, kept carefully to the sides but tried to get everyone joining in.

He said to Haltern, "Where does your brother get his energy from? It's tiring even watching him, but we can't let him win simply because it's his birthday."

"I'm fine watching, sir," replied Haltern nervously.

"I know the feeling. How are the twins?"

Haltern said, "Growing, Your Highness, and loud…"

"Well, they're only a few weeks old. I remember Tain never stopped crying for ages and now look at him."

Haltern did so. "Has the noise ever got any better, Your Highness?"

Arkyn laughed. "No, but I've got used to it. Come on, let's go and find somewhere quieter to perch."

To his own surprise, Haltern nodded. Arkyn was easy to talk to.

Adeone smiled to himself. Arkyn had a quiet but kind streak that meant he couldn't see anyone left out. Haltern was probably the calmest of the Galdwin siblings, but whether that was his nature or decision he wasn't sure. He watched as Louisa took Elantha over to meet Madam Galdwin.

"Lady Elantha, the drawing you did of Louisa is beautiful."

Elantha blushed. "Thank you, Madam Galdwin. It was a pleasure to draw her. I hope you've recovered fully from the twins' arrival."

Madam Galdwin smiled. "I have, thank you, my lady. Doctor Chapa, as well as our own doctor, was most attentive."

Elantha smiled. "The doc's like that. How are the twins?"

Madam Galdwin realised that Elantha constantly turned the conversation away from herself and onto other people without seeming to be evasive. She wondered why and what the young girl might be hiding. So used to her own daughters talking about all their doings, it was strange that this young girl was more interested in everyone else.

Landis, standing next to Master Galdwin, smiled at him. "How are your ears standing up?"

"Just about all right, thank you, my lord. I'm trying to work out which is the noisiest brood…"

Landis chuckled. "Mine are certainly giving yours a run for their money. Young Ira and Elsie seem to be hiding under the tables."

Hearing him, Adeone said, "Shall we join them?"

Master Galdwin snorted, amused. "I'm not sure we'd all fit, Sire."

Halfway through the evening, the door opened and Rhian and Neassa entered quietly. They gave a brief curtsies to Adeone – who shook his head tolerantly at them – before edging around the melee until they'd safely joined the other adults.

Neassa said, "Our apologies for being late, Sire…"

Adeone winked. "I'll cope, Neassa, and although this might look like a battlefield, it is a family gathering."

"I think he wants you to call him Adeone," observed Rhian, staring at the melee.

The King glanced at her. "There was still the possibility of doubt in that, Rhian."

Landis half listening to them said, "Possibilities aren't certainties, Sire."

Adeone shook his head. "You might as well take your cloaks off; we're not going anywhere for a while. Somewhere in that tangle is my son..."

Rhian took his hand and squeezed it. "He's definitely your son, if this mayhem is anything to go by."

Landis and Neassa shared a glance and started talking about everyday matters.

Chapter 62

APPOINTMENT

Pentadai, Week 1 – 5th Cearal, 5th Cearcis 1214
Inner Office

TWO DAYS AFTER the end of the Petitionals, Adeone looked up as Richardson announced a rather uncertain youth. The King scrutinised him in a swift but not condescending manner.

"Come in and sit down, Master Selth. Thank you, Richardson. That will be all for now."

Richardson left as Peter took a seat uncertainly.

Adeone crooked an eyebrow. "Have you concluded your shorthand lessons with His Highness, Master Selth?"

Peter considered. "Y-yes, Sire. He is able to scribe in shorthand without guidance. We have simply been improving speed and technique over recent weeks."

"Good. From my understanding, you've been helping Prince Tain with more than learning shorthand; I'm referring to the composition of official invitations for him. I also understand from Judge Tancred that you've helped to highlight the fact that Prince Tain needs a secretary or, more accurately, an able administrator. Is this true?"

"I d-didn't mean to interfere, Your Majesty."

Adeone smiled. "I never thought that was your intention. You're a trained lawyer, I understand, and a scribe's son. I believe your late father was training you to be a scribe before Judge Tancred persuaded you to follow a different path. Are you methodical and organised?"

"I, erm, I try to be, Sire."

Adeone nodded. "Well, you've juggled studies and teaching, so we'll take that as a definite. There has been a suggestion that, as my son will be the Justiciar, a trained lawyer would be perfect as an administrator, as long as he holds the other skills normally found in clerks and scribes and can work for Prince Tain. From what I and others can see, you fit those criteria, so... Master Peter Selth, might I offer you the position of administrator on Prince Tain's staff? Starting today?"

Peter sat stunned. After a moment he managed, "Sir, as you have just offered the position, of course you might…"

"Ah, I forgot I was dealing with a lawyer. What I meant to ask was, will you accept the post of Prince Tain's Administrator?"

"S…sorry, Your Majesty, force of habit. I would be honoured to accept, but s…surely someone with more ex…experience will be needed?"

Adeone sighed. "Have you ever heard the expression about not looking a gift horse in the mouth? Or even the one about not questioning the King?"

Peter took a deep breath. "My apologies, once again, Sire, but as a lawyer I hunt for the catch in everything, especially after a few discussions with Prince Tain, but that's a good thing… I think. Sorry, sir."

Adeone chuckled. "The catch here is long hours, probably few thanks, no real life of your own, putting up with our whims, and my son's sense of humour. I mentioned the long hours, I think…"

"You did, Your Majesty."

"Good. I did, however, miss out traitors trying to suborn or even kill you, notoriety and infamy," he trailed off and motioned with his hand that the rest could be concluded.

Peter smiled. "I can't see why anyone would ever refuse the post, sir."

Adeone laughed. "It is true, few would: the benefits are supposedly great. Richardson will see you get to know everything about those and all the rest of the paraphernalia over the next two weeks. Firstly, however, I need to take your oath of loyalty. It is not fealty but it can be as strong."

"I understand, Your Majesty. I have made a study of such matters since I was asked to teach His Highness."

"Thank you. Richardson!" When the door opened, the King continued, "Master Selth has just accepted the position of Prince Tain's Administrator. I need to take his oath, and then he's in your care for a while."

Richardson smiled. "Very good, sir. Master Selth, welcome to the FitzAlcis staff."

"Thank you, Administrator, and I much prefer plain Peter."

"That is for His Highness to decide," said Richardson. "I suggest you kneel for His Majesty."

* * *

Later that day, Adeone said, "He's no longer your teacher, Tain, but a member of your staff. Can you adjust to that?"

Tain bit his lip. "I think so, Your Majesty, but I'm not sure exactly what he should be doing…"

"I'll have a word with Arkyn and see if he can spare Edward to explain, shall I?"

"He's busy with the preparations for the Macarian Review; he's leaving at the end of next week."

"Leave it with me."

Arkyn suggested Tain might learn as much about how to interact with an administrator if he actually spent a hectic day in Arkyn's office.

Adeone smiled. "Can you stand it?"

Arkyn sighed. "I might be able to, Sire. There's a table he can use and if he has his lessons with him, he *might* be quieter."

"True. I'll suggest it. Just warn Edward why. I know you have an intuitive understanding of each other but try to remove it for the day."

* * *

The following Tretaldai, Tain settled himself at the table and started reading the Redress Decree. Making notes, he kept one ear open as Arkyn organised details of his trip and meetings. Edward meticulously took notes and explained what had already been done.

Halfway through the morning, the administrator said, "Would you like some refreshment, Your Highness?"

Arkyn nodded. "Please. I'm talking rather a lot today."

Edward smiled. "And you, Your Highness?"

Immersed in law, Tain didn't realise the question had been directed to him, as he'd only heard the honorific.

Arkyn rolled his eyes. "Tain! Edward asked you a question. You're meant to be listening."

Tain bit his lip. "Sorry, Edward… Look, would it be easier to say 'sir'? With both of us in the room it does get a bit confusing."

Edward hesitated. It would, but Prince Arkyn could be a stickler for propriety.

Arkyn said, "It's up to you, Edward. I don't mind in this situation."

Edward inclined his head slightly before saying to Tain. "Then, yes, sir, it might be."

Tain grinned. "Good. What was the question again?"

After lunch, Tain listened more closely. He'd had lessons on what his father and brother did but to see it at close quarters was fascinating.

Arkyn said, "For the first time we're all travelling together. Lord Julius Landis and Advisor Rayburn, along with their staff, will also be accompanying us before carrying on to the Pale Lands, to undertake the provincial visit for Lord Landis; so, it might be a bit crowded for a couple of days on board ship. Right, gentlemen, that's all for today. Take the day tomorrow to see your families. We'll be away for a few weeks again and after last year… Well, I'd be happier knowing you've seen them. Remember, though, no weapons in the city; they're now banned in the Lower City as well as the Administrative Quarter. I don't want any of you under arrest."

His advisors made appropriate noises of appreciation before leaving.

Tain looked up when they'd gone. "Caple doesn't do much of the work, does he?" (Arkyn frowned.) "I'm just saying he doesn't know what's in the reports he has to hand. He has to keep checking them."

Arkyn said, "He can't write them all, Tain, he's my Chief Advisor."

"I'd be surprised, after that, if he'd written one. Sorry, I know they're your staff and I should keep my mouth shut."

Arkyn smiled. "Do you ever though?"

"On occasion. It was only an observation. I'm probably completely wrong. One meeting isn't really enough, is it?"

"You can come back for a couple more."

"No, thank you. Really, I'm quite content."

Arkyn laughed. "Well, that's it for the day, I think. I'll just check. Edward!" A moment later, he said, "Is there anything else today?"

Edward shook his head. "Nothing official, Your Highness. The dispatches from Terasia arrived earlier. There's a letter from the Margrave but I very much doubt that it's official."

"*That's* a safe assumption," muttered Tain.

Arkyn chuckled. "Pass me Wealsman's letter then, Edward. I'll reply tonight. Could you let Kadeem know we're done, please?"

"Certainly, Your Highness." He turned to Tain. "Shall I send your papers to your chambers, sir?"

Gathering his notes together, Tain hesitated. "Would you mind?"

"Not at all, sir. Just leave them there; I'll get them into order for you as well."

Tain grinned. "Good luck but I think they're about right. Thank you."

Arkyn pushed himself to his feet. "Come on, Tain. I've a dinner planned with Irvin, Julius and Emrys. Do you want to join us?"

Tain grinned. "I'd be an odd number."

"That's not the only odd thing you are."

"I'm *your* brother…"

Arkyn groaned. "Do you have to keep reminding me? Thank you, Edward. Take tomorrow off. If there's anything urgent, it can wait."

"I'm content, sir. I don't have family to visit," replied Edward, placidly.

"I don't plan to be attending to my duties on my birthday; if you're not here, no-one can interrupt me easily – so it could be purely selfish."

Edward sighed. "Thank you, Your Highness."

As they left, Tain could have sworn he heard the administrator say under his breath, *'It could be, but it isn't.'*

Once in his sitting room, Arkyn said, "Have you got more of an idea now?"

"Yes. Thank you. Edward's very efficient, isn't he?" observed Tain.

"Yes. I asked him to highlight every aspect today, but it doesn't mean he elaborated any of them."

"Let's hope Peter is as well because I'll be ten times worse than you to keep organised."

"Now you mention it… What? You said it first…"

Tain grinned. "I thought I'd get it in before you did. Who are you taking to head your guards?"

"Lyndon. Why?"

"I think you should take Smithers again… Please. You should have a captain guarding you on official trips…"

"It's not written in any law, is it?"

Tain grinned. "No. I just thought, well, that it might look better."

"It would, but Lyndon should get experience travelling abroad before I promote him when you're fifteen. We'll both need a captain then."

"So, you admit that a captain looks better if we're being official. Take Smithers, Arkyn. I really don't mind."

"Thank you." He glanced round. "Evening, Kadeem. His Highness will be joining me for dinner. Could you offer my invitation to Lord Rale as well, please? His Highness was worried about odd numbers."

Kadeem, who'd been waiting unobtrusively, nodded. "Very good, sir. I'll let Master Linnt know too. Would you prefer to change here or in your rooms, Your Highness?"

Tain, musing on his day, started. "Sorry, Kadeem. Erm, here, if it's not too much trouble. Maybe you should call me *sir* as well…"

Kadeem said, "I shall consider it, sir." He turned to Arkyn. "Your Highness?"

Arkyn laughed. "Ask Edward, Kadeem, and then follow what you think is right. Prince Tain's old enough to make such decisions himself."

When Kadeem had left, Tain said, "Is it a foolish decision?"

"It's an interesting one. I know you dislike honorifics, but they exist for a reason and have their uses; however, I can't see if Edward and Kadeem are discreet when we're together that there's a problem."

Tain nodded. "Thank you." He raised an eyebrow slightly. "So, I'm old enough to make my own decisions?"

"Damn!"

Chapter 63

UPPER HALL

Pentadai, Week 2 – 12th Cearal, 12th Cearcis 1214
Palace – Secretaries Corridor

TWO DAYS BEFORE Prince Arkyn left for Macia, Edward was returning to his room on Secretaries' Corridor when he saw Peter leaving his.

Noticing vague uncertainty, Edward said, "So you've moved in then?"

"Yes, sir."

Edward shook his head. "We're both administrators, Peter. It says so on our doors."

Peter smiled and turned to his own pointedly. "Not on mine it doesn't."

"Trust the joiners to let down my arguments. I'll get it seen to. Are you off to eat?"

"I was, yes, but I'm not sure... I've been part of the FitzAlcis staff for months technically, but I've never eaten here or found my way around properly."

"You've had a busy time since you joined. Let me get changed and I'll show you the way. Have you your tokens?"

"Tokens?"

Edward looked at him. "Like these..." He held out two small pyramidal sticks painted scarlet and banded with gold: one was marked 'Upper Hall – Administrator Edward – Prince Arkyn's Staff' on different sides, the other was marked 'Secretaries Corridor – Room 2 – A'.

"Not my new ones."

Edward grinned. "You'd better get them. They might not believe me."

"I've not seen them yet. Richardson said they would be in my room but I've had a hunt..."

Edward frowned. "They're normally on the occasional table. Did you check there?"

"First place."

Still frowning, Edward said, "No matter. Give me six minutes."

They entered a pleasant refectory where there were both tables set for eating and comfortable chairs to relax in. It reminded Peter in a way of the common room at the Law School but far more polished and refined.

One of the servers, his servant's badge clear on the left side of his chest, hurried over seeing Edward entering. "Administrator! Food or drink?"

Edward smiled as the man's gaze slipped to Peter. "Food please. This is Administrator Selth. He's accepted the post for Prince Tain, Denny."

"Pleased to meet you, sir. Any tokens?"

Peter said, uncomfortably, "Not yet, it seems."

Denny sighed. "Typical Palace efficiency! I heard a while ago that you'd accepted the post. Never mind, sir, I'll see you get them forthwith or I'm not head server. I'll let the lads know the situation. Now, let's see…" He turned to the room, surveying everyone else who was present "…Do you *want* to be bored tonight, sirs?"

Edward grinned. "Not really."

"I'll avoid everyone else then. These places should do nicely. Now, we've a few different soups tonight but I'd recommend the Denshirian Tomato – not too spicy but nicely warming. Fish: we've, no, no you'd be better with the trout. Meat: nice bit of pork with sage and apple and for a sweet we've cakes, creams or there are some decadent meringues. As a savoury, there's always the Low Plainers Toast – lovely that is, rich creamy cheese melted in a pot with ooo so many lovely things added, herbs galore and—"

Edward smiled both at the recitation and at the look on Peter's face. "Sounds admirable, Denny. As for the sweet, we'll have a selection."

Denny smiled. "I'm glad you said that, sir. Now, for drinks…"

When he'd left, Peter exclaimed, "Five courses!"

"Lunch is three." Edward laughed. "Tell me about it. In the orphanage I was lucky to grab a bowl of soup. When I was with the runners and couriers, it was mostly a stew or some such thing. Lower Hall you get two courses. This, this came as a surprise."

"My life's been one course meals. I'm not sure I'll manage all he said."

Edward nodded. "You'll be surprised. How do you like your room?"

"It's surprisingly spacious. I thought the rooms here were only big enough for a bed and a chest, a window if you're lucky."

"It depends on your status. Some have dormitories, some rooms like you describe, others rooms like ours with variations in between. Administrators and FitzAlcis body servants are high ranking – hence we have somewhere to sit as well as sleep. We work long hours and in thanks the FitzAlcis have traditionally given us comforts."

Peter said, "I'd have thought, given the long hours, all we'd want to do is sleep."

"Yes, but sometimes you just can't. Ah, thank you, Denny. You're right, this smells appetising." He caught a sparkle in the server's eye and watched as Peter took a spoonful of soup.

Peter grimaced. "It might look nice, but it's very salty."

Edward chuckled. "Denny!"

Denny grinned. "I have my orders, sir. I can't deny His Highness."

Peter rolled his eyes and shook his head.

"I thought self-preservation was your strength, Denny," commented Edward. "Peter is also a lawyer and will be able to make your life far more difficult."

Waving his hands, Denny said, "Yes, yes, sir, but the Prince…"

"Isn't here and we are."

Denny swallowed; he'd somehow known it would go wrong.

Peter laughed. "Denny… I'd be grateful for some soup that hasn't been laced with salt. The other courses likewise untampered with and I'll let His Highness know that your welcome was exemplary."

Not at all reassured, Denny sagged. "Thank you, sir. The Prince might think I, erm, was a coward and failed if you use the word 'exemplary'."

"His Highness might think a lot, Denny, but I'd be more concerned about what he says."

Setting down a different bowl of soup, Denny left looking a little dejected.

Edward grinned at Peter. "Well done. You've gone from being a nervous, inexperienced official to a force to be reckoned with in all of three sentences."

"As you said, I'm a lawyer!"

Edward laughed. "So I did. Oh dear, I thought he'd noticed… Steward, good evening."

"Evening, Edward. What was all that about?"

"It's not mine to tell."

Peter said, nervously, "It was nothing to worry anyone with, St…Steward."

"I think it was, Selth," retorted the Steward.

Peter shook his head. "I'm afraid not."

The Steward pursed his lips. "I shall find out."

Seeing Denny fearfully watching their conversation, Peter considered the oaths he'd taken, all the conversations he'd had and overheard. Without relish, he said, "I'm not sure that would advantage anyone, Steward."

"Master Selth, it's my business to see that there are no disruptions here."

"Then might I suggest that it is not myself, or Administrator Edward, causing one? The evidence, it would seem, points elsewhere and the jury might acquit the defendant."

"I beg your pardon?"

"I mean to say that our conversation with Denny was private and I will not make any complaint to *anyone* about it."

When he'd gone, Edward let out a long breath. "You just told the Steward to bugger off and mind his own business."

"It appears I did."

Edward caught his eye. "And without reminding him that you work for Prince Tain in a highly confidential post."

"I thought it better to avoid the issue."

"*And* he did what you said."

Peter sighed. "What about it?"

Edward asked mildly, "How old are you?"

"Nineteen."

"I bet you nineteen darl he'll try to get you removed from post."

"I'll not bet, but I think you're right."

Edward grinned. "I wouldn't worry about it. The FitzAlcis like you."

"They don't him?"

"I never *said* that."

Peter eyed him, amused. "There's more to communication than words."

"Oh, stop your lawyer's tricks."

"I'll just finish my soup then, shall I?" asked Peter, chuckling.

"What a good idea," replied Edward dryly.

Lips twitching, they finished their first course.

Denny walked over to clear. After he served the fish, he said, "Erm, Administrator Selth... Thank you. I understand that you're not taking any action."

"How...?"

Denny grinned. "The Steward, bless him... I mean, the Steward is fuming about it, sir. He's wanted me gone for a while."

Peter said, "You did as ordered, as we all do. It's that simple." He winked. "Any chance of some water to drink?"

"Straight away, sir."

When they'd finished eating, they moved to sit in comfortable chairs. They'd barely taken a breath to start a new conversation when Denny was again hovering.

"Drinks, sirs?"

Edward nodded. "My usual please, Denny."

"Right you are, sir. Administrator Selth?"

"What choice is there?"

"Think of a drink from anywhere in the empire and I'm sure I can lay my hands on it. You'd be amazed what we've got. Terasian whiskey or rum from Macia, especially good with Serpent Isle limes, Lufian wine and Pale Landian vodka, Gerymorian sherries, Low Plainers creams—"

Peter smiled. "I get the picture. I've never tried half of those."

"Now's your time, sir. We've more choice here than the King's chambers – mainly because he-who-orders-supplies, that is the Victualler, likes his choice. Looking at you, I'd say you're a rum and lime sort."

"Then I'll try that, Denny, thank you."

Denny was a good judge of taste and Peter happily sipped at the drink knowing he'd just found a favourite of many years. He and Edward talked quietly for a couple of hours before Edward stilled slightly.

"Richardson's here. Him you do call 'sir'."

"I've found that out, don't worry."

Peter watched as Denny greeted Richardson formally before motioning in Edward and Peter's direction. Richardson crossed to them. As Edward rose to greet him so did Peter.

"Sir."

"Oh, sit down, Edward. Evening, Master Selth. I'm glad to see you."

"Good evening, sir, and please, call me Peter – really."

Richardson eyed him. Although Peter had made the request before, Richardson had refused, trying to teach him that the Palace wasn't always accommodating to personal wishes but, now Peter had been released from his charge, he said,

"You won't object if I don't return the favour?"

"Not at all, sir."

"How fortunate." He sat down. "I need a drink." A salver was beside him in a moment. "Very amusing, Denny! How about the bread and meat?"

"It's on its way, but chef's muttering."

"He can mutter. It's all I fancy. How did the soup go down?"

Denny swallowed. "Sir?"

Richardson looked at him. "Prince Tain inherited his sense of humour and the way it manifests itself from His Majesty. I have a long memory."

Denny said, "Administrator Selth surprised and concerned us all. I'll fetch your food."

With a faint grin and crooked eyebrow, Richardson turned to Peter.

"I don't think the Steward was too happy that I didn't lay a complaint against Denny, sir," explained Peter, "but I know His Highness' amusements and can recognise his hand."

"I'm impressed."

Edward smiled. "I certainly was – and highly amused…" By the time Edward finished a summary of what had happened, Richardson was chuckling, much to Peter's surprise.

"Carry on in that vein, Peter, and you'll be fine. Have you settled in?"

"Just about, sir, thank you."

Edward said, "But without a door plaque, appropriate tokens or anything from the Steward about living arrangements, I believe."

Richardson sighed. "One day… Edward, where's Prince Arkyn?"

"At Ceardlann for the night. He's expected back in Oedran tomorrow afternoon."

"Prince Tain?"

Peter answered, "He's also at Ceardlann, sir."

Richardson nodded. "Good. Edward, do you have time tomorrow morning to show Peter what's what and to get that plaque sorted?"

"I can spare a couple of hours, sir. My deputy can sit in the office and field messages."

"Then, Peter, you'd better arrange a time with Edward... Denny! Just what is that?"

A plate with a two-pound loaf and a pound of sliced spiced meats was put down on the table in front of Richardson, along with large bowls of different condiments.

Denny with a grin said, "It's bread and meat, served as the chef ordered."

"Just get him," muttered Richardson in a dangerous voice.

"Do I have to return as well?"

Richardson looked him in the eye. "Don't you want to, little nephew?"

"Not particularly, uncle. I'm a self-confessed coward."

"Then of course you must return. It's character building. Get him!"

"Spoil sport."

"Watch your cheek."

Denny left with a grin, fishing out a mirror from his pocket.

Two minutes later, the unconcerned chef stood in front of Richardson, smiling delightedly. "Yes, *Administrator*?"

"What is this, *chef*?"

"Bread and meat, an unspecified amount, therefore as ordered. I'm sure you'll manage it."

"I'm not. Are you done for the day, cousin?"

"Aye. You were the last one, as ever. I'm sure you do it so I have to work late."

Richardson rolled his eyes. "Stop complaining. Pull up a chair and help me eat this. By the way, this is Peter – he's looking after Prince Tain's professional life."

The chef nodded to Peter. "Like a challenge, do you, sir?"

"Fortunately, I do."

Richardson said, in an official voice, "Denny..."

"Yes, *sir*?" replied Denny silkily.

"See the chef's underlings know he's done for the day and that they can tidy up."

"You do realise that includes me?" he asked with a sigh.

Richardson merely smiled. "Yes."

It wasn't long before Peter and Edward excused themselves. They continued their conversation in Peter's room.

Peter eventually said, "Richardson, Denny and the chef are related?"

"Yes, but Denny isn't related to the chef. Different sides of the family and all the female lines, so surnames are different, confusingly. It's one reason the Steward dislikes Denny so heartily; he thinks Denny reports things to Richardson."

"Does he?"

"Who knows? If he doesn't, he'll be on someone's payroll."

"Hmm. Talking of payrolls…"

"Every Pentadai. See the Treasurer. You're charged a fixed amount from your wages for bed and board as you've a room here, but it's really not much."

"Right. I'm sending my pay home, or to the Law School to finish paying the last of my fees. If I can't get myself…"

"Talk to the scriveners and set an amount to send to each. I wouldn't make it the whole of the amount, just in case it does go astray, but they'll see it's delivered discreetly. The rest take along when you can."

"Do they do that?"

"Yes, for anyone with a token labelled A to C as our time off is limited. I send most of my pay to the orphanage; it reaches there fine. I even get a receipt from the scriveners. Keep some money back for settling your own bills: tailor, cobbler and the like – you have to be presentable. Prince Arkyn's a stickler – even if Prince Tain's more relaxed, don't be caught out."

"Right, it's all a little daunting."

"I know. Ask me if you ever need anything clarifying, or Richardson – he's really not that bad underneath…"

* * *

The following morning, Peter appeared in Edward's office at quarter past eight, looking smart but guarded.

Edward grinned at him. "You're actually nervous, aren't you?"

"Wouldn't you be? I've spent a lot of time speaking with Judge Tancred or the Keeper. It's what I know. The time I've spent with Richardson has been disquieting."

"You'll be fine. You've found your office here, I take it?"

"I've not really had much call for it yet."

"Did you see the Steward at all after you accepted the post?"

"No. Richardson has explained some bits and made sure I'm 'up to

298

scratch' but I didn't know what I needed to ask."

"Understandable. Do you have any scribes at your disposal yet?"

"Disposal?" Peter's eyes were amused.

"Lawyer!" laughed Edward. "Do you?"

"Not yet, no. Will I?"

"Of course. Keep an eye out for some and don't be afraid to mention to Prince Tain if you need more help. Prince Arkyn's always good about it and I expect His Highness will be as well – possibly more so, given the situation. Let's go by His Highness' chambers."

Edward, who hadn't entered Tain's sitting room before, looked around in interest. The room's general arrangement was no different from others, with comfortable seating around the fireplace a dining table behind them and a sideboard against the wall at its head. The room was spacious, with dual aspect windows looking over the city and gardens. "Do you have a key to the bureau?"

"Should I have?"

"Ask His Highness if he wishes you to have one. You'll need to make sure there are adequate supplies of writing materials. If His Highness doesn't wish you to have a key, it will not be a comment on trust but rather on privacy. If you're not furnished with a key, see the carpenter. I'd suggest you get a box made to hold the supply of writing materials, get it inlaid and so on, just so it doesn't look out of place. It might be an idea to get one made anyway. That way, your deputy, when you get one, could keep it supplied, or a trusted scribe could. His Highness' main office, will I take it, be the one at the Courthouse from next year?"

"Yes. I've not got access yet."

"That's understandable and unsurprising. We'll go to your temporary office. Where is it?"

"In the Justice Office—"

"That's a trek! You shouldn't have to cross the Palace. Who allocated it?"

"I presume the Steward, Chamberlain or Officier did. His Highness doesn't have an office yet, so I couldn't be accommodated next to it. It'll only be for a year."

Edward frowned. "You should still be closer to His Highness' chambers."

"I'd have a trek wherever I'm put, one way or another. If not to His Highness to the Courthouse."

"That's what the runners and couriers are for. Or your messenger, for that matter. Have you registered your messenger's name with the Herald? He'll know you've called one and what his name is, but you're meant to let him know."

"Richardson mentioned it, so I have, but I did wonder why, when he'd already know, I had to do so."

"By-law. There're a few here. The lawyer in you ought to look them up."

"I suppose there was an insult in that somewhere."

"Well, if you couldn't spot it, don't let me disillusion you." He laughed. "Come on, let's find your office. I'll know where to find you then."

"That's a good thing, is it?"

Chapter 64
ON THE JUSTICE HALL
Imperadai, Week 3 – 18th Cearal, 18th Cearcis 1214
Fitz's Inn - Schoolroom

TAIN ENTERED the room at Fitz's Inn on Imperadai, glad to see the judge. Once he was ensconced comfortably in his normal chair, Tancred said,

"I thought we could start looking at something new today, sir, but I also have a test for Your Highness at some point."

"I've not done any preparation, Judge. Can't you postpone it?"

Tancred said softly, "Many of life's tests come without warning, sir. Should we not, perhaps, mimic that to offer what practice we can?"

Tain bit his lip. "Maybe, Judge, but can you, at least, give me chance to gather my thoughts?"

"Of course, Your Highness. I thought instead of examining the laws of the empire, we could examine the court you will be in charge of during the majority of trials that you hear. Can you name it, sir?"

"Of course I can, Judge: the Justice Hall."

"Its formal name is *The Hall of the King's Justice*, sir. Maybe Your Highness can tell me by which door you enter?"

"Judge's Door."

"Correct. What is in front of you?"

"My chair, or rather the Justiciar's Seat and the long desk or bar."

"Correct. Why did you correct the possessive?"

Tain grinned. "It's because I'm not Justiciar yet, Judge."

"Good, sir, but did you mean 'it is' or 'it was'?"

"Either. Does it matter?"

"A man of law should always be clear of intent, sir. Occasionally shortened speech can confuse the issue and the meaning of statements. Some lawyers use it to their advantage, but being misunderstood is not always advantageous. There are other ways of conveying double meanings and it can pay to be precise."

Tain enquired, "Is that why you never use such speech, Judge? A lot of people think it's because you're trying to hide your origins."

"I have no wish to hide my origins; there is nothing disgraceful in them."

"I didn't mean that, Judge."

"No, sir, but there are times when saying the bare minimum is more polite than going into detail."

"I'm sorry, Your Honour."

"I know you are, sir. I can see it in your face. Shall we continue with our lesson?"

"Had we stopped, Judge?"

Tancred smiled. "Maybe we had not, sir. So, you are faced with the bar and Justice Hall. What is on either side of you when you enter?"

"I don't know, Judge. Should I? I suppose I should."

"There should be nothing but a member of your guard standing on each side of the door. It adds emphasis. What characterises your entrance, Your Highness?"

"Not tripping up, hopefully."

Tancred shook his head slightly, amused in spite of himself. "That would indeed be advantageous, sir. Do you know how your entrance is heralded?"

Tain sighed. "No, Your Honour."

"That surprises me, sir, with all your reading into the Cearcall."

"Why? Oh, but surely the flute music doesn't sound now?"

Tancred smiled. "That has not been heard since the golden flute was lost but it only sounded for a true Lord of Justice, one of great integrity, impartiality, compassion and knowledge. It is said it also heralds the manifestation of Truth and Justice; however, in the absence of flute music, trumpets sound at the entrance of a justiciar. It is also worth noting, sir, that once you have taken the oath, whether you enter that court as an official, or pass through it as a shortcut, the trumpets will still sound."

"Oh. What if I don't want them to? If I want to be anonymous?"

"There is no way that has been discovered of preventing them sounding, Your Highness. Prince Lachlan searched for one for many years."

"I suppose forewarned is forearmed, Judge."

"In many ways, sir. So, trumpets herald your arrival into the court. What then occurs?"

"I sit down?"

"Very nearly, sir. Every person in the court should rise and greet you appropriately. You should have had a briefing from your lawyers about the case and notes should be in easy reach on the bar, along with fresh parchment, ink, pen nibs and so on. If I might advise you, do not simply sit down straight away. Stand for a moment in front of your chair, give the court a sweeping glance, collecting, as it were, each person with that glance, give a brief nod and then sit down."

"Why, Judge?"

"It marks your presence and sets your authority on the court. Can you explain to me what you see in that glance, sir?"

"The defendant and lawyers for both sides."

"Is there no-one else?"

"Of course, the jury!"

"Scribes, warders and people in the public seats also. Do not forget to collect those in your glance. Where exactly is everyone?"

Tain blushed. "I… I don't know, Judge."

Tancred smiled. "That is why we have these lessons, so you can discover such mundane things, sir. It is nothing to worry about. Diagonally on your left at about forty-five degrees is the defendant."

"In a sort of box?"

"Not in the Justice Hall, sir. It is an ancient hall. He stands on a plinth, or kneels on it, with a warder either side. The choice whether to stand or kneel is the defendant's, but whichever he chooses, he chooses for the duration of the trial. Can you ascertain anything from a defendant's choice, Your Highness?" enquired Tancred.

"No, Judge, facts must decide a man's guilt not supposition and court circumstance. No-one looks their best on trial and it cannot be proof of a state of mind."

"Very good, sir. You might make a judge thinking like that, but some may try to convince you that a kneeling man is guilty and in supplication; a man who stands, defiant in his innocence but both arguments can be reversed. Directly in front of you, perpendicular to the bar, is a table for scribes and on the left of that one, parallel to the bar is the table for the defendant's lawyers and to the right of the scribes' table one for the prosecution. To the far right is the seating for the jury and a scribe at their disposal."

Tain nodded, absorbing the information and drawing a mental picture of the arrangement. "What about my administrator?"

"It is not usual for him to be present, sir, but if he were to be, he would head the scribes' table. Unless you wish him to sit elsewhere. As Peter is a lawyer, at Your Highnesses invitation, he could sit somewhere behind the bar."

Tain absorbed that and nodded. "That all makes sense but what of the witnesses?"

"They stand directly in front of you, sir, at the end of the scribe's table between the lawyers. Try not to be too intimidating."

Tain grinned. "I can't see that being a pleasant spot."

"Your Highness' cynicism is showing."

"Good. Maybe it's in anticipation of this test…"

Tancred smiled. "Who says you have not already had the test, sir? I have just been asking you a wealth of questions."

"Surely, Judge…"

"Not all tests are written, Your Highness."

Chapter 65
FIRST APPEARANCE
Alunadai, Week 5 – 1st Tradal, 8th Middis 1214
Judge Tancred's Office

TANCRED WAS WORKING in his office at the Courthouse when his scribe rather uncertainly announced Prince Tain. Tancred nodded in thanks, rose and bowed as Tain entered the office.

Tain grinned. "I'm sorry to disturb you, Your Honour…"

Tancred smiled. "I am not at all disturbed, Your Highness."

"Are you sure, Judge?" asked Tain with a grin. "After all, disturbance comes in many forms."

"So it does, sir, but I shall amend the statement to 'I am not disturbed by Your Highness' presence'. Everything else, may we leave it to the doctors?"

Tain nodded. "I think so because I'm sure Chapa would say something about my influence on Your Honour. Have you got six minutes?"

"Of course, sir. Is this about your studies or something else?"

"A bit of both, Judge. I've been reading the book you wrote…"

Half an hour later, the scribe re-entered to find the judge patiently explaining the history behind the different types of fealty and how the Cearcall had helped to forge them.

The judge reached the end of his recitation. "What is it, Ryder?"

"The Keeper's compliments, Your Honour, but Court Six…"

Tancred nodded. "I shall be along shortly." When his scribe left, the judge said, "I am sorry, Your Highness, but my presence is required in court."

"I shouldn't have kept you so long. Judge, could I…" Tain hesitated. "Could I come and observe?"

Tancred retrieved his green judge's robes. "What would His Majesty think, sir?"

"Probably 'Thank heavens he's interested'. Please, I won't get in your way, I promise."

Swinging his robes around his shoulders, Tancred said, "You are not trying to avoid anything you should be doing, Your Highness?"

Tain grinned. "For once I'm not, Judge. I promise you, I'm not."

"Then you may come and observe. Unfortunately, I do not have time to brief you on the cases in hand."

* * *

They walked through the Courthouse in companionable silence. The judge's billowing robes caught the eye first and people moved out of his way, normally with a smile on their faces. It was only moments later they realised Tain was with him and then inclined heads and bows followed along with speculative stares. In a year, they'd all be indirectly working for the Prince. Tain maintained a slight smile as they walked past the library and then down the corridor that ran alongside what would be his office before entering Court Six.

The occupants of the court rose when Tancred entered and took his place at the bar, but instead of seating himself as they had expected he said with a voice trained to carry,

"Please all make an obeisance to Prince Tain Lachlan FitzAlcis, who is to be observing the proceedings this afternoon."

Tain entered as everyone's eyes were lowered; he smiled at the judge but Tancred noticed his charge's eyes were uncertain. The judge winked and then seated him before sitting down himself.

"Thank you. You may all be seated. This court is convened for the trial of Thomas Middleton accused of wounding Henry Gardenson with a knife. Prosecution, you need to prove your case absolute. Defence, your client shall be heard with due diligence. Jury, if you have any questions you will have chance to have them asked…"

* * *

When they left the court, at the conclusion of the trial with a guilty verdict having been reached, Tain discovered Peter was waiting for him.

"His Majesty wishes to know if you will be dining with him this evening, Your Highness?"

Tain said, "What's the time?"

"About six o'clock, sir. I'm informed by Master Simkins that dinner will be at seven thirty."

Tain looked at Tancred. "Do you mind if we discuss this another day, Judge?"

Tancred smiled. "Not at all, Your Highness. I hope His Majesty is

304

well when you see him. Could you give him my greetings?"

"Of course, Judge. Thank you." He was about to run off when the judge said,

"Wait for your guard, Your Highness. Haste can be a poor reason for recklessness."

Tain sighed. "Sorry, Judge."

Peter, however, said, "Your guards are waiting by the back door to the Courthouse, Your Highness. It is the closest exit."

"What did I do without you, Peter?"

"You waited around, sir."

Chapter 66

PESKY

Septadai, Week 5 – 7th Tradal, 14th Middis 1214
Ceardlann

TAIN'S MESSENGER, a rainbow-coloured dragon, went by the name of Pesky; it wasn't a nickname but it might have been a description. Tain generally didn't trust messengers knowing the Herald in Oedran, head of the Palace communications and the King's mail routes, could watch them. He had, however, begun to get used to Pesky, and unbeknownst to his family and friends would call him up simply for a chat.

Pesky tried to convince Tain that their discussions were private. "But, princeling, honestly, I can't tell any of the other messengers anything that's said in a link or out of it. Nothing. If I try, no sound comes out."

"Then how can the Herald watch you?"

"I don't know exactly but I don't think he hears what's been said. I think he just knows who's talking to who."

"Whom."

"Oh, very funny, princeling. Correct my language, do. I mean, it's not like I often get chance to perfect it. Someone else around here does all the talking…"

"Who's feeling cross-grained today?"

Pesky might have been small enough to sit in Tain's palm, but his glare was impressive.

"Stop grouching, Pesky, it was just getting interesting."

"I could just go, princeling."

"I could just call you back," retorted Tain, grinning. "Am I really that annoying?"

Pesky lay down, his head resting on Tain's notes. "At least you treat

305

me like I've got feelings. Some think their messengers don't have a brain but we do… All right, princeling, you *can* stop laughing now."

Tain smiled instead. "Sorry, colourful, but are you sure about that?"

"Watch who you call 'colourful'. I can breathe fire, you know."

"Oh, good. I've got some letters to seal. It'll be easier than a candle."

Pesky glared at him again. "That's not funny, princeling… though I can see you think it is. Watch out, Dragoris, is about to appear."

Pesky disappeared, leaving Tain wondering if only one messenger could be near him or whether Pesky didn't want the others of his kind to know they simply chatted.

"Your father would like a word, Prince Tain," announced the red dragon.

"Any idea what I've done this time, Dragoris?"

Dragoris looked momentarily disconcerted. "I have not. Can I form the link?"

Tain nodded. "Of course."

* * *

Adeone's eyes narrowed. "What are you grinning for?"

"I can't remember, Your Majesty, but I've not broken anything…"

"Good. The first of the Yearling Markets in Oedran starts tomorrow. Do you want to be here?"

Tain grinned wider. "Can I? I'd love to look round it."

"Come to Oedran tonight with Cal and Elantha. I've a dinner planned with Merchant Chapa. He can explain how it's entirely his fault…"

"His fault?" enquired Tain.

"Yes, it was one of his many ideas when he was Chief Merchant. It's meant to replicate the Byfa Frander but I think it might be more fun and less trade."

Tain grinned. "I look forward to it."

Chapter 67
THE YEARLING
Alunadai, Week 6 – 8th Tradal, 15th Middis 1214
Prince Tain's Chambers

THE FOLLOWING MORNING, Tain woke with excitement flowing in his veins. He was getting old enough to be included properly in events. He rang for Linnt.

"After my bath I'll need a formal tunic, Linnt. Can you find it for me, please?"

Linnt said seriously, "Certainly. I'll just fill your bath."

Tain reached for a drink, which wasn't there. "Could I also have some water, please, Linnt? You have forgotten it again."

Linnt nodded and left. Tain rose and padded to the window. It was cloudy and close, as though there was a thunderstorm brewing. Being soaked wouldn't be fun.

As Tain shrugged on his tunic, he tugged at it. Had it shrunk? When had he last worn it? The shoulders were tight and the length shorter than it should be. Linnt had probably noticed. Breakfast was more important. He ate the eggs and toast without taking much notice before moving onto a pastry filled with apple, cinnamon and oats. As he was leaving, he picked up a scone and slipped it into his belt pouch. He left his rooms grinning and ran through the Palace. With barely a good morning to Richardson, he was through the Inner Office door and giving his father a brief bow.

Adeone sighed. "Tain, you've got to remember to knock. So, outside and come in properly!" When his son re-entered, he waited for the door to close before saying, "This isn't Ceardlann. I could have anyone with me and although it's nice to know you want to see me, it is an office first and foremost."

Tain nodded. "I understand, Your Majesty."

"Good. try to *remember* as well. Hmm, you're looking very important this morning. Only the grin might give away your state of mind."

Tain said, "It does match yours, Sire."

Adeone laughed. "True…"

* * *

The official ceremony to open the Yearling was held in Alcium Plaza, just below the Administrative Quarter gates in the Lower City. Although all the major thoroughfares of the city were crammed with traders from all over the empire, the actual plaza was relatively clear. Standing next to the King, Tain listened with half an ear and looked around with more interest. He noticed the bunting and atmosphere, the excitement and expectation of the crowd. He smiled to himself as he glanced over the crowd. One man in particular caught his attention. His eyes narrowed and suddenly the man looked at him and moved away.

"Hillbeck…" murmured Tain, motioning with his head and eyes, "He's up to no good."

Hillbeck saw what Tain meant. He turned to the guards. "Men."

Adeone never appeared to notice as the man was cleverly caught in a net of guards and yeomen. Tain watched carefully as, with the conclusion of the King's speech and subsequent cheer from the crowd, the man was disarmed and led away.

A few moments later Adeone said, "Was that your doing, Prince Tain?"

"Yes, Sire. He was gazing at Your Majesty fixedly, as in *very* intently, and, when he saw I'd noticed, tried to get away. Something was wrong."

The King nodded. "Hillbeck."

The senior sergeant of the King's Guard stepped forward. "Sire?"

"See he's lodged safely with Major Wynfeld."

"Very good, sir. If he's innocent?"

"Then I shall be pleased, but he was carrying weapons in the city and that is no longer permitted." When the sergeant had turned to pass on the orders, Adeone said, "Thank you, Prince Tain."

Tain smiled. "It was nothing, Your Majesty."

Adeone caught his eye but to laugh or simply in emphasis of the danger Tain couldn't quite work out.

Standing a couple of paces away, Landis motioned to Hillbeck. "What was that about?" After Hillbeck explained, he said, "See the Major knows I'll want sight of his report." He moved over to his nearson. "Prince Tain, would you like my job?"

Tain shook his head. "I would never be as good as Your Lordship."

Landis squeezed his shoulder reassuringly. "I think you could be, sir. Your Majesty, the crowd is dispersing. Shall we start our walk?"

Adeone said, "Why not? Where's Lady Elantha?"

Landis said, "She is with my children, Sire, and Master Calumiel is with his family. They've been watching from the sidelines."

Tain grinned. "I'm sure they'll find us, my lord."

* * *

They walked around much of the north-western quadrant of the city, looking carefully at most of the stalls, passing comments with the stallholders. Tain found several intriguing items that he purchased, either for himself or as presents. Landis and Adeone chuckled, glad to see his enjoyment. They soon found the Landis family. It wasn't long until Tain spotted Cal and his siblings, and, with a glance at his father, ran to join them. Never far away from each other, they moved their way down the Maclan, between the Macarian and Landis lordships. As they reached The Strait, Landis glanced at the sky.

"Would you care to refresh yourself at Landis House, Your Majesty?"

Adeone considered. "Yes, please. How about this motley crowd?"

"I am sure my house can cope. Your Highness, would you care to extend my invitation to the Galdwins?"

Tain nodded and ran off.

Adeone sighed. "I wish he'd remember to stay closer to his guards."

Of the Galdwins, only Cal, Crispin and Louisa accepted the invitation.

As they entered Landis House, Landis smiled at them. "Welcome to my home. Take your cloaks off and pass them to Backery. He has to have a use, don't you, Backery?"

"Apparently so, my lord. Where would Your Lordship like refreshments served?"

Landis glanced round. "Good question – we're quite a crowd. The larger drawing room, I think.

"Very good, my lord."

As they made their way to the room, the thunder rolled in.

"Just in time," remarked Adeone. "Anyone would think you planned it, Festus."

Landis smiled. "I might work some wonders, Your Majesty, but the weather is one I cannot control."

Tain grinned. "But you can read it, Uncle Festus. I saw you glance at the sky."

"That took no great skill today, Your Highness. I am not an aeromancer."

Adeone looked at him. "No, you're not, are you?" He eased himself into a chair and relaxed. "That's better."

Tongue in cheek, Tain said, "We've the rest of the city to see, Sire."

Adeone eyed him as a small chuckle came from close by. "If you and the others want to, you can explore when the rain's passed. I have other matters to attend to before this evening. And, Master Calumiel, make your appreciation of my son's observations quieter…"

Cal bowed. "My apologies, Your Majesty."

Adeone smiled at him. "I'll cope. Why are you all still standing up?"

After they'd eaten and drunk, the rain was still hammering down. Adeone smiled at Landis. "Shall we go to your study, my lord, and let this lot chatter without us?"

Landis nodded. "It seems sensible, Your Majesty."

Adeone pushed himself to his feet. On the way out of the room, he enquired where Cornelia was.

"Visiting Lady Rhian and Lady Neassa, Your Majesty. I'm glad they took a separate house."

Adeone said, "Yes, so am I, in a way."

Once in the absolute privacy of his study, Landis asked, "Were you pleased Rhian returned with Neassa? You've hardly seen them since."

Adeone eased himself into his favourite chair and accepted a glass of whiskey. "I am feeling a fool for not realising something sooner and I can't work out how to face Rhian."

"Ah. When did you realise, Sire? I saw it months ago."

Adeone smiled ruefully. "When she returned unexpectedly. I must get my head straight and only I can do it."

Landis nodded. "That is understandable but don't isolate yourself. Does Lady Rhian…"

"Reciprocate my feelings? I think she might," said Adeone with a small smile. "I think she might."

"Then maybe you have a decision to make together," suggested Landis.

"Not yet. I must reconcile quite a lot first. My heart and my sons' feelings to begin with."

"You have to talk to them then."

Adeone nodded. "At some point I will if I decide my own feelings warrant it."

* * *

Half an hour later, the rain had eased slightly. A knock at the study door brought an exceptionally grave and damp Major Wynfeld into the room.

Adeone crooked an eyebrow. "Major, I wasn't expecting to see you for a while."

Wynfeld saluted. "No, Your Majesty, and I don't think you're going to like my report."

Adeone motioned to a chair. "What is it?"

Wynfeld continued to stand. "The man has died, Sire. From poison. Self-administered almost as soon as he was in the barracks."

Adeone regarded him. "That is unfortunate."

"Yes, sir. Especially because he screamed rather loudly and drew attention to the fact he was under arrest and would disappear."

Adeone swore. "He's trying to make me out to be tyrannical?"

"He might have been, sir. Or he might simply have been told to succeed or die and was improvising."

Landis said, "Find a lookalike and have them walk out of the barracks."

"Defender, that would be more dangerous. It would become known. If discrediting His Majesty's regime was the aim, and even if it wasn't, they'll use it to their advantage anyway. I think being honest with the facts is the only option open to us. He was taken to the barracks and committed suicide. There are enough of the men stationed at the barracks who saw the truth. They're currently talking about it in the bars around the barracks—"

"Without waiting for me to be told, Major?" interrupted Adeone.

Unable to gauge the King's tone, Wynfeld said, factually, "Your Majesty, I thought it was better that it couldn't possibly have been at your order."

Landis smiled ruefully. "He's got a point, Your Majesty. Is there another promotion waiting for him?"

"No, please, my lord, no," protested Wynfeld. "I'm more than flattered

310

by my current rank and, anyway, the General's not retiring."

"Yet," muttered Landis.

Adeone chuckled. "Stop discomfiting Wynfeld, Festus. Come and sit down, Major, and get yourself a drink. You look like you need one."

Wynfeld, relaxed and, knowing his report was made, sat down – far happier than he had been.

A few minutes later, Landis caught his eye. "Any news on Apposer Nallvir's concerns, Major?"

Wynfeld hesitated. "There is still nothing definite, my lord, but there is more supposition to add to your Apposer's feelings, Sire. Odd meetings between people I wouldn't have expected to be together. Snippets of conversation that appear innocent but are out of place when considered against the people talking. His Highness' notes from the Lufian Review were interesting because no-one put a foot wrong in all the interviews – *no-one* and that's surely odd in itself. Lufian's been quiet for some time, but I am beginning to be uneasy about the peace..."

Adeone nodded. "That mirrors my feelings."

"Thank you, sir. There's just nothing that means you could replace anyone or arrest anyone. I am going to need a lot of time to fathom this out, Your Majesty, and I realise that I've already had a couple of seasons."

Adeone chose his words with care. "Take the time needed to be certain, Wynfeld, and avoid jumping to conclusions. I did that in 1212 and caused a complete uproar over Lord Daioch. I would rather not be in that position again."

Wynfeld nodded. "I will do my best to avoid it, Your Majesty."

"Thank you. Keep the same meticulous records for all other provinces as well, please. Even Areal and Terasia. I trust their governors, but that doesn't mean I trust everyone in power there."

Chapter 68
REVIEW ENDED
Septadai, Week 8 – 28th Tradal, 14th Tradis 1214
Inner Office

THREE WEEKS LATER, Arkyn returned from the Macian Review, uncomfortable at the outcome but determined to stick to his decisions. He made his way to his father's office and handed the report to Richardson before knocking and entering the Inner Office.

Adeone looked over. "I'm glad to see you're back."

"Thank you, Sire. I'm sorry for my report. The Fencible needs replacing."

Adeone got up and poured them both a drink. "Fair enough. I'm sure we'll find a suitable replacement."

"Well, don't make it Lord Longland. He's rather too like Silvano for my liking..."

Adeone smiled. "In that case I'll agree not to. Come and sit down and tell me about it."

Two hours later, Adeone was glad to see the cares drift away from his son's features. "You look like you need a week at Ceardlann."

"Is there anything you need of me here?"

"No. Not at the moment."

"Thank you, Your Majesty. Then I'll go to Ceardlann tomorrow. Tonight, I plan to have a massage and dinner..."

"Dine with me if you want to. Your household will be sorting the detritus of the journey."

"Thank you, father. At least they all returned this year."

Adeone said sadly, "Yes. The memories weren't too bad, were they?"

"A sea journey was very different."

Adeone accepted the face value of the comment. "How did Julius cope in Meith, do you know?"

"Advisor Rayburn mentioned that he'd done better than Julius, himself, thought. The Jarl might have more to say, as I wasn't there."

"Whether it would be about Julius' statesmanship or sense of humour has yet to be revealed though. Has Tain told you about the Yearling?"

Arkyn shook his head. "No. What is there to be said?"

As Adeone explained, Arkyn nodded. "He's sharper than we give him credit for sometimes, father."

"Yes. He's suddenly seemed to grow up. I wake up and my sons are men. It's both pleasing and sad."

Arkyn topped his father's glass up. "I doubt Tain will be sober at seventy. I sometimes wonder if he and I would have been as close if we'd been a larger family."

Adeone looked at him in interest. "Are you close, really, Arkyn?"

"Yes, I think we are. I might groan about him, but I do miss his company when I'm on reviews."

"I'm glad, very glad... I just wish Ella had lived..."

Arkyn cursed his words about a larger family. "We all do, father. She's protected by the stars though."

"As are your mother and grandmother, they also died too young." Adeone took a deep breath to shake himself out of the memories. "Talking of families – have you got your eye on anyone yet?"

Arkyn laughed, embarrassed. "No, sir. Have you?"

Adeone paused almost imperceptibly. Amused, he enquired, "Would it worry you if I had?"

Arkyn scrutinised his face. "Have you?"

Adeone rolled his eyes. "I ask a question, you evade it and turn it round on me; I'll have to have a word with your advisors, Arkyn."

Arkyn laughed. "Sorry, father. It would depend on who it was."

Over dinner, the talk returned to Arkyn's experiences travelling abroad and, although Adeone was very careful not to mention friends made and lost, Arkyn brought up the subject first.

"I was surprised in Macia that I wasn't introduced to many of the younger lords. There were some, but I rather got the impression that the idea I might want congenial company of my own age hadn't crossed the Fencible's mind."

"You're right; he needs replacing."

Arkyn smiled. "Not because of that, Sire. I've been thinking though; Tain's been asking for as long as I've been doing reviews if he can come with me, but I think I'd like him to. Next year's isn't far. In fact, by the Rex Dallin, it's only a day's hard travelling to Oedran. He could be home easily, if need be, and I'd look after him."

"Are you sure? I don't mind, but I wouldn't want him to embarrass himself – or you, come to that."

Arkyn smiled. "I think by the end of this year he'll be more than ready, sir. Judge Tancred's tutelage has steadied him."

Adeone nodded. "Yes, I think it has. He handled himself well at the Yearling. Shall we leave it as a surprise?"

"Yes, that way, if he has a suddenly mad episode, we're not committed…"

"He might be though."

"Father!"

Adeone chuckled. "Sorry. Have you made any decision about when to do the Arealian Review?"

Arkyn said carefully, "I think, if Tain can go with me, I'll humour ReJean, Sire, but I'd like it if you could come to Amphi for the actual day."

"It's your decision, Arkyn, and I'll be there, but might I ask why you've decided to humour ReJean?"

"Because I can't have my birthday celebrations where I really want them; therefore, some more good might as well come out of the situation."

Adeone frowned. "Where do you *really* want them, Arkyn?"

His son looked at him. "Ceardlann and ideally mother would have been there as well. Before you say we can have it at Ceardlann, Sire, I'd be too choked with emotion. I know I would."

Adeone half nodded. "I can understand that but if, at any point, you change your mind, let me know and we'll have it at Ceardlann and the Court can celebrate without us."

Arkyn relaxed, decision made. "Thank you, father. I wasn't sure what your reaction would be."

"As long as I'm invited, I don't suppose the rest matters. ReJean can have the nightmare of the arrangements. Don't make it easy for him."

Arkyn chuckled. "I'll do my best to imitate grandfather, shall I?"

"Maybe not *that* difficult."

Laughing, they continued with their dinner.

* * *

The following day, Tain greeted Arkyn enthusiastically and listened with more attentiveness than in previous years to Arkyn's tales of Macia. Cal also listened with interest, and Arkyn found that his father was right. Tain seemed to have grown up. Cal had certainly matured. Elantha was her normal quiet self, but her hug conveyed she was pleased to see her cousin.

Arkyn caught up with all his brother's news and found that Tain had observed two days in court and enjoyed the Yearling far more than he'd let on to their father. He showed his brother some of the small items he'd bought and Arkyn looked at them in interest. There was an ancient puzzle box to add to the collection that the carpenter had made and a beautiful Denshirian glass desk set – the combination of entertaining and practical made Arkyn smile.

Leaving his brother looking at the items, Tain went and hunted in a drawer and came back, holding out a small package.

"You couldn't be there, Arkyn, so I got you this. From the same stall as the puzzle box."

Arkyn took the box; it was small but beautifully crafted. He frowned at Tain and sat down, carefully lifting the lid. In the centre of the box was what looked like a small case, enamelled in turquoise but not gaudy, about an inch and a half in diameter. Arkyn gently lifted it out and caught a grin on Tain's face.

"I'm safe to open it, aren't I?"

Tain nodded, barely containing his excitement. "Yes, but look carefully at the enamelled design. I know… well, I think I know what this is, but the stallholder *definitely* didn't."

Around the top was an interlocking pattern, any part of which might be an hourglass. He frowned at Tain, who simply carried on smiling. Cal and Elantha were watching intently, completely unaware of what Tain was up to but guessing he was up to something.

Arkyn ran his hands over the case and felt the hint of a design, long since rubbed to invisibility. He tilted it against the light and frowned.

"Tain… If this is what we think it is, where's it been for years?"

Tain grinned. "I don't know, do I? I just bought it!"

Arkyn opened the small case. There was what looked like a normal, if small, timepiece, but the face was different. Instead of numbers, symbols were at the tips of an offset twelve-pointed star. Arkyn lifted it out of the case completely and put it to one side gently. He carried on looking at the case.

"I can't believe this."

"Neither can I, but I didn't have your book *The Items of the Cearcall*, so I only have my memory to rely on and I'm not sure about that."

Arkyn chuckled. "Can't think why."

"Do you want to know the best bit? The stallholder said that, because there were no hands, it would need repairing, but it might be of interest simply because it was old."

Arkyn snorted with laughter. "He really had no idea he had the Amser's Watch?"

"If that *is* the Amser's Watch, obviously not – he certainly wasn't charging enough. It's going to be useless to tell the time with, I'm afraid."

Arkyn shrugged. "I have a normal timepiece. Tain, you can't give me this, you found it."

Tain sat next to him. "I want to. Half the pleasure for me is seeing your face. I've not even told father."

Arkyn laughed. "How did you keep the secret?"

"With practice. Do you think it is the watch? Really? I wondered if I was getting fanciful. I'd have taken it and shown it to Laioril if he'd been here, but he wasn't and therefore I couldn't."

Cal said, "I'd have gone, Your Highness."

Arkyn smiled at him. "Have you learned to control your spirit yet?"

"Just about, sir. It's taken a lot of practice and His Highness has confused everyone by locking us in the drawing room and closing the curtains…"

Arkyn grinned. "I hate to think what they thought was going off."

"They've not dared ask," revealed Elantha. "Arkyn, you do realise we're none of us going to get any peace and quiet again if Cal can just appear at will?"

"That's a good, if worrying, point… Cal, any chance of a promise to only use it to *disappear*?"

Cal smiled back. "Not a chance on Erinna, Your Highness. My Prince's wish might well be my command, but I am more concerned with practicality than his sanity."

Tain snorted. "Has Arkyn got any sanity?"

"I didn't say which Prince, Your Highness."

"I didn't ask you the question…"

Arkyn and Elantha rolled their eyes.

Elantha said, "Cal, would you promise me?"

Cal looked at her. "That's unfair, my lady… How can a courtier deny a lady's wish?"

Tain said, "Quite easily when it's El, the term lady being—" A cushion cut him off mid-sentence.

Arkyn laughed. "You deserved that. Good shot, little flower – perhaps not ladylike but right on target." He picked up the Amser's Watch again, turning it over and over in his hands.

Cal noticed. "What does it do, sir?"

Arkyn smiled ruefully. "I don't think anyone knows, Cal. The stories say that the Amser carried it with him, but that's as much as we know. For all the speculation, it could just be a beautifully crafted timepiece, just as the Memini's Manuscript might be an ordinary diary."

Cal grinned. "And the Skifta's Sword in the Great Hall might just be a sword."

"Arkyn, can I borrow your book on the Cearcallian items at some point?" enquired Tain.

Arkyn nodded. "If you're careful with it." Unseen, he glanced at Cal pensively. Kensal would have been fascinated by the events, not that they could have discussed some of them but if they could, they would have debated the meaning for hours. He wished he could have shown his late friend the Amser's Watch. Kensal might even have been able to use it, or work out what it did, if it did anything. When he could, he slipped out of the room and made his way to the snug. He wanted time alone with his thoughts and once more with his loss. Cal found him there half an hour later and asked if he wanted to talk but Arkyn didn't. He wanted to remember.

Chapter 69

EVENING RELAXATION

Evening

Ceardlann

WHEN ARKYN HAD LEFT for Ceardlann, Edward sorted out the papers and official detritus from the Macian Review. He boxed up all the Prince's notes, labelling the boxes with their contents and putting them in a small archive attached to the Prince's chambers.

Peter disturbed him late in the day. "Are you planning to eat, Edward?"

"When I get chance. Make yourself useful and help me restack this lot."

"I come by for a chat and get roped in to doing your work for you..."

Edward grinned. "Stop moaning. We'll both get food sooner."

"How does that work?" asked Peter, passing him a box. "I could just get food now and leave you to it. I'd therefore eat sooner than you."

"Lawyer. You know what I meant."

Peter laughed. "Yes. How was Macia?"

"Busy. I'm always glad to see Oedran again."

Half an hour later, Denny hurried over as they entered Upper Hall. "Administrators! You're rather late tonight."

Peter grinned. "Blame Edward."

"Oh, it's always my fault. Denny, I'm starving..."

Denny grinned. "Then sit yourself down. Didn't they feed you well in Macia? I've heard foreign climes aren't always good for the digestion."

"They fed us well enough, but I've not eaten since breakfast."

Denny tutted. "Now, now, sir, you should always eat. Keep up your strength. Surely with His Highness elsewhere there could have been chance? ...Well, I'll leave instruction that if they've not seen you by mid-afternoon tomorrow to take something up to your office. If he finds out you're not eating, Richardson will worry... Now, there's a good choice tonight..."

After they'd eaten, they relaxed into comfortable chairs. Peter listening, as Edward talked about Macia and the process of a review, realised his colleague was wont to overwork. Was it natural instinct or borne of the fact that Prince Arkyn worked hard?

After half an hour, Edward said, "So how have you been? Found your way around yet?"

Peter smiled. "Just about. My office has moved as well. I don't know at whose instigation, but I've a small room that wasn't being used in the Privy Wing."

"I'd leave that one to mystery, if I were you."

Peter eyed him. "It was you, wasn't it?"

"Might have been. Are you rejoicing or complaining?"

"I'm not complaining, but I fail to see how one can rejoice at the location of an office."

Edward laughed. "Lawyer. Is it easier?"

"Much, thank you. I'm not as worried if I've got to leave the office for any reason and if there's correspondence there. Most gets sent straight to Ceardlann but there're times when there're invitations and so forth in my office, and I've taken over management of His Highness' personal accounts."

Edward frowned. "That's Linnt's responsibility."

"If he was responsible in doing them, I wouldn't have worried, but I found the ledger left on the side in the crossover room and I'm not sure that it's been kept accurately either."

Edward said, "See if there's a discreet scrivener around to have a look. Or ask Kadeem to glance at them. Are you thinking Linnt's been fraudulent?"

"No, I think he's been haphazard at record keeping. I don't think he's light fingered. Other than that, everything's fine. I'm glad you're back, though. I want to ask you some stupid questions; not having been in the Palace most of my life, there're things that elude me."

"A lawyer admits fallibility?"

"Only to close friends," laughed Peter. "It's little things. Our clothes for example. I didn't expect such a strict dress code."

Edward smiled. "It helps everyone. Black loose trousers with a black, front central buttoned, long line tunic top means a clerk, scribe, secretary or administrator. A white ensemble like the black one is a high-ranking manservant. Cream or grey are footmen…"

"I'd just about worked that out! It's more the significance of things like our belts and badges. How do you know which you're meant to have?"

"If you're ever unsure the Steward holds a list but it's relatively simple. All servants have to wear a badge other than tokens A – C, which include us. C's are secretaries, chief clerks, heads of sections etc. B's are Palace officials such as the Chamberlain and Herald. A's are the administrators and body servants of the FitzAlcis, oh, and the Steward as chief official of the Palace. Secretaries' tunics are hemmed with the appropriate colour for their area of concern – for instance, the King's have tunics hemmed with scarlet, the Justiciar's with emerald. The Palace officials all have separate tunics and so on for their particular job but they are marked out with different headwear – mostly brimless hats with their 'badge of office' sewn into the front of it, or for some skull caps. We get belts, aren't we lucky? Mine has a thin band of scarlet to illustrate I'm Prince Arkyn's administrator, Richardson's belt is scarlet as he's the King's. Yours currently mirrors mine but in emerald – come the Munewid it will mimic Richardson's as you will be an administrator to the Justiciar of Oedran. Have I confused you yet?"

Peter shook his head. "Not quite. It's as complicated as I thought it was though. What do you do if you spot someone flouting the dress code?"

"Report them to their superiors. It needs to be enforced so everyone can recognise who is who, or at least where they rank and work. You shouldn't spot too many though and you have to know who to report and to whom, which means knowing what they should be wearing in the first place. I love the vagaries of this place. Clothing is, however, one of the by-laws of the Palace."

"So I discovered but I couldn't discover any more. How did you?"

"I was a runner from the age of seven, then a courier, before His Majesty asked Richardson to train me to become a clerk. It's a long story, but it means I learnt the Palace rules quickly."

Peter nodded. "You're a foundling-orphan, aren't you?"

Edward looked at him levelly. "Yes."

"I don't mean to insult you, Edward. I was going to say it can't have been easy."

"It's one reason I work absurdly hard. I have more to prove, I suppose."

Peter smiled. "Not to me. I've things to prove as well. A son of a scribe who dared to try to become a lawyer, and ended up as an administrator. We've both broken one mould or another."

"True." Edward laughed. "I'm pleased they appointed you. I don't feel quite so different any more. I've been working with secretaries twice my age and clerks the same age and knowing that by a chance of fate I'm an administrator and they who have had more years' training are not."

"Maybe it's not the training but the application of it that matters. You suit His Highness and work damned hard. Surely that's what's important?"

Edward sighed. "Maybe. So is anything else confusing you?"

Peter grinned. "I'm sure there's plenty…"

Chapter 70
ON RESPECT
Pentadai, Week 14 – 12th Macial, 12th Macis 1214
Fitz's Inn - Schoolroom

"YOUR HIGHNESS, it is not a mark of respect if people obey you, it is merely and only a mark of obedience. You can be obeyed easily enough. You may be obeyed for any number of reasons, including fear, there is nothing that says obedience and respect are dependant."

Tain, settled in his chair at Fitz's, listened with interest to the judge. "Judge, how would I know?"

"You will learn to recognise the signs, Your Highness. Prince Lachlan used to say that people only did as he asked because his brother had proved he wielded a sharp sword. He might have been joking on occasion, and there was certainly more to why people obeyed him than that, but there was one thing I noticed with people working for him: when he was obeyed through fear jobs were done, when he was obeyed because of respect they were done exactly how and when he wanted them to be, mostly with a smile."

Tain considered carefully. "Was Uncle Lachlan a pessimist, Judge?"

Tancred chuckled. "He had that in him to be, yes, Your Highness. He used to say, in private, to his very close friends, that his only use was as a seal."

"He didn't feel he was in the swim of things then?"

Tancred's lips twitched. "I wish someone had dared say that to him, Your Highness—"

"How would he have reacted?"

"I am not sure, sir. When he said he was merely a seal, he tended to be melancholy and in later life we knew his thoughts were elsewhere. I do not think, therefore, that he would have appreciated the pun."

"Oh, right. Then it's probably fortunate he's not here now."

Tancred shook his head. "He would have accepted it from Your Highness, I believe. He had a particularly soft spot for both you and your brother. Somewhere in a box will be the blessing gift he gave you. You should find it soon; it might mean more to you now."

Tain frowned again. "What was it?"

"That is for Your Highness to discover. It was a mark of trust and I do not think you will ever be unworthy of it. Shall we return to our lesson, sir?"

Tain nodded. "If you're not going to solve the mystery for me then, yes, please."

"Respect cannot be inherited, Your Highness, not in its pure form. People may appear to respect you because of your place in society, your family but that is respect of an ideal, not of yourself. Respect for who you are might be a lifetime endeavour because it has to be earned."

Recognising in the judge's words the coalescence of something he'd been trying to work out for years, Tain asked eagerly, "How?"

"Take notice of those who work for you. Appreciate them and their skills. Look out for them. Never simply assume that they must do something. Treat them as people with brains, feelings and needs as well. Make sure your decisions are fair and consistent. Be approachable but also, above all, be yourself, not the title."

"But I am made to feel that I am the title."

"Your Highness, no-one can make you something you are not without your consent, however manifested. Remember, your job is the title, you are yourself; it is a subtle difference."

Tain thought for a long time. "I think I understand what you mean, Judge, but what if I haven't got time, for some reason, to be and do all that you have suggested?"

"If you have people's respect to start with then the odd day when you need to be the stereotypical prince it will be forgiven if you recognise it. You will know when to do so."

"I hope so, Judge. I don't want to make people fear or turn against me."

Tancred looked at him. "I am sure that few will, Your Highness. The respect you forge in your early years as Justiciar, might well carry you over the difficult times which we are sure are coming."

Tain said softly, "He *won't* succeed."

"I truly hope not, sir, for that would be a black day in our history."

Tain sighed. "I'm going to do my best to make sure it doesn't happen, Judge."

"I have no doubt about that, sir. When you begin to sit in judgement as Justiciar, it might be as well to remember that Your Highness is also being judged. There might be adherence to the title, but that is when you make the title mean what it does."

"At the moment, it might as well be tyrant from what I can see."

Tancred looked at him. "That was said with feeling, Your Highness."

"Probably because I feel strongly about it."

"I understand that, sir, but might I recommend that outside of here you phrase your distaste for Lord Scanlon's regime differently?"

"I've a wealth of words to use, Judge, but I will try to be more circumspect."

Tancred chuckled. "Thank you, sir. How have you found Peter as an administrator?"

Tain accepted the change of topic. "Fine, Judge, but then I've nothing to compare him to. He's got different things to do in comparison to Edward and Richardson."

"Not as different as you might imagine, Your Highness."

"Maybe not, but, unlike a manservant, administrators have different spheres in which they work."

"Very true. How large is your household and staff now?"

Tain said, "It's just Linnt and Peter. I suppose father will be increasing it soon."

"It is likely, Your Highness. Will you feel confident dealing with a household and staff, sir?"

"I thought the lesson had finished, Judge."

Tancred smiled. "Your Highness is not yet at Ceardlann."

Tain groaned. "All right, I take the point. I have not considered how I will feel as I have not considered a household or staff."

Tancred inclined his head slightly. "Then might I give you some advice, sir?"

Tain tilted his head. "That is the point of these lessons, isn't it, Judge?"

"Very true, sir. In dealing with your official entourage, it will be important to lay down metaphorical lines and stick to them. You should treat different members and household consistently with their functions. Your manservant, for example, will be more intimate than your administrator but should not *expect* confidences. Your administrator must be as discreet, if not more so, than your manservant. He will hear as much as your man but in a different context. You will need the respect of both of them, above anyone else's – so spend time getting to know them as people. You need to be able to trust them absolutely. You hold the power, but they control who can get to see you and when. Your welfare and how your day progresses is in their hands as much as yours. Try not to stand in the way of that; they are employed for a reason. Make their life consistent and relatively easy and they will respond, hopefully, in like manner. Civilities work both ways and it is always worth remembering them, though, as far as I have observed, none of that should be arduous for Your Highness."

Tain absorbed the advice at his own pace and Tancred waited patiently for him to speak.

"I trust Peter and like him, but I can't say the same of Linnt, Judge. Is that my fault?"

Tancred said carefully, "Without observing you together properly, I could not tell you, Your Highness."

"I suppose that's fair enough and I'm not in Oedran that often to get to know him well. Not like Arkyn and Kadeem. Kadeem doesn't need to be asked for anything, he just knows what Arkyn needs."

"That is the sign of an exceptional manservant, Your Highness."

"Not an ordinary one? I was beginning to wonder."

"Not necessarily, Your Highness." Tancred watched him. "Maybe you should talk to His Majesty, sir?"

Tain bit his lip. "Maybe, but father appointed him and I'm sure it's me."

"I do not think His Majesty would mind, sir. I think he would be more upset if you felt you could not discuss concerns with him."

Dispirited, Tain nodded. "Perhaps, Judge. I'll think about it and see if I can work it out with Linnt first."

Tancred smiled. "I am sure there will be ample opportunity soon, sir."

Tain looked intrigued. "Judge?"

"His Majesty has agreed to Your Highness observing the court each Alunadai. Or at least most of them. If there are any significant cases that I could hear, the Keeper has kindly said he will consider my name as the judge for the case."

Tain leaned forward, all unease gone. "Really?"

"Really, Your Highness."

"I'm looking forward to it already."

Tancred smiled. How times had changed; two years before, the idea would have been abhorrent to the Prince.

Chapter 71
VIAN
Imperadai, Week 15 – 18th Macial, 18th Macis 1214
Court

DURING THE THIRD WEEK of autumn, Adeone was at Court, peacefully seated at the dais in the King's Hall, watching a troupe of dancers from Denshire perform intricate and sensuous moves when in front of him appeared a small black griffin. He eyed him with amusement.

"He knows how to pick the times, Magucan," it was said softly, almost in a whisper.

Magucan inclined his head slightly, "Shall I tell him you'll speak to him later, Majesty?"

Adeone smiled. "It might be wise. I shouldn't be too long."

As the messenger disappeared, Landis, sitting on Adeone's right, said conversationally, "Wealsman?"

Adeone nodded. "Kristina's nearing her time."

Half an hour later, Adeone congratulated the dancers on a superb performance and mentioned some of the younger lords wouldn't be feeling well that evening and quietly withdrew. He made his way through an almost silent Palace, acknowledging the salutes of the guards but keeping an eye out and an ear tuned for trouble. The Palace might be his main place of residence but it didn't make it any safer. He made it to the King's Corridor before a voice said,

"Has Percival been in contact, sir?"

"He's tried to be – the middle of the entertainment. I couldn't tell Magucan to open the link. Why, Arkyn?"

"I simply wondered, Your Majesty." There was a hint of a smile on his face, tempered by serious contemplation.

They made their way in companionable silence to the King's sitting room and Arkyn poured drinks whilst his father contacted their friend.

* * *

Adeone took in Wealsman's appearance as the link formed: shadowed eyes red from rubbing, hollowing cheeks and more than usually disordered hair. "Tell me."

"Kristina went into labour yesterday. It's been protracted. We've a son but she's very ill, exhausted. The doctor feared for her life at one point."

"She's survived though, Percival. It's not easy but she's still with us."

"Yes."

"Is the doctor there still?"

"Yes."

Adeone looked at him. "Get a sleeping draught and go to bed."

Wealsman swallowed. "I daren't, in case she needs me..."

"She'll be more distressed if she sees you like this, you know that as well as I do. You can't look after her properly if you're half asleep—"

"Did you ever listen when people tried to make you rest when Ira was ill, Adeone?" asked Wealsman, more bluntly than he'd intended.

The King sighed. "You know I didn't. Percival, I *can* be high handed about this..."

Wealsman smiled slightly. "You wouldn't do that to our doctor."

"Watch me. All right, I'll let you off the sleeping draught. Have a bed made up in Kristina's room and go to sleep there. You'll be on hand if she wants you, but you'll get your rest as well."

Wealsman yawned. "Right, sir."

Adeone shook his head slightly. "Congratulations on the birth of your son. I told you you'd have one. You've all the headaches to come."

Wealsman said, "Talking of headaches, you should hear my daughter in a tantrum. I think naming her for Your Majesty was a bad idea."

Adeone eyed him. "How is it you can meld honorifics and cheek so smoothly that I can't object?"

"Practice." He yawned. "Adeone, I've asked Arkyn to be nearfather again... I know it's not traditional, as such, but I'd like you to be Vian's nearfather also. We named Adeona for you, but I wish I'd also asked you to be hers. I think there's so much you can do for any child, especially when you ignore the King part."

Adeone said gently, "Thank you, Percival, I'd be happy to accept but on one condition..."

Wealsman's eyes narrowed; he knew his friend's conditions of old. "What's that?"

"Well, two conditions. One, no-one knows as such. I wouldn't want

324

anyone surmising that you don't trust Arkyn. I know that's not why you've asked me, but there's always someone nasty willing to make the most of every opportunity and normally they're named Scanlon in our case. Secondly, you stop trying to dig yourself into and then out of a hole. It might be amusing to listen to, but I can't laugh when you're so tired."

"Thank you, I appreciate it."

Adeone nodded. "I thought you might. I'll send a blessing gift... I'll also tell Ernst that you're not to be at your desk for two weeks and that he's to let me know if you are. He can cope with running Terasia for that long, and Kristina and your children will appreciate your company. Don't try to object, Percival; it's not going to work."

Wealsman looked at his friend. "One of these days, I'll find a way round you in one of these moods."

Adeone grinned. "I hope not. You need a break, Percival. Just take it."

"Thank you, Your Majesty," said the Margrave.

"Far too official, Wealsman," observed the King.

Percival grinned. "It takes one to know one, Adeone."

"Oh, go to bed." Adeone chuckled, whilst nodding at Dragoris to close the link.

* * *

When the link broke, Arkyn looked over. "Did you accept, father?"

"Yes, but only on the condition that it's private to our families. Otherwise, it might appear he's lost trust in you."

"Nonsense, sir... No, I suppose it could, but we'd know that it wouldn't be that."

"We would, but it's amazing what rumours can do," remarked Adeone. "I'll let Ernst know Percival's taking a fortnight off and then we can enjoy a drink." When he came out of the link with Percival's Deputy Governor, he found a replenished drink to hand and also biscuits and cake.

Arkyn grinned. "I took the liberty of ringing for Simkins, sir."

"A good idea. So, what are we going to get Vian as a blessing gift?"

"I have no idea. I thought Adeona and Samara were complicated enough, but I now think a boy is even worse."

Adeone chuckled. "Well, he's Percival's son – do we *have* to be sensible?"

Arkyn laughed. "Possibly not..."

* * *

In the end, Adeone sent a beautifully crafted mobile, whose hanging components could later be removed to create toys. Arkyn sent an ornate and intricate chest. As he wrote in his letter to Percival and Kristina, Vian could keep his treasures in there and it might hold all the other blessing

325

gifts he would receive. Percival read the letter to Kristina when she was recovering, and she said quietly,

"And people say nearfathers should be close at hand… You know he's never missed writing to Adeona every month and the letters are to *her*, even though he knows I have to read them to her."

Percival grinned. "He and Adeone aren't as different as they try to make out. They've both got a caring heart. I'm glad Arkyn persuaded me to ask Adeone to also be nearfather to Vian."

His wife smiled in return. "Yes. Does he know it was Arkyn's idea?"

"No. I'm not going to enlighten him quite yet… I'll save it for an appropriate moment. I hope Arkyn has children of his own soon."

Kristina smiled. "Let him find a lady to love first, Percival."

"It does help," said her husband, placing a gentle kiss on her forehead.

Chapter 72
JUDGE'S DECISION
Pentadai, Week 18 – 12th Meithal, 19th Easis 1214
Fitz's Inn - Schoolroom

THREE WEEKS LATER, Tancred bowed as Tain entered the schoolroom at Fitz's and was immediately concerned by how pallid he was. Tain didn't, however, mention it and so the judge started their lesson as though he hadn't noticed. At lunchtime, the Prince hardly ate anything. An hour later he was sick and Tancred rang for Fitz.

"We will need a coach, Fitz; His Highness is unwell."

"Right you are, Judge. I'll sort out the one here and take His Highness back to Ceardlann. Someone should be with him in the coach, though, and there's only his Oedranian guard here."

Tancred looked at the Prince, turned to the window and back. "I'll go."

Fitz aware of the judge's feelings when it came to Ceardlann asked, "Are you sure?"

"Yes."

Fitz left and Tain whispered, "I'd be all right, Judge."

"I am sure you would, Your Highness," replied Tancred sharply, "but I have made my decision and you are not well enough to convince me otherwise."

* * *

When they reached Ceardlann, Tancred helped Tain down and watched as Joe helped him inside. The judge took a deep breath, squared his shoulders and followed. He was met by a worried Comptroller.

326

"James, it's good to see you under any circumstances."

"Comptroller, nice as it is to see you also, once His Highness is settled, I shall leave him to your care."

The Comptroller pursed his lips. "We'll argue that point later. I've let His Majesty know you're to be here. He said something like 'about time'."

Tancred swallowed as they made their way up the stairs. "I never intended to return, Comptroller."

"We all know that, Judge, but you're here and part of you must have wanted to be. Your old room is being made ready for you; so, welcome back. Now, we've an invalid to see to and Chapa's on his way…"

Tancred sighed. "I see I am being bullied."

"Glad you recognise it. Saves me time," replied the Comptroller with a private smile. The years of absence rolled away and he could almost feel the valley welcoming the judge again. He'd had many pleasant evenings in Tancred's company and had been sorry when the judge had made his farewells in 1205.

They entered Tain's room and Tancred smiled to himself, Lachlan's old room, but there weren't that many to choose from.

The Comptroller took charge. "Nip and see to a warm bath, Joe. It might help the stomach upset. Right, Your Highness, any fever?"

Listening, Tancred wondered why the Comptroller had bothered sending for Chapa at all. He settled himself in the window seat and waited. Once Tain was bathed and in bed, the Comptroller looked at him,

"Do you mind staying here, Judge?"

"Not at all, Comptroller."

"Your Highness, don't let him run off."

Tain said, "I'm not sure I could stop him, Comptroller, but I'll try."

Six minutes later, Tancred was quietly reading to Tain when Arkyn entered the room. The judge got to his feet and bowed.

Arkyn smiled at him. "Good afternoon, Your Honour. Thank you for coming with him."

Tancred said softly, "He was in no state to return on his own, Your Highness. There was no-one else, other than Fitz and he was busy driving the coach."

"Keep telling yourself that, Judge. We've let Madam Tancred know where you are. She seemed concerned for my errant brother but pleased you were here."

Tancred sighed. "I made Prince Lachlan a promise, sir…"

"He never foresaw you teaching me, Judge, or that I'd be living here," stated Tain. "He wouldn't consider that you're forsworn in the usual sense."

Arkyn nodded. "Circumstances have overtaken you, Your Honour. There is no, erm, dishonour in you being here. You're more than welcome."

"My presence seems to be so welcome that people are forgetting His Highness is ill," replied Tancred regretfully.

"He's exceptionally quiet; everyone's recovering their hearing."

"Arkyn!" exclaimed Tain.

Arkyn sat by his brother. "I hope you're not contagious."

"I must have eaten something."

"Food probably…"

Tancred closed the door on their wrangling.

Cal, turning the corner of the landing, asked, "How is he, Your Honour?"

"Not feeling his normal self, Master Calumiel. He has a slight temperature and a stomach upset."

Cal said, "Can I go and see him?"

"I cannot stop you, but it might be better to ask the doctor when he has seen His Highness."

"I'll do that then."

It wasn't long before horse's hooves heralded the eccentric attitude wrapped up in a body that was Doctor Chapa.

"Judge, nice to see you. Is he being good in bed?"

"He is in bed at least, Doctor Chapa. Can I do anything?"

"Come and tell me what happened."

* * *

Early in the evening, Tancred was comfortably ensconced with the Comptroller reminiscing when Adeone breezed into the office.

"Thank you, James. Comptroller, Rhian's with me – she insisted and she's taken lessons off her mother. Can you see a room's prepared for her, please? I'll just go and make sure that Tain's being sensible, and then we'll find ourselves a drink and a comfortable chair, James."

Long after everyone else was in bed, Adeone and Tancred were in the snug talking, unaware of the time. Adeone talked about things he never would have done in Oedran, not even to his closest friends. Tancred realised just how unencumbered Adeone felt when he said,

"When my mother died, I was truly lonely and I never grew close to Uncle Lachlan until after that. He seemed to notice, whereas my father was distant – it wasn't that he didn't care, it was just he couldn't talk about it and I needed to talk. I spent so long in Uncle Lachlan's office. I didn't know Festus then… I got to know an awful lot of things then that I'd never have come close to knowing otherwise."

328

Tancred nodded. "Prince Lachlan was also lonely at that time. Marni had gone very suddenly. He never did say why but he was distraught. Saying he had wrecked their lives. He felt things deeply. Even when most men would see it was not his fault, he could not accept it."

Adeone sighed. "I think that's a trait in my family, James. Who was Marni?"

"His pet name for his mistress – I cannot recall her real one. He once asked your father if he could marry her and King Altarius said no. She was cisan, you see. He was devastated. I met her a few times but she kept quietly in the background; his confidant and companion for when he needed to be himself."

Adeone searched his memories. "I vaguely remember her or someone, anyway. I wonder where the lady is now."

Tancred smiled slightly. "Wherever she is, if she's still alive, I hope she's content with life. She was younger than Lachlan; I remember that much. He met her by chance one day."

"It seems the people we are closest to we meet like that. He had a habit of making up pet names for people, didn't he? When Tain was born, and we chose Lachlan as his second name, I remember my uncle was touched but he said straight away that young 'Tailan' would go far. He asked, *'What is the point of a one syllable name? You can't shorten it effectively.'* Whenever he was in private, he always referred to Tain as Tai, or Tailan. I wonder if my son recollects it at all. He was five when uncle died."

"He died too young," said Tancred sadly. "A life of official duties and worry took it out of him. He suffered with headaches for years."

Adeone sighed. "I remember. I see his character occasionally in Tain and I hope with all my being that Tain doesn't suffer the same."

Tancred said softly, "So do I, sir, but I do not think Prince Tain will. Not to the same depths. I do not mean he is unfeeling, but he has good friends around him and a brother he cares for and who cares for him. Prince Arkyn let us get him settled earlier, but he was straight there afterwards."

Adeone smiled. "That's nice to know. I'm going to let them go to Amphi together next year. ReJean's asked for the review to be right at the beginning of the year and Arkyn's said he doesn't mind as long as Tain's there. Arkyn will come of age in Amphi but he said as he couldn't be here at Ceardlann then there wasn't much difference between Oedran and Amphi and therefore he might as well humour ReJean."

Tancred listened carefully. "I think that says a lot about both the Princes, sir. When exactly would they go?"

Adeone frowned and looked at his empty whiskey glass. "Just before the Munewid, Judge. That way they can preside at the Amphi celebrations."

Tancred nodded. "So Prince Tain's cisan-age celebrations will be in Amphi as well…"

Adeone groaned. "How did I forget that, Judge? We'll have to tell him, or see if he wants to celebrate there."

"I think His Highness will be accepting of the situation, sir. His brother will be with him and it is my understanding that Lady Phylicia ReJean is the same age…"

Adeone sighed. "So is Cal. They might have wanted to celebrate together. I'm not good at this… I curse ReJean for complicating it all."

Tancred topped up the King's glass. "I am hardly surprised, sir, and I hesitate to add another complication but *traditionally* His Highness would take his oath on his fifteenth birthday…"

Adeone groaned. "I'll consider that with a clear head. This whiskey is feeling potent."

Tancred smiled. "It might be the amount rather than the drink. I think I have also drunk enough. Shall we wend our way to bed, Sire?"

"Only if you call me Adeone."

"Adeone."

The King pushed himself to his feet and Tancred steadied him, considering he had not seen the King so tipsy for a long time. He glanced at a timepiece and looked again. It was close to two in the morning and they'd sat down after dinner. No wonder they were feeling the effects.

Chapter 73
LAUGHTER
Hexadai, Week 18 – 13th Meithal, 20th Easis 1214
Ceardlann

ADEONE WOKE LATER than normal the following day and groaned; maybe the judge being at Ceardlann was a bad thing, at least for his head.

Simkins said conversationally, "There's what the doctor might call a cure in the glass next to you, sir."

Adeone rolled over and swallowed it without question. "Thank you."

"The judge mentioned you might need it, Your Majesty. He also sent his apologies."

Adeone chuckled and wished he hadn't. "Right. How is Prince Tain?"

"Feeling better, sir. Lady Rhian's been to see him and made him stay in bed."

Adeone sighed. "I wonder if I should emphasise that or sympathise,

Simkins?"

"I am tending to the latter option, Your Majesty…"

Adeone looked at him. "Lady Amara's daughter?"

"Exactly, sir."

"That's my aunt and cousin, Simkins…"

Simkins smiled. "Sorry, Sire, but this *is* Ceardlann."

Adeone said, "Good point. Right bath and breakfast, I think."

Feeling more reasonable, he walked along to the Princes' sitting room and opened the door. No-one was there. He stood for a moment, turned on his heel and walked to his younger son's room. When he entered, everyone bar Tain got to their feet.

"Does this count as restful, Tain?"

Tain grinned. "Probably not, father, but I was bored."

Adeone shook his head. The 'cure' was working. "Don't let me interfere then. Is there any point me staying?" (Tain nodded.) Adeone walked over to him and gave him a hug. "Good, but it's a bit crowded in here…"

Rhian got up. "I'll go and find somewhere else."

Arkyn also got up. "Me too."

Elantha hardly seemed to have heard. "No, Judge, don't move, please."

Adeone glanced over. "Little flower?"

"Sorry, Uncle Adeone, I wasn't listening…"

Tancred said quietly, "Her Ladyship is taking my portrait, Sire. I am quite flattered, no-one else ever has."

Adeone smiled. "Then don't move or she'll not finish it and there should be a portrait somewhere of you. In fact, we'll have an official one taken as well."

Tancred stilled. With only faint wryness, he said, "Thank you, Sire."

Adeone winked at Elantha. "I have my uses. Now, see if you can try to get him to stop using honorifics."

Elantha smiled. "We keep trying with Cal, but he doesn't and I think the judge is the same."

"It was worth a try. Who's left? Morning, Cal."

"Good morning, Your Majesty. May I stay here, please?"

Adeone looked at him. "Of course. There's something I wanted to ask you and Tain anyway."

Tain groaned. "I suddenly feel worse."

Adeone chuckled. "It's nothing bad. Tain, Arkyn's going to do the Arealian Review at the beginning of next year. It means he'll come of age in Amphi…"

"He can't do that, father."

"That was my reaction but he wants to do it. I'll let him explain why; however, he's asked that you travel with him and I've said you can. No, be sensible, lie still, you're ill. I'll be there for his birthday, but there are added complications to this. The celebrations for your cisan-age birthday would be held in Amphi and I wouldn't be able to be there…"

Tain bit his lip. He wanted to travel so badly but he didn't want to hurt his father's feelings. "I'd like you to be there, father, I really would, but I can understand why you can't be. I'd like to see Amphi and I'm better travelling with Arkyn, aren't I?"

"You are, but we could always go together for his birthday and I can leave you there for a bit afterwards."

"Your Majesty, what did you want to ask me?" enquired Cal.

Adeone looked at him. "Whether you'd like to go as well."

Cal sighed. "I would, sir, but I know my parents would like me at home for my birthday."

"We enjoyed our joint birthday party this year…" declared Tain. "Father, could we have an early birthday celebration? It could solve everything."

Adeone looked at him. "It's unusual."

"Yes, but I'd have to take my oath on my birthday and it would put the dampeners on it, really. If we made it a week before or something, there'd be no clash with Court functions here. Arkyn and I could have a joint banquet, Cal could be there…"

Adeone mused over the idea. "That could work."

Tain grinned. "I could come back from Amphi with you after Arkyn's birthday. By which time he'll be in the middle of the review and I'll be getting in the way. I could meet some of the Amphi judges…"

Adeone ruffled his hair. "There's a brain in there somewhere, I'm sure of it now."

Tain smoothed his hair down. "Take pity on an invalid, father."

"You're not doing badly for someone who's ill."

Cal laughed. "I think he's feeling better, Sire."

Tancred said softly, "So do I. Maybe we should resume our lesson."

Tain groaned theatrically.

Adeone looked over at the judge. "Strange that, James."

"Strange indeed, Your Majesty. I do not think His Highness appreciated the idea at all. I might be hurt."

Tain grinned at him. "The idea isn't you, Judge."

"Thank you, sir. I think that was a compliment."

Adeone shook his head slightly. "There is a slight problem we've yet to overcome, Tain. When you take your oath. It should be on your birthday and you should be in Oedran afterwards."

Tain bit his lip. "Damn."

"Don't swear."

"You and Arkyn do, sir."

Adeone eyed him. "We're older and have more to curse."

"I do not know if this will help, Your Majesty, but there is no fixed day on which His Highness must take the oath," advised Tancred conversationally, still posing for Elantha. "Only tradition dictates it should be on his birthday. He could take it tomorrow. It is only the post of Justiciar of Oedran that begins when he is fifteen. He could assume some of that with no oath taken. Again, it is only tradition that he takes the Judge's Oath in the Justice Hall before becoming Justiciar of Oedran."

Adeone turned to him. "You've just ripped everything I thought I knew about this to shreds, James."

"I was going to mention it last night, Your Majesty, but events rather overtook us."

Adeone smiled. "So they did. What would you suggest, *Your Honour*?"

"That His Highness takes his oath early. A couple of weeks might suffice. It shows faith in him. If Your Majesty explains the situation to the Keeper, he is not likely to worry overmuch that His Highness is not present for a week or so. He has coped so well for years that it is normal for him. His Highness will soon dispel any negative connotations from him not having been here for the first fortnight."

Tain said, "There's nothing to stop the Keeper sending me documents in Amphi. I'm more than happy to deal with them there."

Tancred's lips twitched. "There is not, Your Highness. Oh, I beg your pardon, Lady Elantha."

Adeone watched the two of them. "James, I have never regretted choosing you to teach Tain and I want you to know that."

Tancred contemplated him. "Never, Sire? Not even when—?"

Adeone shook his head. "Never!"

Tain smiled. "I couldn't have wished for a better tutor either. El, make that portrait honest. Twinkling eyes, slight smile, tolerant persona…"

Cal said quietly, "I'm not sure a persona can be drawn, Your Highness."

Adeone laughed. "We're making James uncomfortable and he's only just returned here."

Tain tilted his head. "Has he? It feels like he's always been here."

Tancred sighed. "Am I going to be allowed to go home?"

Tain scrambled out of bed and gave him a hug. "Only if you promise to come back."

Tancred grimaced in apology at Elantha, who shrugged resignedly.

Returning the hug, the judge said, "I think I shall have to; Lady Elantha might not then commit a treasonable homicide."

Adeone chuckled. "Tain, get back into bed. Doctor Chapa's still here somewhere and I'd rather not be berated by him. Cal, make sure he's sensible. I've just got to go and see Arkyn. El, good luck, little flower. I have this feeling that you might need it. I'll be riding back to Oedran this evening, James, if you wish to come, but you may stay here for as long as you like."

Tancred smiled. "Thank you, Sire. I will accompany Your Majesty."

"Good but, if you carry on that obsequiously, you might not reach Oedran. Just a warning…"

Chapter 74

A WHISPERED WISH
Mid-morning
Ceardlann – King's Rooms

LEAVING HIS SON'S ROOM, Adeone made his way to his dressing room. He took out a box he'd not handled for years, ran his hands over it and hesitated, but it was as though a reassuring hand was placed on his shoulder, giving him support to follow a wish. He opened the lid. There, carefully arranged, was some of his late wife's jewellery. He ignored the majority hunting for one piece in particular: a thin, delicate, whisper of a gold chain. He found it and ran it through his hands. There was no pendant to clutch at his memories and he snapped shut the box. Just because he'd retrieved it didn't mean he had to do anything with it, did it? No, but he'd set everything in motion. Was it too soon? Not for *him*, but maybe it would be better not to highlight anything. He took a ring from his finger and weighed it in his hand; looking out of the window towards the forest. He rubbed at his naked finger. Re-entering his dressing room, he rootled in an old box. Discovering a plain gold band, he slipped it on. That felt better, as though nothing had been lost. Threading the original ring onto the chain, he retrieved a small velvet pouch. The chain went in the pouch and that went into his belt pouch. He walked downstairs with a heavy heart as though he'd just ended something, which, in a way, he had, he told himself regretfully, but it was time.

Spotting David, he asked where Arkyn was. A few moments later, he entered the drawing room, still lost in thought.

"Father, is everything all right?"

Adeone glanced at him and he saw Rhian as well. Absentmindedly he said, "Yes…"

Arkyn saw his father's eyes linger on Rhian. There was something in the look he couldn't name, but he could begin to understand. He smiled gently to himself. "Is Tain feeling better?"

Adeone shook himself. "He seems to be…" He explained what had been decided and Arkyn nodded.

"He even makes sense occasionally. It sounds like a good plan, father."

"Doesn't it? Compelling even." The sun dancing through the windows invited him outside. "I'm going to go for a walk. Dispel the last of this headache. Do either of you want to come?"

Rhian smiled. "I will with pleasure. It's a long time since I was in the Rex Dallin."

"You know you're always welcome, Rhian."

Arkyn said, "I'll stay here, father, and make sure Tain's sensible… or rather stays in bed for a bit longer." He walked companionably with them to the front doors and watched them leave with a small smile.

From beside him, the Comptroller said, "Shall I send a guard, sir?"

Arkyn continued to watch his father and cousin's retreating figures. "No, Comptroller. I don't think that would help at all."

Without knowing he had a destination, Adeone guided their steps until they entered the Great Meadow, a mile from Ceardlann. His gaze was drawn to an ancient lone oak.

Rhian said, "The Wishing Tree?"

He smiled. "Which apparently grants wishes for the valley inhabitants…"

"Mind over matter?"

"I sometimes wonder."

They strolled towards it; old, majestic, rooted into the fertile earth of the Rex Dallin it stood proudly, not troubled by time or human frailties.

Adeone said gently, "I've always seen oaks as dependable, strong characters."

"Yes, I know what you mean. Even the saplings have something stately about them."

Adeone nodded. He slipped his hand into Rhian's without thinking as they crossed to the oak.

She squeezed it. "What is troubling you? Something is."

He looked at her. "I am not sure I can explain." He paused. "We are bound—"

She smiled ruefully. "We *are* bound, Adeone."

Adeone started. "By more than familial ties, I was going to say."

"What makes you think I wasn't?"

Adeone glanced up into the branches. He made a wish, not knowing why he did it; it was woven in his mind. With Rhian's hand in his, he willed it to be true. He wanted what remained of his life to be happy, without great loss. A fleeting light passed over his face. Rhian touched his cheek; his eyes met hers, mind made up. He wouldn't put her through everything an announcement would entail. This would be for them – companions and confidants, as Lachlan and Marni had been.

He kissed her for a long moment, releasing many of his pent-up feelings. His heart told him what he wanted, but he would take the time to let things develop. Their marriage would come later. He sat with his back against the bole of the tree, pulling her down next to him. They gazed over the meadow and down to the river.

"I should have returned before," she whispered.

He slipped an arm round her and didn't say anything. Her body against his pressed his belt pouch into him. He struggled to move it round on his belt, and Rhian stayed his hand with hers.

"Let me."

Two minutes later, he opened it and took out the small pouch. "Rhian, will you give me your Dallin?"

Rhian frowned. "Of course, if you want it, but I didn't think..."

He put a finger on her lips. "Not like that. I've something for you and you won't need the Dallin afterwards."

Rhian's eyes scoured his face, and, recognising only concern, rummaged in her pocket and drew out the gold True Dallin that granted entry to the Rex Dallin. Half-heartedly, she passed it over.

Adeone took it and slipped it into his pouch. He leaned over and, kissing her, was free of troubles. Moments later, he slipped the chain and ring over her head.

"Keep it safer than you did the Dallin."

Astounded, she looked at the filigree ring and then held his gaze.

"I mean everything it implies, Rhian, but it needs to be safe. You'll know when to—"

She touched his lips lightly with a finger. "I do, but that will be a long time yet... I don't want a fuss..."

"I didn't think you would. We can keep this between us. A pompous wedding ceremony isn't us, is it? The ring's merely my promise to you."

"Thank you." Two minutes of silence later, she said, "Maybe we could return after the Munewid? It would be simpler."

He slipped his hand into hers. "Do you mind?"

"No." It was whispered, her promise of intent and for the future. One day, they would be married.

PART 5

Chapter 75

A LESSON IN UNDERSTANDING
Late Morning
Ceardlann

WHEN ADEONE AND RHIAN entered Ceardlann, it appeared deserted. Everyone was ensconced in Tain's room. Adeone sent for Chapa.

"Can he at least get up, doc?"

Chapa smiled. "Of course, sir, I just thought people might appreciate the peace and quiet."

"They're hardly escaping his company; I think you'll agree."

"I try to help, sir, I do try but some people just can't be helped."

Adeone laughed. "Cousin, try harder to sound longer suffering. I'm not sure there was enough nuance in that."

Chapa grinned back. "I'll try it another time, Adeone. Now, how are you? I've been trying to get chance to ask for a while."

"You're here to see to Tain."

"I wasn't necessarily meaning your health," stated Chapa lightly.

"Ah. I'm fine. I'm at Ceardlann, it always helps."

"Mind if I retire here?"

"Yes. I'd never get any peace…" replied Adeone without considering if the doctor was being serious. He smiled. "But you can visit whenever you wish, as long as I'm in Oedran, for the same reason…"

Doctor Chapa chuckled. "There are times I think you don't appreciate my company at all."

"Company and care are two very different matters, cousin. Shall we go and cheer Tain up?"

"If we must."

Lunch was a hectic affair and Adeone caught Chapa's eye ruefully. Chapa raised an eyebrow without saying a word. Shortly after lunch, he left, pointing out that Tain seemed perfectly well again. Adeone tried to persuade him to stay until he and the judge left, but Chapa mentioned he'd drop in on Fitz and reassure the old guard on his way to Oedran. It was another way of saying that he planned to spend the afternoon reminiscing over a replenishing mug of ale.

Walking round the corner of the house, after Chapa had left, Adeone saw Tancred strolling through the gardens. Unobtrusively, he ambled over.

"Mind if I join you, James?"

"Hmm. Oh, I beg your pardon, Your Majesty. Not at all, sir."

Adeone looked at him. "James…"

Tancred said softly, "A place truly without rank?"

"If I had my way."

The judge sighed. "It is terrifying for some people."

Adeone frowned. "James?"

"I was born in a small room, in a small dingy house, in the wharf quarter of the Ryson lordship, sir. I was almost the lowest of the low. I never expected anything in life but to be pushed around. My brother was executed for treason; we may now understand that, but, for most of my life, there has been guilt and confusion in my mind. By chance, I became acquainted with Prince Lachlan and because of that I came here, where no-one of my kind ever had before. It was daunting, it still is. I walk these grounds and consider what I have lived through and where I have lived, and it is not comparable. I have seen wonders and experienced life at the bottom and rising high. I have experienced in life more variety than many a man and yet I am considered a friend by the FitzAlcis. It is unsettling. There is always doubt there. Here, in this beautiful place, that tears the heart from you and heals it at the same time I am to be considered equal? That frightens me, Sire, and what frightens me more is that here I could almost feel it when I look at Prince Tain. He feels almost a part of me now. I cannot watch him hurt without it cutting me. Prince Lachlan's friendship and Your Majesty's regard have meant much to me, but I have always known you are of the FitzAlcis. Yet, here especially, I see His Highness as himself. For one born as I was, that is terrifying. I understand Calumiel Galdwin more than anyone else at such times. I am glad I have returned, but I shall not do so again. Please do not try to change my mind, Sire. I am not taking this decision lightly, but I know for myself it is the right one."

Adeone considered one of his few confidants. "James, I will always respect your choices and, if you are adamant, I shall say nothing on the matter, nor shall I say anything again if you ever change your mind, but this I must say, if not for myself, for Tain: in this life we are all frightened by circumstances beyond our control. It is our friends who soothe those fears. I understand your feelings more than I think you can ever believe, but, even if you still see me as your King, do not harden your heart so to my son and see him only as your Prince."

Tancred knelt and kissed the King's signet ring.

Adeone bit his lip and guided Tancred back to his feet. "Not here, James…"

"It is only here that it says truly what I feel, Your Majesty. In Oedran it is merely seen as a mark of obedience."

Adeone said simply, "Let's get a drink – though hopefully not as much as last night."

"Forgive my blunderings, Sire."

"I didn't see or hear any blunders… but I may just take the decanter away from you."

Tancred chuckled, a warming laugh. "A king, Your Majesty, should never have to fill his own glass."

"Then that tradition is all the better for the changing," said Adeone dryly.

Laughing, they made their way companionably back to the house.

Chapter 76
ON RESPONSIBILITIES
Pentadai, Week 22 – 12th Seral, 5th Seris 1214
Rex Dallin – Pillars of Alcis

A FEW WEEKS LATER, Tain rode to Fitz's in a pensive mood, though he couldn't quite work out the reason for it. He and Cal had spent the last hour with swords drawn and daggers in their hands, testing each other's mettle. Cal had, as always, disarmed him more than he had disarmed Cal, but that was simply an annoying fact of life. It wasn't at the base of his feelings. Bandit splashed into the ford at the Pillars of Alcis, and Tain reined him in. He turned in the saddle, viewing the Rex Dallin. Why was he so torn on leaving the valley? He spent days frustrated by the fact he had to stay there, but, when he was away from it, he wanted to return to its simplicity. He watched the river swirling around Bandit's fetlocks.

Patting the horse, Tain said softly, "Come on, Bandit, neither of us can return yet."

The horse let out a gentle nicker, as though agreeing and then, urged on by Tain's heels, moved forward and out of the ford on the road to Dellwood. Barely had they cleared the slight rise than men were shouted to attention.

Tain glanced over. "Morning, Smithers."

"Good morning, Your Highness. At least, I trust it's a good morning?"

"So far – possibly. Is the judge at Fitz's?"

Smithers smiled. "Yes, sir. Safely delivered there and, when we left him, in perfect health."

In Fitz's stableyard, Tain reined in and dismounted smoothly. He said a quiet word to Bandit before passing the reins to one of his guard, glancing around the stableyard. A cart stood laden with trunks and odd pieces of furniture. Did Fitz have visitors?

"Who else is here, Smithers?"

"I'm not sure, sir. We'll check."

"No, it's all right, thank you. I'm sure I'll be safe enough with you by my side."

Smithers fought to control a smile. "Your Highness is too kind."

"It's a failing of mine."

Tain and Smithers entered the kitchen and stopped abruptly. Tain even paused in removing his riding gloves.

A curt gentleman was saying, "I don't care to dine here. There's a room with a table and chairs at the end of the upstairs corridor. I'll dine there, alone. There's only an old buffoon there. He can find somewhere else."

Tain took a second to collect his thoughts. "Who are you, sir, to throw your weight around in this manner?" he demanded, finishing removing his gloves. The voice of authority he'd heard in his father and brother came naturally to him in a way he'd not known before. Was it the situation or his age, his understanding that soon it would be required more often?

"Says a spotty oik. I'm Lord Longland of the Macian Isles. Who do you think you are?"

Tain put a hand out slightly to stop Fitz and Smithers saying anything. "I'm surprised to see you here. I would have thought you'd have been presenting yourself at my father's Court in Oedran, my lord. Obviously, you must have business on the mainland that prevents such courtesies. What is that business?"

Lord Longland reddened. "I was on my way to Oedran, sir."

"I'm sure you are – *now*. His Majesty will wish to meet you. Prince Arkyn will, no doubt, be interested to renew your acquaintance also. I hope their experience of your manners is not the same as I've witnessed. You will take your meal wherever Fitz is good enough to place it and desist from describing any more of his guests as either 'old buffoons' or 'spotty oiks'. After all, you have managed to insult not only myself but a close and valued friend of His Majesty." He turned to Fitz. "I'll take myself out of your way, Fitz. We'll ring as usual for lunch."

Fitz suppressed a smile. "Of course, Your Highness. My apologies for the situation that greeted your arrival, sir."

Tain smiled. "I do not believe it to have been of your making. Captain Smithers, don't get *too* comfortable."

Barely had Tain reached the other side of the hallway door when he heard Fitz saying,

"Would you care to eat in here now, my lord?"

He chuckled as he walked to the room he and the judge used.

* * *

Tancred bowed as Tain entered, noting the Prince's preoccupation. "I presume Your Highness has encountered Lord Longland?"

"Yes, Judge. Did you also have the pleasure?"

"Not so that he would have noticed, sir. If Your Highness wishes to talk to His Majesty, our lessons may wait."

"Thank you, Judge. There're a couple of things bothering me."

* * *

Adeone glanced up as Pesky popped into existence on his desk. He simply raised an amused eyebrow.

"The princeling would like a word, Sire. Don't ask me what about, he never tells me anything…"

Adeone chuckled. Two moments later, he said, "Tain, any reason Pesky's feeling aggrieved?"

"Probably, I'll find out later. Lord Longland is at Fitz's, sir."

"What on Erinna is he doing there? Is Smithers with you?"

"He's with Longland, sir. I don't know what His Lordship's doing here. After a brief discussion, he said he was on his way to Oedran but I doubt it. I think he only said that because he realised that the spotty oik was your son…" A grin flittered across Tain's face. "I don't think he appreciated me asking his business without introducing myself properly. He'd called the judge an old buffoon and was being obnoxious to Fitz, so I wasn't too bothered about pleasantries."

"Did you lose your temper?"

"No, sir. I utilised my vocabulary instead. I'd rather someone else told you what was said; I simply thought you might be interested in Longland's arrival and location, Sire."

"I am, very. I'll deal with it. Just concentrate on your lessons – or at least try to."

Tain grinned. "I'll try, father."

Once the link closed, Adeone contacted Wynfeld and Smithers. Longland would be escorted to Oedran before Tain concluded his lessons.

* * *

After spending the rest of the morning looking at his formal duties at the King's Court and his precedence there, Tain was glad when Fitz brought in lunch.

Without even being asked, the former captain said, "His Majesty has been in touch, Your Highness, and your guards are keeping Lord Longland under observation."

343

"Thank you, Fitz. Have you any idea how he ended up here?"

"Not exactly, sir. I rather suspect some jokers at the port, or Two Ways and Cilford, might be responsible. His Lordship appears to have a knack for alienating people. I rather suspect that he might have managed it with someone he asked to point him in the right direction."

"Any idea why he's visiting the mainland?"

"A supposition only, Your Highness. I think he might be looking for marriage prospects. His wife died last year."

Tain snorted. "Good luck to him with that attitude."

"Quite, Your Highness. I think being escorted to Oedran to explain himself to His Majesty might well make him reconsider his behaviour. Ring when you want this lot out of the way, sir. Judge."

Once the meal had been demolished and cleared, Judge Tancred looked at his charge. "What would you like to continue with this afternoon, sir?"

"I suppose this morning's lesson, Judge. Maybe, though, we should move on to my duties as Justiciar?"

"Maybe so, sir. Your actual duties are a subject for other lessons. Your responsibilities are pretty simple. As Justiciar, you are appointed to see that the laws of the empire are upheld, that the process of justice is free from corruption and that new laws are formed as the necessity arises. The last is also the domain of His Majesty, but when he proposes new laws, he will generally seek advice from the Justiciar or other judges in the empire."

"It doesn't sound like much, Judge."

"Again, Your Highness, the explanation is brief in comparison to the execution of such responsibilities. They will seem far weightier in time than they appear now. If it was only Your Highness dispensing justice then they would be pretty simple to uphold; however, Your Highness will need to influence and control people as far away as Terasia and as close to home as Carnford, not to mention Oedran itself. Your judges should follow your lead but there will be times when you will need to emphasise your decisions. There are procedures for that and we can discuss them later, if you wish."

"I think it might be helpful, Judge."

* * *

Talk swung back and forth until hooves and military attire was heard in the stableyard. Minutes later, the tread of boots resounded in the corridor and a captain entered. He saluted smartly as Tain got to his feet.

"Captain?"

"I'm here to escort Lord Longland to Oedran, Your Highness. His Majesty suggested that you came and explained matters to His Lordship."

Tain took a breath. "Lead the way."

As Tain left the room, the judge accompanied him. Tain was pleased of the support though wondered if it might appear that he couldn't be trusted to do anything without his tutor.

In the stableyard, the guards saluted as Tain walked out. They were behaving impeccably to enhance his authority, it seemed. No doubt they would gossip about the incidents when they went off duty but, for the moment, they were playing things by the book.

Predictably, Longland was objecting to the idea that he was to be *chaperoned* to Oedran.

Arms behind his back, Tain said, "My lord, your King's instructions are quite clear on this matter. You will be escorted under guard to the Palace of Oedran. You will then have an audience with His Majesty. Where you can explain matters. You were a little out of your way – that is, if you still claim you were on your way to Oedran. A mile more on this road and you would have been arrested and tried for treason. I'm sure you have no wish for that. I can assure you there will be no chance of you getting lost again."

Longland frowned. "Am I under arrest, sir?"

"An interesting question. You are certainly detained until His Majesty has a satisfactory explanation. You are not, however, currently charged with anything under the law. That, of course, could change. All that is required currently is that you accept the guidance of your escort and that you do so with relatively good grace. I would suggest you also curb your abrupt and insulting manner."

"You must—"

Judge Tancred said, "My lord, please remember it is Prince Tain you are addressing."

Longland's face flickered to a sneer before he controlled it.

"As I mentioned, curbing your insulting manner might be wise," observed Tain.

"Your Highness, I am not happy with this situation."

"Most of this situation, my lord, is of your own making; therefore, if it vexes you to such a degree, you might consider how in future you could avoid a repeat incident. For now, Your Lordship should be on the way to Oedran. His Majesty does not like tardiness and will have many audiences your behaviour has postponed."

Looking bilious, Longland swung into the saddle of his horse and moved off. The captain saluted Tain and motioned his men forward. Once out of sight, Tain let out a long breath.

"Odd. He didn't take his leave of me, Your Honour."

Tancred chuckled. "I cannot imagine how he came to so forget himself, sir."

"Imagination and knowledge are two very different matters, Judge."

"Indeed they are, Your Highness," admitted Tancred, lips twitching. "You handled that remarkably well. There was just the right level of authority to deal with a man of uncertain temperament."

"You mean he was stroppy and recalcitrant. I wasn't overbearing?"

Tancred said softly, "I do not think you were, in that circumstance, sir. His Lordship might be having a bad day but there was no need for his behaviour."

Tain sighed. "Thank you, Judge."

"Not at all, sir. Shall we obtain a drink from Fitz before we resume?"

* * *

Whilst still seated in the warm kitchen, Tain took a sip of mint tea. "Judge, what will my responsibilities be away from Court but to the King?"

Tancred looked at him. "I wondered if we would reach this today, sir. You have your responsibilities as a son and those will not feature here; they are for Your Highness and His Majesty to discuss. As a prince, your responsibilities are to ensure that people remember the King is the King, to watch for his safety and wellbeing but to obey his orders. Basically, enhance His Majesty's standing and protect him."

"Is this another case of simpler said than done, Judge?"

Tancred nodded. "Very much so, Your Highness. Do not, however, worry about it. In time, you will find your own place and work out your own rules."

Tain sighed. "That's what Uncle Scanlon's done, isn't it?"

"No," snapped Fitz. "He's become a traitor. You never will."

Tain looked at him. "How do you know?"

"I've seen you all growing. Your father, uncle, brother and yourself. There ain't a bone in your body that's like your uncle. So stop guessing at the future, stop fearing it, live it instead."

Tain snorted. "At times, Fitz, I think your respectful attitude is simply an act."

Fitz laughed. "Your Highness is a person same as anyone else. Sometimes things need to be stated plain and simple. Hey, Judge?"

"On occasion I would agree with you, Fitz," replied Tancred, "but maybe one needs to be sure of one's reception."

Tain smiled. "I can stand the truth from both of you."

Fitz winked. "That's fortunate, sir, but we're worrying the judge."

"I rarely do anything else, Fitz."

Tancred said softly, "Nothing could be further from the truth, Your Highness."

Tain grinned at him. "Apparently, Judge, you're not a courtier."

"Then that must have been the truth, sir."

Chapter 77
A DIFFERENT VIEW
Septadai, Week 25 – 7th Ralal, 7th Ralis 1214
Prince Tain's Chambers

ON THE SEPTADAI after the Mundimri of 1214, Tain was in Oedran and Peter was briefing him on the case he was to observe the following day. Halfway through the briefing, Linnt abruptly announced Cal. Tain grinned at his friend, motioned to the chairs and continued listening to Peter.

"We can stop, Your Highness," offered his administrator.

"No, it's all right. I'm not sure when we'd get chance to complete this in time."

So Peter continued. Cal listened with half an ear and retrieved the plans of the Palace that had been delivered in the autumn but which they hadn't had chance to look at properly. He frowned. They were all numbered but out of order. Tain must have been impatient and started the hunt for the Viewing Gallery entrance without him. It was unusual but not surprising.

Tain glanced over as Cal reordered the plans, but, aware of his earlier to words to Peter, carried on listening to his administrator, who ended with the normal question.

"Is there anything requiring clarification, Your Highness?"

Tain shook his head. "No, Peter, thank you. That's all for now."

His administrator left and Tain grinned at Cal. "Sorry about that…"

"It's fine, sir. It's strangely interesting to listen to occasionally. Were the plans delivered out of order?"

Tain frowned. "No. I checked them but I didn't start looking at them."

"A mystery then. Never mind, where shall we start?"

"King's Hall?"

Cal found the plan and they pored over it. It gave nothing away. Tain groaned.

"That would have been too easy, I suppose."

Cal laughed. "Of course…"

Two hours later, Tain put the final plan down. "Not a clue on any of them…"

"No. Shall we go for a ride and clear our heads, sir?"

* * *

When they returned, they found Arkyn, drink in hand, happily ensconced, examining the plans.

Tain said, "Make yourself at home."

"I did. What are these for?"

Tain passed Cal a drink and explained.

Arkyn chuckled. "It won't be shown on these. They're copies and, anyway, the plans themselves are nowhere near old enough – the originals, that is – copies of copies of copies, each one simpler than the last because it's only a copy. You need some ancient plans, don't you?"

Tain said, "Obviously that thought never occurred to me—"

"Was that meant to be sarcastic?"

Cal grinned. "I'd say it *was* sarcastic, Your Highness."

Tain continued, ignoring them both, "Father said that there weren't any older plans."

Arkyn smiled. "Really. Does father know everything, Tain? Cal, who would you go and ask if you wanted a really old document?"

Cal smirked. "The archivist?"

"Exactly and when Kensal… was spending every hour he could in the archives he came across some old plans of the Palace, when it was being built. You need to go and see the archivist."

"That'll take ages," grouched Tain. "They'll be buried again…"

"If you want to see them, he'll have to shift stuff until he finds them. Plain and simple."

Tain's face became animated. "Arkyn…"

Arkyn sighed, saying to Cal, "He's got an idea, hasn't he?"

Cal grinned. "It has been known—"

"Shut up the pair of you and listen—"

Arkyn said, "That's not very polite."

"Succinct though, Your Highness," observed Cal.

Tain scowled. "Well, if you don't want to know…"

Arkyn smiled. "Go on."

Tain turned to Cal. "Shift?"

Cal sat there for a moment, puzzled, then a small grin spread over his face becoming wider every moment.

"Isn't that cheating?" enquired Arkyn mildly.

Tain shook his head. "I'd say it's using the resources to hand."

* * *

Cal appeared in the small gallery, its carved and fretwork screen masking

348

him from the hall below. The dark, gloomy and dusty room was hung with scarlet velvet drapes. They must be over five hundred years old and the fabric was so friable some had already collapsed to dust. Several chairs – upholstered in what had been jewel-toned silk – were dotted around the room, all facing the screen. A sturdy oak table was pushed aside, chairs were skewed, one overturned. Haste was shadowed in their positions. Whoever had been here last had left swiftly.

He glanced around the room again. A step peeked out from below a drape. Afraid to move the material, Cal shifted behind it. He stumbled and made himself fall forward instead of back into the material. He fell heavily on his hands, grazing his knees. Winded, he gathered himself. This was no passage, no door. Stairs led up, not down. He pushed himself to his feet. No-one had trod this stair for centuries. Twelve steps later, dust teasing his senses, a stone wall faced him. He looked back down the stairs. Sconces still held their ceramic lamps, wicks long turned dark. The dimness of the stair stole into his unease. He needed to find how to leave. The wall was probably a door. He turned back. There were ledges on each side, holding candlesticks of twisted iron. Cal, aware that time might have rusted metal as it had decayed cloth, carefully pulled the left-hand stick. Nothing happened. He pushed it. Nothing happened. He twisted it. Nothing happened. He turned to the one on his right. His eye fell on a worn scratch in the ledge. He pulled. The stone wall in front of him moved out. He pushed at it gently and it swung as freely as a pendulum. He stepped beyond the door into a servants' passage. Narrow, often dark and gloomy servants' passages hid in the walls. Corkscrewing staircases within them caused as many issues as they solved. Cal exited at the very top of one of these onto a square landing. He stood for a moment, his eyes adjusting to the gloom. Voices wafted up to him. He recognised one but caught only the end of the conversation.

"I'm doing what I can. There's never enough time."

The Viewing Gallery door swung to behind Cal as he started to feel for the handle of the door that would lead him out to the formal corridors of the Palace.

"Can I help?"

Cal gathered himself. "No, thank you, Linnt, I was just exploring," privately cursing he hadn't thought to check if anyone was close by.

Linnt nodded and held the door open for him. Glancing at where the lad had been standing, he thought he saw the shape of a door where there was none. What was that about?

They were on the third floor of the Privy Wing, close to Arkyn's chambers. Cal took in the location without seeming to notice it. To divert suspicion, he said, "Were you coming to see Kadeem, Linnt?"

Linnt never hesitated. "Yes, Master Calumiel."

"Maybe you'd be kind enough to say that Prince Arkyn will be with His Highness for some time?"

Without waiting for a reply, Cal walked away and let out a long breath. He made his way to a deserted spot and shifted back to Tain's chambers.

* * *

Tain looked up. "Well?"

Cal grinned. "It's dusty... *Very* dusty. There's a tiny staircase that goes up..."

"Up?"

"Yes, up, I told you it wouldn't be simple. It exits into one of the servants' ways. Near Prince Arkyn's chambers... Linnt saw me shortly after I exited from the Viewing Gallery stair. I don't think he realised anything was wrong. I told him to tell Kadeem that you'd be here for a while, Your Highness—"

Arkyn smiled. "Quick thinking."

Tain nodded. "He occasionally manages it. Cal, we could watch the Court tonight..."

Arkyn shook his head. "You'll stir up all the dust and start sneezing. Anyway, you're in court tomorrow."

Tain sighed. "I suppose you're right, but it's not as much fun."

Arkyn grinned. "I don't know. You know you've found the entrance."

Cal said, trying to put his idea into words, "We've found the *exit*, sir, but not how to make it an entrance... That is, it looks like just a plain wall. There's no handle or mechanism I could see."

Arkyn grinned. "Father's theory about a secret lever must be right then and it won't be too far from the door, I expect. Finding it without bumping into servants might be interesting though. Shall I ask the archivist for those plans?"

Tain grinned. "Could you? He's more likely to listen to you."

Arkyn, his insides knotting up at the memories of Kensal, said, "I'll go now," wanting to get it over with. He'd considered momentarily sending Edward or asking Tain to send Peter, but he had to face up to the memories at last.

Chapter 78

ARCHIVES

Afternoon
Palace of Oedran – Archives

ARKYN LEFT his brother's rooms knowing he was doing the right thing. Halfway to the archives, doubts crept stealthily into his mind and he was almost at the archives when he faltered. He stopped, oblivious to his surroundings, images assailing his memory, images of Kensal talking, laughing and debating and that final of all images, the light dying in the young lord's eyes as his life had ebbed out. The Prince was rooted to the spot for a couple of moments until Lyndon said,

"Your Highness?"

Arkyn took a deep breath and Lyndon realised that he had interrupted something, but he had no idea what. He followed as the Prince continued the last few yards before, at a word from Arkyn, waiting outside as the Prince entered the archives.

The first room was dim, very little natural light was available, let alone permitted to enter the rooms: light could damage so a heavy dullness pervaded. It suited Arkyn's mood and he was glad of the gloom. Two clerks sat at one of several desks, immersed in their jobs and, for a moment, Arkyn envied their simpler life but realised they'd have troubles of their own.

Matching his voice to the atmosphere of the room, he said to the room at large, "Is the archivist here?"

"He's in the office marked 'Archivist'!" snapped one of the clerks looking up.

"Of course," replied Arkyn, glad Lyndon had remained outside. He paused and caught the other clerk's eye. That clerk had an inkling, if not a certainty, about who he was. The Prince in Arkyn said, "Maybe you could just inform him that Prince Arkyn would like a word."

"Now look here…"

Arkyn glanced at the second clerk, who was torn between warning his companion and watching the natural outcome. "Might I suggest you warn him?"

Hearing the wry humour in Arkyn's voice, the second clerk said, "Of course, Your Highness, but I think it would be better for me to simply tell the archivist you're here."

"So it may." Arkyn turned to the first clerk. "Are you always so sharp, even sarcastic, when a request is made?"

"My apologies, Your Highness."

Already strung out, Arkyn stated, "I don't believe your apologies answer my question."

"Erm… Yes, I am, when the answer is obvious."

"Any answer is obvious when you know it. Maybe I should ask of you if you still have your job?"

"I guess the answer is 'no' and quite frankly you can stuff the job. I'm sick of it anyway."

Arkyn crooked an eyebrow. "As you have just resigned, I shall not detain your departure, but the answer to my question was actually the opposite of your assumption."

The man sank onto a chair. "What have I done?"

"You have overreacted and caused adverse consequences. Now," Arkyn sat opposite him, "Why are you sick of your job?"

The man said crossly, "What do you care?"

"Obviously enough to ask and not to report your manner to your superiors. Nor will anyone else here, but if you continue in that attitude there will be repercussions."

The clerk looked at the Prince. There wasn't much of an age difference between them. He had to say or do something to explain, apologise or just get out of the room with his life intact. "I became a clerk because my father was one and his father was one but the work is boring and I'm not suited to it. All I hear is 'work your way up and it has its compensations'. It's nonsense. I know flannelling when I hear it."

"I'm sure we all do. Very well. What makes you think that you can jump straight to the interesting bits?"

"I don't think there are any, frankly. Even the *compensations* wouldn't be worth that – backhanders only go so far."

Arkyn stilled. "Frank is a word you utilise, it seems. What would you do if you discovered a high-ranking official was corrupt?"

"You mean they're not? I'd find someone to report it to. Why should they get away with things that we can't?"

"A valid question but if His Majesty discovers anyone is corrupt, I can assure you they leave their post."

The man snorted. "Right."

"I shall assume your current discontented mood is the reason you call into question His Majesty's integrity, but I cannot let it pass. I'm afraid you've had your chance to modify your behaviour." He turned to the second clerk who had returned with the archivist. "Get my sergeant, please. He should be outside." (Lyndon entered and saluted.) Ignoring the pallor of the clerk he'd been talking with, Arkyn said, "Please escort this clerk from the Palace and inform his superiors that his conduct was found seriously wanting."

Lyndon glanced at him, inwardly confused. Arkyn was obviously emotional to the practised ear but he didn't normally react so pointedly.

The clerk said, "Your Highness—"

"I don't want to hear another word out of you," snapped the Prince. "You had your chance to explain, to redeem your manner and you didn't take it. You exacerbated the situation. I was willing to overlook you insulting me, but I shall not overlook your aspersions about His Majesty! Be glad I'm not arresting you for treason. Get out! Lyndon…" Arkyn jerked his head and Lyndon escorted the clerk out.

The second clerk remained motionless, silent, with eyes downcast.

Arkyn, however, looked at him. "You are?"

"Tinkery, sir."

"Thank you. You didn't see, hear or witness any of that – or at least, you're not to gossip about it. A simple explanation that he was exceptionally rude should suffice. Archivist, maybe we should adjourn to your office."

The archivist merely bowed slightly and motioned with his hand.

* * *

Once in his office, the archivist said, "Hang on, Your Highness, let me clear a chair of documents."

A few seconds later, Arkyn sank gratefully onto it. "Please be seated. I'm sorry for what occurred."

"I'm not. Young Welard's a right termagant. His immediate superiors won't be sorry. They only tolerated him because his father is a senior clerk in the Steward's Office."

"Thank you. I came because Lord Kensal once told me he'd found some early plans of the Palace. Architectural plans."

The archivist frowned. "Oh, yes. I remember. They showed the Privy Wing was early, or at least some of it was – the area where Your Highness' rooms are in particular… The plans should be in the Kensal Room, sir." He saw the haunted look on the Prince's face. "It was jokingly named that when His Lordship was here. I made it permanent when he died: a small token to his memory. Would Your Highness care for a tour whilst we locate the plans?"

Arkyn swallowed but nodded. "It might help."

"Aye, it might. I miss him and his help. You've no more friends staying who might like to work here, have you, sir? He'd never be replaced but I do miss his help. I miss his absurd sayings about libraries, for a start."

Arkyn laughed. "Yes, so do I. Whenever I hear the word 'library' or 'archive' I think of Kensal. His last words included a phrase about a library."

"What were they, Your Highness?"

Arkyn became the Prince, the memories still too raw. "They weren't for the repeating, Archivist. We shall locate the plans."

The archivist led the way. The archives were various rooms and the Prince noted that they all seemed to be in complete confusion until they reached the Kensal Room: here all was neat and ordered.

"He did all this?" enquired Arkyn.

"Yes. He borrowed a clerk to help with the cross-referencing and labelling work but he catalogued and sorted all this out."

"Sicla! No wonder he was here such a lot."

The archivist searched for the plans. He found them quickly. "I'll lay them out and find a better light, sir."

"I'm going to borrow them, or rather Prince Tain is. Don't worry; he'll take good care of them and will return them as soon as possible. Are there any other documents about the building of the Palace?"

"I shall locate what we know we have, sir. Will a copy suffice?"

"If it is accurate. Thank you, Archivist. I should not interrupt your day any further."

* * *

Arkyn returned to Tain's chambers in a thoughtful mood. Had he overreacted due to emotional complications? He could never have let the comment about his father pass. He had a duty as a son, and as a Prince, to make sure no aspersions were cast on the King, whether privately, politically or publicly. He tried to shake himself out of the preoccupation but it didn't work and when he re-entered Tain's sitting room his younger brother said softly,

"That bad?"

Arkyn swallowed. "Yes, especially thanks to a fool of a clerk."

"What happened, sir?" enquired Cal.

Arkyn glanced at him and at Tain and explained.

By the end of the recitation, Tain was thoughtful. "Stop worrying about it, Arkyn. You couldn't have done anything else, not once he'd said or given the impression that father accepts corruption. I'm sure that something will be said to the Steward, who will take delight in reporting the incident to father, but since when did father accept that sort of tale-bearing? You acted as an official and that's that. You are, after all, an official, aren't you?"

Arkyn caught Cal's eye. "He really does know how to make me feel better about things, doesn't he?"

Cal chuckled. "Brotherly love, sir... Not to depress you further, but I think he's right for once."

Tain said, "What do you mean, 'for once'?"

Arkyn laughed. "Well, it's such a rare occurrence. Do you want to look at these plans, or are we going to be throwing insults at each other all afternoon?"

"We can always do both…"

"And mostly we do," said Cal, wryly.

The old plans were just that: old, delicate as though dust composed them and the slightest touch would be the whisper that set the particles blowing in the wind. His brother handled them with more care than Arkyn expected.

Tain rang the bell and, when his manservant entered, said, "Linnt, you're back. Can you ask Peter to join me please?"

After Linnt had gone, Arkyn frowned. "Yes, why did he leave these chambers when you were here?"

Tain shrugged. "Who knows. He never says."

Cal murmured. "Probably for self-preservation reasons."

When his administrator entered, Tain said, "Peter, could you get these plans copied for us? They're so delicate that I'm afraid of destroying them, but really accurately copied. Every little mark on them. There's no point it being a copy otherwise…"

Peter smiled. "Of course, Your Highness. When would you like them done by?"

Tain considered. "Next time I'm in Oedran for more than a day? I think it'll be in about an aluna-month; do you think that would be all right?"

Peter nodded. "I think that should be ample time, Your Highness. Where do the original plans belong?"

Arkyn replied, "Pass them to the Palace Archivist, please. He knows."

"Very good, Your Highness. I'll just find a tube to keep them safe."

Tain smiled. "That's a sensible idea. I wish I'd thought of it. There's some more here that could do with the same treatment."

Peter nodded. "I'll find a temporary one for now and, if Your Highness wishes, I'll ask the Palace Carpenter to make some wooden ones."

Tain grinned. "An even better idea. Thank you, Peter."

Peter bowed and left. Tain carefully sorted the plans into two piles and with Cal and Arkyn's help ordered the most recent set. Peter returned, after a seemingly short time, and knelt by the low table. He pulled the first tube apart in the middle and very carefully rolled the ancient plans up. He held the roll tightly and reached for the tube, but Tain was holding it for him.

"Oh, thank you, Your Highness." He carefully placed the furled roll in the tube and closed it. The procedure was repeated with the new plans before Peter picked up both. "I'll have them labelled as well, Your

Highness. Where would you like them returning to when finished?"

Tain looked round his sitting room. "Good point. I suppose the bureau, if they'll fit in one of the drawers."

"Very good, sir. Your Highness. Master Calumiel."

After he'd gone, Arkyn said, "He really is very good, isn't he? He keeps you in line so easily, Tain."

Cal grinned. "Someone's got to."

"My bad name was happily sleeping. There's no need to wake it up," muttered Tain.

* * *

Adeone heard about the incident in the Archives but on receiving the whole story from all who were there told the Steward, and through him Welard senior, that as Arkyn hadn't ordered Clerk Welard's arrest he wouldn't, but he was sorely tempted to. Arkyn breathed a sigh of relief and let the incident drift into memory.

Chapter 79

TAILOR

Septadai, Week 32 – 28th Anapal, 14th Anapcis 1214
Prince Tain's Chambers

"LINNT, have you spoken to the tailor recently?" enquired Tain, squeezing into a tunic.

"No, sir. There's been no need."

"Really? The fact I need some new tunics obviously is not important. Ask him to come here this evening, please."

"Very good, Your Highness."

That was it. No apology. In fact, no emotion whatsoever.

That evening, the FitzAlcis' tailor bustled into the Prince's chambers with a smile.

"Still growing then, Your Highness?"

"Looks like it, tailor."

"Well, can't say I mind, keeps me and mine in a job. This is my nephew, he's my new assistant. I hope he's got neat writing. Can we start? Oh, dear, dear, these really are a bit tighter than they should be, aren't they, sir? I don't think I'll be able to let them out, so I'll have to take a new set of measurements, if you don't mind, Your Highness? We'll also have to look at what you want exactly from your formal wear come next year. But first, your measurements – got your modesty cloth on? Don't want

356

to embarrass the lad here. Now, arms out…"

Twelve minutes later, Tain resumed his tightening tunic and the tailor said, "So just a bit of growth, sir. I'd say you've put on a couple of inches and some muscle since I last saw Your Highness."

"I can't help it, tailor, it's perfectly natural."

"Aye, sir, I know. Now, is Your Highness in the mood to examine some ideas for tunics?"

Tain grinned. "I might stand that."

The tailor smiled. "Now, sir, I've brought a few samples. Obviously, the greatest change come your birthday is the fact your formal clothes will become those of the Justiciar of Oedran. With regard to the formal emerald green stripe, there's several ways I can apply it. I'd be interested to know which you'll prefer. We can dye it on white, appliqué it on other colours or even stitch it in. Alternatively, a thin cord could be used and there're many more options, each one obviously has a different cost associated with it but then Your Highness needn't worry about that. We'll let His Majesty's scriveners deal with that. If you'd like to have a look…"

Tain nodded and a couple of minutes later said, "I like the look of the appliquéd silk but don't think it is *right*. It needs some definition. How thin does this green cord get?"

"I can have some made thinner for you, sir. What is Your Highness thinking?"

"That a border using the cord is set either side of the green silk."

The tailor nodded. "We should be able to do that, sir."

"Good. What else have you got?"

"A few designs I thought Your Highness might be interested in. Ignore the colours we can use any that Your Highness wants but try to make my life interesting…"

Tain grinned. "I'll try, tailor. I like some of these interwoven lines."

"Yes, sir, so do I. Technically they're 'Pale Landian' patterns, but mostly people refer to them as 'Landian'. Again, there's several ways of applying the design but I thought this one especially might interest you. Obviously, depending on the colour Your Highness would like, it can be formal or informal. I had thought of that design for the hem of a tunic. I don't know what Your Highness thinks about that?"

"Sounds good to me. Make sure there's a nice belt to complement it and don't let the jeweller bully you too much. I don't want jewels on every bit of clothing I possess."

The tailor smiled. "I'll do my best, sir. Do you want a complete new wardrobe of summer tunics and hose for the Munewid? I'll do a couple of winter tunics immediately."

Tain grinned. "It might be an idea as I'm outgrowing everything I currently have."

"I'll do what I can. How are your shoes fitting? Should I ask the cobbler to visit?"

* * *

The tailor requested an audience with Adeone thinking that he ought to check that what had been agreed was all right with the King.

Adeone saw him as soon as he could and opened proceedings with his normal relaxed manner, when dealing with family matters. "Don't tell me, he's still growing."

The tailor smiled. "I'm afraid so, Your Majesty. I just need to check Your Majesty's happy to let me make a whole new wardrobe for His Highness and to ask the cobbler to go and take a new set of measurements."

Adeone sighed. "Of course. He *should* stop growing soon… Do a few tunics as soon as possible. He's going to be in Amphi for a week and a half at the beginning of next year, so see there are some formal tunics ready to be packed. Did you deal directly with Prince Tain?"

"Yes, sir. I also believe he sent for me."

Adeone eyed him. "So what aren't you telling me?"

The tailor hesitated. "It's not my place, Sire."

Adeone eyed him. "When I ask a question, it is your place to answer it."

The tailor considered for a brief moment. "Master Linnt should have noticed His Highness was outgrowing his tunics a while ago, Your Majesty. I don't believe he did."

Adeone nodded. "Thank you. You see, it can be your place."

Chapter 80
ON FORMALITY
Hexadai, Week 35 – 20th Bayal, 13th Bayis 1214
Prince Tain's Chambers – Sitting Room

TAIN SMILED as Linnt announced Judge Tancred. It had been decided as Tain was in Oedran to dispense with Spellen's lessons and concentrate on Tancred's expertise whilst it was closer at hand.

Tain jumped up. "Come in, Judge. Could we have some tea please, Linnt."

Linnt said, "I'll have to send for some."

Tain grimaced. Once the manservant had left, he muttered, "Organisation isn't his strong point, Judge."

"It was not that which was primarily concerning me, Your Highness."

Tain eyed his mentor. "That doesn't mean it wasn't worrying you, Judge."

"Very true, Your Highness. I even believe you could make a lawyer with a reply such as that."

"So what exactly was bothering you, Your Honour?"

"Cannot Your Highness work it out?"

Tain frowned. "Arkyn thinks that Linnt shouldn't be my manservant."

"What does Your Highness think?"

"That I'm to blame. I can't be easy to work for."

"That has not been my experience, sir. My experience has been, in fact, quite the opposite."

"You don't work for me, Judge," said Tain, defeated.

"If we are to speak precisely, Your Highness, neither does Master Linnt until you are of your age, that is twenty."

Tain walked over to the window; he gazed unseeingly at the view and sank onto the window seat, his head in his hands.

The judge watched him for a couple of moments. "Your Highness might not be of age, but it does not mean that you have no authority here within your chambers. It is a myth that the authority one has is based on age. There is a certain measure that comes with a certain age, but you are still a prince of the FitzAlcis, whatever your age. I might go as so far as to say it is only your authority in the empire that is dependent on your years."

Tain blinked. "Thank you."

Tancred said, "What *is* troubling you, sir? I can tell something is."

Tain hesitated and excused himself. Whilst he was gone, Linnt returned and placed the drinks on the sideboard.

"Thank you, Linnt. Might I give you a piece of advice?"

The manservant glanced at the judge. "Can't see how I can stop you."

"Quite. Remember that the man you serve is a prince and modify your manner accordingly."

"He hasn't complained."

"However, it has been noticed. If you continue to show a lack of respect, there are things I shall be compelled to do that, for your sake, I would prefer not to."

Linnt merely said, "I hope the drink is to your liking, sir," and left.

A few moments later, Tain re-entered the room and collapsed into his chair, his eyes red. Tancred simply handed him a drink and sat quietly opposite his charge.

"He didn't address me correctly, did he, Judge?"

"No, Your Highness," answered Tancred, unsurprised Tain had been mulling the problem over.

"I've never really minded, not deep down, if you know what I mean."

"I do, sir. Might I, however, suggest that in this instance, it is not what you mind that matters? Honorifics exist for many reasons, but mainly as a mark of respect and an enhancement of authority."

"I find them so burdensome."

"That is hardly surprising, sir, at your age. It is better to ignore their existence than insist on them not existing. To do the latter is to inadvertently invite scorn and to undermine His Majesty's authority."

Tain grimaced. "I understand that, Judge. I've had many lessons on why honorifics exist; it doesn't mean I have to like them."

"No, Your Highness, it does not. Liking, though, is not the same as accepting. You might dislike something, but you may still accept the fact of its existence."

Tain said, "I suppose so, Judge. Yet here, in my own chambers?"

The judge put his drink on a table and formed his words carefully, "There is a difference, sir, between how friends and employees should address Your Highness. For employees, it should always be formally."

"For friends it should not?"

All too aware that Cal addressed his charge formally, Tancred said, "We should respect our friends' decisions without trying to influence them to our own ends but I might also add that only in private, away from servants' ears as well as less intimate acquaintances', should informality be appropriate."

"Can you tell Cal that?"

"I believe that Your Highness has tried on many an occasion and where Your Highness fails, what makes you suppose I should succeed?"

Tain sighed. "Hope."

"A commodity that, from my experience, is inexhaustible."

There was a knock at the door and Linnt announced the King with an exaggerated formality.

"James! I'm glad to see you. I hadn't realised you'd be here. Tain, do you mind me interrupting?"

"Not at all, father. The judge is trying to convince me of the proprieties of formal modes of address."

Adeone sat next to his son. "What sparked this lesson then, James?"

The judge never seemed to hesitate. "Matters of the moment, Your Majesty."

"Ah, one of those lessons. They never end; I still receive them regularly. Tain, I wanted your advice. Cal's never going to tell me anything he needs, so I was wondering if you thought a dagger would be a good cisan-age gift."

Tain grinned. "Yes, *I* do, but I'm not sure what his father will say."

Seeing the spark of amusement in Adeone's eyes, Tancred said, "I think, Your Highness, that if it was a gift from His Majesty, Master Galdwin would have to accept it."

"I would not like to discomfort him," replied Adeone, still with the glint in his eyes.

Tain mulled that over for a brief moment. "He's been discomforted for years, father. Why dispel the prejudice?"

Adeone laughed. "That's just the sort of thing uncle would have said. I believe you must be responsible, James."

Tancred smiled. "I think it is an inherited trait of the FitzAlcis, Your Majesty."

"You mean it's my fault?"

"Far be it from a mere judge to comment such on Your Majesty or your family, Sire."

"Definitely saying it's my fault. I suppose it is. Most things are sooner or later. I'll leave you to conclude your lessons. James, come and see me later. I could do with a talk."

When his father had gone, Tain said, "Do we have to return to my lessons, Judge?"

"What would you rather be doing, Your Highness?"

"It's a nice day; I wouldn't mind a walk in the grounds."

* * *

Once outside, Tain breathed deeply. "Judge, I understand everything there is to understand about formality's existence, but I can't accept it as easily as others do. I just want a spot of normality."

"What is it exactly that bothers Your Highness?"

Tain frowned and walked for some moments in silence. "The implied fear behind the formality. I think it is since I recognised that it isn't all about respect or even something that just is."

Tancred nodded. "I can understand that, sir. Initially, it may be many things: fear, respect, tradition, to name but three. For the moment, with regards to Your Highness, it is more to do with His Majesty than with yourself, at least for those who do not know you. For those of us who do, it is more respect than anything else."

"Cal though…"

"Master Calumiel made his decisions for private reasons, sir; is it right, as a friend, to try to force change?"

Tain stopped in his tracks. "I hadn't thought of it as forcing him into actions before. I suppose that is rather low of me."

Tancred looked at him. "You have tried to change a friend's ways, sir,

361

for personal reasons. That is all, Your Highness."

Tain smiled sadly. The rebuke cut deep but, for the first time in a long time, he didn't fight it, for he'd truly come to value and appreciate the judge's opinions and advice.

* * *

Two hours later, Tancred was announced in the Inner Office.

Adeone looked over in relief. "James, you always appear when I need a break. Come and have a drink and tell me what had upset my incorrigible son and why you ended up repeating lessons he's doubtless had before."

Tancred accepted a drink. "I am not certain what exactly upset His Highness, Your Majesty, but the subject of formality was brought up because of Linnt's lack of it."

Settling into a chair, Adeone said, "Ah. Was it a marked insolence?"

"I would say it was a noticeable one, Your Majesty."

"What do you think of Linnt, James?"

"I think he is very different from other servants I have known in the FitzAlcis' employ."

Adeone said, "I won't get angered by the truth, James. I didn't pick him. The Steward recommended him."

"In that case, I would question whether the Steward knows his job or whether he has been coerced into action," remarked Tancred, "because Linnt is not a manservant, Your Majesty. That much is clear."

Perplexed, Adeone exclaimed, "What on Erinna makes you say that?"

"His manner, sir. Any manservant would never dream of having to send for something as predictable as drinks, and he certainly would not highlight the fact he was sending for them in the first place. His manner of talking would be more deferential than equal also. If others have not noticed it, I may have caught Master Linnt at a bad time."

The King sighed. "No, Judge. I think you're spot on. I just hadn't spotted the cause, only the effect. I shall do yet more discreet enquiries. I won't deprive a man of his living without certainty."

"Sir, I do not mean to be impertinent but to leave him so close to Prince Tain, if he is not as he portrays, may be dangerous if he hears enquiries are being made."

"I take the point. We have to work out Tain's staff as well, James."

"Your Majesty?"

"Well, I can't do it on my own and you know the Oedranian Courthouse. We need to leave time for checks to be made so there isn't long."

Tancred said, "Very good, sir. I shall try to have suggestions to Your Majesty by next week, if that suffices?"

"Admirably, James."

Chapter 81

TUCHLIN OR NOT
Cisadai, Week 41 – 2nd Geryal, 9th Souis 1214
Inner Office

LANDIS ENTERED the Inner Office without fuss but looking grave.

Adeone laid his pen aside. "I suppose I've done something wrong?"

Landis smiled. "I'm not sure I'd recognise it if you had, Sire. I've just been talking to Ifor. He's worried that he's about to be given far too much work."

"I can't think why he'd think that with the Tuchlin having announced he's retiring."

Landis eyed him. "Will you choose Ifor?"

"Yes. He's known it since he was here in 1212. He could refuse, as Faran has, if he really doesn't want the responsibility."

Landis accepted a drink. "Your Majesty, if you offer it, he will accept, but that doesn't mean he wants the responsibility."

"Are you telling me I shouldn't offer it to him?"

Landis shook his head. "No. I happen to think that he would be a good governor. I suppose I'm trying to say it might be wise to persuade him first and not assume."

Adeone smiled. "I've been trying to persuade him for years, Festus. It's never worked."

"Hmm. I wonder. There's a name that springs to mind who might help convince him, but they don't know each other."

Adeone was confused. "Who?"

"The Margrave, Lord Percival Wealsman..."

Adeone sighed. "Yes, I do know his name. It's a good point."

"Especially as he had no warning that Arkyn was handing him the job."

"He had just been doing it for months," pointed out Adeone.

"Ifor's been Deputy Governor for years. It might be worth considering."

"I'll speak to Wealsman. The announcement will have to be made soon. I want to stop political manoeuvrings."

"I doubt anyone is in ignorance of whom you'll choose. Anyone with an ounce of sense realises that a Representative who is life-bound is the safest governor you could have. When exactly is Aldwy retiring?"

"Munewid Eve. He said it seemed like as good a time as any. It's neat at least. Was that all you came for, Landis?"

Festus smiled. "Not exactly. Tain's growing quickly, isn't he? He's invited Julius and Julia to dinner..."

Adeone groaned. "Is that a cause for celebration or concern, I wonder?"

"We'll find out in due course. Anything been turned up on Linnt?"

Adeone shook his head. "No, everything checks out. If he's not modified his behaviour by the end of the year, I'll replace him. I've not been happy for a time and James is also worried."

"So are Prince Arkyn, Kadeem and Simkins. William's not too impressed either," said Landis referring to his own manservant.

Adeone's brows knitted. "When's William run into him?"

"When you came to dinner for Marcelea's birthday."

"Ah. What did he say?"

Landis smiled. "Something along the lines of, 'If he calls that service, he missed off the word bad'."

Adeone snorted. "How old is his second son now?"

"You're not pinching all my best servants, Adeone."

"Kadeem has been perfect for Arkyn and I was just wondering…"

Grinning, his friend said, "Hands off. I need them as well; I've far too many children reaching their adolescence."

Adeone laughed. "Good point. Have you found anyone for Lord Rale?"

"Yes, they're getting on well. One of Uncle Iris' footmen applied when he knew we were hunting. He'll do well enough."

"Good. I'm pleased. Now, whilst you're here…"

Landis said, "You know, traditions could be changed, Sire, and I *could* walk out of here with less to do than when I came in."

"Planning on resigning a post?"

Landis looked at Adeone's grinning face. "No."

"Then that tradition won't be changed."

"I suddenly need a few days at Ceardlann, Your Majesty."

"You'll not get any more peace there, Festus."

Landis smiled. "I know. So what do you want me to do, Sire?"

Half an hour later, as the conversation was drawing to a natural break, Landis said, "Joking aside, can you spare me for a few days to go to Ceardlann? I'd like to talk to the terrors."

Adeone looked at him. "You *want* the mayhem?"

Landis said musingly, "I do, or at least I think I'd enjoy the visit."

"Then don't let me stop you. I'll join you for a day and then leave you to Tain's tender care."

"Tender?"

Adeone simply raised an eyebrow.

Chapter 82

MELLOW MOOD

Pentadai, Week 41 – 5th Geryal, 12th Souis 1214
Ceardlann - Snug

THE EVENING of the day Landis and Adeone reached Ceardlann, Adeone eased himself into his favourite chair in the snug and watched the flames of the fire, clearing his mind of all his cares. A knock at the door heralded his manservant.

"Can I get you anything, sir?"

Adeone glanced over, completely relaxed. "I'm not sure."

Simkins smiled. It was nice to see the King's face without worry. "How about a footstool, cake and company, Sire?"

Adeone nodded. "Sounds admirable but quiet company. I'm feeling mellow. No need to disturb Landis."

His legs were lifted on to the footstool and six minutes later the company and cake had arrived.

"Get yourself a drink, Comptroller."

"Thank you, sir. Simkins mentioned you were feeling mellow."

"Yes, and I have no idea why. What news is there?"

"The Wanda are back. Miranda's been stocking our medicine cabinet for us and has sent the normal bottles of wine for yourself and Lord Landis. The Chief said if you appeared he'd welcome a word…"

"What have I done?"

"Good question: he never normally hunts you out, does he?"

"No, but we've had some interesting conversations over the last couple of years. How are the terrors?"

"Well enough. Prince Tain's lost the child but found himself, I think. His mischievous streak is still there but controlled. Master Calumiel's also matured; he's a steady character for all his mischievous side still rivals His Highness'. Do you know he told Laioril he never wants to leave the valley? He's been accepted as few are here."

Adeone smiled. "I'm pleased. He will have to leave soon. When Tain takes up his duties, their childhood will truly be over."

The Comptroller nodded. "I realise, sir. I shall be sad to see them leave. Their presence has been pleasant. What of Lady Elantha? Will she stay with us?"

"I would hope so, at least for a few more years. I'm not even going to suggest anything else to Scanlon. He's never cared for her as a daughter; he left her to Aelia and then Ira. To my mind his claims might be paternal by right but not endeavour, as I've said before."

The Comptroller nodded. "I couldn't agree more. She's a lovely girl."

"She's her mother all over again. I wish Aelia could see her…"

"She'll be watching over her from the heavens. She was far too good for Scanlon." He paused. "I'm sorry, Sire. I shouldn't have said that."

"Tonight, I don't care, Comptroller. You're right. I feel most strongly for Cornelia though when I think of the Rales. Of her siblings, she's the only one left and I know she thinks of Aelia and Finn a lot. It's hard being the only one left."

"She has her children and her niece and nephew – not to mention Lord Landis."

Adeone smiled. "Yes. How she copes with Festus, I sometimes wonder."

"You take him out of her hair often enough, sir."

"Too often really… I sometimes wonder if Scanlon thinks I'm stupid. Finn's accident was no such thing, and I doubt Aelia's was either."

The Comptroller said, "I don't think anyone believes Lady Aelia had an accident, Adeone. She knew what she was doing."

Adeone sighed. "True. Maybe with Finn it was all too co-incidental, but I doubt it. There were too many odd circumstances and Malinda was tricked into remarrying, I'm sure of that. Finian says her letters don't say much and, from a mother to her son, that is odd. I might insist on Malinda visiting Finian, discreetly, of course. I don't want to stir that hornet's nest too much."

The Comptroller topped up the King's glass. "For tonight, leave your worries behind, Adeone. Think of yourself."

"Sorry." He looked at his companion. "What will I do without you here?"

The Comptroller smiled. "Find someone else whom your family has complete trust in? I am sorry I never had children now, but I didn't expect my brother and nephew to die; I thought there was plenty of time."

"There still could be."

The Comptroller shook his head. "No, sir, I will not marry simply to have a son for my own ego. Just find me a successor before I get too old to pass on this house's secrets. That is all I could ever ask."

Adeone put his head back on the chair. "I shall give it some thought. Anyone in mind?"

"No, Sire. It should just be someone who loves the house and valley. It would be an advantage if they were born here but as long as you trust them enough to grant them entry, it shouldn't matter."

Adeone looked at him and smiled. "An idea forms. Man or woman? I'm not sexist."

"That, I think, would depend on whether Your Majesty wishes the post to be hereditary. Personally, I think it should be."

"Then it will be."

The Comptroller smiled. "You take my views far too seriously sometimes, Adeone. It is *your* home."

As though it was a stray thought, Adeone said, "No, it's our home. You and your family for generations have lived, loved and died here. It's our retreat and you've made it what it is. Never say I take your views too seriously because that isn't possible."

The Comptroller asked softly, "How much have you drunk, Adeone?"

"Not enough."

Chapter 83
RIDDLES AND ENIGMAS
Hexadai, Week 41 – 6th Geryal, 13th Souis 1214
Rex Dallin

"**H**AVE YOU had any more dreams, lad?"

Having woken early, Adeone decided to see what the Chief wanted, rather than return to Oedran, and the question as they walked towards the river didn't surprise him.

"Plenty, Chief. All more vivid and strange than the last. Their meanings puzzle me."

"Your dreams may be strange, but you do not need to understand them. Meanings can be misinterpreted, simply record them."

"There is one, Chief, that haunts my waking hours also. It is an image of a crossbow bolt in a hand I have seen before but cannot name."

"To name it would be unbeneficial, I suspect. It is not, I take it, your own hand?"

Adeone laughed. "No, Chief, it is not. Look, mine are not highly scarred or worn. They carry not the lines of recognition that the dream one does."

Laioril took the King's hand. "No but your lifeline is long."

"Shall I live to old age?"

"Nay, lad, lifelines are not so easily read. Mine is long and so is yours, but I suspect that is where the similarity ends. A venerated palmist once said that the line may continue after death for some, or it measures what is in your life rather than the length of it."

"Chief, it's called a *life*line."

"Aye, lad, but I think he was right. Your line suggests to me that even when you've died, your name will live on, that your deeds here on Erinna will be remembered for many yet unnumbered years. Your star will shine brightly in the heavens, never to be dimmed; it is that life your line represents.

Maybe your time here will be short, maybe it will be long, but your memory and destiny shall stretch beyond it. Fate is controlling you now."

"Some people would just have said I'd live till old age and would have cheered me up. So, what do you think yours represents?"

Laioril smiled. "When I was a young man, someone believed that my lifeline was a herald to posterity, that my name would be remembered and that my descendants would repeat it with pride. Times have changed and much changes with time. Many, myself included, forget that and I changed too late. My time for posterity has gone. Infamy or fame does not interest me and I have no descendants; I am happy wandering the roads of Erinna. My lifeline is long due to my age alone. Once I pass to our ancestors, I shall rest forgotten. My stories will pass and quietly lay themselves down beside me to sleep."

Adeone smiled. "I doubt they ever will, Chief, so stop being morbid." He asked with a laugh, "How old are you now?"

"As old as my tongue and a little older than my teeth, it is an age which doesn't change and so has many benefits."

Adeone sighed. "Maybe I should start using it then. Do you think I should forget these dreams?"

"No. Record them. They will eventually make sense. Tell me, though, how often do the youngsters feature?"

Adeone shot him a sharp look. "All the time. Why?"

"How often is young Cal in them?"

Adeone paused. "How?"

"Watch that boy carefully, Adeone. You need his skills, *all* of them. He has more of the future in his hands than we can realise. Engender trust and secrecy."

"I have no need to; it is already there."

"Good, because magic is moving, it is on the wind, there is a tang in the air and a sizzle on the breeze, it awaits only the age of youth."

Adeone blinked. "I think you've finally cracked, Chief."

Laioril smiled. "Magic is not coming again; it has arrived."

"Chief, the rebirth of the Cearcall has been predicted for centuries."

"Cearcall? Pah. I speak not yet of twelve but of one, for one began it. He must have left his beginning and found his end. His death unfolded, yet not believed. He must be young yet old, laughing yet solemn. His life for a time seen yet hidden as one hides a trait one dislikes."

"Some of that sounds familiar."

"Aye, lad, I'm sure it does. Are you afraid of magic?"

"I am, yes. Is that strange?"

"In a king, no; in you, perhaps. You have friends who utilise the Ullian

Legacy, do you fear them?"

"No, but I'll not use them to rule. I, myself, am a medium and try to avoid the perspective it gives me."

"That, lad, is admirable, but it might be foolish also. The day will come when you mustn't hesitate but must use what is to hand. You know more men and women of magic than you recognise. The near future will not be a footnote to history."

Adeone had enough. "Chief, you need to lie down in the cool and I need to return to Oedran and not with a head full of riddles and enigmas."

"Sorry, lad. I forget how strange I sound," admitted Laioril. "I see the world differently to others. Come to camp for a short time, please."

Adeone looked at him. "No more nonsense?"

"This *is* me, lad, but I'll do my best."

* * *

Once in the Chief's tent Adeone lay back gazing up at the canvas. Laioril watched him.

"You need a good night's sleep, lad."

"Dreams keep interrupting it and drink hasn't helped."

"Ah. Headache?"

"Blinding one."

Laioril said, annoyed with himself, "I probably didn't help. Wait here." A few minutes later he said, "Drink this… it's one of Miranda's special brews. She might even know the ingredients, though hopefully not personally."

Adeone held out his hand. "Thank you. My head is splitting."

Laioril nodded. "I should have realised. Sit up, close your eyes and think of nothing at all."

Adeone took the remedy and did as suggested. Laioril sat behind him and, as he'd done for Cal, sent him to sleep, ignoring the fact Adeone had mentioned returning to Oedran. Once Adeone was comfortable, he walked out of the tent.

"Sayre, nip and tell the Comptroller or Simkins that the King's not going to be awake for a few hours…"

Sayre nodded and walked off. Miranda walked over to the Chief.

"What was in the cup, lass?"

"A cure. He shouldn't be drinking to sleep."

Laioril said sadly, "His dreams aren't easy and he worries too much."

Half laughing, half serious, Miranda said, "He needs a woman to keep him sensible."

"Don't we all, lass?"

"Can't say I do, Chief."

* * *

Four hours later, Adeone surfaced muzzily from sleep. His headache gone.

Laioril murmured, "Don't sit up suddenly, lad. Here, sip this. You should tell someone when you're ill."

"The doc fusses."

"That's his job, lad; you pay him for a reason."

"It doesn't mean I have to appreciate it."

Laioril chuckled. "True. Miranda reckons you need a woman to keep you sensible."

Adeone sat up. "I've found one but it's complicated, Chief. We don't want the whole ceremony and palaver that would result if it was known."

Laioril said, "You don't have to play the world's games, lad. If you love her and she you, it is only your own expectations that matter."

"My sons?"

"Their feelings are important but they would not apply pressure for you to be anything or anyone other than you are. They love you dearly and your happiness matters to them as much as theirs to you. Is a marriage to be had?"

"Not with pomp and I will not ask anything of her that she does not wish to give."

"For yourselves and not the empire?" (Adeone nodded.) "Then my blessings go with you both. Tell Rhian I'm pleased."

Adeone shook his head. "What gave it away?"

"That would be telling. Now, lad, you'd better get to Oedran and may your sanity go with you."

Adeone smiled. "I lost that many years ago in this tent."

"Didn't we all?"

Chapter 84
REALISATION
Mid-morning
Rex Dallin

LANDIS SMILED to himself as he returned from a morning ride. There was a lot to be happy about: not least the day was warm and spring had truly arrived. The buds on the trees were exploding into a green hue where merely a fortnight before there'd been stark branches.

Riding to the stables, he dismounted lithely and nodded to the chief groom. "Any idea where Prince Tain is, Alfred?"

"I believe he's in the training yard, my lord. Shall I ask the kitchens to have refreshments at the ready?"

Landis grinned. "It's a nice day; ask them to bring us some out please. The lads need fresh air."

"Aye, well, they're getting that."

Landis leaned on the fence of the training area. He nodded appreciatively and caught the eye of the guard tasked with teaching the Prince how to fight. The man made his unobtrusive way over.

"How are they doing?"

The guard hesitated. "Very well, my lord, but then I expect you can see that for yourself."

Landis smiled. "Any objection if I…" He motioned with his hand.

"None at all, my lord. Will you need my presence?"

"Only if you wish to stay. If not, I'm sure you have more than enough to do."

After the guard saluted and left, Landis continued watching the fight until Cal disarmed Tain.

"You *always* manage that!" exclaimed Tain.

"Then watch your left side better, sir."

Still grumbling, Tain picked up his sword and saw Lord Landis.

"Uncle Festus, how long have you been there?"

"Long enough. You're doing very well."

"No, I'm not. Cal's still beating me," grumbled Tain.

"True but only on that bout. It doesn't mean the war is lost. How would you fancy beating me?"

Tain sighed. "I know I wouldn't manage it, so why bother? Try Cal!"

"Your Highness, you did once tell me not to let you win," said Cal.

Tain grimaced. "At least that is one thing you took to heart. Can't you get rid of the honorifics as well? I'm going in for a time. No, Uncle Festus, I'd rather be on my own and Cal's worth a fight."

Landis shook his head slightly. "Whoever taught you the double meanings of words and phrases ought to be shown the error of his ways."

Tain's lips twitched. "It was you, Uncle Festus."

Landis nodded. "I rather thought it might have been. Now, come here."

The hug lasted a long moment. Feeling better, Tain said, "Really, Uncle Festus, give Cal a bout. It'll be good for him to lose."

"That's what friends are for, is it?" enquired Landis.

"At the moment, yes. I've not succeeded at anything this morning, so I'll just go and see about lunch."

Once he'd gone, Landis looked at Cal. The lad had grown and it didn't take long to realise it wasn't only in height. After the first bout, which

Landis found a harder fight than he'd expected, Cal retrieved his sword.

Landis said, "Using honorifics doesn't seem to be pleasing Tain."

Cal grinned. "No, that was because I'd disarmed him and Your Lordship was watching."

Landis shook his head. "No, it wasn't. Ready for round two?"

The clash of swords reverberated and Cal said, "Maybe not, but… he's still our Prince."

Landis parried. "Can you… imagine what… his reaction would… be if I… did the same?"

Cal jumped backwards before thrusting forward. "I've not known… him as long… my lord," he stumbled, his sword flying out of his hand as Landis tripped him up.

"I wouldn't necessarily say that, young Cal. You've lived with him; I've only seen him at times. Seriously though, you've got to make some decisions before the Munewid. If you need any advice, you know where to find me."

Cal weighed his sword in his hand. "What kind of decisions, sir?"

"Soon you're going to be the friend of the Justiciar of Oedran, not merely an underage prince. There are many differences. Tain's going to be living in Oedran; whether Oedran's ready is another matter. How will you treat him then?"

"Hopefully, the same as I always have, sir."

"Is Oedran the right place for that? I wouldn't beat him quite so openly for a start."

Cal frowned. "He'll be annoyed if I let him win."

"All too true. Then save the battles for private locations. How are you planning on addressing both him and Arkyn in Oedran?"

"Correctly, my lord."

Landis nodded. "In private?"

Cal frowned. "As I ever have, sir."

"Then you'll make their lives very lonely. Have you never considered the barrier an honorific causes?"

Cal paused. "Yes, but it's simply a lengthening of their name, my lord."

"If it only was. Look, Cal, you are who you are. You've made decisions based on many factors, factors which I doubt you'll ever explain – so be it – but listen to me, decide where the boundaries truly are and learn that informality has its place as much as formality does. If I hadn't learnt that, I doubt my friendship with His Majesty would have flourished as it has. Ceardlann and the Rex Dallin are special and unique places, but you'll soon be facing the world beyond as a confidant of princes. It will not be kind to you."

Cal sheathed his sword. "I don't know what to do. I feel lost whenever I'm in Oedran."

"Let's go for a walk… In what way lost?" Landis motioned towards the trout stream.

Cal hesitated. "I've read the protocols for the Palace and yet, although I can obey them, they don't feel right. They're staid, I suppose."

"So they are. How often have you been at the Palace?"

"A few times but not lots."

"Very vague. You should be fine if you keep that up. Seriously, half the so-called protocols aren't observed. If you observed all of them, it would mean contradicting yourself. I'm sure the stewards have wanted any excuse to make people's lives harder. In brief, when in a public area always use people's titles and honorifics, never discuss anything even vaguely important or that can be used against or to disparage the FitzAlcis and remember to make sure that you're presentable. When in private rooms with servants present, observe the same conventions. When in private rooms with the FitzAlcis only, let your conscience guide you, but remember that you are one of the few men who will treat them as people, and formality can be a curse."

They walked in silence for a few moments. Landis giving Cal time to absorb everything he was saying. The stream beside them gurgled its way to join the river, sunlight reflecting off the ripples, weeds wafting in the flow. Cal watched them.

"I wish we could stay here. It's so much simpler."

"How's everyone treated you when you're in Oedran?

Cal paused. "Differently. The guards and couriers have been odd… they keep calling me 'sir', I can't get used to it, but the others almost seem to be laughing at me."

"Who do you mean by the 'others'?"

"The Steward, Captain Pixney even Linnt."

Landis stopped walking. "Linnt?"

"Yes. I can just see amused tolerance in his eyes. I'm used to spotting it in the Comptroller's after all."

Landis chuckled. "So am I. Tell me something, Cal, has Spellen ever talked to you about what you can expect as a close *friend* of the FitzAlcis?"

Cal shook his head. "No, sir. Mainly, I think, as he doesn't know."

"That's a good point. You have a greater status than I suspect you'll ever admit to. You will, in part, set the authority of your friends. If, for example, you disparage them, others will also, if you argue over much with them in public, others will see and say they don't deserve respect for even their friends don't respect them. You will be one of the few men who will be allowed to tell them anything like the truth. I suspect if you told Prince Arkyn, for example, that he ought to get an early evening, because he's not looking well, you'd be listened to, whereas most people would simply receive directions for the door. You could go to the Steward and request things for them and the Steward would, I suspect, grumble but obey – most men would just obey. You will act almost as an unofficial official. So, for example, when I see His Majesty and I realise he's not feeling his best, I suggest to Richardson that he should cancel meetings. Normally Richardson will do so…"

"But you're His Majesty's Defender…"

"A supposedly ceremonial post only. No, I used to tell Richardson before Adeone was King. People will do as you say, Cal, because you're their confidant. Oh, they might be wary, even complain but mostly people will follow your advice or requests. The Court will accept you very gradually but you'll have a unique status there."

"I wasn't expecting to attend Court. I'm just a merchant's son, my lord."

Landis nodded. "Basically yes but actually no. You're a friend of princes – that's a status of its own. Remember that you'll be more to them than all their staff and all the officials. I'm not trying to scare you, though I see I'm succeeding. Cal, I know how much you care for your friends and how much they care about you. That should never change, but, in Oedran, learn to be a bit of an official as well. People will give you that status anyway."

Cal said, "Oh. I just thought I'd be there when they weren't seeing to anything."

"So you will, but you've still got to walk through the Palace to get to them. That walk can be more important to both them and you than all the private hours spent together."

"Right, my lord."

"You'll be fine, as I said, you know where I live – come and talk, if you ever need to."

Cal nodded. "I will, sir, thank you." He paused. "There's just one thing, I'm not Prince Arkyn's confidant."

Landis laughed. "Yes, you are, Cal. You most certainly are."

"What about Lord Irvin, Lord Julius and there was Lord Kensal?"

"Friends, certainly, but not confidants – Kensal was becoming one and had he survived then, yes, possibly. Arkyn confides in very few people and you are one of those. Julius is his nearcousin, they are thrown together because of mine and His Majesty's friendship and, yes, they are close, but there is a restraint there that he does not have with you. He talks with Irvin, but he never tells him how he's feeling deep within himself. Does he tell you?"

Cal paused again. "I suppose he does, yes, but I hadn't, that is, I didn't think it was anything unusual."

Finding a suitable spot, Landis sat down. "It is almost unique. Arkyn keeps his feelings so closely wrapped up that even the King is uncertain of them at times. Before you came here, Arkyn was close to a breakdown; he'd lost his confidant and he couldn't talk to anyone else he was close to because they were all suffering the grief of Ira's passing. Wynfeld sorted him out on that occasion and it's primarily for that reason that Wynfeld has risen so rapidly, though the King doesn't consciously realise it. Wynfeld couldn't continue to be that confidant though, Cal, the brothers needed another and it might have taken time but for Arkyn, as much as for Tain, you are that confidant. I'm their nearfather; they come and see me for support, not to confide. I'm there if they want to but they know that I'm their father's friend. There's always a suspicion that I'll tell Adeone."

"Didn't you once?" enquired Cal, picking at the grass.

Landis sagged. "I had no choice: Adeone exercised his right as my liege. When he realised what he'd done, he was more than contrite."

"Will I ever be expected to swear fealty, my lord?"

"I rather suspect the decision will be left up to you, Cal. You're not a lord, therefore it's not obligatory. Would you want to?"

Cal took a moment to answer. "What exactly would it entail?"

"Hasn't Spellen…"

"Yes, my lord, but that's all theoretical, isn't it? There's surely more to it than the ceremony and knowing you've got to be loyal."

Landis laughed. "Far more, Cal. Some would say your life is not your own. They can call you to fight, even if you don't agree with the dispute. They can demand you answer questions, lay your soul bare, even force you to tell the truth. Depending on the level of fealty, even your life could be dependent on your thoughts. It can insinuate into every facet of your life; however, if you're not part of the militia or a guard, it generally means nothing substantial until you're under suspicion of treason. One swears to protect the FitzAlcis and empire; to stay out of trouble, that's all you must do."

Cal nodded. "As a normal Oedranian you make that promise anyway."

Landis smiled. "Not everyone, Cal. You'd be surprised. People turn against the empire for many reasons."

"What like, my lord? The promise of money?"

"That's certainly a powerful motivator, but so is position and status. Support the wrong faction and everything you have could be lost. We're living in uncertain times. If Scanlon, for example, succeeds, I'll lose everything I have, even my life and lordship. The fact my life is at risk has been proved before now. Then you get the motivators of fear and love. Threaten someone close to the person you want to use and they'll normally do what you want—"

"Have you ever?"

Landis eyed him. "No, not unless I've absolutely had to. I prefer to persuade by other means. Lord Scanlon, however, has and uses and abuses the technique regularly because he has found it to be effective."

Cal nodded. "Am I in danger?"

Landis looked at him. "Why do you ask?"

"Because I think you'll tell me the truth. I know the Princes are and the King is. I've noticed Your Lordship is and, after everything you've said, I suspect I am."

Landis sighed. "Yes, you are. A very real danger, Cal. You're the same to the Princes as I am to the King."

"Is my family?"

Landis sighed. "I shouldn't be telling you, but yes, they are. The King's made sure that there is protection around them, but they are very much in danger, Cal. Sooner or later, Lord Scanlon isn't going to be able to ignore your presence."

Cal nodded. "Then, my lord, can you give me some weapons training?"

The sudden change of direction perplexed Landis. "Me? Why?"

"Because I can disarm the guards, but I can't disarm you and I'd like to."

Landis laughed. "All right. I must admit, you gave me a harder fight than I was expecting. Shall we go and start?"

Cal grinned. "Yes, please."

"You're not at all fazed by what I've told you?"

Cal shook his head. "No, my lord. I've suspected a lot of it but no-one's ever actually told me it. It's nice not to be treated like a child."

Landis nodded. "I can appreciate that. Let's see what you're made of."

Chapter 85
WEAPONS
Late Morning
Ceardlann – Training Yard

LANDIS RE-ENTERED the training yard as the guard was tidying up. He said simply, "Lay out Master Calumiel's weapons, please, and then ask the Comptroller for mine." Crossing to a trestle table set up under a simple awning, he motioned Cal to follow. "Take off your sword-belt. We'll start from scratch."

Cal fumbled with the old buckle.

"Hmm. We'll get that fixed as well. You can't fight well if your weapons aren't in good order and that includes their impedimenta. What's the belt like…?"

Cal passed it over hesitantly.

"Not the best I've seen. We'll worry about it another time. Daggers?"

Half smiling, though he didn't know why, Cal passed over the first one.

"Not a bad balance, but the blade needs sharpening – though perhaps not today if you're to be attacking me with it. Do you care for these yourself, Cal?"

Cal shuffled his feet. "Not really, my lord."

Landis eyed him. "Start. I'll have a kit prepared for you and the guard can show you how to sharpen and care for your weapons. They won't look after you if you don't look after them."

"I know that but unfortunately lessons get in the way."

"And when you've finished your lessons, life will. Start now, young Cal, no excuses."

Cal nodded. "I will."

"Good," replied Landis, oddly believing him. There was a different set to the young man now. "Hmm… What do you see that's wrong with this dagger?"

Cal took it back. "Nothing really, sir, except it's not sharp."

"Comfortable in your grip, is it?"

Cal considered. "It could be better."

"There's no room for *could* with weapons. When they're your weapons, they should be moulded to you. We'll talk to the blacksmith shortly. Firstly, though, there is one thing that can be done. That hilt needs rebinding; it should feel better straight away. How do you feel about ornamentation on weapons?"

"Negatively, my lord. They should be functional."

"Good, lad. Jewels or ornamentation cut into your hands, never a good thing. There is a place for ceremonial weapons, but it isn't in a decent armoury or fight."

Cal grinned. "About that fight…"

"Yes, that's where your training has gone wrong. The fight is the event, but you've got to get the preparation right. It's fine for the Princes to concentrate on the fight, but they'll have men to care for their weapons. We don't have."

Cal looked at the Lord of Oedran. "Surely Your Lordship could have?"

Landis said, "Except I value my life. My weapons have saved me on numerous occasions. More than Adeone knows—"

"You haven't told His Majesty when you're attacked?"

Landis eyed him. "Worrying him even more? Have him give orders that will damage his reputation because he feels responsible? No, young Cal, I do not tell him every time I am attacked."

"Who do you tell, my lord? Not that it's my business…"

"These days I trust Major Wynfeld. Ah, thank you…" The guard had returned with Landis' weapons and his manservant. "William, ask the Comptroller to see that the blacksmith is available today, please."

William nodded. "Right you are, my lord."

As Landis' weapons were laid out, Cal studied them with interest.

"I'm travelling light," quipped Landis.

Cal grinned. "Of course you are, my lord. There's no need for weapons here in the valley."

Landis clipped him round the head. "I've still got to get here. Name those you can."

Cal did so: sword, short daggers, poniard, wrist knifes, a narrow 'saddle sword' that could be tied behind a saddle and hidden by a cloak and a small pistol bow that could be hidden in a saddlebag.

"Good. Have you ever acted as a combatant's squire?"

"No, sir."

"First time for everything then…"

Cal looked back at the table. Considering what he'd put on when, he armed Lord Landis.

"Good. Not bad at all. Guard, do the same for Master Calumiel, whilst I just mark out our area."

He took the post and nail and marked a large circle in the centre of the training yard and two smaller ones at diagonally opposite points inside it. He grinned to himself.

A voice said, "Uncle Festus, what are you doing?"

"Confusing the issue, Tain. Cal's asked for some weapons training."

"I thought he was more sensible; never mind, another illusion ruined."

Cal walked over and inclined his head to Tain.

Landis glanced at him. "Practise informality, Cal. You'll need to."

Cal didn't dare look at Tain. Landis winked at his nearson.

"Now, we need the ring. Don't scuff the marks on your way to practise archery."

"Who said anything about archery?" protested Tain.

"I did. Go on."

Without true malice or rancour, Tain grumbled, "Anyone would think

I was born a prince; *he* doesn't need to practise *his* informality."

Cal's lips twitched and Landis watched him.

"Right, young Cal. The aim of this bout is to disarm me without leaving your small circle – if you do, for any reason, then you *mustn't* leave the larger ring or you forfeit the bout to me. Understand? If you end up in the outer circle, I'll think of a forfeit."

Soon, there was only the clash of swords and the twang of a bow as an arrow was released.

Half an hour later, Landis nodded appreciatively. "Good. That will do for now. Take a breather. William, Joe and David are hovering with refreshments. I take it David is looking after you these days."

Cal grinned. "He's trying to: the first morning he forgot to wake me until Tain asked where I was – I didn't mind in the slightest though."

Landis chuckled before walking over to the table and divesting himself of his wrist knives and sword. He left his daggers where they were. William handed him a drink and he accepted it with a word of thanks. He took a second from the tray and crossed to Tain.

"Right, sir. Get that down you."

Tain grinned. "Thanks, Uncle Festus. Cal's good, isn't he?"

"Very; however, your archery leaves a little to be desired."

Tain sighed. "I know. It's odd but I know, I feel, my aim is good but the arrow rarely hits the centre of the target."

"You're not so far off, though, as to be worrying for my safety. Notch your first arrow and take your stance."

"I've had lots of lessons, Uncle Festus."

"Not with me you haven't. Take your stance."

Tain did as requested, and Landis walked around him slowly. He put his hand against his nearson's back.

"Relax, sir. Let the tension from the string. Good. Your stance is as good as I've seen, so that's not your issue. Now, don't be self-conscious. I'm going to stand out of harm's way but to the front of you. I want to see what happens when you release the arrow."

"You're very trusting, Uncle Festus."

"Do I have need to worry, Tain?"

"Not today."

Landis smiled. "Then let's start."

Tain had released two arrows when Landis said, "Interesting. Release another three, sir."

Tain did so and saw the smile spread over Landis' face. His nearfather waved William over, whispering instructions. The manservant left. Landis turned back to Tain. "Your grouping is excellent, Your Highness. Lend me your bow. Yes, not a bad weight." He hummed as he selected three arrows and landed them in the centre of the target.

"That's not fair, Uncle Festus."

"Yes, it is. Look at the distance between those and yours. Yours are offset to the right. Every single one. Take your aim again but mirror that distance and aim that much to the left." He smiled from behind Tain as his nearson did as requested. "Good, lad. Now, release the arrow as normal."

Tain did so and the arrow landed next to Landis'.

Tain sagged. "I've done that before, but it doesn't always work. It's never the same amount."

"Of course it's not, sir. The breeze confuses the issue. We'll solve the reason for your archery issue today. I lay you five to one."

Tain grinned. "I shouldn't bet."

"Then if I don't succeed, sir, I shall cancel your lessons for a few days."

"That's almost worth me failing on purpose."

"I shall know if you do, sir, and I'll make sure Spellen gives you twice as much to do."

"I suppose you'd call that double or quits."

Landis laughed. "I might well. I shall go and continue my lesson with Master Calumiel. Come and watch for a time. After all, he has had a break and you have not."

Landis rearmed. "Joe, His Highness' arrows need retrieving and when William returns, whistle."

"Whistle, my lord?"

"To get my attention. I know you can whistle loudly."

"I shall not ask how, my lord."

Twelve minutes later, William had returned and Landis had called a halt. He walked over to his manservant and took a bandage and eye patch from him. Right, you lot, disappear. You too, guard."

They all left exchanging glances and Landis smiled to himself; they were curious and would hang around but he had obeyed a fuzzy convention.

"Now, Tain, you're not going to appreciate this but just trust me. You're right eye dominant, aren't you?"

"Er…"

"Which eye do you close when you take aim?"

Tain considered. "My left."

"So you're right eye dominant. Good. Do you have to be so tall? Sit yourself down…"

"Uncle Festus, what are you doing?"

"Prevention as a cure. I'm going to bandage your left eye; I'm doing it so that you can't carry on opening it as you release the arrow and re-aim subconsciously."

Tain sighed. "I'm going to look like a fool."

Cal grinned. "Nothing like looking what you are, sir."

Landis chuckled. "Cal, there're a lot of weapons around here, and he knows how to wield them."

Cal fought down a laugh. "Sorry, Your Highness."

Tain grinned at him and as Landis bandaged his eye said, "This is you practising informality, is it?"

Cal smirked. "There's more than one type of informality."

Twenty-four minutes later, as almost every arrow hit its target, Tain was convinced. He grinned and took off the bandage.

"Now I don't have to have my lessons for a few days."

Landis ruffled his hair. "No, I said that if I was wrong you didn't have to. Get practising."

Tain groaned.

"However, I might just cancel them for Alunadai."

"I'm in court then, Uncle Festus."

"It could be cancelled."

Tain shook his head. "No, thank you, Uncle Festus. I'll find a different day and have it owed."

Landis laughed. "You *do* take after Adeone."

Chapter 86
SEAL

Septadai, Week 42 – 14th Geryal, 21st Souis 1214
Prince Tain's Chambers

A WEEK LATER, Tain answered the knock on his door with a simple command to enter. Linnt abruptly announced the Palace Signumery before perfunctorily leaving.

Tain got up and smiled, waving to a seat. "Come in. I believe you've some sketches of what my seal could look like?"

"Yes, sir. Your father's and brother's are constrained by tradition, but Your Highness may develop your own."

"Do I... That is, my seal as Justiciar. Is it the same as I'll use for private correspondence? I keep forgetting to ask."

"An interesting question, Your Highness. The Office of the Justiciar has its own seal: at the centre the Tree of Law, its trunk crossed by the sword of Justice, encircled by the chains of justice set within a triangle representing the cloak of Truth; at the top of the triangle, a single moon, representing the fact that all are judged by the same laws; at the bottom left of the triangle is the star of the empire and at the bottom right three links of a chain, the middle one broken to more accurately represent Mercy's effect; outside of the triangle, on the left side is the word 'Justice', on the right 'Office' and at the bottom 'Oedran'. That seal is set on any documents emanating from the Justiciar's Office; however, documents requiring your seal also will carry the seal we're about to design. Normally it's small – it has to be carved or etched into a signet ring as well as the desk seal – it is normally a monogram of Your Highness' initials within a recognisable border of some description. It is always circular – ladies seals are triangular and most official ones square – governmental and regional anyway. High offices such as His Majesty's and the Justiciar's may take whatever form the incumbent wishes, over time these have become circular for those Offices of the FitzAlcis that exist."

Tain nodded. "So my seal will be small, circular and a monogram and goes on both private and official paperwork. Can I take a look at your proposed designs?"

He glanced over them and frowned. None of them grabbed his mood, character or attention. They were drawn many times larger than they'd be in reality, with a real size example in the corner of the page.

Tain bit his lip. "There's something missing. I don't know what."

"They're all standard examples, Your Highness."

"I am sure they are, but they don't feel right. I like this monogram," he indicated a strong angular T with a flowing F where the crossbar of the F became the crossbar of the A with the stem of the T forming the right-hand side of the A. The continuation of the F above the crossbar of the T meant that there was a lopsided L. It satisfied every capital letter in Tain's name.

He continued, "I just feel there should be more to it. Any fool with a passing skill could forge it. A simple dotted border is good but still a bit plain."

Fafnir appeared and Tain excused himself.

"Prince Arkyn would like a word, sir."

"Can you tell him I'm busy please, Fafnir? I'll chat to him later."

Fafnir said, "Very good, sir," and disappeared.

Tain was still looking at the spot he'd gone from. In the brief moments before he'd gone, he'd been haloed by one of the further drawings.

"Pesky."

The small rainbow dragon came tumbling through the air. "Princeling?"

Tain caught him. "I've got company."

"So I see, or would if turned round. Message to deliver?"

"Nope."

"Link to form?"

"Nope."

Pesky looked hopeful. "Chat?"

"No."

The dragon sagged. "What then?"

Tain grinned. "See that seal drawing that is on the top of the pile?"

Pesky turned. "Do you want me to destroy it?"

Tain didn't even look at the Signumery's face. "No, I'd like you to lie down at the bottom of the monogram, so I can see what a dragon would look like there."

"You really know how to enhance the dignity of your messenger, princeling."

"If I'd got a dignified messenger, I wouldn't have to enhance it. Just get on with it, Pesky."

Grumbling, the small dragon did so. Tain looked at the effect and grinned. He turned to the Signumery.

"What do you think to a miniature dragon lying below my monogram, or above it?"

The official looked surprised. "I don't know, sir. It's not been done for centuries."

"Hmm. I wonder why. Still, other than the fact it makes my seal harder to forge, my messenger is a dragon, if a little cross-grained and colourful. It also provides a nice illustration and makes my seal different."

"The use of such devices used to be widespread, sir; however, during, or more accurately after, the Age of Tyranny, they became frowned upon. Their use declined to the point they were considered outlawed. They are not, however, illegal, but they do require the King's agreement."

"Please have the drawings made. I'll talk to His Majesty when we've a design I like."

The Signumery collected everything together, disturbing Pesky.

The messenger said, "Oh, don't mind me. I suppose I should just move or disappear now."

Tain grinned. "Pesky, just move, don't disappear. I'll only call you back in a couple of minutes."

Pesky padded off to one side. He put his head down on his front claws and watched as the Signumery left. When the door closed, he perked up. "You want a picture of me on your seal?"

"Alcis knows why. Were you acting up on purpose?"

"Of course. Have to have some fun, princeling. Will your father agree?"

"Can't see why not."

* * *

Looking at the next designs, Tain wondered if the artist had enjoyed experimenting with something different. Dragons had been draped over and under the monogram, they'd been put standing on each side. Wings enfolding the monogram, which was drawn on the chest of the dragon. Tain, much as he admired the skill and the time that had gone into some designs, settled on his original idea. The selected monogram sitting above a curled up dragon, haloed by a simple dotted border. Should he push it further?

"How about including a motto as well?"

"Has Your Highness decided on one?"

It took him two days before he chose, 'Duty before self'. He discussed it with Tancred and his father, who, although both were surprised, had agreed it was understandable and acceptable. Tain had it drawn in the border of his seal and nodded when he saw the finished result. It felt complete.

He took the design to the Inner Office and waited for the King to finish his meeting.

Adeone saw his grin. "Planning mischief?"

"I think I might have succeeded without planning, Your Majesty."

"How? Why? Do I really want or need to know?"

Tain bit his lip. "I've got a final design for my official seal."

"Oh yes? I have heard it's going to be unconventional. Don't worry, I've not been shown it, but it is amazing what people think I should know."

Tain laughed and unrolled the design. Adeone walked over and examined it closely.

"It's different, I'll grant you that. Is that meant to be Pesky? Oh. An interesting idea and I think it suits you. A simple monogram would have been a bit boring. I can't see anything to question or that I want changed. Tell them to produce it. The drawings will need sending to all Chief Judges and my Representatives. They can have copies taken to distribute to the relevant offices."

Tain sighed with relief. "Thank you, father."

Chapter 87

CONSIDERATIONS

Pentadai, Week 43 – 19th Geryal, 5th Geryis 1214
Palace of Oedran – Imperial Garden

LANDIS TURNED a corner in the Imperial Garden and was faced with the smile of his elder nearson. Bowing, he smiled back. Arkyn greeted him pleasantly and invited him to join him on his saunter. They made their way into the wider Palace grounds. Spring was represented in every flowerbed. Daffodils and crocuses bloomed, amongst new shoots and fallen blossom.

"You've been wanting to talk to me for some time, Lord Landis."

Landis eyed him. "What gives Your Highness that idea?"

"Because you've been trying to bump into me outside of the Palace and Court for days. You could have asked or come to Ceardlann."

Landis smiled. "Your Highness, have you been purposefully leading me a dance?"

Arkyn grinned. "Yes."

"I suppose this is your latent sense of humour? Couldn't you have spared my feet?"

"I didn't think it was latent. Sorry, Uncle Festus. How may I help with what's bothering you?"

Landis paused. "It's going to sound awfully officious now. Have you considered the changes the next year will bring for you, sir?"

"In what way, Lord Landis?"

"You'll be of your age, sir, a prince with all the authority of one."

"I hadn't noticed a lack of authority now."

"Quite, Your Highness, but you are, to some extent, still learning."

Arkyn's eyes narrowed. "Come to the point, Landis."

"Do not be surprised if your father gives you less authority once you are of age, sir. He has passed you much over the last few years to prepare you for anything that might come your way. In the new year he is likely, I do not speak from prior knowledge, to pass you less."

Arkyn eyed Landis, inwardly amused but outwardly preserving an official mask. "Your concern surpasses your normal endeavours. Does His Majesty know you are talking to me like this?"

"No, but then I am your nearfather, Your Highness," admitted Landis uncomfortably.

Arkyn raised an eyebrow. "A fact I had hardly forgotten. Tell me, Uncle Festus, what do you think father's response to this would be?"

"I would rather not imagine, sir. I'm sorry—"

"Don't be. I wondered who would be the first to broach the subject. I *know* half of my authority has been granted because I'm still learning. To tell you the truth, I'm quite looking forward to the rest."

Landis shook his head. "There are times I think you and Tain aren't so different."

Bright eyed, Arkyn faced him. "Maybe we're not, Uncle Festus, just our futures change the men we are."

"Or the thought of them, sir. Are you, may I ask, inwardly laughing at me at the moment?"

Arkyn openly grinned. "Not at you, Uncle Festus, merely at the situation. It will be strange next year; I'm to be in Amphi when I come of age."

Landis said softly, "Are you disappointed?"

"A bit. I do not regret the decision, but there is a small part of me that wishes to be here."

"I'm sure ReJean will make the day memorable and enjoyable, sir."

"It's not the same though, is it, Uncle Festus?"

"No, it's not the same, but when you return there will, I'm sure, be ample celebrations and there is the banquet in a few weeks."

"I wouldn't have the celebrations, just the company. As you say, though, the day will probably be quite different to how I currently expect."

Landis smiled. "I think so, sir, but then Amphi isn't that far away, and that's all I'm saying."

"Don't get my hopes up for no reason, please. Father is travelling and I am content with that."

"All right, forget I said anything. Shall we return to our original discussion?"

"I'd rather not."

Chapter 88

AMENDMENT

ARRIVING IN OEDRAN, Tain found Peter and Linnt waiting in his antechamber. "Refreshment, please, Linnt. Peter, you always have a pile of documents to hand; I think I appreciate how my brother feels when he sees Edward now."

Peter smiled as he rose from his bow. "One day, Your Highness, I shall not have."

"It isn't today though. Come on through and let's get started."

Peter briefed Tain on the cases for the following day. Tain took copious notes and Peter smiled. The Prince's shorthand was good and almost up to the speed of a scribe.

When they concluded, Tain said, "So, what's in the rest of those papers?"

"Laws and amendments proposed for the new year, Your Highness. They are split into those passed and those still to be decided."

Tain nodded. "Why has the judge sent me those not yet passed?"

Peter said, "They would be under your seal, Your Highness, if they don't pass by the Munewid."

"Then I'll have a read tonight before I see him tomorrow."

* * *

Tancred turned to Tain, who was sitting beside him making notes. "Shall we have the last case, Your Highness?"

Tain looked up. "You don't need my permission, Judge. I'm only here to observe."

"I thought I would practise, sir."

"Which is the next case?"

"A young man accused of theft, one Bradach."

The judge watched the Prince's face as the defendant was brought in. He reckoned they were of an age. Tain listened with a will as Tancred opened proceedings unorthodoxly,

"So, lad, can you tell us why you are here this time?"

"Well, you see, I picked a pocket, didn't I?"

"Or two by my notes here. How do you plead?"

"Guilty, ain't I? Can't argue with the yeomen, can I?"

The judge glanced at Tain., "Does Your Highness wish to ask the defendant anything?"

Tain, with all the directness that was to characterise him, said, "Just one thing, Your Honour. *Why* did you pick a pocket, Master Bradach?"

The judge smiled. In one question, Tain had put his finger on the hardest point to justify. The prosecution and defence counsels looked disconcerted. They waited for the defendant to speak.

"Why, sir? Well, I suppose, you could say I needed to."

"Why?"

"Well, because I'm poor, ain't I? The rich are there to provide, as it were."

"Surely though if you rob them then they'll be poor."

"Yes, but it'll take a long time for that to happen, and I was hungry. Needed the dal, didn't I? Never pick the same pocket twice, do I?"

"No, because then it's empty. What's dal?"

Judge Tancred said lightly, "It is money, Your Highness. Dal is the slang term."

"Thank you, Judge. That was all I wanted to ask."

The judge continued with the brief trial. Bradach and Tain continued to watch each other. They lived in the same city but a world apart. They couldn't comprehend the other's life. Yet there appeared to be some sort of connection or understanding between them, possibly created by their age. The judge reached the point of sentencing.

Half-heartedly, he said, "Bradach, there has been an amendment to the law since your last trial. The sentence for pick-pocketing, after the first conviction, is now the removal of a hand."

Tain turned to him when Bradach's face whitened. In a more authoritarian voice than he had used before, he asked, "When *exactly* did that amendment come into force, Your Honour?"

The court held its collective breath. How would Tancred phrase his answer? The lawyers exchanged knowing glances.

Tancred did so succinctly and honestly. "The Justiciar has had it put before the Etanes but has instructed us to implement it immediately, sir."

"Then it is not current law, Your Honour – until the Etanes pass the amendment, that is; if, in fact, they do pass something so unfoundedly barbarous. As it has not been passed, and as, therefore, you would be guilty of a crime yourself, you will ignore this *amendment*."

"It is the Justiciar's instruction, Your Highness."

"That may well be the case, Your Honour, but it is not the law of this city or this empire. Your oath was to serve that *law*. You *will* ignore this *proposed* amendment or I shall have to have you arrested. If it had been a death sentence, would you have played a game with the lives of the citizens of this empire?"

The judge gave a small nod of acknowledgement. "You are of course right, Your Highness. Bradach, you have a three-month sentence instead."

Bradach sighed with relief and – to the surprise of the court, Judge and Tain – said, with little hint of the street child, "Thank you, Your Honour. Thank you, Your Highness."

Tain nodded as Bradach was led out of the court. It had been the last case of the day and Tain and Tancred returned to the latter's office.

* * *

When the door had closed on the rest of the world, the judge chuckled.

"Well done, Your Highness. The reasoning you voiced was extremely well presented."

"Thank you, Judge."

"It will be all over the Courthouse before many more minutes have passed though."

Tain laughed. "Good. There's just one thing: I can't believe you'd have enforced that amendment."

Tancred looked at him shrewdly. "I would not, sir, but I have to be seen to be trying to. I must thank you for 'persuading' me to ignore it. I am afraid I used your honesty and compassion to prevent me having to implement it. I rather suspect no other judge will now dare follow Lord Scanlon's orders in this – it is too close to Your Highness' birthday."

"I knew you were up to something when I read those amendments and cross-referenced with the trials in hand. How often has Bradach been up before you?"

"A couple of times, he is harmless enough."

Tain turned the talk to the other cases he had observed. When he left, Tancred became serious. Scanlon wouldn't be happy when he heard of the day's events. Tain was already showing his mettle and he wasn't even a justiciar yet. He had single-handedly shown Scanlon's methods for what they were. There would be repercussions. No matter how much he, Tancred, had the protection of King Adeone, Scanlon had already tried to bring him down and discredit him once. That had failed. Tancred pondered that his own extraordinary luck was probably running out. When he got home that night, the judge took out his requests and bequests and made sure it was as he wanted.

* * *

The following day, Tancred went to see King Adeone in a sober frame of mind but with a pleasant purpose.

When Tancred was seated, Adeone said mildly, "Your Honour, is it fair to test Tain in front of a court and use a defendant to do so?"

"No, Your Majesty, but it was the ultimate test. I would say His Highness is ready for his oath."

Adeone smiled and, getting up, poured two drinks.

"Good. Thank you, James. I think you have made our next Justiciar into the man he is. You should be rightly proud of yourself and him."

"I am not the only man to have helped mould His Highness' character, as I have said before, but I thank you for the compliment, Your Majesty."

Adeone sighed. "Take the credit, James. Tain's investiture will be on Hexadai. I'll contact the Keeper. Lord Scanlon is far enough away to not make it back in time; therefore, we need a judge to take the oath…"

Tancred shook his head slightly. "Oh, no, you don't, Your Majesty. You could take it."

"I will be taking one oath, but I cannot take the Judge's Oath."

"Yes, you can, Sire. You devolve the power to His Highness but—"

"James Tancred, you *will* be taking my son's oath, without argument.

389

That, if you continue to quarrel, will be the order of your King…"

Tancred eyed him, amused in spite of himself. "As a judge, I answer to the Justiciar, Sire."

Adeone leaned forward. "Shall we ask him, James?"

Tancred sighed. "No, Sire. I shall take His Highness' oath."

"I thought you'd see it my way. I don't like bullying you though."

Tancred twitched rueful lips. "I do not much like being bullied, Your Majesty, but I accept this is a good cause."

"That's fortunate. Make sure Tain knows the ceremony. You've only two lessons left with him."

Tancred said quietly, "I will miss our discussions."

"There is no need for those to end, James. Someone needs to keep him on track until he's twenty."

Tancred made a noncommittal movement of his head. "I can only try, sir. Isn't Their Highness' birthday banquet on Hexadai?"

"Yes. Might as well save the cost of another."

Tancred laughed. "Your Majesty, you sound far too cheerful for that to be true."

Adeone grinned openly. "Shall you tell Tain, or would you like me to?"

Tancred considered that. "Together?"

* * *

Tain whitened and sank into a chair. "Judge, I'm not ready."

Tancred knelt by him. "Do not start doubting yourself now, Your Highness. It is not the time and it is ill founded."

"Better than him doubting himself after his birthday," murmured Adeone with wry humour.

He might as well not have said anything. Tain and Tancred were locked in an unspoken conversation.

Tain swallowed. "Thank you, Judge."

Tancred said softly, "My name is James, Your Highness."

"Mine is Tain."

"Maybe one day, sir…"

Tain smiled. "Maybe one day, Judge…"

Watching them, Adeone rolled his eyes and walked away.

Chapter 89
INVESTITURE
Hexadai, Week 46 – 13th Lufial, 6th Lufis 1214
Prince Tain's Chambers

Tain woke, already shaking. Had he had a choice? No, not one he'd ever have taken. Was he ready? No, but that apparently didn't matter. Other people thought he was, and it was their thoughts that mattered, not his own. He couldn't stop shaking as he got up and got ready for the biggest day of his life so far and, unbeknownst to him, several other people were nervous as well.

Arkyn awoke and smiled sadly. Tain had grown up. Today was proof and he thought wryly they'd never have the same relationship again.

Adeone rose quietly, his feelings under strict control; there was no room to show his sadness at having to force the future on his younger son, who had already left childish thinking behind him in the pursuit of ideals of others' making. He looked in the mirror and nodded. It would have to happen.

Tancred dressed with extra care and fastidiousness. He took the cane the Prince had had made for him in his hand and wondered at its significance. If there was any or if it was simply as it had seemed, a gift of respect.

They all breakfasted together, talking of everything but what was going to happen.

Tain's tunic was plain, but formal enough with its emerald green banding on the hem and cuffs. He walked with a measured pace across to the Courthouse. The streets had been cleared of all traffic, they were swept clean but people lined them: people, guards and yeomen and, amongst the milling crowd, many of Wynfeld's men, discreetly placed to make sure nothing untoward could happen. The day was kind: there was no rain and no burning sun. The clouds scudded overhead, blowing with them the last days of spring. Tain swallowed. He wished he were elsewhere, but he fixed his gaze ahead. He was taking this walk alone; his father, brother and mentor, along with all the judges and Lords of Oedran were gathered and waiting for him.

He entered the Courthouse at the main doors: their great imposing majesty swinging aside as he approached. As he entered the atrium the Keeper, clad in teal robes; bowed, precisely, exactly and with a small smile to lighten the moment. Tain gave a slight bow back, a nod of respect, which surprised some of the many watchers. Here were gathered the lawyers and scribes.

The Keeper stepped forward. "Prince Tain Lachlan FitzAlcis, welcome. Is it your pleasure to take upon yourself the solemn duties of a Lord of Justice?"

"It is my pleasure, Keeper of the Hall of the King's Justice."

The Keeper smiled at that. So the new Justiciar knew his full title, did he? That *was* interesting.

"Then does it please you to pass into our most ancient court?"

"It would please me greatly but more so if you would walk with me."

Again, Tain smiled to himself. Who said traditions couldn't be changed? He and the Keeper would have to work together, maybe they should start.

The Keeper knocked on the Justice Hall's doors, and they opened wide. Tain turned to the people in the atrium.

"The Justice Hall is open to all. It would please me if you wish to be there that you enter in an orderly manner and take your places quietly." He didn't dare catch the Keeper's eye as he walked forward, as he meant to go on, with slight authority.

Adeone had heard his son's words and smiled to himself. Tain really had put the magic amongst the mundane.

Tain entered the Justice Hall between the tiered public seats. All the other furniture had been moved aside and where the Justiciar's Seat would normally be, a stone plinth was visible. He looked at it and glanced at his father standing just beyond it. Taking a deep breath, he walked forward at a gradual pace, no hint of his nerves and fears, nothing to give away just how daunted he was by what he was doing.

He reached the plinth and knelt on it, closing his eyes for a brief second. People were entering the Justice Hall behind him. In the Justice Hall, beside those dear to him, were the Lords of Oedran and other high officials. His nerves were taut but he still had them under control.

When the rustle subsided, the King stepped forward. "My son, will you accept the post of Justiciar of Oedran and thereafter the Empire?"

Tain looked his father in the eye. "I will, Your Majesty."

"You must swear the Judge's Oath and once sworn it is for life. I ask again, Prince Tain Lachlan FitzAlcis, do you wish to accept the post of Justiciar of Oedran and thereafter the Empire?"

Tain said, clearly, resolutely, "I do, Your Majesty."

"Do you acknowledge that the power hereafter granted is ultimately gifted to you by the King?"

"I do, Your Majesty, and I say if my lawful King wishes to reclaim it, he may." That caused a murmuring. "It is not my power by birth-right but by gift. I hereby acknowledge that."

Adeone regarded him. Would his sons ever follow the conventional script? "Be that as it may, I do confer this power to you once your oath has been sworn, for as long as you shall live or until a descendant yet to be born assumes the duties in his turn."

Tain said, "Your Majesty, I shall not be covetous of power and will relinquish it when requested by my lawful King."

Tancred was thinking, *'Lord Scanlon is* not *going to like this.'*

Adeone took two paces back. "Who here will take the Judge's Oath?"

Tancred knelt. "If it pleases Your Majesty, I am willing."

"Judge James Tancred, you are most welcome here and may take the oath."

Tancred took a deep breath and stood. This was no normal Judge's Oath for all the pretence was made that it was. He stepped forward and bowed once more to Adeone. The King motioned him forward and stepped aside.

Tancred moved until he was facing Prince Tain and again bowed. Tain smiled at him and there was just the hint of wry humour there.

Tancred said in a loud enough voice to carry but not to shout, "Prince Tain Lachlan FitzAlcis, the oath you wish to take is of great moment and should never be taken lightly: your words will bind your future. You have said to His Majesty you wish to take it. The Judges of Oedran are willing for you to take it, but it is your future and no pressure must be brought to bear. Do you take it in full understanding of its meaning and with a heart willing to accept its strictures?"

"I do, Judge Tancred."

Tancred stepped forward and Tain raised his hands. There was no backing out now. Tancred enfolded the young man's hands in his own and they both felt strangely reassured. Age and youth met in an ancient hall looking to the future.

"Prince Tain Lachlan FitzAlcis, do you here swear to serve Truth and Justice?"

"I do so swear."

"To let no personal loyalties or friendships overrule your duty to Truth and Justice?"

"I do so swear."

"To pass fair and just judgement on any person brought before you and not to condemn the innocent but to let them regain their freedom with characters unbesmirched?"

"I do so promise."

"To obey and enforce this empire's laws regardless of rank or personal feeling?"

"I do so promise."

Tancred took a deep breath, now for the one that no other judge ever had to answer. "Do you bind your life to Truth and Justice; to always serve them and to never falter in your allegiance to them? To serve them no matter what is asked of you?"

Tain closed his eyes, found a peaceful place in his mind, reopened his eyes saying, "I do so swear and bind."

Tancred carefully released Tain's hands and took an emerald green robe from one of his colleagues. Draping it across his own arms; he held it out to the King.

"Your Majesty, His Highness has sworn the Judge's Oath."

Adeone stepped forward so that he was face to face with the judge but sideways on to the Justice Hall.

"Is that his judge's robe, Your Honour?"

"With Your Majesty's pleasure it is the robe of our Justiciar."

Adeone looked into James' eyes and smiled. Tancred inwardly cursed. The *King* wasn't about to change the script, was he?

Adeone glanced at Tain and back at the judge. "It is more than my pleasure, Your Honour. It is my wish. It is also my wish that you – who has taught and guided my son for so long, who has earned the right, and deserves the honour – robe my son on this day."

Tancred took a deep breath. He had to reply; the King had spoken in an official ceremony and he *couldn't* refuse. "Your Majesty, your words do me an honour unlooked for, and one that I cannot at this moment fully comprehend; however, for the honour of all Judges of Oedran I shall robe His Highness."

Adeone was thinking, *'If only they were all honourable.'* He said, "For *yourself*, Judge Tancred. Prince Tain Lachlan FitzAlcis, Justiciar of Oedran and hereafter the Empire, you may stand."

Tain got to his feet. He stepped forward, off the plinth, and held his arms behind him. Tancred pulled the robe on and fastened it with the clasp embossed with a tree. He stood back two paces and bowed. Tain inclined his head slightly in respect.

"Your Honour, I hope I am worthy of your teachings." He turned to his father and knelt. "I am Your Majesty's servant."

Adeone leaned forward and helped him to his feet. As the script had already been changed, a bit more alteration would hardly matter. "You are my *son*, Prince Tain."

Tain looked at him and smiled slightly. He turned to the Justice Hall.

His speech would be brief.

"May our future be just and merciful and may truth be heard within this hall and throughout the empire."

A cheer erupted when they realised that was the whole of his speech but whether for the shortness or the sentiment Tain wasn't sure. As the cheer subsided, a fanfare of trumpets reverberated around the hall as though welcoming and heralding Tain in one go – yet there were no trumpeters present – and the ancient magic of the Justice Hall was felt and heard by all who were there.

The new Justiciar of Oedran walked resolutely through Judge's Door, held open by the Keeper. His family and mentor followed. He turned right into what would be Peter's office and then through into his own. Once there and with the door closed, he sank onto a chair, shaking. Adeone undid the clasp of the robe and, kneeling by him, pulled him into a hug, saying, gently,

"You did exceptionally well, Tain, and your mother would have been exceptionally proud of you."

Arkyn said, thoughtfully, "I don't think I should have told you so much about impromptu changes to the established scripts."

Tancred held out a drink.

Tain broke the hug, took the drink and looked at the judge. "Thank you, James."

Tancred smiled. "It was my pleasure, Tain."

Chapter 90
AFTERWARDS
Late Morning
Prince Tain's Chambers

TAIN RETURNED to the Palace by coach and made his way to his rooms. He'd be glad to be able to sit and absorb what had happened. He had to come to terms with it in his own way, with the fact it had happened.

In his sitting room was the one other person who he wanted to see. Cal was waiting patiently and bowed as Tain entered.

The Prince said, "Were you there?"

"Hidden at the back, sir. With a good view though. Congratulations, Justiciar."

Tain grinned. "Not in actuality, for a couple of weeks."

"From something the judge said, you are the Justiciar now. Lord Scanlon just won't acknowledge it and so it was easier to pretend otherwise for a couple of weeks. I overheard a discussion at Ceardlann."

"Thanks for putting a larger burden on me."

Cal grinned. "Someone's got to have your best interests at heart."

* * *

An hour later, the door opened and the Landis twins entered. They both made an exaggerated obeisance and Tain retaliated by throwing cushions at them. One which landed squarely on Julius' back and the other sailed over Julia's head to catch the closing door. Tain momentarily considered it was a pity it hadn't hit Linnt.

Julia said, "Congratulations, sir."

"Thank you. Were you there?"

"No."

"Thank heavens for that."

Julius grinned. "I was. It was an interesting ceremony. Do you plan to carry on by confusing everyone, Your Highness?"

Tain shrugged. "I took lessons off my nearcousins."

"Then it's all our siblings' fault. It can't be ours. We're models of respectability."

Sitting in the window seat, Cal chuckled. "Lady Julia, really?"

Tain muttered, "Evidence withstanding."

Julia managed to say, "There speaks our Justiciar," before Julius said, "What evidence? We're always very careful."

They started laughing and Tain realised he'd needed something to make him relax properly. He rang for Linnt and asked for refreshments.

When the door closed, Julius said, "What is his problem, Your Highness?"

"Who knows, he's just like that." Tain added with a smile, "It could be the fact his first name is Gab," before continuing, "I keep thinking of talking to father but I never seem to do it. I've not had to put up with him day in, day out, I suppose."

Julia nodded. "It would make a lot of difference if he were at Ceardlann as well…"

Julius laughed. "No wonder he's miserable. Gab Linn…"

Tain grinned. "There's a silent T on the end. I think his parents had a dry sense of humour myself."

Julia chuckled. "Yes. Especially as the anagram once meant illegitimate but maybe he doesn't know."

Tain laughed. "It's an ironically appropriate name though, he never says much. What's the anagram?"

The door opened and the gentleman in question entered.

Julia looked at Tain. "I'll tell you later, Your Highness. The surprise

396

will make it pleasanter."

Linnt had barely left before Adeone and Arkyn entered the room and they spent a couple of hours as family, nearfamily and friends without other cares.

* * *

The banquet that night was truly spectacular. Tain and Arkyn were congenial and laughing, and Tain felt the stress drift from him. Adeone had invited all the children of the Lords of Oedran over eight to Court to share in the evening, and it meant that most of the Landis siblings were there and Lady Elantha also. Cal had been formally invited and so his father couldn't refuse to let him attend. It was the first time he'd experienced Court and it wasn't going to be an evening he would forget. It was also the first time the Court had seen him and there were speculative whispers taking in everything from his clothes to his manners: some simply curious, most judgemental. Cal didn't take long to understand why Arkyn saw Court as a chore most of the time. For Tain it was still a novelty but Cal realised there was danger here for them all. At one point he caught the King's eye and bowed slightly but Adeone simply nodded, recognising in the lad's stance the understanding that was being formed.

Watching Elantha chatting with her Landis cousins, Adeone's smile spread. When he could, he said, "Are you all right, little flower?"

"Yes, Your Majesty."

Adeone smiled. "Good. You should come to more banquets."

"Can I come to the Munewid one? Please?"

Adeone sighed and looked at her. "All right, you may, until midnight."

She gave him a hug that didn't go unnoticed before saying, "Promise?"

Adeone laughed and hugged her back. "I promise."

"Thank you, Sire."

He watched as she ran off and shook his head at the thought of Scanlon's indifference.

The following morning Tain and Cal returned to the Rex Dallin for the last time before their birthday, feeling decidedly free, happy and excited for the future.

Chapter 91

AN END AT A BEGINNING
Cisadai, Week 47 – 16th Lufial, 9th Lufis 1214
Outer Office

THREE DAYS LATER, a servant approached Richardson, asking for an audience with King Adeone. Richardson refused. The servant held out a King's Token half apologetically. Richardson scrutinised him suspiciously but went to enquire if Adeone would see him. The King's Token was either a fake or lent. The first was treason, the second only permitted in exceptional circumstances.

Divested of everything but his tunic, the servant was shown into the Inner Office. Adeone simply raised an eyebrow in invitation.

"Sire, forgive me for disturbing you. Judge Tancred lent me the token."

"Why couldn't he come himself, John?"

The servant glanced uncertainly at Richardson. Adeone took the hint and dismissed his administrator. Tancred's name and his own knowledge of the footman was enough.

"Well?"

"He's dying, sir."

Adeone blanched. "What? Why wasn't I informed?"

"He didn't wish you to be, Your Majesty. Someone wanted him to know about it before he died but he didn't want Your Majesty to—"

"You are telling me James is being poisoned?"

"Yes, Sire."

Adeone let the breath escape from his body in a hiss. "I'm coming."

* * *

When Adeone reached Tancred's house he was shown straight to his friend's bedchamber. He dismissed everyone else. Obviously jaundiced and close to death, James tried to sit up, at which point Adeone snapped,

"Don't be such a bloody fool! Can't the doctors do anything?"

"No, sir. Lord Scanlon would only find another opportunity. No, Sire, please listen. I have taught Prince Tain too well. Lord Scanlon objects already. Tain is gaining too much respect even now. When he defied, or rather had me defy, that amendment of Lord Scanlon's, I did so but I knew my days were numbered. By Alcis, sir, I wish I could see Tain bring down Lord Scanlon. Sorry, I know it would be your son against your brother."

"There's no need to be, James. I wish you could as well. Please, let the doctors help."

"No, Sire. I am old anyway. I wanted to implore one thing—"

"Anything and more, old friend."

"Do not let Scanlon take over Prince Tain's education. Tradition says his mentor should be there until he is twenty, but that lad can manage perfectly well on his own now. I am leaving him my library. Do not let Scanlon get hold of it. There are copies of ancient law. It has been a good hobby. Lachlan left me some."

"All of that is a given, my friend. Scanlon won't get a say in Tain's education. That I *can* promise you. I'll have your library taken to Ceardlann."

"Thank you, sir." James stared off into the distance. "He has been like the grandson, I never had."

Adeone swallowed. "You mean as much to him. Can I get him here?"

"No. I would not have him see me like this. Not now."

Adeone kissed his hand. "I need to say this. You are the nearfather I never had. More than any other, James. I will never forget everything you did for me, for Tain, for us all. I won't let your memory die."

Tancred closed his eyes, whispering, "That's what the Justa said."

Adeone hesitated. "Prince Emlyn? James? What?"

"He stood there, in his ethereal robes, and told me my legacy would never die. It would be etched deep into the foundations of peace. Will you find me in the heavens when your work here is done?"

"As quickly as my spirit will fly."

Judge Tancred's eyes closed as he sighed his relief. Adeone waited with him until he had fallen into a deep sleep. He wanted to stay until the end, but the doctor said it might be many hours. He left, giving instructions he was to be informed of any change. When he reached his office Richardson cancelled the immediate meeting. Adeone simply sat for six minutes, looking out of the window before turning to his desk and setting several matters in motion.

Four hours later, John came from Tancred's household to say the judge had died. Adeone's heart shattered. It was truly the end of an era.

Chapter 92
NEWS
Afternoon
Ceardlann

LEAVING HIS OFFICE, Adeone informed Richardson that he was going to Ceardlann far more bluntly than normal.

For once he didn't enjoy the ride and idly considered the irony that Tancred had once made the same journey to inform him of a death. He galloped into the Rex Dallin and, free of all guards, carried on the gallop to Ceardlann.

Ceardlann, home, was alien to him. As he walked through its unimposing doors, he ignored everyone and everything. Finding Tain at his books, a simple flick of the eyes dismissed Spellen – Cal also left, leaving father and son eyeing each other. Adeone held out an arm, enveloping Tain in a hug as his son reached him.

Thoroughly disconcerted, Tain said, "What's the matter? Nothing's happened to Arkyn, has it, father?"

Adeone swallowed. "Not to Arkyn, no. Tain, my son, there's no easy way for me to say this, but James died earlier."

Tain stilled. "No! He can't have! Father, he can't have. No!" He glanced at his father, whispering, "He wasn't even ill. He can't be dead. He can't!"

"He was taken ill two days ago. He didn't send to me or you'd have been there. These things can be swift and he was elderly."

"No... I... Father, I think I want to be alone."

Adeone gave him a hug. "I'm staying here tonight. If you need to talk, find me, wherever I am."

Tain nodded, walked away and sat in the window seat, tears silently overflowing.

Adeone closed the door on the room and looked at Spellen. "He is not to be disturbed. Judge Tancred died earlier. Go and see your family in Oedran. I'm not sure if Prince Tain will resume his studies. Cal, I need a word." Adeone led the way to his study and closed the door pointedly. "Sit down." He passed the perplexed lad a drink. "You're nearly of cisan-age, enjoy it. Tain was very close to James, wasn't he?"

Cal swallowed. "Yes, Sire, I think he was."

"So I thought and James was close to him, that's been proved by his bequests... Never mind, I shall tell Tain first... but maybe you could help with a different problem. I need a room here that can be secure, private and yet accessible. Any ideas?"

Cal thought. "How about one of the tower chambers, Sire?"

"Not a bad idea. The first-floor room might well do. We can change it from a bed chamber easily enough..."

Some time later, there was a knock at the door and Tain entered, looking particularly despondent. Cal got up, eying him, concerned. Tain tried to smile but couldn't manage more than pursed lips, which quivered with every moment. Cal simply left, squeezing his friend's shoulder in passing. Adeone simply pulled Tain into a hug and held him for several minutes fighting back his own emotion.

"How did he die, father?"

"I'm not sure. I've yet to speak to the doctors properly."

"He was murdered, wasn't he? And it's my fault."

"No, it isn't. Why would it be?" enquired Adeone.

"That trial and amendment, my investiture. I showed Scanlon up and I made it known it was thanks to the judge's teaching. It is…"

Tain was crying, and Adeone wrapped him in another hug. Why hadn't he told Tain the truth? Was he trying to save the guilt? The deception hadn't worked, but he didn't want to confirm it.

Finally, Tain collapsed into a chair and looked bleakly at his father.

"I don't know if I can face next year, father. I feel lost without James."

Adeone passed him a drink and sat opposite him. "I can understand that but he'd never have taken your oath if he didn't think you were ready."

"I'm not convinced, and I never truly was."

"As I know and can see. There are many times in life when feeling inadequate is perfectly normal, but rarely correct. I believe that this is one in your life."

"Thank you, father, but… Oh, what does it matter? You'll just tell me I'm a fool."

"Of course it matters, and, anyway, being a fool has stood you in good stead all your life so far. Tain, nerves are nothing if not normal. You've a couple of weeks to grasp all this. Would it help if you were to meet with your staff before you got to Amphi? We've finalised the details…"

Tain shook his head. "I don't think it would. Not at the moment."

"Then we'll leave them be for a time. Tain, James left you a bequest."

Tain glanced up. "Oh. What is it?" He was half afraid of the answer as though it was an unexpected test.

Adeone regarded him. "He's left you his library complete: everything that is in the library and his office – other than the furniture belonging to the Courthouse."

Tain swallowed, emotion welling inside him. "Now I am truly scared."

Adeone smiled. "He must have thought you'd appreciate it."

With a catch in his voice, Tain said, "I do but… I'd rather he was here."

"You and me both, Tain. I always viewed him as a good friend, never as a servant or official. He might have been your tutor, but he was never less than my friend. The closest I ever had to a nearfather as well."

Tain moved to sit by his father. "I had almost forgotten that."

"Grief strangles many senses. I didn't expect you to remember and merely said it to get it straight in my own head. We will have to pay our respects to the family."

Tain nodded. "I'd like to see Madam Tancred, not merely write. Would that be permitted, sir?"

"Yes, but give her a day or two."

"Then I'll write today. I feel I should do something."

Adeone gave his son a one-armed hug. "I'm sure she'll appreciate it."

Tain stared straight ahead, blankly. Then he focused. "I'll go and write now, whilst I feel like this. Will you excuse me, father?"

Adeone nodded. "Of course." He watched his son leave and pondered on his fortitude. One of the mainstays of his life had been stripped away from him again. He considered the problems that Tancred's untimely death had caused and was determined to make sure Tain would know as few as possible. He pushed himself to his feet and gazed unseeingly out of the window, swallowing back his own grief. He closed his eyes. James should never have died in the manner he had.

Chapter 93
FUNERAL
Tretaldai, Week 47 – 17th Lufial, 10th Lufis 1214
Judge Tancred's House

THE FOLLOWING MORNING, Adeone called in on Madam Tancred before returning to the Palace, asking if there was anything he could do to help.

She swallowed and in a moment was crying on the King's shoulder.

He held her. "He shouldn't have died, Bets. I don't know what else I can say." She tried to pull herself together and was surprised when Adeone whispered, "Gather yourself slowly. I don't mind."

In that moment, she saw what James had seen for years and pulled away. She smiled ruefully. "I am sorry, Sire."

"There is no need to be. Tain would like to see you when you feel up to receiving visitors. There's a letter from him."

"How is he?"

"Emotional. We all are. Have you decided when the funeral is to be?"

"Two days, Sire."

Adeone said softly, "Would you think me high-handed and rude if I put the City Alcium at your disposal?"

Madam Tancred whitened. "Sire?"

"James was respected and honoured throughout the city, high and low alike. You might be surprised at how many people turn out and, apart from that, I'd consider it an honour if you could bring yourself to accept."

Madam Tancred looked at the King. "But… We're not fit for it, sir."

Adeone smiled at her. "I think you are; I think James deserves the honour: he made history in this city and empire and he's made the future. For his memory, will you accept?"

Madam Tancred clutched her throat. "Put like that, sir, I don't see how I can refuse."

Adeone said quietly, "Thank you. I'll send the Moonshi along."

She hesitated. "You meant so much to James. You and Prince Tain. I know it was mutual. I could see it. Will you..." She half turned away before taking a deep breath. "There needs to be pall bearers. I don't know... I know it's wrong to ask but if you weren't...well..."

He took her hands. "I would be honoured, Bets, but I can't." Tears pricked at his eyes. "I wish I could but I can't, and nor can Tain."

She nodded, flushing. "I'm sorry to have put you in the position."

"No. Don't be sorry. I'm truly honoured."

* * *

The following afternoon Tain arrived in Oedran with Arkyn. Rather more subdued than normal, they walked through the Palace from the stables to the Inner Office. Richardson announced them without question. As they entered, Adeone rolled up the documents he was dealing with, moving out from behind the desk to greet them with hugs. Tain accepted it, glad of the support. Arkyn though felt tenseness in his father and frowned.

"Your uncle arrived last night. He's passing through," said Adeone aware he'd been rumbled.

Tain swallowed. "He's not going to be at the funeral tomorrow, is he?"

"No. He's leaving for Black Hills first thing in the morning. Can you promise me to stay out of his way today? Both of you?"

The brothers nodded. Arkyn caught his father's eye and had the strangest feeling there was more than the usual caution there.

"Thank you." Adeone collapsed onto the couch. "We can't dine together with him here."

Tain hesitated. "I don't want to be alone at the moment..."

"Then you'll have to annoy me," said Arkyn with a smile. "Shall we invite ourselves to dinner at Landis House?"

"That is an excellent idea," said Adeone. He saw his younger son's face. "They know you're grieving. I'll keep your Uncle Festus busy here. Let Cornelia and your nearcousins distract you."

Tain swallowed. "I want to see Madam Tancred as well."

"I would leave it a few days. I know why you want to, but it is a busy time for her." He hesitated. "She wanted us to help bear James' body to the City Alcium—"

"I'll do it," said Tain immediately.

"I had to refuse." He saw anger and confusion in his son's face. "I

403

would have accepted in a heartbeat for James, but we cannot be seen to bear the weight of the dead on our shoulders. The symbolism of that—"

He broke off abruptly as Arkyn slumped forward, head in his hands sobbing as he hadn't for years.

Adeone wrapped his elder son in a hug. "We bear the weight in our hearts, not on our shoulders. I know, son. I know. We can't let it be seen."

Tears starting in his own eyes, Tain hugged his brother from the other side, realising how much Arkyn had hidden. The pain of their sister's and mother's deaths, the horror of Kensal's, Marsh's, Thomas and Alan's murders, the responsibility he'd felt for Axton's suicide. He'd carried it all. Carried the guilt of ordering executions and surviving when others had died. The wound had been opened and was bleeding afresh.

Tain didn't need to be told that Arkyn was unable to control the waves of despair that a simple phrase had unleashed. When his brother brokenly apologised, he grasped his hand tightly whispering that grief was grief, whatever the cause, however manifested. His own wound gaped as guilt burned within. Arkyn sensed it and squeezed his hand just as tightly.

Watching them, strangled by grief, Adeone whispered, "Your greatest strength is each other. Never let it falter. I wish Scanlon and I had found what you have."

Arkyn wiped his eyes. "You've got us, father."

Adeone simply hugged them tighter.

* * *

The following evening, Madam Tancred could never believe how many people were there when she walked with her husband's body into the crowded Alcium Plaza. It was as full as it had been at the Yearling. She noticed judges and lawyers her husband had worked with, but there were so many people she could never have known them all. Her son walked beside her, dumbfounded. Behind them walked the King and Princes. They'd insisted on being behind and Madam Tancred found that as disconcerting. James was borne to the Alcium on the shoulders of fellow judges, lawyers and Peter Selth, who had been humbled by Tain's suggestion that he represented both of them and all of Tancred's many students across the years.

The words were said, the pyre was lit and Madam Tancred watched the only man she had ever loved be consumed by the flames. She turned from the sight, caught up in emotion and the moment. Prevented from stumbling, she was sobbing onto the shoulder of a young man. When she could, she looked up and found Prince Tain holding her, watching the flames with tears running down his cheeks.

"I hope I do you proud," he whispered to the night.

Chapter 94
AMPHI

THE FOLLOWING WEEK, the Princes reached Amphi and had a day to settle in. ReJean, having noticed Linnt had no deputy asked a footman to undertake the role – considering it better than a strange manservant having to cope alone – when he took the message from Adeone asking him to do just that because of an 'oversight' he smiled to himself. Tancred's death had no doubt caused much upheaval.

On Munewid Eve, Arkyn entered Tain's rooms, dressed for the banquet to find his brother, still in a normal tunic, staring out of the window.

"Tain! It's quarter past eight. You've got quarter of an hour to get into hall looking like a prince – or as much of a prince as you can."

Tain ran out of the room. Arkyn turned to Linnt.

"Get your incompetent presence with His Highness and, next time, make damned sure I don't discover such a situation again."

* * *

Twenty-four minutes later, ReJean was greeting them. Moments later, Arkyn introduced Tain to a couple of Arealian lords he'd met before and then looked for the Governor. He was taking a message off a courier and Arkyn turned back to the lords.

"SICLA! Your Highness…"

Arkyn frowned. "Your Excellency, there is surely no need to shout."

ReJean said, "There is. Can I have a word with you, please, sir?" When Arkyn reached him, he said, "Our food-taster has died of poison."

Arkyn whitened and ran a hand over his head. "You're right, there was reason to shout. What food?"

"Dais."

Arkyn took a lungful of air. "Your Excellency, have all food destined for the dais destroyed. All of it."

Tain crossed to them. "What's happening?"

"In a moment, Tain."

ReJean said, "What shall we eat, sir?"

"The same as everyone else, ReJean. Your food-taster: if he had a family, send them compensation. He might have been employed for this eventuality but not every food-taster dies and you have to admit it is probably because of mine and my brother's presence."

"There is no guarantee of that, sir."

Tain said, "I think there is, Your Excellency. Have the kitchen staff questioned, gently. They'll not reveal anything if they're scared and they will be scared. I think we should perhaps carry on our conference later. We're drawing a bit of attention."

Arkyn smiled. "Tain, it's not your birthday for another few hours."

"You seemed to be too busy being shocked."

* * *

They had dined, and the dancing had long since started, when an incident occurring at the end of the dais caught Tain's attention. Excusing himself, he went to discover what was happening and, recognising an all too familiar face at the centre of the melee, said,

"Let him through, please."

The Amphi guards looked uncertain. "We were told to apprehend anyone without a right to be here."

"I have just given him that right. Let him through."

Once on the way to Tain's seat, Cal put a restraining hand on his friend's arm. "Sir, I need to speak to your brother and yourself alone."

"I wondered what you were doing here. I thought you were accompanying Elantha tonight."

"Plans change, Your Highness."

Tain looked at his friend's drawn face. He called Arkyn over.

"Can we go somewhere private, sir?" enquired Cal immediately as Arkyn reached them.

Astonished to see him, Arkyn replied, "Not without a lot of awkward questions. Whatever it is, will have to be said here."

Cal pursed his lips slightly and shuffled his feet slightly. In handing over a letter to Arkyn, he managed to position himself so he blocked Arkyn and Tain's faces from the majority of the room beyond. Arkyn glanced at the seal: his cousin's. He read the letter, blanched and the parchment dropped from shaking fingers. One handed, Cal caught it and passed it to Tain, whilst his other hand hovered under Arkyn's elbow to support him. Tain read. He paled as shock shot through him.

"You know what this contains?" Tain demanded, his voice official and strained.

"I was there," murmured Cal.

Tain nodded. He glanced at Arkyn. "I'll announce this. Cal, he needs to sit down." He turned and found Kadeem within call. "Get silence in here *now*!"

Kadeem spoke to the Master of Ceremonies. As silence spread through the hall, Arkyn seated himself. Cal passed him some wine and for once Arkyn sipped it feeling the warmth of the alcohol bringing colour to his cheeks. Tain continued to stand, one hand on the back of his brother's chair. At a significant look, Cal stood back. Silence fell. Tain spoke.

"Your Excellency, my lords, ladies and guests, it is my sad duty to inform you of the death of King Adeone Altarius earlier this evening..."

CHARACTERS

FAMILIES

FITZALCIS	KING ALTARIUS APOLINAR	King of the Oedranian Empire 1168-1204
	KING ADEONE ALTARIUS	King of the Oedranian Empire 1204-present
	QUEEN IRA	*King Adeone's wife (deceased)*
	PRINCE ARKYN ADEONE	King Adeone's eldest son
	PRINCE TAIN LACHLAN	King Adeone's younger son
	PRINCESS ELIZA ELANIA (ELLA)	*King Adeone's daughter (deceased)*
	PRINCE LACHLAN AMARUS	*King Altarius' brother (deceased)*
	LADY AMARA TALITHA	King Altarius' sister
	LADY NEASSA RATHGAR	Lady Amara's elder daughter
	LADY RHIAN FAIRSON	Lady Amara's younger daughter
	LORD PEAGA RATHGAR	Lady Amara's grandson
	LORD SCANLON AMARUS	Justiciar of the Empire
	LADY AELIA	*Lord Scanlon's wife (deceased)*
	LADY ELANTHA	Lord Scanlon's daughter
	PRINCESS LILITH	King Altarius' cousin. Lives in Bayan
	LORD GALWOOD	Princess Lilith's son
	KING ALDEN AND PRINCE EMLYN	FitzAlcis twins from history. They perfected the system of king and justiciar
LANDIS	LORD FESTUS LANDIS	Lord of Oedran, Defender of the King's Life, Chief Advisor, nearfather to Adeone's children
	LADY CORNELIA LANDIS	Long-suffering, hardworking Lady of Oedran
	LORD JULIUS AND LADY JULIA	Eldest children, twins
	MARCELEA, ANTONIA, LUCIUS, IRA	Younger children

IRIS	LORD IGNATIUS IRIS	Lord of Oedran for the Low Plains, King's Counsellor
	LORD IRVIN IRIS	Lord Iris' grandson
RALE	LORD FINIAN RALE	Lord of Oedran
	LORD FINN RALE	*Lord Rale's father (deceased)*
	LADY MALINDA ATGAS	Lord Rale's mother - remarried
PARA	LORD PARA	Lord of Oedran for Anapara
	LORD KENELM	Son
	LADY MALANDRA	Daughter
FARAN	LORD FARAN	Lord of Lufian, Adeone's friend
	LADY FARAN	Lady of Lufian
	LUCILLE, ELEANOR, CAITLIN, MELANIE	Daughters`
TANCRED	JUDGE JAMES TANCRED	Prince Tain's mentor. Adeone's friend.
	MADAM ELIZABETH TANCRED (BETS)	James' wife.
	PROFESSOR THOMAS TANCRED	Son. Lecturer at the Law School. Lives apart.
	JOHN	Footman
	MAISIE	Maid
GALDWIN	MASTER GALDWIN	Cloth Merchant, Cal's father
	MADAM GALDWIN	Cal's mother
	CALUMIEL (CAL)	Eldest son. Lives at Ceardlann. Princes' friend
	HALTERN, LOUISA, CRISPIN, TABITHA, ELSIE	Younger children
WANDA	LAIORIL	A chief of the Wanda
	MIRANDA	Wise woman of the Wanda
	SAYRE	Man of the Wanda
SELTH	MASTER SELTH	Scribe to Judge Tancred
	MADAM SELTH	Wife of Master Selth
	PETER	Eldest son, Law School student
	GEORGE, JO, HARRIET	Younger children

KING'S RETINUE

RICHARDSON	King's Administrator
SIMKINS	King's manservant
DOCTOR CHAPA	King's Physician and cousin
CAPTAIN PIXNEY	Head of the Palace Guard
SERGEANT HILLBECK	Head of the King's Guard
SERGEANT KILBRIDE	Sergeant of the King's Guard
KENTON	King's Secretary
ADVISOR RAYBURN	King's Deputy Chief Advisor, King's Military Advisor
ADVISOR SPELLEN	Tutor to Prince Tain and Cal
MERCHANT ANNATTO	Tutor to Cal
APPOSER NALLVIR	King's Apposer

ARKYN'S RETINUE

KADEEM	Manservant
EDWARD	Administrator
ADVISOR CAPLE	Chief Advisor
THOMAS	Kadeem's deputy
ALAN	Footman
GUNN	Edward's deputy
SIMON	Groom
CAPTAIN MARSH	Captain of the Princes' Guard
SERGEANT SMITHERS	Sergeant of the Prince's Guard
HALIEN	A guard

TAIN'S RETINUE

GAB LINNT	Manservant

SCANLON'S RETINUE

BANTLING	Advisor
DYER	Administrator

CEARDLANN

COMPTROLLER	Gentleman in charge of Ceardlann
SUSAN	Housekeeper
COOK	Cook
JOE, DAVID	Footmen
MARIA	FitzAlcis Nurse
ALFRED	Chief groom

LANDIS HOUSE

WILLIAM KADEEM	Lord Landis' manservant
BACKERY	Footman
CLODACH	Chief Groom

IN THE EMPIRE

TERA	LORD PERCIVAL WEALSMAN	Margrave of Terasia
	LADY KRISTINA WEALSMAN	Wealsman's wife
	ADEONA WEALSMAN	Wealsman's daughter
	ERNST	Deputy Governor of Terasia
	PENROD SILVANO	Young lord. Heir of Lord Silvano.
OTHER	LORD EAMES	Sagamore of Lufian
	LORD TYLER GALWOOD	Exarch of Bayan
	LORD CAMLYN	Lord of Bayan
	MELLONIA CAMLYN	Lord Camlyn's daughter
	LORD ALDWY	Tuchlin of the Low Plains
	LORD IFOR DAIOCH	Deputy Governor of the Low Plains. Life-bound to Adeone. Wed-brother to Landis.

IN OEDRAN		
COURT	LORD KENSAL PARCHI	Guest of Court, Arkyn's friend
	LORD FAIRSON	Lord of Oedran for Tradere
	LORD RYSON	Lord of Oedran for Gerymor Provost of the Law School
	LORD LUX	Lord of Oedran for Lufian
	LORD TERAN	Lord of Oedran for Terasia
	LORD RATHGAR	Lord of Oedran for Bayan
	LORD ANGUIS	Lord of Oedran for Serpent Isle
	LORD CEARIS	Lord of Oedran for Denshire
	LORD RUFUS RATHGAR	Husband of Lady Neassa
	LORD CHANDER, LADY CHANDRA	Eldest children of Lord Teran, twins.
PALACE	STEWARD	In charge of day-to-day running of the Palace
	CHAMBERLAIN	In charge of the individual rooms in the Palace
	HERALD	Mail routes, runners and couriers
	SIGNUMERY	In charge of official seals
	ARCHIVIST	In charge of the official archives
	CAPTAIN PIXNEY	Captain of the Palace Guard
	DENNY	Chief Server of Upper Hall
	CASWAL HILLBECK	A courier. Susan's son. Hillbeck's nephew.
CITY	MERCHANT CHAPA	Merchant of Oedran and King Adeone's cousin
	KEEPER OF THE JUSTICE HALL	Superintendent of the Courthouse of Oedran
	BRADACH	An inept young thief
ARMY	GENERAL PATURN	Head of the King's Army
	MAJOR WYNFELD	Major of Oedran
	MAJOR AXTON	Major of the Northern Empire
	CAPTAIN BEAVER	Captain of Intelligence
	SOLDIER JOST LYNDON	Barracks' Gate Guard

DELVINGS

Lexicon

OF THE MOONS

ALUNA	The larger of the two Erinnan moons
ALUNA-MONTH	Four weeks
ALUNAN	The higher section of society
ALUNAN-AGE	Twenty years old. Alunan become adults in law
CISLUNA	The smaller of the two Erinnan moons
CISLUNA-MONTH	Three weeks
CISAN	The lower section of society
CISAN-AGE	Fifteen years old. Cisan become adults in law

FOR THE ANCESTORS

ALCIA	A guardian of the ancestor's memory
ALCIUM	A place to remember the ancestors, for blessing new life, for contemplation and for funerals.
MOONSHI	Chief Alcia in Oedran

ON RELATIONSHIPS

NEAR*	Named when a child is born, *nearparents* act as mentors for a child and would act as guardians should the child be left orphaned. Nearparents' children are *nearcousins*, unless the child lives in the same house, then they're *nearsiblings*
WED*	This prefix denotes relatives married into the family, rather like the suffix *in-law*

IN OEDRAN

KING'S ADVOCATES	A group consisting of the King's Defenders, heir and Representatives in the empire
TRINICULUM	A formal dining room at the Palace
ETANES	The law-making body, made up of the Lords of Oedran and twelve cisan members
EALDORMAN	The person keeping order in the Etanes debates
YEOMEN	Law enforcers

STREET SLANG

DAL	Money
RES	Crescent – smallest denomination of coin

HONORIFICS

SIRE, MAJESTY	The King
GRACE	The Queen
HIGHNESS	Princes
ELEGANCE	Princesses
EXCELLENCY	King's Representatives
BENEVOLENCE	Moonshi
GREATNESS	Scanlon
MY LORD	Lords
MY LADY	Nobel Ladies

FEALTIES

FEALTY	A declaration of loyalty from one person to another: a declaration to take up the fight for the liege by the vassal
TRUTH-BINDING	In addition to fealty, the vassal swears to speak to the truth to the liege when required.
SPEECH-BINDING	In addition to truth-binding, the vassal swears never to reveal anything confidential, never to say anything to annoy the liege, to speak only for them not against them.
HONOUR-BINDING	In addition to truth-binding, the vassal swears only to work for the honour of the liege, not against them.
LIFE-BINDING	Melding all aspects of truth, speech and honour bindings, the vassal ties their life force to the wishes of the liege. If they annoy their liege, they feel pain. If they commit treason, the vassal will die immediately.
VALLEY-BINDING	Specific to the Rex Dallin, this binding is said to be life-binding but may stop short of death.
OTHER BINDINGS	There are oaths which fall short of the recognised fealties, that are sworn when taking on specific duties or when an employer requires it.

OTHER

GUDDLING	Catching fish with one's hands by searching under stones and the bank of a watercourse

The Cearcall and Ull's Legacy

At the beginning of the reckoning of years, the Majistar Ull brought magic to Erinna. Twelve star sapphires controlled the creation of the magic. Ull gifted the star stones to twelve individuals, each with a magical spirit. For six hundred years they, and their successors, controlled magic on Erinna, formed laws around it and maintained peace. In the year 600, they died, blown to the winds when magic, wielded by the Tribility who held three spirits, destroyed the Cearcall Tower in Denshire. Since 600 magic has been weaker, almost dormant. Some stones were lost, their location hidden by history, along with some items related to the members of the Cearcall.

Title	Spirit	Stone Colour	Item
AMSER	TIMER	TURQUOISE	AMSER'S WATCH
BERAN	BEARER	BLACK	BERAN'S PENDANT
ESPIER	ESPIEN	YELLOW	ESPIER'S GLASS
JECI	ILLUSIONIST	BLUE	JECI'S RING
MEITHRIN	HEALER	PINK	MEITHRIN'S VIAL
MEMINI	MEMOR	GREY	MEMINI'S MANUSCRIPT
RHEOL	BALANCER	WHITE	RHEOL'S NEEDLE
SENNACHIE	SEER	GREEN	SENNACHIE'S BOWL
SENTIRE	SENSOR	RED	SENTIRE'S KNIFE
SKIFTA	SHIFTER	PURPLE	SKIFTA'S SWORD
SUNDRIAN	SPLITTER	ORANGE	SUNDRIAN'S WHISTLE
WRIGHT	MANIPULATOR	BROWN	WRIGHT'S BOX

Each magical spirit manifests differently from healing hurts to splitting the mind, from creating illusions to manipulating objects.

More than one person at any one time can hold a spirit, but only one spirit wielder can possess the star stone and unlock its full power.

Each spirit has a collection of *hues*, lesser forms of the spirit, which may manifest in anyone.

People who wield magic are said to be affected by Ull's Legacy.

Provincial Information

Province	Capital City	Lord of Oedran
ANAPARA	OEDRAN	PARA
AREAL	AMPHI	RALE
BAYAN	GARTH	RATHGAR
DENSHIRE	CEARDEN	CEARIS
GERYMOR	RY	RYSON
LOW PLAINS	EYLLYN	IRIS
LUFIAN	LUFIA	LUX
MACIAN ISLES	MACIA	MACARIA
PALE LANDS	MEITH	LANDIS
SERPENT ISLE	ANGUIN	ANGUIS
TERASIA	TERA	TERAN
TRADERE	BYFA	FAIRSON

Province	King's Representative	Chief Judge
ANAPARA	DOMINI OF PARAS	CHIEF JUDGE (PARAS)
AREAL	GOVERNOR	KENNER
BAYAN	EXARCH	ESCHERVIN
DENSHIRE	VISIR	HAKIM
GERYMOR	DEY	BORSHOLDER
LOW PLAINS	TUCHLIN	DOMESMAN
LUFIAN	SAGAMORE	DEEMSTER
MACIAN ISLES	FENCIBLE	DOMARE
PALE LANDS	JARL	LAGHMAN
SERPENT ISLE	PASHA	TUOMARI
TERASIA	MARGRAVE	TERAZI
TRADERE	SATRAP	ARCHON

Province	Symbol	Colour
ANAPARA	THREE CROSSED ARROWS	PURPLE
AREAL	A KEY	SILVER
BAYAN	A BIRD IN FLIGHT	ORANGE
DENSHIRE	A TWELVE-POINT MYSTIC ROSE	BROWN
GERYMOR	A SET OF SCALES ON A GEM	WHITE
LOW PLAINS	AN EYE	GREEN
LUFIAN	A FLOWER AND SNOWFLAKE	BLUE
MACIAN ISLES	A TRISKELE OF THREE SPIRALS	RED
PALE LANDS	A VIAL	PINK
SERPENT ISLE	A CURLED SNAKE	YELLOW
TERASIA	A BEAR'S PAW PRINT	BLACK
TRADERE	AN HOURGLASS	TURQUOISE

Notes on Time

WEEKDAYS		FESTIVALS		
	ALUNADAI		MUNEWID	FIRST DAY OF SUMMER
	CISADAI			FIRST DAY OF THE YEAR
	TRETALDAI		MUNPYRAM	FIRST DAY OF AUTUMN
	IMPERADAI		MUNDIMRI	FIRST DAY OF WINTER
	PENTADAI		MUNLUMEN	FIRST DAY OF SPRING
	HEXADAI		*These festivals are known as Alcis Days*	
	SEPTADAI		*and are marked by both moons being full*	

ON TIME

1 MINUTE	=	60 SECONDS
1 HOUR	=	72 MINUTES (12 X 6 MINUTES)
1 DAY	=	24 HOURS
1 WEEK	=	7 DAYS
COURT CYCLE	=	12 DAYS
1 FORTNIGHT	=	2 WEEKS

Season	Aluna-month	Week	Cisluna-month	Season	Aluna-month	Week	Cisluna-month
SUMMER	CEARAL	1	CEARCIS	WINTER	RALAL	25	RALIS
		2				26	
		3				27	
		4	MIDDIS			28	NORIS
	TRADAL	5			ANAPAL	29	
		6				30	
		7	TRADIS			31	ANAPCIS
		8				32	
	LOWAL	9			BAYAL	33	
		10	LOWIS			34	BAYIS
		11				35	
		12				36	
AUTUMN	MACIAL	13	MACIS	SPRING	TERAL	37	TERIS
		14				38	
		15				39	
		16	EASIS			40	SOUIS
	MEITHAL	17			GERYAL	41	
		18				42	
		19	MEITHIS			43	GERYIS
		20				44	
	SERAL	21			LUFIAL	45	LUFIS
		22	SERIS			46	
		23				47	
		24				48	

POSTSCRIPT

To you, my reader…

Thank you.

I hope you enjoyed *Tragedy*, the fourth book in the *Treason and Truth* series.

Please consider leaving an honest review of this book wherever you feel most comfortable. Reviews really help readers find their next book and help authors find their next reader.

Acknowledgements

Authors rarely get to publication without help and support. They sit and write in snatched hours or minutes. Sometimes stories flow unceasingly from their fingers, clamouring to be heard amongst the din of everyday life. When the last scratch of the pen and click of the keyboard is done, then comes the editing, the interior design, the cover…

My journey has not been solo. From my friends and family who have read, re-read and given me honest feedback to you, the reader that got this far, I say thank you.

This book is dedicated to Mark, whose friendship and support has been far more important than words can express.

Explore Erinna

Please visit https://erinna.co.uk for more about the Erinnan Legacy or sign up to The Court Newsletter for freebies and news.